Detective Inspector
Huss

Detective Inspector Huss

Helene Tursten

Translated by
Steven T. Murray

First published in the English language in the United States in 2003
by Soho Press, Inc.
853 Broadway
New York, NY 10003

Library of Congress Cataloging-in-Publication Data

Tursten, Helene, 1954–.
[Krossade tanghästen. English]
Detective Inspector Huss / Helene Tursten ;
[translated by Steven T. Murray].
p. cm.
ISBN 978-1-56947-370-2
I. Murray, Steven T. II. Title.
PT9876.3.U55K76 2003
839.3'74—dc21   2002026920

10   9   8   7   6

To Hilmer and Cecilia

Detective Inspector Huss

NOBODY SAW HIM FALL through the dense November darkness. With a dull, heavy thud he hit the rain-wet pavement. Even though it was still rush hour, there were few people on the street. The pedestrians huddled beneath umbrellas turned inside out and scrunched their chins into turned-up collars for a little protection from the icy, whipping rain. Everyone who could was driving a car or jammed into the steaming warmth aboard a bus or streetcar.

An elderly woman pulling a stubborn, soaking-wet dachshund on a leash stood closest. The howls that she and the dog uttered announced to those people in the vicinity that something serious had happened. Hurrying pedestrians slowed their pace. Curiosity got the upper hand, and they were drawn toward the site of the accident.

A white Mercedes was carelessly parked by the curb. A man in a light-colored overcoat had just rushed around the car and opened the door on the passenger's side when the lady with the dachshund started to scream. The man turned quickly, squinted through the rain, and caught sight of the heap thirty meters away. He kept his grip on the open car door, slowly tilted his head back, and looked up at the top floor of the imposing apartment building. A faint moaning sound rose from his throat, but he remained catatonically still.

Without putting on her coat, the small woman in the passenger's seat jumped nimbly out of the car and ran over to the motionless figure on the ground. Her slenderness was emphasized by the stylish Chanel dress she was wearing. She had mastered to perfection the art of running in high heels. She elbowed her way through the crowd frenetically and reached the inner circle.

Chapter One

THE PATROL CAR WAS the first to arrive on the scene. The ambulance came a scant five minutes later. As far as the ambulance medics could tell, there wasn't much for them to do. The two police officers attempted to hold back the sensation-hungry spectators who suddenly were stoic enough to defy both wind and rain. One of the officers got into the car and called for backup.

"Send the crime scene team to the corner of Aschebergsgatan and Molinsgatan. A guy jumped from the fifth floor. Looks like it's that big-time businessman, Knäck-something-or-other. His wife and son are here, in shock. We need another ambulance for them. Oh, I see . . . von Knecht."

DETECTIVE SUPERINTENDENT Sven Andersson had just reached his old Volvo 240 and was putting his key in the lock when he heard a familiar female voice shouting, "Sven, wait! Case in progress!"

Annoyed, he turned to her and sighed. "What is it now?"

The detective inspector's voice revealed a slight hint of titillation when she said, "Richard von Knecht jumped off his balcony!"

"Richard von Knecht! *The* Richard von Knecht?"

"Yes. It sounds unbelievable. Was there a stock market crash or something?"

"Hop in the car. Did you get an address?"

THE RAIN was pouring down, and the superintendent had to put his windshield wipers on high to be able to see out. Göteborg was really living up to its nickname of "Soaking-borg." The week before there had been total winter chaos with half a meter of snow; the whole city had been paralyzed for several days. The result would undoubtedly be a high birth rate the next August. Now it was a few degrees above freezing with not a snowflake to be seen.

Detective Inspector Irene Huss phoned her teenage daughters and told them that she'd be late. They were used to it by now, after her many years with the Crime Police. They promised to take the dog for a walk and feed him, and to let their father know. Krister was no doubt used to it, too. As was usual, he would make a good dinner for his daughters. Everything had been organized to run smoothly in the family, even without her help.

She must have sighed audibly, because Superintendent Andersson turned to her and asked, "Is something bothering you?"

"No, nothing. It's depressing weather. Depressing, with scattered suicides. Depressing. Depressing!"

The superintendent nodded in agreement and stared gloomily at the black rain being flung against the windshield by the gusty wind. He broke the silence and asked, "How could Dispatch be so sure that it was really Richard von Knecht who jumped?"

"According to the officer on duty, the wife and son were down on the street. Apparently, it was the son who called the police."

"Do you know what floor he fell from?"

"No, but it seems it was high enough."

They sat in silence for a few minutes. At last the superintendent cleared his throat and asked, "Do you know anything about Richard von Knecht?"

"What most people know. Aristocratic family, and wealthy. Talented businessman, stock market speculator, and one of Göteborg's biggest celebrities. According to *Aftonbladet*'s financial section he's a business genius, but my husband says he's just had incredible luck."

"Is Krister an expert on business and the stock market now, too?"

"No. Although he does own twenty shares of Trygg Hansa, which he received as a bonus when they reorganized a few years back. He's still the chef at Glady's Corner."

"That's supposed to be a great place. Very trendy, I hear."

"You bet."

Through the slapping of the windshield wipers they could now see the flashing blue lights of the emergency vehicles. The crime team was there and had blocked off a large area. The site of the body's impact was illuminated by a soft light streaming from the glass in the front entrance of an exclusive menswear store. The door was set into the corner of the building's granite foundation. Superintendent Andersson had a vague memory that there had been a pharmacy on this spot when he was a boy. But he wasn't quite sure, since he had grown up in

Masthugget, the neighborhood that was torn down during "urban renewal" in the sixties.

Above the door the corner extended into an oriel. There was an oriel on the corner of each floor, whose bay windows faced in three directions, except for the top floor, which sported a balcony crowned by a turreted roof. It was from there that Richard von Knecht had plunged to the street. Superintendent Andersson let his glance pass over the remains, but he quickly looked away. Inspector Huss also shuddered when she saw what von Knecht looked like. It was not a pretty way to die, she thought. One of the crime scene team came over to them.

"The medical examiner will be here any minute."

"Do you know which one is coming?" asked the superintendent.

A shrug was the reply. With Inspector Huss in his wake, Superintendent Andersson walked over to the parked patrol car. He bent down to the officer in the driver's seat.

"Hi, Superintendent Sven Andersson from Homicide."

"Hans Stefansson from PO-One. So they've already called in you guys?"

"Yes, it's unusually quick. We were contacted barely fifteen minutes afterward, which would mean that he jumped at five forty-five P.M. Is that right?"

"No, we were the first on the scene, at five thirty-five on the dot. He must have floated on down max five minutes earlier. My partner and I were on Korsvägen when the call came in. I would think the correct time of impact would be five-thirty."

Their conversation was interrupted by the arrival of Medical Examiner Yvonne Stridner. She was a professor of forensic medicine and undeniably one of the country's most talented pathologists. But Superintendent Andersson had a hard time working with her because Professor Stridner was a woman who demonstrated her expertise gladly and saw no reason to hide her light under a bushel. Inspector Huss herself had been involved in several cases in which the hypotheses of the police were turned completely upside down by Yvonne Stridner's definite forensic opinions. And so far she had always been right. But that wasn't it as much as the fact that she was authoritarian and pedantic that made it difficult for Superintendent Andersson to accept her. Huss had a strong hunch that, deep down, the superintendent did not regard forensic medicine as a proper job for a woman.

The white Ford Escort with MEDICAL EXAMINER painted on both front doors had been parked at the outer perimeter of the blocked-off area.

Out sailed the professor of forensic medicine. Even those who had no idea of her profession stood aside in deference to her commanding presence. Her flaming red hair was exquisitely set off by her soft mustard-colored woolen coat. She strode up to the body, took off her coat, and asked an officer to hold it. Underneath she was wearing a clean white lab coat. She opened the little bag she was carrying, pulled on a pair of latex gloves, and squatted down next to von Knecht's remains. The crime scene technicians had just rigged up a floodlight, giving her a better view. She hadn't cast a single glance around her. Professor Stridner was wearing a pair of plastic protectors over her expensive leather shoes. There was a good deal of blood around the body, mixed with a lot of other material and diluted with rainwater. Slushy.

In order to feel that she was being of some use, Inspector Huss decided to start questioning the police officers present. The commander of the unit, Håkan Lund, she knew well. Fifteen years earlier they had both been rookies in what was then the third precinct, today Polisområde 1, Göteborg's downtown area. Lund wasn't much taller than she was—five-nine at most. But his waistline would soon be approaching his height if he didn't watch out.

The crime team had received their instructions. Håkan Lund turned to Irene Huss and said easily, "At your service, Huss! Is Violent Crimes already on site?"

"Hi, how are you doing? Yes, we were called in early this time. When did you get here?"

"We got the call from Dispatch just after five-thirty. We were inside the station but left right away. 'Top priority! Richard von Knecht is lying dead at the corner of Molinsgatan and Aschebergsgatan!'"

"How did it look here?"

"Chaos! The vultures had gathered. We almost couldn't get through the crowd. But we pushed and shoved and got them driven back and set up barriers. We cordoned off a large area, as you can see. A few people did try to get under the crime scene tape, but I yelled right in their faces. Literally!"

Inspector Huss could imagine the scene vividly. Quickly she went on to ask, "Who identified Richard von Knecht?"

"His wife and son. When we got through the crowd a woman covered in blood was standing here wailing. Some guy was trying to prop her up. That was Fru von Knecht and her son. From what I understood, they happened to be right here on the street when he fell," said Lund sympathetically.

"Where are they now?"

"The ambulance took them off to Sahlgren Hospital. But you won't be able to talk to her for a couple of days, and the son was chalk white in the face. He even threw up before they got into the ambulance."

Lund looked serious, but suddenly brightened up and exclaimed, "Hey, I know someone you'll be interested in meeting. Come on!"

Irene followed him over toward the crime team's van. With a histrionic gesture he opened up one of the side doors and said, "This is Fru Eva Karlsson. Fru Karlsson, this is Detective Inspector Irene Huss."

He turned to the little old woman in the light-gray trench coat, who nodded mutely in greeting. On her knees sat a brown dachshund. It clearly did not suffer from muteness. Over the dog's frantic yapping Irene could hear Lund saying, "This is the closest witness we have. She was standing about seven meters from the point of impact."

Irene turned to the woman. A trembling, thin white hand was held out toward her. Cautiously, she took the fragile, ice-cold hand in hers. In a soothing tone of voice she began, "Fru Karlsson, I'd like to hear a little about the tragic event you were witness to this evening—"

"Frightful! I'm almost seventy-seven years old, and this is the most appalling thing that has ever happened to me in my whole life! To watch a human being smashed right at my feet! He almost fell right on top of Snoopy!"

A thin white finger pointed accusingly at the remains of Richard von Knecht. Irene gave up at once. It would be best to drive the old lady home and try to interview her later.

Over by the body, Stridner had begun packing up her things. With a practiced motion the professor tore off the rubber gloves, took off her lab coat, and stuffed all of it into her bag. She had already removed the plastic protectors from her feet. Without looking at him, Stridner made a queenly gesture with her arm to the young police sergeant, who had been patiently holding her coat for more than a quarter of an hour. She seemed only now to notice all the people standing around her. She called out, "Is there anyone from Violent Crimes here?"

Superintendent Andersson slumped, sighed, and shambled over to her.

"All right, Andersson. Come and look. Don't step in the blood," said the pathologist.

Inspector Huss stole after her superintendent. Stridner had taken a pen from the outside pocket of her bag. She pulled briskly on one end and produced a meter-long lecture pointer. It was perfectly in character for Yvonne Stridner to go around with a pointer in her bag. She said urgently, "Look there at the top of the right hand. I've turned his hand forward so that the light falls on it. Look!"

She gestured with her slender pointer. The two detectives looked. Running across the entire back of the hand was a deep groove. It wasn't as incised as a knife wound, but it had clearly been caused by something relatively sharp.

Andersson ventured to ask, "Couldn't he have gotten that from the fall?"

"No. Too distinct. The wound was inflicted by an instrument or weapon. Since I happen to know . . . knew . . . von Knecht, this death affects me personally. I'm actually supposed to be teaching graduate students all morning tomorrow, but I'll see to the autopsy myself. I'll start by eight at the latest and will let you know after eleven."

"Isn't there a chance you could take a look at him tonight?" Superintendent Andersson gazed at the professor without much hope. She fluffed her red tresses with her fingertips. Her hairdo had been thoroughly soaked while she was doing her preliminary investigation. "Not necessary, Andersson," she replied curtly. "It's almost certain that this is a homicide."

Irene Huss stared incredulously at the pathologist. Rage began to rise inside her: being condescended to stimulates the release of adrenaline in most people. She interrupted the conversation acerbically. "Wait just a minute! What are you basing this on? And how did you know von Knecht?"

The pathologist gave her a surprised look, as if only now noticing that another person was present. Sven Andersson muttered Irene Huss's name and title in explanation. Before Professor Stridner managed to reply, some ambulance men came over and asked whether it was all right to take the body to Pathology. The ME nodded. She gestured toward the main entry.

"We'll wait over there so we won't be in the way. And we can get out of the rain."

In a troop they walked over to the building entrance, a solid door with beautiful incised glass in the top half. There was no list of names of the people who lived in the building, only a coded intercom system. You had to know the proper code to get hold of any of the residents.

Yvonne Stridner came straight to the point.

"We weren't close friends, von Knecht and I. He did some sailing with my husband. My ex-husband, to be more precise. My present husband doesn't know the von Knecht family at all."

So the frosty medical examiner was married, and for a second time. Irene's ire was replaced by astonishment.

Oblivious to the inspector's surprise, the professor continued.

"It must be fifteen years since I last saw them. But I'm convinced that Richard never ever would jump from a balcony twenty-five meters up! Even if he wanted to commit suicide. He was terrified of heights, you see. When he was out sailing, if a sheet or shroud starting getting tangled on the mast, he never wanted to climb up and fix it."

"How did your ex-husband know Richard von Knecht?"

Again it was Irene Huss who asked. Yvonne Stridner gave her a sharp look but nodded in comprehension of the reason the question had been asked.

"They belonged to the same crowd during their high school days. They stuck together through thick and thin over the years. Over time, various girlfriends and wives joined the group. We were invited to the spring bonfire celebration and the New Year's party held every year. Otherwise we girls stayed pretty much on the sidelines. It was like a men's club, or a fraternal lodge."

"How many years did you socialize with the von Knechts?"

"Tore and I were married barely four years. I met them probably ten times. As I said, this was fifteen years ago. After our divorce I lost contact with the von Knecht circle."

Irene could see that the professor was beginning to glance at her elegant wristwatch and knew that she had to hurry and get to the last important question. Quickly she asked, "Who was included in this men's club?"

Now Yvonne Stridner looked annoyed. Maybe she thought she had been too communicative.

"They were men who are quite prominent today," she said brusquely. Then she thought for a moment and her expression brightened. "Let's do this. I'll make a list of all the men in the group. You'll have it tomorrow with the preliminary autopsy report."

She hurried off toward the white Ford Escort. Irene watched her go and said, "She's actually quite human."

Andersson snorted. "Human, her? She's got the emotional life of a backhoe!"

Inspector Huss smiled, concluding once again that the superintendent didn't forgive or forget easily.

"How are we going to get into the building then? This is a real Fort Knox if you don't have the code or the keys," she noted.

Superintendent Andersson didn't seem to be listening; for a long while he stood, lost in thought. Finally he took a deep breath and said, "It's going to take some time before the superintendent at headquarters gets hold of the prosecutor and gets his permission for a search warrant. In the meantime I'll just have to stay here and wait for the warrant and a locksmith. HQ will also have to track down the phone number of someone in this building who can let us in. Maybe you could drive up to Sahlgren Hospital and check on how the wife and son are doing. My first thought was to borrow the key from the wife so we don't have to damage their lovely front door."

A weary and bitter undertone revealed that Andersson was more affected by the events than he would admit.

"Okay, I'll run up to emergency. The car keys, please," she said.

Irene reached out her hand and took the keys, still warm from his pocket. She walked off toward the old Volvo.

AS USUAL, finding a parking place was hopeless, even though evening visiting hours at the hospital were almost over. Huss showed her police ID to the guard and was allowed to drive in. That didn't always happen when the police showed up in plainclothes and didn't have someone in the car who needed patching up.

Since it was a normal Tuesday evening and still relatively early, it was quiet in the big emergency room. Irene went up to the nurses' counter and saw a blond male nurse sitting there, talking on the telephone. They had met several times before in the line of duty. He waved cheerfully in acknowledgment and signaled that he'd be off the phone soon.

Irene looked around. Right outside the counter was an elderly man on a gurney. His face was a horrible shade of gray; she could hardly see his lips in that pale face. He lay there with his eyes closed and didn't seem to be conscious of his surroundings. On a chair next to him sat a short, plump woman patting his arm unceasingly. She was sniffling quietly but didn't speak to him. Over by the waiting room a youth sat with a wad of bloody paper towels wrapped around his hand. An older gentleman whom Irene recognized from the "A-team" bench in Brunnsparken lay snoring loudly on a gurney. He didn't seem to be in such bad shape because the blood around the gash on his forehead had already started to congeal. A young woman sat stiffly on her chair staring into space. Except for the old man's snoring it was almost peaceful in the ER.

Nurse Roland finished his phone call and waved Huss over from the corridor with a blithe "Hi there, Irene! Long time no see! I bet I can guess why you're here."

"Hi! Have you seen Fru von Knecht and her son?"

"I sure have. The medics came in and brought me out to the ambulance. They had a feeling that it was probably best to take her straight to Psych. And in the condition she was in, I agreed with them."

"How did the son look?"

"He just sat there staring into space. Of course he's had a great shock too. Would you like a quick cup of coffee before you dash off?"

Roland gestured invitingly toward the employees' lounge. Irene could feel her body longing for a cup of coffee but declined. Time was passing. She started to walk toward the exit as an odd figure came through the double doors. He was tall and incredibly skinny. His rat-colored hair was thin and straggled down the back of his leather jacket. On his feet he wore a pair of indescribably dirty and ragged jogging shoes, and only his jeans could compete with them in filthiness. His thigh-length leather jacket was of a sixties design and had probably been bought at the Salvation Army or picked out of a Dumpster after someone had cleaned out an attic. But it wasn't his slovenly clothing, which had seen a few too many winters, that made Irene gape.

His skin was so yellow that it was almost greenish. The guy had jaundice of the most fulminating kind. Without a word the yellow-skinned man ripped off his jacket. The front of his T-shirt was drenched with blood. His stony pupils, surrounded by the sulfur-yellow whites of his eyes, stared straight at the inspector. He grabbed hold of the bottom of his T-shirt and pulled it up.

Then Irene yelled, "Roland! Hurry! Roland!"

Nurse Roland stuck his head out the door of the nurses' station. After more than ten years on the job in the ER, he had no problem evaluating the situation instantly.

"Damn, that's a loop of intestine hanging out his belly!"

He dashed back into the station. Irene heard him yell on the intercom, ". . . abdomen slashed open. He's a walking case of HIV and hepatitis!"

He bolted like a shot out the door. On the way he swept on a yellow protective coat, plastic gloves, and a pair of safety glasses. Just as he reached the stabbing victim, the man's eyes turned upward and rolled into his skull as he collapsed onto the floor.

Down the corridor quick steps were heard approaching. The emergency personnel walked as fast as they could while trying to pull on some protective gear.

With a careful evasive maneuver the inspector slunk out into the black November damp. Now it felt good to be outside in the cold. The wind had let up and the rain hung like an icy fog in the air. She went over to her car and drove through the hospital grounds.

PSYCH EMERGENCY was locked, of course. Irene had to ring the doorbell. A tall, muscular nurse in a white uniform came and opened the door. He towered in the doorway, his shoulders almost filling it. He had sharply defined, powerful features and very dark skin. Could he be from India? He was certainly ten years younger than Irene. But he was one of the most beautiful men she had ever seen.

"Hi, what do you want?" He had a deep, pleasant voice with no accent.

"Detective Inspector Irene Huss, Crime Police. I'd like to have a few words with the son of Richard von Knecht. No, not an interrogation, nothing like that. I know he accompanied his mother here an hour ago. We need some help with a case. Their ambulance had already left by the time we got to the scene of the accident."

Irene showed her police ID. The nurse, whose name tag said THOMAS, nodded and smiled. She followed him to the cramped waiting room. He said in a low voice, "They were placed in an examining room immediately. Have a seat if you like, and I'll go tell Henrik von Knecht that you want to speak to him."

Again he gave her an irresistible smile before he turned away. Irene saw his broad back disappear down the corridor. He knocked on a door and opened it. Sobs could be heard from within. The nurse was inside for barely a minute. When he emerged a pale man most likely in his thirties accompanied him. There were flecks of blood on the man's light beige overcoat, mainly on the sleeves and across the chest.

From inside the examination room a loud wail was heard. "Don't go, Henrik. Don't leave me here!"

Henrik von Knecht closed the door and leaned his forehead against it for a moment. He straightened up quickly, took a deep breath, and followed the nurse. They were about the same height. But everything about the dark-skinned nurse that implied strength, warmth, and radiance seemed to be the exact opposite in Henrik von Knecht. He was indeed tall, but slightly stooped. His elegant topcoat hung loosely on his gaunt body. His blond hair was thin on top. To conceal this he combed his long shock of hair in front straight back. His face was angular. It was actually a pleasant face, but his pallor and the light-colored coat gave him an oddly washed-out appearance.

He walked up to Irene. His gruff voice rasped when he said expectantly, "Yes, what do you want?"

"My name is Detective Inspector Irene Huss. We would be very grateful if you would help us with something."

"What's that?"

"We need to borrow the key to your parents' apartment."

He jumped as if she had slapped him hard.

"The key? Why?"

"So we don't have to call a locksmith in order to enable us to search the apartment. It's a necessity in cases like this. It would be nice not to ruin the lock. Or the door."

He looked as if he was thinking of protesting, but instead gritted his teeth and turned on his heel. Over his shoulder he said, "Mamma has the front door key in her handbag."

He vanished into the examination room. Irene could hear an excited muttering of voices inside and loud sobbing. After almost five minutes Henrik von Knecht emerged. His face resembled an eroded marble statue. From inside the room Irene could hear a tense, shrill female voice: ". . . back the keys. Even if they're . . ."

The flow of words was cut off as von Knecht resolutely pulled the door shut.

Chapter Two

HENRIK VON KNECHT DIDN'T say a word during the five-minute car trip. He sat with his head bent forward, his forehead in his hands, and his elbows propped on his knees. Inspector Huss didn't ask him to put on his seat belt, but let him sit there, lost in his grief, in silence.

When they turned onto Molinsgatan, Irene Huss saw that it wasn't just Superintendent Andersson and the crime scene technicians who were gathered outside Richard von Knecht's building. Two people she recognized quite well were squeezed into the doorway of the menswear store. She drove by them and turned left on Engelbrekts- gatan. Huss lightly touched Henrik von Knecht's arm, which made him jump as if she had wakened him.

"Where are we going?" he asked in confusion.

"I thought I'd drive around the neighborhood and park on Asche- bergsgatan. There are two newspaper reporter guys waiting on the cor- ner by the menswear store. Can we get into the building through a back courtyard and open the front door for the others from inside? That way you can ditch the hyenas," she said.

A tense expression passed over his face, and he seemed to awaken. "Park here on the right side by Erik Dahlberg's stairs. Take one of the two outer spots," he directed.

They were lucky; one of the spots was vacant. Irene looked at his blood-flecked beige overcoat. She asked him to remain seated while she stepped out and opened the trunk. In it she had an old, greasy blue Helly Hansen jacket and her daughter's black cap, embroidered with NY. She handed him the garments and said, "Take off your overcoat and put these on."

He changed quickly inside the car, without revealing what he thought of his disguise.

They crossed the intersection at a brisk pace. This was the critical moment. She had to force herself not to look toward the corner fifty meters away. With strained composure they kept going for another twenty meters or so. Henrik von Knecht stopped at a massive wooden doorway, took a bundle of keys out of the pocket of his tailored trousers, and unlocked the door. One of the photographers poked his head around the corner, but he didn't seem to react to the contrasts in von Knecht's attire.

They slipped in through the doorway and wound up in a storage area. It was a combined bicycle and garbage room consisting of a passageway about twenty meters long equipped with locked doors at either end. Five green garbage cans stood close to the street entrance.

They hurried through the room, turned the lock of the inner door, and stepped into a small, square, back courtyard. It was dominated by a big tree in the center, and illuminated by an old-fashioned streetlight. Flower beds bordered the walls. On each wall there was a little entry door with a window, and each door was lighted by a bright exterior lamp. Henrik von Knecht strode directly to the one on the left, unlocked the door, and held it open for Irene Huss. He reached out his hand toward the glowing red button to turn on the stairway lights.

"Don't turn on the lights! Or the reporters will see that something's going on," she snapped.

She took out her little high-intensity flashlight from the pocket of her poplin jacket. With the beam pointed downward she started up the five narrow steps, went through a low doorway, and stepped out into a large stairwell. In the beam of light the floor's variegated marble gleamed. To her right she could see the light from an elevator window. She turned off the flashlight and they headed off toward the stairs, which led down to the front entrance. When she was opposite the elevator door she could see the upper part of the front door's beautiful incised-glass pane. She took a few steps forward and glimpsed the heads of the superintendent and the techs outside. Cautiously she stepped to one side of the broad stairway, grabbed the carved banister, and glided down the ten steps to the front door. She padded across the soft carpet in the foyer, pulled open the door behind her colleagues, and loudly urged, "Hurry! Come inside before the ambulance chasers get here!"

"Hurry? How the hell are we going to do that when we've just pissed our pants?" asked Police Technician Svante Malm.

Superintendent Andersson later claimed that he had never been so close to a heart attack in all his life.

They slipped in through the door before the tabloid reporters at the corner figured out what was happening. Irene turned on the stairwell lights. The superintendent blinked his eyes angrily and snapped, "What the hell are you doing?"

Irene didn't reply, but gazed up in wonder at the walls of the stair-well. The frescoes were amazing, with children romping among wood anemones and an allegorical figure of Springtime, flying in a cart drawn by huge exotic butterflies. It was all done in light, elegant, springlike pastels. On the opposite wall was a full Midsummer Eve celebration done in considerably richer and more intense tones. Grown-ups and children danced in the summer twilight, and the fiddler sawed away at his instrument for dear life. His face was shiny with sweat; his eyes glistened with the joy of making music.

"Carl Larsson did the paintings, in the early eighteen nineties."

The police turned their faces to the top of the stairs, where the voice had come from. In his disguise, Henrik von Knecht looked undeniably bizarre. He peered down at the four officers and nodded to Irene before he continued.

"Inspector Huss was kind enough to help me get past the press. Shall we go upstairs?" He gestured toward the elevator door. The police trudged up the stairs and squeezed into the tiny elevator. A brass plate said MAX. FIVE PERSONS. Irene sincerely hoped that meant full-grown persons. She made a point of introducing Henrik von Knecht to the other three: Superintendent Andersson and the crime scene techni-cians Svante Malm and Per Svensson. The latter was carrying the heavy lighting equipment and various cameras.

The elevator took them up to the fifth floor without a hitch. They stepped out and walked over to a huge carved double door. A slender wrought-iron grid in the shape of entwined French lilies covered the door's cut-glass window. The carvings on the lower half of the door rep-resented leaping and gamboling deer. Svante Malm put his lips together to whistle, impressed by its magnificence.

Irene thought that Henrik von Knecht seemed to have recovered a little of his spirit during their game of hide-and-seek with the press. But when they stepped out of the elevator the rigid expression was back on his face. Superintendent Andersson saw it too.

"You don't need to go into the apartment with us," he said kindly.

"But I want to!"

His reply came like a cobra strike. The superintendent was surprised, and he hesitated. "I see, all right. But you have to stay right next to us. You can't touch anything, sit on any chairs, or turn on any lights. Of course we're grateful that you can guide us through the apartment. How big is it?"

"Three hundred fifty square meters. It takes up the whole floor. The other three flats in the building take up a whole floor too. Pappa bought this building in the late seventies and had it renovated very carefully. It's on the National Register, of course," he informed them.

"So there are only three other apartments in the whole building?"

"Right."

While they were talking, the superintendent had put on a pair of thin rubber gloves. With a gesture he asked Henrik von Knecht for the door key. He took it and unlocked the door.

Gingerly gripping the very end of the door handle, he pressed it down and opened the door to the apartment.

"Don't touch any light switches in the hall. Turn on your flashlights," Svante Malm exhorted. He sighed and went on, "The laser is broken, so I'll have to use the good old powder method."

As soon as the technician said this, he began to search for the light switch with the beam from his flashlight. When he found it just inside the door, he asked Irene to keep her flashlight pointed at the switch while he blew metallic powder over the entire plastic switch plate. Carefully he brushed away the excess, pressed a thin plastic sheet over the surface, and then peeled it off. A look of astonishment spread across his long, narrow face.

"Completely blank. Not a single mark! Someone has wiped the switch plate clean," he said, astounded.

"That's probably why it smells like Ajax," said Irene.

She sniffed the air. There was something else. A cigar. That explained the Christmas mood that had stolen over her unconscious when they stepped into the hall. A memory from her childhood Christmases. Her mother's Ajax and her father's Christmas cigar. She turned to von Knecht.

"Did your father smoke cigars?"

"Yes, sometimes. On festive occasions . . ."

His voice died out to a whisper. He swallowed hard, for he too had noticed the cigar smell. Barely moving his lips, he whispered to Irene, "Why are they taking fingerprints?"

She thought about what the medical examiner had said, but decided to evade his question. "Just routine. We always do this when we're called to the scene of a sudden death," she explained.

He made no comment but clenched his jaws so hard that the muscles bulged out like rock-hard pillows along his jawline.

Svante Malm turned on the light in the hall, which was airy and of an imposing size. The ceiling had to be four meters high. The floor was made of light gray marble. To the right of the door paraded five built-in wardrobes with doors carved of some dark wood. The one in the middle was adorned with an oval mirror that took up almost the entire door panel. Despite this, one of the biggest and most ornamental mirrors Irene had ever seen loomed up on the opposite wall. Below it stood an equally ornate gilt console table. Superintendent Andersson turned to von Knecht.

"Can you give us a rough idea of the apartment's layout?"

"Of course. The door next to the mirror leads to a toilet. The door after that goes to the kitchen."

"And the door opposite the kitchen, next to the wardrobes?"

"It leads to the guest suite on this level. There's also a separate bathroom with a toilet in there. Straight ahead we have the door to the living room. All the way in, to the left, is the stairway to the upper floor. Up there are the library, a small den, sauna, bedroom, TV room, and billiard room. And a bathroom with a toilet and Jacuzzi."

Svante Malm had stopped in front of a shiny polished bureau with gilt fittings, rounded lines, and checkerboard veneer in alternating light and dark wood. With reverence in his voice he said, "I just have to ask: Is this a Haupt bureau?"

Henrik von Knecht snorted involuntarily. "No, the Haupt is in the library. Pappa bought this one in London. The insured value is five hundred fifty thousand kronor. Also a fine piece," he said.

None of the policemen could think of anything to say. The superintendent turned to Irene. "You might as well stay here with Henrik while we take a look around," he said.

"I'd like to come with you. There could be something that's out of the ordinary," von Knecht quickly countered.

He jutted out his chin and his mouth took on a stubborn look. Andersson gave him an appraising glance and nodded his assent. He turned to the crime scene technicians.

"Let's check the balcony first," he decided.

As a group they headed for the wide entrance to the living room. They stepped cautiously onto the vast, soft rug in the middle of the hall floor. Irene couldn't help stopping to admire its shimmering gold pattern, which depicted a beautiful tree with birds and stylized animals, surrounded by a climbing plant like a grapevine against a dark blue background. She could feel von Knecht looking at her.

"That's a semi-antique Motashemi-Keshan," he said knowledgeably.

She had a fleeting vision of her latest investment on the rug front, a rusty red rug with small primitive stick figures in the corners. The salesperson at IKEA had assured her that it was a genuine, hand-tied Gabbeh, for the reasonable price of only two thousand kronor. She loved her rug and thought that it lit up the whole living room from its place beneath the coffee table.

Suddenly she had the equally fierce and foolish impulse to defend her rug. With more vehemence than she intended, she snapped, "Are you some kind of museum guy, or what?"

"No, but I deal in antiques," he replied curtly.

They stood in the doorway until Henrik left the living room. In the flashlight beam Svante Malm was performing his fingerprint procedure on the big light switch panel, with the same negative results. Irene could sense that they were in a very large dining room. Light from the street filtered in through the sheer, drawn curtains. Windows seemed to run from floor to ceiling along the entire outer wall. Why did it feel like they were in a church? Since there weren't any prints to be found, Malm flicked on the lights. Shiny, heavy brass chandeliers illuminated a huge dining room. They were all surprised and oddly awestruck, but the superintendent collected himself and said, "All right, then. Has everyone put on their plastic booties?"

The stairway began right next to the light switch panel and led up along the wall where they stood. With Andersson in the lead the techs quickly climbed the broad marble staircase.

Henrik pressed the last button on the panel, and with a soft hum the thin champagne-colored side drapes slid open.

She had envisioned it all wrong. The tall windows were not windows, but French doors to the balcony. And they didn't stretch from floor to ceiling. The height of the ceiling at the outer wall was indeed eight meters. But above their heads the ceiling was only four meters high, stopping abruptly a few meters farther toward the windows. Irene walked into the room and looked around. What was the ceiling in this room was of course the floor of the upstairs level. Where the upper-level floor stopped, there was a lovely wrought-iron railing. It extended on two sides of the dining room. High above her head vaulted the stuccoed ceiling. No wonder she had the feeling of being in a church. From the ceiling hung three colossal chandeliers. The entire room was oblong, but it looked narrower than it was because marble pillars stood in rows supporting the upper floor.

Her colleagues walked with purposeful steps along the railing, over to the corner of the balcony in the big open library. She returned to Henrik, and they walked silently up the wide staircase together.

On the upper floor the odor of cigars was very strong. They followed the railing up to the airy library. To the left Irene saw a corridor with several doors. This must be where the other rooms and the sauna were, she realized. The sauna . . . She slowed her steps and stopped. Underlying the cigar smell was a familiar fragrance.

She took a deep breath and turned to Henrik. "Do you know what this smell is?"

He sniffed the air and nodded. "Eucalyptus. Pappa took a sauna. That's why he had on his dressing gown," he replied with a slight quaver in his voice.

She had a fleeting vision of the scene: the crushed body of Richard von Knecht dressed in a thick dressing gown of wine-red velvet terry cloth, his naked legs contorted and white in the floodlights, and the brown leather slippers lying a few meters from the body. She shuddered and concentrated on her colleagues standing by the door to the balcony.

The three men silently faced the locked door. Slowly Superintendent Andersson turned around and said solemnly to Henrik von Knecht, "Unfortunately, I must prepare you for the fact that there are strong indications that your father was murdered. The balcony door is locked from the inside, the key is in the lock, the handle is pulled down. And there's no handle on the outside."

This was too much for von Knecht. He dropped to his knees inside the balcony door with his hands to his face and broke into quiet, dry sobs.

Irene called for help, for someone from a squad car to drive him home in his white Mercedes.

BEFORE THE cruiser arrived, Inspector Huss asked him whether he could try to answer a few questions. He nodded affirmatively.

She began neutrally, "Where do you live?"

"The Örgryte neighborhood. On Långåsliden."

"Do you have anyone who could stay with you tonight, or would you like us to contact someone?"

"My wife is home."

"Oh."

Irene could hear how stupid her remark sounded, but she was very surprised that von Knecht had a wife. She quickly tried to cover up her reaction.

"Does your wife know about what happened this evening?"

He shook his head without taking his hands from his face.

She went on, "If I understand correctly, you and your mother were in the street at the time your father fell. You were getting out of a car, is that right?"

For a long time he remained sitting silently in the same position. Irene began to wonder whether he even realized she had asked a question. She considered reformulating it when he removed his hands and looked straight at her. Again she saw the rigid mask. Even though his eyes were shining with tears, there was a layer of ice beneath the tears. He rubbed his face in a weary gesture.

"Pardon me . . . What did you ask me?"

Irene posed the question again. He took a deep breath before he answered.

"We parked around the corner, on Aschebergsgatan. I didn't notice that anything had happened as I hurried around to open the door for Mamma. Then I heard a scream. I could see that . . . something was lying on the ground, and people were running over to it. Mamma ran there. She started screaming. I called the police from my cell phone. Well, you know the rest."

"Where had you and your mother been?"

"We had decided to meet at Landvetter Airport. She came in on a plane from Stockholm that landed fifteen minutes after my own flight from London. It was a pure coincidence that our flights were arriving at the same time. We discovered it last Saturday when we had a party here. Mamma and Pappa were celebrating their thirtieth anniversary . . ."

He swallowed hard and fell silent. Huss realized that he wouldn't be able to say much more.

"We can postpone the rest of our talk until tomorrow. Would you like me to come to your house or will you come down to the station?"

"I'll come down to the station."

"How does eleven sound? Bring your wife too."

"We'll try to be there at eleven."

"It's about time for us to go downstairs. The officers in the squad car can't come through the front entrance, as you know," she said gently.

She escorted him down in the elevator. He muttered his thanks and disappeared out into the darkness between the two waiting uniformed officers.

IRENE HAD to stop and admire the skillfully laid marble floor. The pattern was a black swan surrounded by pink and white lilies. It was the most beautiful floor she had ever seen. Carl Larsson on the stair-well walls, as an extra bonus, didn't hurt the overall impression either.

In her many years on the police force, she had passed through hun-dreds of stairwells, most of them depressingly dilapidated, with the smell of piss and cooked food slamming visitors in the face like a kind of urban tear gas. The walls were scratched up and the graffiti shrieked COCK, NIGGER GO HOME, KILROY WAS HERE, and other cheery messages. Filthy stairs and front doors that had been kicked in were part of the usual picture. The police are seldom called to stairwells with marble inlay on the floor and Carl Larsson paintings on the walls.

THE BALCONY door was open and the techs were busy securing evi-dence. One obvious item was a meat cleaver. Not the size used by a butcher, but rather a smaller kitchen variety.

"This was lying on the floor of the balcony, right next to the wall. It was sheltered by part of the roof, so we'll probably find something of interest on it," said Andersson.

The superintendent was more excited than he wanted to show. His cheeks were flushed a bright red.

Irene said softly, "Are you okay? I mean . . . your blood pressure?"

"Why the hell are you bringing that up now?"

The superintendent was thrown quite off balance and looked annoyed. No one wants to be reminded of the incipient infirmities of old age. Hypertension was one of his. The techs looked up from their tasks in surprise. With great effort Andersson controlled himself and lowered his voice.

"The sauna was turned on. I got overheated when I looked inside," he said without convincing even himself.

Irene decided to drop the sensitive question of her boss's blood pres-sure. "Was the heating unit still on?" she wondered.

"No, it was off. And here's the explanation for the cigar smell."

Andersson pointed at the gray cylinder of ash left by a cigar that lay in a blue crystal ashtray, placed on a smoking table inset with a round copper disc. Beside the ashtray stood a short whisky glass with a trace of amber-colored liquid in the bottom. The smoking table stood between two sofas, which stood perpendicular to each other. They looked invit-ingly comfortable and were covered in soft wine-red leather. The sofa nearest the balcony was placed with its back to the wrought-iron rail-ing, one end facing the balcony door. A wing chair was ensconced in front of the big mullioned window, upholstered in leather that matched the sofas. The halogen reading lamp next to it resembled a flesh-eating plant made of brass. The other sofa faced the balcony door, with its back to the stairway and the bedroom corridor. The placement of the ashtray and the whisky glass indicated that Richard von Knecht had been sitting on the latter sofa. The superintendent pondered the scene.

"Why was he sitting on the sofa and not in the wing chair?" he wondered.

"Check the speakers. One is in the corner and the other is on the other side of the balcony door. I'm guessing the sound is best right here on this sofa," Irene replied.

She walked over to the CD player, which was hidden behind smoky glass doors in one of the bookshelves. With a pen she carefully pushed a button, and the disc slid out. Without touching it she read aloud: "*The Best of Glenn Miller*. So Richard von Knecht sits here, fresh out of the sauna, smoking a good cigar, drinking a shot of Scotch whisky, and listening to Glenn Miller. Suddenly he's supposed to jump up, cut his hand with the cleaver, and throw himself off the balcony! It doesn't sound very believable. Stridner was right, it wasn't suicide."

"Don't forget that the balcony door was locked from the inside and the key was in the lock."

"I wonder what happened."

"That's what we're paid to find out," said the superintendent dryly.

He turned toward the balcony and asked in a loud voice, "Svante, is there much blood on the balcony?"

Svante Malm stuck his freckled, horsy face through the door. "No, so far we haven't seen any. Could be some spray, but nothing you'd notice right off."

"Apparently, he wasn't killed with the cleaver on the balcony but was actually shoved over the railing. Funny he didn't scream. Did any of the witnesses say whether he yelled before he fell to the ground?" asked Andersson.

Irene thought of the little old lady with the dog.

"I spoke with the closest witness, an elderly lady with a dachshund. She was quite upset that von Knecht almost landed on her dog. But she didn't mention any scream. Surely she would have said something if he'd screamed as he fell. But she was obviously in shock. I'm interviewing her tomorrow."

"Okay. We'll keep looking around."

Tall built-in bookshelves dominated the library. They extended from floor to ceiling and had glass doors. The sofa group stood in the middle of the area. A smaller reading group in one corner consisted of a glass table and two wing chairs, in the same leather and design as the sofa group. There were no bookshelves around the big window or by the balcony door. Modern art hung on the walls instead. Below a brilliantly colored oil painting, depicting a green monster head with yellow eyes, stood the piece by Haupt. You could hardly call it a bureau; rather, it was a secretary on tall, ornate legs. Below the writing surface were three drawers in a row, and above it an elegant rolltop. It was a disappointment. The bureau in the hall was grander. But evidently that wasn't what determined its value, as Irene gathered from Svante Malm's reaction. On the other side of the window hung two paintings that even the superintendent's untrained eye could tell were Picassos. There were clear signatures on each.

"Cubist style. I recognize it from the descriptions of paintings that were stolen from the Modern Museum in Stockholm. Nothing is where it should be. How do they expect you to see two eyes when the nose is in profile?" said Andersson.

He eyed both paintings critically. They were considerably smaller than the monster painting, but surely much more valuable.

"We'll take a look around. And we won't touch anything, and only use flashlights."

This last he directed at Svante, whose face was again visible in the balcony doorway.

THEY WALKED toward the corridor on the upper floor where the other rooms were located. The first room proved to be the den, slightly smaller than an ordinary living room. In the beam of light they could see more bookshelves with books and binders, a small sofa group, a large desk, and a separate computer table.

Everything looked very clean and neat. Andersson's flashlight stopped at a framed poster over the desk. It depicted a ballerina in a calf-length tulle dress. She had assumed a pose with one leg raised at an angle in front of her, and her arms and torso stretched forward. In large type the poster announced: THE NUTCRACKER. MUSIC BY TCHAIKOVSKY AND WITH ORIGINAL CHOREOGRAPHY BY L. IVANOV.

Surprised, Andersson said, "Did von Knecht like ballet?"

Curious, Irene stepped forward and read in the beam of her penlight: "JOIN US IN CELEBRATING THE NUTCRACKER'S 75TH ANNIVERSARY, 1892–1967, AT THE GRAND THEATER IN GÖTEBORG. Yes indeed, obviously he was interested in ballet," she declared.

"We'll do a quick search through the apartment now. The techs will have all night to secure evidence. I'll meet with them early tomorrow morning if they've found anything of value . . . well, that's a damned stupid thing to say in these surroundings!"

He snorted lightly and Irene felt her heart warm. He too was affected by the objects around them.

They left the den and went into the next room. It turned out to be the famous sauna, completely tiled from floor to ceiling. At the back of the room was a solid Plexiglas wall with a door, also of Plexiglas. Inside were benches at different levels, with a large sauna heating unit against one wall. Outside was a shower with glass walls and sliding doors. Two teak deck chairs with thick cushions and a small table made up the furnishings. There was a strong scent of eucalyptus. Irene shone her light in the shower and saw that the walls and floor were still wet.

"Nothing more of interest. Let's move on to the next door," said Andersson.

Behind it was a separate toilet with a large marble washbasin. The last door on the right side of the corridor led to the billiard room. A large billiard table occupied the middle of the room. On the walls the racks of cues were a nice counterpoint to the art.

They crossed the hallway and entered the largest bedroom either of them had ever set foot in. An extra-wide king-size bed with a yellow silk bedspread and heaps of pillows was the focus of the room. It was surrounded by shining wooden cabinets and chests of drawers; the walls were covered with paintings. Here you could actually see what the art was supposed to represent. Naked bodies, mostly female. There were also a few men pictured. Some of the paintings by the bed were down-right pornographic, or perhaps erotic, since the copulating couples were partially clothed. What clothing they still had on was old-fashioned; the women wore corsets, crinolines, and bonnets. Irene inspected with interest some advanced lovemaking positions portrayed in a number of small Japanese prints. A door on the wall facing the wardrobes proved to conceal a large bathroom. The bathtub was a corner model, apparently the Jacuzzi that had been mentioned.

The superintendent stifled a yawn with the back of his hand and said, "It's ten-thirty. We'll have to settle for a quick once-over of the rest. By the way, did you notice one thing? Where are all the curious neighbors who should be running in and asking what happened? There are three other apartments in this building, after all."

"I'll do a quick round of knocking on doors."

Huss left the von Knecht bedchamber.

She came back sooner than she expected. Andersson was surprised when he ran into her in the downstairs hall again.

"Not a single neighbor is home. It's dark and quiet in all three apartments. And I rang the bells and knocked on the doors," she assured him.

Andersson looked pensive.

"That explains the lack of curious neighbors. And it made things easier for the killer. Headquarters couldn't get any of the neighbors on the phone either. By the way, I looked into the last room upstairs. A TV room. Nothing of interest. Just a bunch of pictures and a giant TV."

He nodded toward the kitchen door.

"Let's look it over."

The kitchen was ultramodern, probably at least fifty square meters. In the middle of the room there was a huge cooking island with an enormous copper ventilation hood. The upper and lower cupboards had carved doors of red-toned cherry wood. On the floor a silk rug lay upon dark red-glazed parquet that gleamed. In front of the stove and around the kitchen island reddish brown tile had been laid. The walls were light colored, almost white. Beams ran across the ceiling, glazed the same color as the floor. Everything was clean and in immaculate order. The door of the dishwasher was ajar. Cautiously the superintendent poked the end of his flashlight inside and looked around.

"Dishes done. No dishes on the drainboard," he declared.

"Sven, look above the counter," said Irene. "There are kitchen implements hanging underneath the ventilator hood."

Five centimeters above the edge of the hood ran a rod that was soldered fast. It had small hooks on it, and various kitchen implements hung on them. They didn't see any meat cleaver. Andersson looked a little perplexed and asked, "What do you use a meat cleaver for?"

Irene was amazed that he didn't know, but restrained herself.

"One side has a sharp edge for chopping off tendons and gristle. The wide, flat part you use to pound the meat to make it thinner and more tender. I wouldn't think it would be used much these days. Usually meat is already cut up and tenderized when you buy it."

"We'll have to compare the wooden handle of the cleaver with the handles of the implements hanging here. It seems to be the same style. And here's an empty hook," said the superintendent.

"I get the feeling these are only for decoration. The tools don't seem to have been used. I've certainly never seen a more virginal whisk! And look how the wooden handles match the cupboard doors exactly," Irene snorted.

She pointed to a door on the far wall. "I wonder where that leads?"

"Looks like an ordinary door to the kitchen stairs. The techs will check it out tomorrow," Andersson decided.

He stifled another yawn before he went on, "I think we've been pretty thorough even though it's just the preliminary survey. Anything we've forgotten?"

Irene understood that the superintendent's question was rhetorical, but that door was bothering her. An image from her memory had been insistently pricking at the back of her mind, and now it popped up. She remembered the four doors downstairs off the little square courtyard in back. The five stairways of all the main entry halls opened onto it, if she remembered it correctly. She hadn't seen anything that looked like back kitchen stairs. There was every reason to look behind the door before they left, she thought.

Andersson sighed but lumbered over to the door with her. With a cautious shove she managed to open it. Behind it was no kitchen stairway, but a large scullery. The beams of the flashlights played over broom closets, a clothes dryer, drying cupboard, and a washing machine. On the latter a red light was blinking, indicating that the wash was done. Again Irene used her pen, so that she wouldn't leave any fingerprints or wipe off any that were already there, as she opened the lid of the washing machine.

"A sheet. He put a sheet and towels in the washing machine before he met his killer," she said dramatically to the superintendent.

They went back out through the kitchen, stepped over the rug in the hall, and inspected the guest suite. Inside the door was an airy bedroom with a queen-size bed. They glanced quickly in the guest bathroom, without finding anything of interest.

Chapter Three

IRENE HUSS DROVE HOME through the midnight stillness of Göteborg. Here and there electric candlesticks had begun to appear in windows, although it was more than a week and a half until the beginning of Advent. Was it because of the Christmas decorations in stores being displayed earlier and earlier, or was it merely a sign of the longing for light in the dense winter darkness? Speaking of light, Jenny needed a new candlestick for her window. The old one had short-circuited last year. Was it Jenny or Katarina who said that she'd rather have a birch-bark star? Sometimes it was hard to remember which of them said what. Even though the girls were twins, they were so unlike in every way that people hardly believed they were even sisters. Jenny was most like Krister, a little uncommunicative and just as blond. But she hadn't inherited her father's interest in food, devoting herself instead mostly to music. Katarina was dark like Irene, extroverted and sporty. She had started going with Irene to the dojo when she was ten. Now she was thirteen and was about to be certified for a green belt, *ukemi-waza.*

Irene had been seventeen when she got hers. At nineteen she became the Nordic female champion in judo, and two years later the European champion. Of course in the women's competitions there hadn't been much significant opposition in the rest of Europe seventeen years ago, but it had still given her high status at the police academy.

Her fellow students still talked about the time an instructor came to the academy to address "the need for the police to know some basics of self-defense." He was a cocksure Stockholmer who intended to show the puny police cadets how a real ninja hero defended himself.

He called up the skinniest boy in class, a wiry kid from Småland who never in his life had trained in any martial arts. On the other hand, he did belong to the Swedish national team in table tennis. The cadet was told to put a choke hold on the instructor from behind, and he obediently complied. Quickly the instructor grabbed the Ping-Pong player's left hand, turned ninety degrees toward him, pressed his hand hard against his shoulder, and put him down on the mat with an *o-soto-otoshi*. There was just one problem—you don't push down wiry cadets from Småland any old way you like. Especially if they're on the national Ping-Pong team. The cadet flared up and resisted, and then his shoulder dislocated. It hurt like hell and the poor guy lay there writhing on the mat. Instruction was halted as the student was taken to the emergency room to have his shoulder reset.

Irene was outraged. During lunch she made a decision. It was against the ground rules of the sport, but the instructor had to be put in his place. He had used a move that belonged to a blue belt, much too high a difficulty level for a beginner.

After lunch the instructor came back to the gym. With a smirk he said he hoped that "this little incident hadn't scared them off from further practice." No one answered, and the mood was gloomy. Quickly the instructor turned to his students and said, "Anyone figure out the hold and want to try?"

Ha, right into the trap! Irene stood up before anyone else could volunteer. With feigned shyness she lowered her eyes and said in her thickest Göteborg accent, "I guess I could give it a try."

Tension was mounting among her fellow cadets, but the instructor didn't notice. He was clearly annoyed when he saw that she was almost ten centimeters taller than he was. Resolutely he raised his arms so he could put a choke hold on her from behind. In a fraction of a second she had tensed her neck muscles, taken a step back with her left leg, and hooked his leg. She pulled his legs apart with a quick sweep, let him fall, and stepped back.

The cheers and applause went on and on.

The flattened instructor tried to regain the initiative as he lay on his back on the mat. "Good, very good! Anyone else want to try?"

The booing that greeted his remark was too strong to drown out. He slunk out the door. That was the first and last time they ever saw the guy.

Irene, amused by the memory, almost missed her turn onto Västerleden at Järnbrotts Motet and headed out toward Särö instead. Her eyelids felt heavy, and she longed to be home in bed.

INSIDE THE front door sat Sammie happily wagging his tail. He jumped, leaped, and wriggled with his whole body to show his boundless joy that she was home. Suddenly he stopped and pressed his nose tight against the door. He gave her a pleading look. *Out. Have to pee. Right away!*

With a sigh she put on his leash and went out in the night. After a few meters she remembered that she didn't have any poop bags left in her pocket. If something happened now, they would have to rely on the darkness and the late hour and quickly slip away from the scene of the crime.

"WAS THIS the reason you were so late last night?"

Krister held up the *Göteborg Post* to Irene's bleary gaze. She was sitting at the breakfast table, trying to wake up. It was almost seven o'clock. Her daughters plopped down at the table. The morning shower fight had ended with Katarina first, Krister second, Jenny third, and herself last. Krister was trying to find a new thermostat for the downstairs shower. It was hopeless to have only one, when all of them had to leave at the same time in the morning. Now it was her turn to shower. But hadn't her husband just asked her something? She saw the black headlines screeching across half the front page: RICHARD VON KNECHT DEAD AFTER FALL FROM BALCONY. Lower down on the page, in smaller type: "Police tight-lipped. Accident or suicide?"

She managed merely to nod in reply. Before she left the kitchen, she said over her shoulder, "I have to take a shower. Dear, make sure the coffee is strong!"

She stood under the water for a luxuriously long time. Feeling much brisker, she went back to the bedroom and threw on her clothes: black Levi's, black turtleneck, and a bright red V-necked Pringle sweater. Well, a Pringle knockoff, at least. Thin blue eyeliner to match her eyes, a little black mascara, and a light spray of Red Door. Now she was ready to move mountains!

The girls had breakfast ready when she came down. Their bus would be leaving in fifteen minutes. Katarina scrambled around looking for her school bag while Jenny sat at the table. She made an effort to gather her courage. Finally she blurted out, "Do you think I could have the money to buy an electric guitar? Or maybe as a Christmas present?"

"An electric guitar?" her parents echoed in unison.

"Yes. A band at school needs somebody who can play guitar and sing . . . so they asked me. One of the guys plays guitar for the same teacher as I do."

"Are any boys from your class in this band?" asked Krister.

"No, three boys and a girl from ninth grade."

"Ninth grade! But you're only in the seventh, sweetie pie."

"I'm not a sweetie pie!"

She jumped up from her chair with tears in her eyes and whirled out of the kitchen. Katarina stuck her head in the kitchen doorway and said in surprise, "What the heck was that about?"

"She wants an electric guitar so she can play in a band at school," sighed Krister.

"Oh, I get it. The White Killers. They're not so bad. Sometimes they play in the courtyard at lunchtime," Katarina informed them.

"White Killers? What kind of name is that for a band? Are they satanists or what?" Krister had an unusually long fuse, but now he was starting to lose his temper.

"Well . . . more sort of punk rock, like . . . maybe . . . Punx Not Dead, Pappa!"

With a gleeful grin Katarina bounced out to the hall and the girls took off running to the bus stop.

Irene could hear the weariness in her own voice as she moaned, "Give me strength! White Killers! Will you be home tonight? I don't know when I'll be back. This von Knecht case is hot. There's plenty to indicate that he was murdered, but we're lying low until the autopsy is done. It seems nothing has leaked out to the press yet. They're going to tear down police headquarters when they hear this!"

"Home? Probably not before six. But that works out fine, since Katarina has judo tonight. So I can try and talk to Jenny. Hurry up now, let's get going."

They took Sammie for a quick walk before they dropped him off with the dog-sitter, a retired widow. She supplemented her pension by taking care of four dogs, for payment under the table. Jenny and Katarina usually picked up Sammie on their way home from school.

THE DAY was already in full swing at headquarters when Irene Huss showed up just before eight. The annual flu season was approaching, but so far it was mostly autumn colds that were taking their toll. The Violent Crimes Unit had three inspectors out sick. It wouldn't be easy, but Superintendent Andersson was going around trying to pry loose some officers from other units.

He was talking with the superintendent of General Investigations, Birger Nilsson, who reluctantly spared an inspector when he realized that von Knecht's death would soon be the cause of even bigger headlines. Accident or suicide is one thing, but murder is something else entirely. Intrigued, Nilsson began asking for more details, but Andersson, feeling stressed, replied curtly. He knew that his new investigative group was already gathered and waiting for him at their first meeting.

"ALL OF us in this room will be working exclusively on the von Knecht case. Any other ongoing investigations will be set aside or turned over to other investigators. Has everyone seen the headlines in the morning papers about von Knecht's 'accident'?"

The seven around the table nodded. Andersson took a deep breath and unconsciously rose up on his toes before he continued.

"It was no accident or suicide. It was homicide!"

The effect, naturally, was an astonished murmur. The superintendent called for silence and began to report on what he and Irene had seen the night before. There wasn't a sound during his entire presentation. He concluded by passing on what the techs had reported about an hour earlier, which was news even to Irene.

He said, "You probably all know Police Technician Svante Malm. You do too, don't you, Hannu?"

This last was directed at Hannu Rauhala, the inspector on loan from General Investigations. No one in Violent Crimes had met him before. Rauhala nodded.

"He just informed me that there's blood and hair, probably from von Knecht, on the flat end of the meat cleaver. On the sharp edge they found blood and skin fragments, also apparently from the victim. The length of the cut on the back of the victim's hand matches the length of the cleaver's edge. The comparison tests were ready by seven this morning. Svante and Per worked in high gear all night. There were absolutely no prints on the handle. It was carefully wiped off, and from the smell we don't need any tests to tell us that a dash of Ajax was used."

He stopped and looked around the table. On his right sat Irene Huss, who only raised one eyebrow slightly at the last piece of information. Next to her sat Tommy Persson, Irene's fellow student from the academy and one of her closest friends. Then came Hans Borg, who still looked tired and worn out from his wife's fiftieth birthday party over the weekend. Birgitta Moberg next to him could hardly be accused of looking tired. Her brown squirrel eyes were fixed in fascination on the superintendent. She was cute, blond, and cuddly. Plenty of guys in various departments had tried to make a pass at that little angel, who looked as if she had just left the police academy. But she was actually over thirty and possessed both brains and claws. Most of them made only one attempt. Among those who had tried was Jonny Blom, the man next to her. At an unforgettable Christmas party the year before, his wife and four kids had figuratively been shoved down his throat by Birgitta. The newest inspector in the department was Fredrik Stridh. He had worked with them for a year now and made a very good impression. The last man, sitting to the left of the superintendent, was Hannu Rauhala, who was of Finnish extraction. He looked inscrutable and slightly exotic with his slanted ice-blue eyes, platinum-blond hair, and prominent cheekbones. It was hard to tell how old he was, but probably somewhere around thirty.

Andersson clapped his hands together and said energetically, "We have to work fast because the media don't know it's a homicide yet. The press conference is set for one o'clock. We've been promised a preliminary autopsy report by eleven."

The superintendent paused and thoughtfully surveyed his inspectors.

"Von Knecht was, after all, a real big shot throughout Sweden. Offhand, the only thing I recall is his sixtieth birthday party a few months ago," he said, hesitating.

Everyone around the table nodded. It had been a celebration that echoed all the way up to the Stockholm tabloids. Everyone who was anyone in the financial and jet-set worlds had gathered at von Knecht's fashionable country estate.

Andersson went on, "Irene and I were impressed by the apartment, but his shack outside Marstrand is at least three times as big. It's located on a peninsula, and von Knecht owns the whole area. He's got a private harbor too. The acreage must be several hectares. My sister has a summerhouse at Åstol. I've seen his place from the lake, when I was out fishing with my brother-in-law. Anything else we know? Irene?"

"His wife's name is Sylvia. His son is named Henrik and he's married. I only know the names, no personal data yet. Oh yes, Henrik said that his parents celebrated their thirtieth anniversary last Saturday. And of course you all know that this is one of the richest families in Sweden. Richard von Knecht had unbelievable success on the stock market during the go-go eighties. I don't know much else. Maybe we should get some help from one of my old pals who's a reporter at the *Swedish Ladies' Journal*. I'm sure she could help us dig up some old gossip."

Andersson didn't look too thrilled at the thought, but finally shrugged his shoulders and said, "Well, the main thing is to work fast. Maybe that will get results. In the meantime I want you to handle the interview with Henrik von Knecht and his wife this morning and try to get hold of the old lady with the dog. Those of you who can, meet me here ten minutes before the press conference. Tommy, Hans, and Fredrik will drive out and start interviewing the other tenants in the neighborhood, in case they saw or heard anything. Birgitta, you stay here for a while so you and Irene can dig up a little more on the residents of von Knecht's building. Henrik von Knecht should know who they are. Then go out and try to get hold of them. Either at work or wherever these people spend their days. They have to be somewhere!"

He took a deep breath and tried to determine who didn't have an assignment yet. When he figured it out he said, "Hannu, you collect all the statistical data from various databases; General Investigations is good at that. Complete background checks on all family members. When we know the names of the other residents I want their backgrounds too. Jonny, get in touch with the Financial Crimes Unit and find out what they know about von Knecht. As for newspapers, we should probably contact the *Göteborg Post*. They must have a pile of material. Anyone here have any contacts at GP? Ah, Hannu—okay, you take care of that too. Have I forgotten anything?"

"What are you going to do yourself?"

Of course it was Jonny who asked that question, in his smug way. Actually, he was probably quite pleased with his relatively simple assignment. The superintendent slumped a bit and sighed, apparently without noticing it. "I've been called before the chief. He wants a report. Then I'm going up to Pathology to meet with Madame Professor."

Irene couldn't help being annoyed for Yvonne Stridner's sake. "As a matter of fact, she's a professor in her own right; she didn't marry into the title," she said sharply.

If Andersson heard her he didn't let on. He made a point of looking at the clock above the door. Everyone could see that it was getting close to ten o'clock, so they had to get busy.

IRENE HUSS started by calling the *Swedish Ladies' Journal* in Stockholm. Finally Sofie's rough, smoky voice came on the line.

"Yeah, Sofie Ahl here."

She was surprised and happy to hear it was Irene on the other end. After a little general gossiping and banter, Irene mentioned that she'd like some old clippings on the von Knecht family. The news of the sensational death had been the lead story even for the major Stockholm papers. Sofie turned professionally inquisitive, but Irene wriggled out of it by telling her that "the autopsy isn't done yet, but we're trying to work up the background . . . looking for a possible basis for suicide . . .

"Go as far back as you can," she went on. "Though I'm sure that starting with the midfifties should be plenty. Maybe I could call you this afternoon and get a summary?" Irene suggested.

"No, that won't work. I've got to go out on a job. But let's do this: Give me your fax number and I'll put one of our interns on it. We'll call it a research project. She'll fax down what she finds to you, and then you can go through it. I'm sure it won't be necessary to send it all, but she can certainly pick out what might be useful."

"You're an angel, Sofie."

The next name on her list was the dachshund lady, Fru Eva Karlsson at Kapellgatan 3. Irene took a deep breath before she dialed. The phone rang ten times before the receiver was lifted on the other end. A thick mumble was heard, but Irene took a chance that she had reached the right person.

"Is this Fru Eva Karlsson?"

"Yes, who is this?"

"Detective Inspector Irene Huss. We met yesterday evening after the terrible . . . accident."

"Oh, don't talk about it! I was asleep when you called. I had to take a sleeping pill last night."

Fru Karlsson went on at length about her many years of insomnia and the various types of tablets she had tried over the years. Irene had a feeling that it was a good idea to listen. If nothing else, it would give the woman time to wake up.

At last she interrupted, "And how's your dog?"

"Thanks for asking, Snoopy is lying right here and feeling so goody-woody, aren't you, Snoopy-Woopy?"

Resolutely Irene asked the next question before Fru Karlsson wandered off again into doggy world. "You're the closest witness we have. Are you still sure that you didn't hear any scream before—or during—his fall?"

There was a long silence.

"No, I'm sure I didn't hear any scream. He just plopped right down in front of me. Oh, now I can see it all again!"

"Fru Karlsson, could I come up and have a chat with you this afternoon?"

"Dear girl, of course, that would be fine. But call first."

"I promise I will. Thanks again."

SHE HAD to grab a quick cup of coffee before eleven o'clock. She rounded the corner of the corridor at full speed. The ensuing collision between the superintendent and herself was forceful, but she hoped it wouldn't leave any lingering marks. And the bright red color of his face would probably fade eventually.

Testily he cried, "Watch where you're going! Oh, it's you. Good. Now we'll get to the bottom of things!"

She had seen him angry many times before, but never like this. With all the outer signs of an incipient stroke he fumed, "The telephone just rang. When I answered, it was a reporter from the *Göteborg Times* calling, that Kurt Höök guy. You know what that jerk said? 'How can you be sure that von Knecht was murdered?' At first I was completely thrown off guard, but then I said, 'Who told you he was murdered?' You know what he said then? 'An informed source.' What do you say to that? I'm going to make sure that source dries up, once and for all!"

"Do you know who it is?"

"I have my suspicions. Who said they knew someone at GP? If someone has one contact in the newspaper world he could have more," fumed Andersson.

"Sven, come with me and have a cup of coffee. What if it isn't Hannu? Just because he knows somebody at GP doesn't mean he knows anyone at GT."

The superintendent protested vehemently but finally admitted that Irene might be right.

Muttering and swearing to himself, he followed her reluctantly to the staff lounge. They greeted two other inspectors who weren't involved in the von Knecht case. Otherwise they were alone. They sat down at a table some distance from their two colleagues. Irene had just bitten into her roll when the chief of General Investigations, Superintendent Birger Nilsson, came into the room. He caught sight of Irene and Sven, broke into a big smile, and headed for their table by the window.

"So you're sitting here drinking coffee," he said cheerfully. "You can take it easy for a while. I think the von Knecht investigation is going to be tough. Keep Rauhala as long as you need him. By the way, you never told me . . . Sven. How can you be sure that von Knecht was murdered?"

Word for word, it was the exact phrase that Kurt Höök at GT had used. Superintendent Nilsson leaned nonchalantly on the table, with one hand in his pants pocket, and exuded an amiable interest. Irene didn't dare turn her head to look at Andersson, but she could sense the throbbing vibrations of suppressed rage emanating from him. That's why the neutral tone of the beginning of his sentence was a surprise, but the rest of it certainly wasn't.

"Well, you see, my dear colleague—I plugged up a leak in his ass from which he'd bled to death, and I'm ready to do the same for you. This source is now dried up for good."

It was a daring shot in the dark, based on pure instinct, but it hit the bull's-eye. Nilsson's face looked as if he had been stripped naked; the embarrassment of guilt was obvious. All trace of easy confidence had vanished. Without a word he disappeared through the door.

The two inspectors at the other table looked as though lightning had struck their coffee mugs. Andersson made a dismissive gesture to them and tried to explain his behavior. "Okay, this is how it is. Early leads are gold for the evening press. They pay a hell of a lot for a scoop. You know as well as I do that some of our colleagues like to make some extra dough by tipping off the press. The press conference on the von Knecht case is set for one o'clock, a little too late for the evening papers. I went and borrowed a guy from General Investigations this morning. At that time Birger Nilsson couldn't even remember my name."

It would be a mistake to claim that the two inspectors looked as if they were any wiser, but they did their best. The color of Andersson's face slowly started to return to normal. He stretched.

"Since you both heard Nilsson's question, I hope you keep your lips sealed for another two hours," he said sternly.

They muttered, "Of course" and "Sure, absolutely," but still looked extremely confused. Irene wasn't sure they understood what they had to keep their lips sealed about.

She quickly finished off her coffee and hurried back to work.

HENRIK VON Knecht and his wife were waiting in Irene's office. Henrik looked hollow-eyed and horrible. He had changed into black slacks and a navy-blue cardigan. Even though his shirt was white and fresh, the overall impression was reminiscent of a newly risen vampire. The woman on the chair next to him was stunningly beautiful. Irene vaguely recognized her, but couldn't place her. She was also dressed in navy blue. In her case it was a suit made of soft Napa leather, with a short straight skirt and big gold buttons on the jacket. Her black boots alone, with their stiletto heels, would cost Irene a month's salary. Her hair was shoulder length and colored a deep mahogany; her eyes shimmered like the ocean, an incredible shade of turquoise blue. The shimmer came from the tears filling her eyes, but only the tears revealed that anything was amiss. Otherwise she was utterly composed and sat with her hands calmly resting on her knee. Discreet makeup emphasized her beauty. It may have been skillfully applied foundation that gave her skin its silky luster. A touch of rouge heightened the glow high up on her sculpted cheekbones.

Suddenly the crisis of turning forty came roaring down on Irene like an express train. No matter what she did, she would never be able to look that captivating after staying up all night. It wouldn't even matter if it was a night of red-hot love that had kept her awake; she would still look like a wreck. As Sofie Ahl once told her, "You know that your fortieth birthday is coming by the way you pack for a trip. In your twenties you just stuffed a bag of toiletries in the outside pocket of your backpack. At forty your whole pack is a vanity case."

Henrik saw how the inspector was staring at his wife, and with a sigh he said, "Good morning, Detective Inspector. Yes, you've seen her before. She's the 'Sun Shampoo Girl.' Although that was a few years ago."

"Good morning. How are you? Forgive me for staring, but I was sure I recognized you, I just couldn't figure out where from," Irene said quickly.

Gratefully she grasped the straw that Henrik had unwittingly handed her. She went over to the young woman and shook her hand. It felt limp and damp.

"Detective Inspector Irene Huss."

"Charlotte von Knecht."

Her voice was deep and sensual; it didn't match her handshake.

"This is not an official interview, of course. I just need some help with background facts to try to sketch the chain of events leading up to the tragic death," Irene began.

The turquoise irises watched her intently. Henrik's eyes were like two dried clay balls. Both of them nodded, however. Irene had a sudden impulse and asked, "How old are the two of you?"

Henrik replied hesitantly, "I'm twenty-nine and Charlotte is twenty-five. What does that have to do with Pappa's death?"

"Background information. When will you be thirty?"

"April fifteenth," he said curtly.

Which would mean that Sylvia von Knecht had been pregnant at her wedding thirty years earlier.

There was only a difference of four years between Henrik and Charlotte, but if they had to guess, most people would have said ten years. Charlotte looked a little younger and Henrik considerably older, closer to thirty-five. Irene turned to Henrik and continued, "When was the last time you saw your father?"

"At the party last Saturday."

"Was that the last time you talked to him?"

"No. He called me at lunchtime on Sunday. I had taken him some catalogs from auctions I'll be attending at the end of the month. In Stockholm. From November twenty-seventh to December third there's an auction every day, but at different auction houses. For some reason I forgot to bring the catalog from Nordén's. Their international top-of-the-line sale is set for November thirtieth. Pappa wanted that catalog. There was a little Flemish baroque bureau he was interested in. At that auction I myself will be bidding on a Tang horse."

More bureaus were probably the last thing Richard von Knecht needed, but she began to realize that practical considerations were not the point. And what in the world was a Tang horse? It went against the grain for her to admit her lack of knowledge. So she quickly asked, "And you, Charlotte, when did you see your father-in-law last?"

Charlotte took a deep breath through quivering nostrils, fixed a steady turquoise gaze on Irene, and replied with a light catch in her voice, "Last Monday afternoon. At lunchtime. I drove over to give Richard the catalog Henrik just mentioned."

"Did you stay long?"

"No, I didn't even go into the apartment. First of all, he had a cold, and besides, the cleaning woman was there, straightening up after the party. I just told him 'Thanks for the party' and 'Get well soon' or something like that."

"How did he act? His mood and manner, I mean."

One mahogany lock of hair slid rapidly back and forth between her fingers as she pondered her response. The desk lamp cast reflections in the delicious dark blue pearl lacquer of her improbably long and well-kept nails. She gave a little shrug and said, "The same as usual. A little tired after the party and maybe from his cold."

"He didn't seem nervous?"

"No, not that I noticed."

"Exactly what time was it when you arrived at Molinsgatan?"

"About twelve-thirty, maybe fifteen minutes earlier or later."

"How did you get in the building? Do you know the code?"

Charlotte abruptly stopped twirling the lock of hair.

"Yes, naturally we know the code. How else would we be able to get in?"

"Neither of you has a key to the apartment?"

Henrik cleared his throat and said, "No. Mamma and Pappa have only one spare set of keys. We keep it when they're away for a while. Otherwise no."

Irene turned back to Charlotte.

"Where do you work? In case we have to reach you during the day."

"I'm home most of the time. I'm a photo model."

Henrik gave a little snort. She pretended not to hear but went on, "The modeling business is tough. I had just started acting school when I met Henrik."

"Do you have any children?"

Charlotte took in a quick breath.

"I found out last Saturday that I'm pregnant," she said after a pause.

"Oh, congratulations!"

Irene smiled and looked from Charlotte to Henrik, but realized that she could have saved her congratulations. Each sat, stiffly erect, not looking at the other. Maybe two powerful emotional events so close together were too much? First the news of her pregnancy and then the murder only a few days later.

As if she read her mind, Charlotte jumped up from her chair and said in a stifled voice, "Excuse me, where's the bathroom? I feel sick."

AFTER ESCORTING Charlotte to the nearest toilet, Irene returned thoughtfully to her office. There was something in the tension between this couple that didn't make sense. So she wasn't particularly surprised when she found Henrik slumped deep in his chair with his hands over his face. Without a word she sat and waited. After a minute he took his hands away and directed his claylike eyes at her. They were completely dry and dead, with no hint of moisture.

Tonelessly he said, "You must think we're behaving oddly, but we've been living under incredible pressure. The last twenty-four hours have been pure hell!"

He took a deep breath and went on, "Charlotte and I have had a little problem. She's been feeling lonely since I travel so much. It's been a tough autumn, with arguments and quarrels. Last Thursday we agreed to separate for a while, but we decided to keep up appearances during Mamma and Pappa's party on Saturday. Friday night when I came home, Charlotte announced that she'd been to her gynecologist, who told her she was in her second trimester! We went back and forth about it all weekend. On Saturday night we celebrated Mamma and Pappa's thirtieth anniversary, and on Sunday my plane left for London at three in the afternoon. Then when I came back Tuesday night, this happens to Pappa! I'm totally beat."

Irene felt sorry for the lanky man across the desk from her. But at the same time it was important to get as much information out of him as possible in this early stage of the investigation. Henrik seemed to need to talk, and to trust her. Every good interviewer notices things like that.

She asked in a cautious, low voice, "Have you and Charlotte reached any decision?"

He nodded. "Yes, we're going to try to stick it out. For the sake of the child and the family. Maybe when Charlotte is busy with the baby she won't feel so bored at home."

Irene could remember how she practically knelt down to kiss the floor in the locker room when she finally went back to work after nine months at home with the twins. Krister had stayed home the next four months, and then the girls started day care.

Out of the corner of her eye she noticed Charlotte come through the door and decided to change the subject. "Who are the other residents in the building on Molinsgatan?" she asked.

"Valle Reuter, a stockbroker, lives on the second floor. His name is Waldemar, but everyone calls him Valle. On the third floor are Pappa's old classmate Peder Wahl and his wife, Ulla. They have a house in Provence where they live most of the year, enjoying their retirement."

"But he can't be much older than sixty if he went to school with your father, right?"

For the first time in their whole conversation, the hint of a smile tugged at the corners of Henrik's mouth.

"Peder and Pappa sold one of the biggest construction and real estate companies in Sweden when the market was at its hottest. With more than a hundred million kronor in hand, Peder decided it was time to take life a little easier. He has three daughters, and none of them had the least interest in going into real estate."

"You didn't either," Charlotte interrupted.

Henrik pressed his lips together but continued as if he hadn't heard his wife's comment. "The apartment below Mamma and Pappa's is empty. Tore Eiderstam, the attorney, used to live there."

Tore . . . Tore, the attorney . . . Irene had a fleeting recollection of Yvonne Stridner's ex-husband. She said casually, "Wasn't he married to pathology professor Yvonne Stridner?"

"Ha, Tore's been married several times! But now that you mention it, you're probably right. I remember a discussion Mamma and Pappa had once. Mamma said something about how disgusting she thought it was that someone in their circle of friends carved up corpses all day. That was the first time I ever heard the word *necrophiliac*."

Irene realized with a dash of sympathy that Yvonne Stridner must have had a rough time in this social circle. Now she noticed that Birgitta Moberg had quietly entered the room. Irene introduced her to Charlotte and Henrik.

Quickly she summed up for Birgitta what Henrik had told her about the occupants of the second and third floors.

"And we were just talking about the fourth floor. The attorney Tore Eiderstam used to live there, an old friend of Richard von Knecht. 'Used to,' you said—where did he move to?"

"Eastern Cemetery, the Eiderstam family plot."

Neither Irene nor Birgitta could think of anything to say. Henrik went on after a short pause. "He dropped dead of a heart attack in September. The final divorce papers from his last wife had just arrived. He had two children from previous marriages, and they were clearly his heirs. It took a long time, but now the apartment is empty. Someone new is moving in on December first."

"Do you know who?"

"I do. Ivan Viktors, the opera singer. He's also one of Mamma and Pappa's old friends."

"Have you heard how your mother's doing?"

"She's starting to recover. I promised to drive her home this afternoon."

Irene nodded and gave the matter some thought. This afternoon the techs would be pretty much finished with the apartment. The little she'd heard about Sylvia von Knecht told her that the woman would certainly be upset over "trespassing" by the police. Not a very suitable atmosphere for gathering information.

To feel them out she said, "When are you going to pick her up? Which hospital ward is she in?"

"She wants to be picked up at three-thirty, because then she'll be home in time for her afternoon coffee. She's in Ward Five."

"If I were to go over and talk to her around three, would that be all right with you?"

Henrik just shrugged. Irene made a little note on the pad in front of her: "Call PS ward 5. Sylvia v. K. 1500?" Then maybe she'd have time to drop by and see the little dachshund lady Eva Karlsson beforehand. It was right on the way to Sahlgren Hospital. New note: "Call Eva K. 1400?"

She looked up from her notepad and turned to Charlotte. "Did you hear from your father-in-law again on Monday?"

"No."

"Did you meet him or speak with him on Tuesday?"

"No."

"Do you know the cleaning woman's name, Charlotte? The one who was at the apartment when you arrived?"

Both of them shook their heads. That was one thing they agreed on, at least.

"Thank you both for being kind enough to come down here. We'll be talking to you again during the course of the investigation. If you think of anything, just call me or any of the other inspectors. Or Superintendent Andersson, of course. There are eight of us working on this case. There will always be someone here to talk to you," Irene concluded in a friendly tone of voice.

She stood up and held out her hand to Henrik. His was ice cold. He only gave Irene's fingers a light squeeze before he quickly released his grip. Charlotte gracefully offered her well-manicured fingers, but her handshake felt like a moist towelette.

ALONE IN the room again, Irene called the psychiatric ward and got permission to talk to Sylvia von Knecht on her room telephone. Her voice sounded slurred and dull when she answered. There was a slight, barely noticeable trace of a Finnish accent.

"Well, it's probably best to get it over and done with. But if you ask me why he jumped, I have no answer for you. He seemed completely normal lately. And he was so lively at the party last Saturday . . . oh!" she broke off in the midst of a sob.

It wasn't ideal to tell Fru von Knecht by telephone that the police suspected murder. But the press conference at which it would be announced was going to be held in an hour. There was a chance that

Sylvia might hear it on the radio news before three o'clock. It was probably best to beat the media. Knowing how they usually behaved, Irene wanted Sylvia to be aware of the risk of a bombardment with questions by scandal-mongering reporters. They would be after her the minute she closed the door to the psych ward behind her. A homicide in that milieu had a hundred times more news value than a simple suicide.

Irene cleared her throat and said, "Fru von Knecht. What I'm going to say will no doubt come as a shock to you. We have certain leads indicating that your husband was the victim of a homicide."

Silence on the line. Finally, an unexpectedly sharp reaction. "You mean murdered? He was murdered?"

"Yes, there are strong indications that—"

"Thank the good Lord! What a relief!"

Whatever Irene had expected, it certainly wasn't this remark. She tried not to show her surprise, but continued in a neutral tone, "There will be a press conference at one o'clock at police headquarters. Superintendent Sven Andersson will have to notify the press that we are working on a homicide, not a suicide. You need to be prepared because the reporters might get pushy."

"They always are anyway. Imagine what a bunch of crap they would have written if Richard had committed suicide. And his insurance . . . Well, there won't be any problem with that now. A murder is horrible, of course, but at least it can't be blamed on the family. No one can protect themselves from madmen. Was it three o'clock you were going to be here?"

Bewildered, Irene confirmed the time. Not until she hung up did it occur to her that Sylvia von Knecht hadn't asked why the police were so sure it was murder. Part of her odd behavior could be due to various medicines she may have received in the psych ward. But her reaction was still extraordinary.

EVA KARLSSON, the dachshund lady, sounded considerably more spirited than she had the first time Irene called her that morning.

"Yes, of course, it's so nice you want to drop by. Two o'clock will be fine, and I'll have coffee ready," she chirped happily.

Irene's protests were kindly but firmly overridden. With a sigh she hung up. It might be tight trying to make it up to Sahlgren by three; she would have to be stern. Elderly ladies who lived alone had an unfortunate tendency to regard the police as their best friends.

Unfortunately, the police were also often their only friends.

It was ten minutes to one, and high time to get hold of the super-intendent. Andersson wasn't in his office. His secretary said that Sven had driven up to Pathology to meet a professor. He had promised to be back by quarter to one but hadn't shown up yet.

At two minutes past one he came charging through the doors.

Chapter Four

SUPERINTENDENT SVEN ANDERSSON WAS pleased with himself for putting that pompous colleague from General Investigations
up against the wall. That should plug the next leak "from a well-
informed police source"! Superintendent Birger Nilsson wasn't the only
one making a little money on the side. There were several colleagues
who lined their pockets in this manner, but it felt good to have leaned
on at least one of them. Should he report it? Hardly enough evidence,
all circumstantial, just a lucky shot. Internal Affairs would want proof.

He happily whistled "Lili Marlene" off-key to himself as he backed
out of his parking spot at headquarters. The sky was still a solid gray,
but at the moment it wasn't raining. The temperature was just above
freezing, so this evening they could probably expect black ice on the
roads. The Traffic Division would be busy with all the cars sliding off
the road. "Snow tires? But officer, I keep regular tires on all year long
and never have a problem."

The garlands of lights over the pedestrian malls were already in place,
and most shop windows had their Christmas displays up. The holiday
shopping season was jumping the gun a bit this year, since retailers had
to suck as much as possible out of people now that income tax refunds
weren't paid out at Christmas anymore.

Ah, Christmas. This year he was looking forward to it. His sister and
brother-in-law had invited him out to Åstol for the holidays. His niece
and her two little boys were coming too. Just so this investigation didn't
drag on for too long. Andersson stopped whistling and sighed loudly.
Irene had said something about a "clash of cultures," and he could
see that there might be plenty of opportunities for that sort of thing
in this case.

The social classes he usually worked within had absolutely nothing
in common with the exclusive apartment he had visited last night.
Murder scenes were normally shitty, stinking crack houses. The victim
had usually been stabbed after some dope deal gone wrong. Another

common scenario was encountering a man stinking of alcohol at the crime scene, blubbering with remorse because he "happened to" kill his wife. Glamorous TV murders like the von Knecht case almost never occurred. But when they did, the police were completely at a loss. Suddenly there were all kinds of tender toes they had to avoid stepping on. They couldn't proceed in their usual way with the investigation. Police Commissioner Bengt Bergström had made a point of emphasizing this during the "little information meeting" they'd had just before Sven Andersson headed off to Pathology. In a low, confidential tone of voice Bergström had said, "Keep in mind that this involves an old established Göteborg family. We have to be extremely careful with anything that might come out during the investigation. You're an old fox and known for employing your own tactics—and very successfully, I might add—but I would really appreciate receiving regular updates from you during the course of the investigation, blah blah blah . . ."

With growing distaste Andersson realized that Bergström knew full well that he wasn't going by the book, but he was trying to hide it behind flattery and feigned familiarity. In Sweden it wasn't normal to give police commissioners information while an investigation was in progress. Usually they received one partial report during the course of the investigation, and then a final report.

Andersson slapped his palm against the steering wheel and sputtered, "Murder is murder, and a killer is a killer! Even if he pisses in a gold chamberpot, he's still a killer."

The woman standing by the crosswalk, where Andersson had stopped for a red light, gave him a quizzical look. Embarrassed, he realized that he had been talking out loud, but thank God the windows were rolled up.

Why was he sitting here getting all worked up? Was it because he was afraid he wouldn't be able to solve the case? Maybe, but he knew that the upcoming meeting with Professor Stridner was also making him uneasy. She was organized and accomplished. But she showed no respect for him. Or anyone else, for that matter.

I'd have to wait for that until I'm lying there like a—if not neat then interesting—corpse on the stainless-steel autopsy table, he thought.

THE AUTOPSY assistant was a huge bodybuilder who had worked in Pathology for many years. He gave Sven Andersson a nod of recognition and pointed up the stairs when the superintendent asked for Yvonne Stridner.

She was sitting in her office, dictating into a little tape recorder the size of a cigarette pack.

". . . the liver is somewhat hypertrophied, although there is no visible sign of steatosis. In view of the size of the liver, this is probably a beginning stage. Sent to Pathological Anatomical Diagnosis."

She clicked off the tape recorder and gave Andersson a sharp look. And she recognized him at once.

"So you've decided to come over yourself, Andersson? I just finished the autopsy and was thinking of calling you up. Now I won't have to," she said with satisfaction.

The superintendent said hello and then asked her the important question at once. "Has the cause of death been determined?"

"Yes, beyond all doubt. He died from the impact of his fall."

"Does that mean there's still a possibility it was a damned suicide?"

"Not at all. There is a severe contusion on the back of his head. On the os occipitale there is a small fracture from a powerful blow, sufficient to cause unconsciousness but not death. The interesting thing is the location of the blow. Right above the hollow at the back of the neck, at the rear wall and base of the cranium. It's located a little obliquely to the left. This opens up two possibilities. One: Von Knecht knelt down in front of his executioner with his head bowed. The killer was unmoved and swung the cleaver from directly above in a wide arc, so that the blow landed somewhat below the base of the skull. But if so, Richard must have been bowing deeply. Hardly credible. Possibility number two: The murderer has a good backhand, and is right-handed."

"Backhand?"

"Tennis stroke, in this case. The power in the blow came from below, obliquely to the killer's body and directed upward. It's difficult to put sufficient power into such a blow, but a good tennis player should be able to put enough force into it to knock someone out."

"From what I understood from Svante Malm, the incision across the back of the victim's hand was made with the blade of the meat cleaver that was found on the balcony. How does the wound at the back of his head look?"

"It matches the cleaver's dull edge exactly. I've checked it."

"But weren't the techs here by seven this morning? And they took the cleaver back to the lab."

She gave him a withering look. "Who wasn't here by seven o'clock?" she snapped.

She took a deep breath and let her gaze wander out through the filthy window. "For me, this is science: I have to know the cause of death. What can the body tell us about the living person? Can it tell me anything about the killer? It's your job to figure out who murdered him and why."

The superintendent decided to stay on Professor Stridner's good side. It was important for him to obtain as many facts as possible right now. An autopsy report wouldn't be ready for a few days. Without showing how much self-control it took, he said in a neutral tone, "I'm very grateful that you attended to the body so quickly. I'll do my best to provide an answer as to 'who' and 'why,' but without your help that will be impossible."

The professor pursed her lips, but she shifted her gaze from the dirty window and deigned to look graciously at Andersson again. Satisfied, she said, "You're probably right about that. By the way, did it ever occur to you that it might not be von Knecht who was lying on the sidewalk?"

Andersson sat dumbfounded, wearing a slightly sheepish expression. Stridner challenged him, "Did you get a good look at the body yesterday?"

"He was lying on his stomach. It was dark," Andersson replied evasively.

"Precisely. He landed flat on his belly. His skull was shattered and in a terrible mess. I've reconstructed the lower jaw and parts of the upper jaw. The forensic odontologists are coming after lunch. And then . . . *voilà!* My little surprise for you!"

She reached across the desk and picked up a manila envelope, which she waved triumphantly in the air.

The superintendent had a hard time hiding his conviction that things had now gone too far. He had always had trouble talking with this woman, but what he intuitively sensed now was that she was totally insane.

Stridner saw what he was thinking. Laughing, she opened the flap of the envelope and pulled out a green piece of cardboard. It was folded in thirds, and each part had small rectangular windows in it, filled with shiny dark celluloid. They were dental X rays. In the corner was a small cardboard label with the text: RICHARD VON KNECHT, 350803.

Andersson was embarrassed and managed only to mutter, "I see . . . all right . . ."

Stridner frowned and jokingly waved the X rays at him. "I don't hear you saying, 'Amazingly fast work, Yvonne!' or 'But how in the world did you manage to get his X rays already?' or the most obvious, 'How did you get hold of his dentist so quickly?'"

This was her point, and she was savoring the moment. Andersson sighed and raised both palms in a gesture of resignation.

"Okay, okay. Amazingly fast work . . . Yvonne, and all that other stuff. I bow to you. But I'd appreciate an answer to my questions, plus facts about von Knecht's general condition."

"Oh, you certainly are a demanding man."

Mischievously she gave him another gleeful look. She was truly enjoying her little joke. With a glance down at the papers on her desk she became the efficient pathologist again. For his part, Andersson preferred this Yvonne Stridner.

"As you may recall, I promised you a list of the von Knecht crowd. I haven't had time to write it down, but I'll give you the names before you go. One of the names is Sven Tosse. He's one of Göteborg's most talented dentists. Among his patients are both myself and the von Knecht family. This is probably the only common point of contact we have left since my divorce from Tore. His practice is only a stone's throw from here, on the other side of the street. At Kapellplatsen."

Andersson had pulled a dog-eared notepad out of his pocket and with a stump of a pencil wrote down the dentist's name and address.

"I called Sven this morning. Naturally he had seen the news of Richard's fall in the paper and was deeply shocked. He sent over his nurse with Richard's X rays, and now the forensic odontologists will take care of the rest."

"Do you have any doubts that it's von Knecht's body?"

"No, but it's important to cover all bases, since his face was so damaged. Would you like to see him?"

Andersson was unprepared for the question, but quickly shook his head. Autopsy rooms were not pleasant places. Not to mention what usually lay on the table. No, if he could avoid it he preferred not to enter any autopsy room. The bodies he had to look at in the course of his work were bad enough. Although their interests did often coincide, of course, Stridner could keep her corpses to herself.

She stated dryly, "It probably wouldn't do you much good to look at the body. It was a long drop, certainly more than twenty meters. Well, here's the data."

She put a pair of reading glasses on her nose, cleared her throat, looked down at her stack of papers and read: "Height, one hundred eighty-three centimeters. Weight, eighty-two kilos. His age we know, and it corresponds with the body. He was in good shape for his age, good musculature."

She gave Andersson a knowing glance over the top of her glasses before she looked down at her papers again.

"I won't go into all the multiple fractures. In brief, I can say that almost every bone in his body was broken. With regard to his condition otherwise, I found some slight arteriosclerosis in his coronary artery, which would definitely increase the risk of heart attack in the future. A healed fracture of his right tibia, his shinbone, that is. The wound looked old. His liver was somewhat enlarged, with incipient fatty degeneration, but moderate so far. A clear indication of a certain level of alcohol intake," she declared.

"Was he an alcoholic?"

"Absolutely not. Their livers are striated with visible fatty necroses. Even though Richard had recently started to drink more, his liver still had many years left. Apparently he could have lived long enough to die from something other than liver problems. Which he did, of course. And a person can have fatty degeneration of the liver for years without being troubled to any appreciable extent. It's when liver function begins to fail and we get a conversion to cirrhosis that problems arise. Real problems! But Richard had a way to go yet. I will venture to state that much, even though I'm no expert in the chronological progression of alcohol damage. I sent blood samples in to be tested for alcohol content and also the contents of his stomach. He had eaten a substantial meal, apparently a late lunch. The time of death we know, of course."

Andersson's stomach knotted up when he thought of von Knecht's surely excellent lunch that now lay quivering like a disgusting sludge in a glass jar at the lab.

Stridner gathered up her papers and took off her glasses.

"That's how far I've gotten," she said.

"How about the slash on the back of his hand? Was it a bad cut?"

"Yes; it wasn't very deep but it must have hurt terribly. It's actually curious that he had no defensive wounds on his forearms. There should be some if the fall was preceded by a struggle. But that doesn't seem to be the case."

Both of them sat and pondered this puzzle for a bit. Finally Andersson said, "It must mean that he was clubbed from behind as he stood leaning over the railing. He never had a chance to defend himself against his killer."

Stridner nodded and a hard expression came over her face.

"That's probably how it was. A cowardly murderer. But then murderers always are. Cowards."

She gave Andersson a dark look as though he were personally responsible for the existence of these killers. She continued more pensively, "Or desperate. Fear can drive people to murder. But the most common motives no doubt are revenge or jealousy and perhaps greed. I wonder what it was that drove Richard's murderer?"

She fell silent again. With a deep sigh she leaned back in her chair and gave Andersson a quick glance.

"The list. You wanted to have the list of those boys. Can you write it down?" she asked in a tone that made it clear that she had no intention of doing so.

The superintendent nodded and got ready with his stubby pencil.

"You don't have to write down my ex-husband Tore Eiderstam because he died last September. Or Per Nord, he died of leukemia five years ago. And now Richard . . ."

She paused for a moment, took a deep breath, and went on, "Sven Tosse, my dentist, and also that of the von Knecht family. He and Sylvia von Knecht were engaged, by the way, before she met Richard. Richard was up in Stockholm for a few years, but he had to return to Göteborg immediately when his father died."

Andersson was writing as fast as he could. Stridner paused tactfully and waited until he finished the sentence.

"Then we have Valle Reuter. He's one of our biggest stockbrokers, in more than one sense. He's the broker for the lot of them, just as Sven is their dentist. His brokerage firm is called Reuter and Lech, as I recall."

Again she had to wait for Andersson to catch up. With an oath he snapped the point of his pencil. Without a word Stridner handed him a white mechanical pencil with GÖTEBORG MEDICAL ADMINISTRATION printed on it.

"Press on the eraser, then the lead will come out. Now where was I? Oh yes, Valle. He lives on the second floor of von Knecht's building. He's married to Leila. They have a son who's a doctor. I had him as an undergraduate a few years ago."

She seemed to be thinking of whether she knew anything else about Valle Reuter, but couldn't recall anything.

"The next man is Peder Wahl. He's married to Ulla, Sven Tosse's sister. They live on the third floor, but I think they have a vineyard in France where they spend most of their time."

"What kind of work does he do?" asked Andersson.

In reply, Stridner just raised one eyebrow ironically. Andersson had a feeling that he'd asked the stupidest question of the day, but he couldn't figure out why. It was best to move on. He looked down at his notepad and said, "I have three names now. Sven Tosse, Valle Reuter, and Peder Wahl. Is that the whole crowd?"

"No. Ivan Viktors, the opera singer."

Andersson gave a start. It's not often that you run into your idol in a homicide investigation.

"He retired from the world's opera stages after his wife died of cancer a year or two ago. There's one more name, Gustav Ceder. He's a banker and lives in London. I met him only once."

Stridner sat twisting a dark red lock of hair as she absentmindedly gazed out the window. It couldn't have been the sight of the gray buildings of Vasa Hospital that transported her into such a dreamy state. It was her memories. She had been a fantastic help. He ought to tell her that. His glance fell on the clock. He blurted out, "There's a press conference at one o'clock!"

He jumped up as if his chair had suddenly become electrified.

She flinched, brutally awakened from her reverie. Deliberately she said, "Surely there's no reason to worry. It's only a quarter to."

"I'm the one who's holding it! I'll call you this afternoon."

"It's better if I call you when the test results come in."

But she was talking to an empty doorway. She could hear Andersson rushing down the stairs. He made good time, considering his physique. She shook her head and said to herself, "If you keep that up, we'll be seeing you sooner than you think."

Chapter Five

THE PRESS CONFERENCE WAS a tumultuous affair with journalists all shouting at once. Andersson had participated in press conferences before, but he had never experienced anything like this. Somehow he managed to get through it, answering as best he could about what he knew while leaving out certain facts for "investigative reasons." A guy with a crew cut from TV 4's local station wanted to know how the killer managed to get out of the building and avoid discovery, even though the police were on the scene so quickly.

Andersson put on an inscrutable expression and snapped brusquely, "The technicians have not yet concluded their examination of the crime scene."

It was high time they found out the answer to that reporter's question. So it was with great satisfaction that he saw Svante Malm sitting at the conference table in the room that served as investigation central. Malm had put up photos of von Knecht's smashed body on the bulletin board. Among them were several blowups of the wound on the back of his head. There were pictures of the cleaver too.

"Hi, Malm!" Andersson tried to assume a cheerful tone, but when he saw Malm's pale grimace that passed for a smile, he regretted it. Instead he said lamely, "You and Per have really done a great job."

Malm looked like he could fall asleep at any moment. He rubbed his eyes and said, "I'd just like to report what we've found so far. One of you will have to take notes."

Andersson gestured to Irene Huss to do so.

"On the balcony we found the cleaver. The sharp edge corresponds to the cut on the hand, and the blunt end matches the cross-shaped wound on the back of the neck. Professor Stridner helped us check it out this morning. It's a small meat cleaver, taken from the utensils in von Knecht's kitchen. The implements hang inside the stove's ventilation hood. The handle of the cleaver was wiped off with a rag dipped in a solution of Ajax. Not any of the working surfaces, just the handle.

The cleaver lay next to the balcony wall, so no rain could reach it. We found blood and hair on the cleaver, apparently from von Knecht. The analysis isn't finished yet," Malm rattled off. He paused briefly and gave a big yawn.

Andersson was careful to ask, "Was the balcony the scene of the murder?"

"Yes. There was no sign that the body was dragged out onto the balcony before being shoved over the railing. Keep in mind that von Knecht wasn't a small guy. It's hard to drag an unconscious body. On the other hand, we have a theory about how it all happened. The balcony is turreted, with four columns supporting the little roof. On one of the columns we found a fresh palm print from von Knecht. His right hand. The cut was on his right hand. We think that von Knecht was standing on the balcony with his back to the balcony door. Maybe he was holding on to the column—the print is actually quite high up. The perp hits him on the back of the neck from the rear, but he's not knocked out; he keeps hanging on to the column. Then the perp slams the sharp edge onto the back of his hand and he instinctively releases his grip. A hard shove on his back and Richard von Knecht takes his last flight."

It was utterly quiet in the conference room when Malm painted this picture of von Knecht's last minutes of life. Irene felt a chill on the back of her neck. Suddenly the killer's presence was completely palpable. Before, he had almost vanished amid the antiques and sensational headlines.

Besides Sven Andersson, Svante Malm, and Irene Huss, Jonny Blom was the only other person in the room. The others hadn't returned yet.

Andersson decided it was a good sign. They were gathering information and the investigation was proceeding. He hoped. Aloud he said, "That sounds plausible. And Stridner pointed out that he didn't have any defensive wounds on his forearms."

Irene looked up from her notepad.

"He knew the killer. Trusted him. Didn't mind having him stand behind him when he went out on the balcony and leaned over the railing. Remember, he was afraid of heights."

Malm continued, "What's even more remarkable is that all the light switches and door handles were wiped off with a rag soaked in Ajax. The whole upper floor is extremely orderly and clean. We probably won't finish up the lower floor until late tonight. Åhlén and Ljunggren have taken over. They'll be checking the elevator and stairs. Even though it poured almost all last night, it might be an idea to go over the courtyard and the trash rooms."

"I'll talk to the guys about that. Go on home now, Svante, and get some sleep," said the superintendent.

After Malm disappeared down the corridor, Andersson remained seated for a while, in deep thought. He was brought back by a tap on the door. A secretary came in and handed him a note. He read it quickly. From the furrow between his eyebrows Irene understood that he wasn't completely pleased with what it said.

"Are we going to have to wrangle with another old crone now? I didn't mean you, Irene, but the prosecutor in charge. It's going to be Inez Collin. It was bad enough with Stridner, but now we have Collin too," he said and sighed heavily.

Irene noticed Jonny and Andersson exchange a knowing look. She was perplexed, because Inez Collin was regarded as a very capable and judicious prosecutor. Tough but clear as glass. Again the problem of attitudes toward middle-aged, competent women. Why were they so intimidating? She realized that she herself was well on the way to joining this group of women. But Andersson never seemed to feel threatened by her, even though she was a bona fide expert detective. Evidently because he knew her and liked her, in his eyes she never grew older. That was a comforting thought.

Andersson said, "I'll see to it that everyone in the group is informed that we'll meet in this room at five o'clock. What are you doing this afternoon, Irene?"

"Talking to Fru Karlsson, the dachshund lady. Then I'll drop by Sahlgren Hospital and talk to Sylvia von Knecht at three."

"Okay. Jonny?"

"I'll keep on checking with Financial. Richard von Knecht obviously figured in a number of shady deals. Last year he declared an income of nine hundred eighty thousand kronor."

Almost a million. Both Andersson and Irene were impressed, but hardly surprised.

Jonny continued triumphantly, "But do you know how much his declared net assets are? Hold on to your hat: a hundred and sixty-three million! But Financial thinks he has a bunch more offshore and profits that never show up in Sweden. Who could track that down?"

It was such an inconceivable amount of money. Anyone would be lucky to win a million kronor, rich if he had two million, and Croesus if he had ten. But 163! A person with so much money—and apparently even more on top of that—what would he have left to strive for? What kind of goals would he have in life? What would give life excitement and meaning? What was it that had given von Knecht's life that extra spice? Antiques?

Irene was jogged out of her thoughts by Jonny's voice. ". . . has tried for many years. But it's hard, because he was an early player in the Southeast Asian markets. His assets are probably plowed into companies like Toshiba and Hyundai. Financial will try and pull out as much as they can."

"You might as well look at the rest of the family's income and assets too. By the way, I got a list from Stridner of the other people in the von Knecht crowd," said Andersson.

He pulled out his crumpled notepad, paged through it, and read aloud: "Sven Tosse, dentist. He has a practice on Kapellplatsen."

"Then I can talk to him on my way back from the hospital. Although it isn't far to walk to Tosse's office from Fru Karlsson's," Irene said.

She decided to try to squeeze in Tosse before she went to Sahlgren.

"The next names are Waldemar and Leila Reuter. Birgitta Moberg will probably run into them, since they live on the second floor in von Knecht's building. Von Knecht has really gathered his old pals around him, because on the third floor we have the couple, Peder and Ulla Wahl. But apparently they live in France most of the time."

The superintendent broke off and leafed through his notepad again before he went on. "Gustav Ceder is the name of a guy who evidently disappeared from their social circle. He has lived in England for years. Jonny, can you check him out too, so we don't miss anyone? The last man is Ivan Viktors. I'll take him myself."

Irene put in, "Did you know that Viktors is going to move in to the empty apartment below von Knecht's? And that Waldemar Reuter lives alone on the second floor?"

"Who told you that?"

"Henrik von Knecht. And Henrik's wife Charlotte is pregnant."

"I see. We'll have to go over everything in much more detail this afternoon when we all meet."

Andersson stood up to signal that the meeting was over. Irene glanced at the clock and saw that there was no time to get any lunch before her meeting with Eva Karlsson at two o'clock.

SHE FOUND an empty parking space right outside Fru Karlsson's street door. Only a few minutes late, she rang the bell next to the nameplate

N. KARLSSON. Since that was the only Karlsson in the building, she took a chance. When she heard the creaky voice of an old woman on the intercom, she knew she had guessed right.

A buzzer sounded. She pushed open the heavy old oak door. The entryway was dark, so she pushed the button for the stairwell light. The floor and steps were of stone, but there were no marble swans here. The stairwell seemed to be newly renovated, with pale yellow walls and a green stenciled border halfway up. There was a small elevator too. It groaned quietly up to the fourth floor.

Eva Karlsson had opened the door a crack but pulled it open when Irene stepped out of the elevator, greeting her warmly. "Welcome, my dear!"

Irene had a vague feeling of being invited to a coffee klatsch. Which was actually the case. Of course she had noticed the bakery right next door, but never in her wildest dreams had she expected Fru Karlsson to order one of everything they had. At least that's what she seemed to have done. The cakes and pastries were set out on thin paper doilies placed on crystal cake dishes. The gold-rimmed coffee cups were delicate, with carefully folded party napkins placed beneath the plates. On the little pedestal table in the parlor there was also a silver coffee service with sugar bowl and creamer. A sofa and two easy chairs uphol-stered in yellow silk fabric, which looked terribly uncomfortable, were grouped around the table.

Snoopy was lying on one of the armchairs, and he didn't look as if he intended to move.

With a shaky hand Eva Karlsson made a sweeping gesture encom-passing the whole room before she said, "We moved here nine years ago. I think the move used up the last of my husband's energy, because five months later he passed away. Nine years . . . imagine how time flies!"

Irene seized her chance. White lies seldom caused her any pangs of conscience. "Speaking of time, I can only stay for half an hour. I have an appointment at three. But it's just around the corner."

She added this last when she saw the expression of dismay come over Eva Karlsson's face. Unable to conceal her disappointment, the thin little white-haired woman said, "Well then, do sit down and don't waste any more of your precious time! The coffee is ready."

She vanished down the dark hallway, and Irene could hear a distant clatter from the kitchen. It was located in the back, facing the court-yard. Fru Karlsson came in with the coffee and began to foist the pas-tries on her. Irene was thankful that she hadn't eaten any lunch. Including the rolls and sponge cake, there were twelve varieties.

The elderly dachshund owner was voluble on every topic except the occurrence the previous evening. Irene had to hear about her childless but happy marriage, her years as a librarian at the public library, and the inexhaustible source of joy Snoopy had been for the past eight years. Feeling slightly desperate, Irene said no thanks to the tenth pastry—shortbread with raspberry jam—and decided to get to the point. She pushed away her coffee cup and turned into a police officer. In an official tone she said, "Fru Karlsson, I have to leave in a few minutes. You haven't recalled anything new, now that the first shock has faded? You're still sure you didn't hear any scream?"

Realizing that the coffee party was over, Eva Karlsson slumped forward. With a slight quaver in her voice she said, "Dear Irene, please don't act so formal with me. It feels so . . . foreign."

Irene didn't reply but she could see how much it cost the old woman to try to remember what had happened the night before. Fru Karlsson cast a pensive glance at the window in the den. She wasn't thinking about the acute need to have the windows washed; it was a real attempt to concentrate and think. Now she couldn't avoid it any longer. Her white-haired head nodded softly as she said, "He didn't scream. I'm absolutely positive."

Which also meant that Richard von Knecht was unconscious when he fell and struck the sidewalk. The pastries made a collective somersault in Irene's stomach at the thought.

Snoopy was snoring loudly in his armchair and didn't notice when Irene got up and thanked Fru Karlsson for the coffee and pastries.

SHE LEFT the car where it was. She wouldn't find a parking place any closer to Kapellplatsen than this. The ones at the square were always taken by customers going to the bank, the state liquor store, or the small shops.

She entered the flower shop and asked where Dr. Tosse had his office. The friendly middle-aged woman pointed with a dirty thumb toward the escalators. She was busy planting hyacinths in a big basket. For the first time this year, Irene started to feel that Christmas was on its way. It had to be the scent of hyacinths, she thought, because outside an ice-cold drizzle was falling.

She took the escalator up one flight and found the door to Sven Tosse's reception area. A shiny brass plate informed her that she was in the right place. She rang the bell, and in a moment a young dental assistant in a pale pink dress opened the door. Her smile was both warm and professional as she asked, "Hello, how can I help you?"

"Detective Inspector Irene Huss. I'm looking for Dr. Sven Tosse, regarding the murder of Richard von Knecht."

The assistant's violet-blue eyes became as round as her mouth. Quickly she stepped aside and silently ushered Irene into the waiting room. She vanished hastily down the corridor toward an open door, from which the whining sound of a dental drill could be heard. Irene gave a shudder. It was the sound and the smell. They were always the same in dentists' waiting rooms. But that was the only similarity with other dental offices she had seen.

This waiting room was empty. A large handwoven wool rug in muted autumn tones lay on the floor. On the walls hung large prints. A bulging brown leather sofa and four matching armchairs, two small glass tables, and a tall étagère for magazines lent the room an air of luxury. Yet it felt homey. The waiting room was separated from the reception area by a glass wall against which stood a fantastic saltwater aquarium. Blanketing everything was the pleasant sound of subdued classical music.

The sound of the drill had stopped. From the doorway came the assistant and a thin, wiry man with steel-gray hair. He appeared ten years younger than his sixty years. The look he gave Irene was sharp and intensely blue. It matched his light blue dentist's smock. In his eyes she could also clearly see uneasiness. He stretched out his hand, shook hers with a painful grip, and introduced himself. With a nod he invited her to follow him to the staff room.

Noticeably upset, he said, "If you'll excuse me, I have a patient in the chair. This won't take long. What was it you told Mia? Richard was murdered? Impossible! Although suicide is just as unlikely. Are you sure that he was murdered?"

"Yes, quite sure. He was knocked unconscious and pushed off the balcony," Irene replied.

She paused. Tosse merely closed his eyes and nodded.

"We understand that you and Richard von Knecht were good friends," she went on.

"Who said that?"

"Medical Examiner Yvonne Stridner."

"I see, Yvonne. Then she must have mentioned that Sylvia and I were engaged when she and Richard met. It was hard for me back then, but he was a better catch than I was. I met Inga, my first wife, only a few months later, so we buried the hatchet. We went to their wedding, and they came to ours the following summer."

Irene suddenly had an idea.

"Were you at their party last Saturday?" she asked.

"Of course. Inga didn't come, though; we've been divorced more than twenty years. Ann-Marie, my second wife, was with me."

"Was everyone from the old gang at the party?"

"Yes. But far from all those who attended the wedding were present last Saturday. There were more than a hundred guests at the wedding. Last Saturday it was about twenty."

"Were the ones who live in France there too?"

"Yes. Peder and Ulla Wahl. Ulla is my sister. They wanted to see their new grandchild. But they went back to Provence on Monday."

"Did Richard von Knecht seem the same as usual?"

Tosse thought for a long time before he replied. "Yes, he was the same as ever. Happy and in high spirits. He loved parties. It was a great party. The only ones who didn't seem to have a good time were Henrik and his wife. Maybe they thought we were a bunch of old fogies."

"And Sylvia von Knecht?"

"Exactly the same. But she's a little . . . special."

He fell silent. Before Irene could come up with another question, he extended his hand and shook hers in another viselike grip.

"Well, now I have to get back to my patient. Catch the killer; nobody should have to be the victim of a murder. Not even Richard," he snapped.

Irene didn't have time to ask him to explain his last remark in more detail before he disappeared. Irene massaged her right palm and fingers. Dentists have strong hands.

The lovely Mia showed her to the door. From down the hall she could hear the speedy whine of the drill.

OUTSIDE, THE drizzle had changed to a cold breeze with an occasional drifting snowflake.

A windy Göteborg, cold and raw with the temperature around freezing, feels just as cold as minus twenty Celsius in Kiruna up in Lapland. If not colder. Irene tucked her chin down into the top of her jacket.

She was going to be a little late for her meeting with Sylvia von Knecht, but all in all she was satisfied with her ability to keep to her schedule today.

It was a quarter past three when she walked through the glass doors to Ward Five at the hospital. The corridor was deserted. The walls were painted a dirty yellow color and the floor was gray linoleum. A sign that said NURSES' STATION was visible up ahead. She went over and found a nurse in her fifties dressed in white sitting behind a counter. She was absentmindedly staring at a monitor.

Irene cleared her throat. "Excuse me. Where can I find Sylvia von Knecht? Detective Inspector Irene Huss."

The nurse started, turned to Irene, and gave her an annoyed look. She snapped, "Yes, I'm wondering that myself. Where is Sylvia von Knecht? And all our other patients."

Had there been a mass exodus from the psych ward? Or was this one of the patients who had put on a white smock and seated herself at the computer?

The woman turned back to the screen. "This is the problem! I managed to knock my coffee cup onto the keyboard. Thank God there wasn't any coffee left in it, but the entire current patient list disappeared. All I can find is the one for April nineteen ninety-three! God knows what key I hit. Maybe several. Darn it! The Countess is in two one," she said all in one breath.

After a confused moment Irene understood that she had received an answer to her question. "The Countess" must be Sylvia von Knecht. "Two one" must mean room two, first bed.

She knocked lightly on the door marked with a scratched and barely legible "2" before she stepped inside. In the bed near the door lay an elderly, emaciated woman gazing vacantly at the ceiling. Her yellowish skin seemed to be stretched tight over her skull with no musculature in between. She had no teeth and her lips had caved in, so her mouth appeared to be a straight line. Without blinking even once, she lay staring up at absolutely nothing. A tube was stuck in one nostril. It was taped to her cheek so it wouldn't fall out.

In the corner by the window sat Sylvia von Knecht. No lamp was lit. A gray afternoon fog had begun to creep in from the sea, lending the room an unnatural murk. The only bright thing in the room was Sylvia's hair, which was thick, shoulder length, and platinum blond. She looked like an ethereal elf, seated, dressed in a dark suit and white silk blouse. Her hands were clasped on her knee. The small, fragile woman sat absolutely still and looked at Irene.

"Are you the one who's the cop?" she asked.

Her voice sounded pleasant with its slight hint of a Finnish accent, but her tone was sharp. Irene felt like a tardy schoolgirl who ought to be bringing a note from home. She nodded and was just about to introduce herself when Sylvia went on, "Huss, that's what it was. Why are you so late?"

Irene quickly took refuge in her police role and replied in measured tones, "Detective Inspector Irene Huss. I've been interviewing a number of witnesses this morning in order to gather facts and information. It took longer than expected."

She had no intention of apologizing!

Sylvia von Knecht said tonelessly, "Henrik is coming to pick me up in half an hour. I refuse to stay here another night. First they tried to put me in a room with four beds. Not on your life, I said. Then they put me in here with that zombie over there."

With a graceful gesture she pointed to the woman in the neighboring bed.

"Oh well, there's no need to worry about her. She hasn't moved or said a word in several years, the nurses say. She has to go back to long-term care as soon as there's room. They force-feed her through the tube in her nose. Apparently it goes all the way down to her stomach. It's incredibly disgusting, but it doesn't really matter. I don't feel like eating anyway. Although I did want to stay for afternoon coffee."

Irene steeled herself for this interview with Sylvia von Knecht. Stiffly she began, "We're trying to find out what motive there might be for the murder of your husband, and—"

Sylvia von Knecht interrupted her. "How do you know it was murder?"

She had clearly been thinking about it since their telephone conversation that morning. Irene took her time reporting the facts that had been uncovered so far.

During the whole account Sylvia von Knecht sat quietly with her hands clasped at her knee and her head bent slightly forward. Her hair fell like a curtain in front of her face. Irene couldn't see her expression.

When Irene finished speaking, Sylvia raised her head. There were tears in her eyes and her voice quavered with emotion as she said, "To think that something like this would befall our family. It's despicable! I refuse to believe it! Who would want to murder Richard? Why?"

"Those are precisely the questions we're trying to answer. Fru von Knecht . . ."

"Call me Sylvia, I'm not that ancient."

Ancient was certainly not an accurate description. According to their information, this woman was a few years over fifty, but she looked not a day older than forty. At least not in the dimness of the room.

Before Irene managed to repeat her question, Sylvia answered it herself. "No, I don't have the foggiest idea. Richard never received any threats. Although big businessmen who are successful always make enemies."

"Would he have told you about it if he were being threatened by someone?"

"Yes, he would have, absolutely!"

Why was she lying? Irene noticed the way she tossed her head, which was much too defiant to be convincing. She decided to come back to the subject, but not just yet. Instead she asked, "When did you make the trip up to Stockholm?"

"Last Sunday, at two o'clock."

"Where did you stay in Stockholm?"

"Hotel Plaza. My mother and Arja accompanied me on the plane. Arja is my sister. We had tickets to the evening performance of *Cyrano* at the Oscars Theater. The next morning Mother and Arja took the ferry over to Helsinki. And I went to the House of Dance."

"The House of Dance? What's that?"

"Don't you know? It's a place in Stockholm where all types of dances are performed. It's the cornerstone of dance in Scandinavia, I might add. I'm a choreographer, as I'm sure you know. The House of Dance will celebrate its fifth anniversary next year, and one of my ballets is going to be staged. It's an awful lot of work, but great fun. I've already been up there twice this fall to go over my conception. Now we've reached the point where we can start selecting the dancers."

Irene noticed how Sylvia's voice changed when she began talking about dance. This was true passion; she could hear it. It was news to her that Sylvia was a choreographer, but it was probably best not to reveal that fact, or that she had never heard of the House of Dance. To change the subject, she asked, "Did you speak with your husband on Monday or Tuesday?"

"Tuesday, around noon. I knew that he was starting to get a cold on Sunday, but he felt really bad on Monday. That's what he said, anyway. But evidently it was just an ordinary virus, because by Tuesday he was feeling better. He planned to go to his Tuesday lunch with Valle."

"Valle? Do you mean Waldemar Reuter?"

"Yes, that's what I said! They've eaten lunch together every Tuesday for more than twenty years."

"At the same restaurant?"

"No, I think it varied. I'm not quite sure."

"How was his mood when you talked to him?"

"The same as usual. He sounded a little tired and had a stuffy nose."

"What did he say? Can you remember?"

Sylvia seemed to think for a moment. Finally she shrugged and then said indifferently, "He told me about his cold and that he had stayed indoors all day on Monday. The cleaning woman had been there to clean up after the party. I think she had her daughter with her."

"What's the cleaning woman's name?"

"What does that have to do with anything?"

"She may have seen or heard something significant. We have to interview everyone who was in contact with your husband on those last few days."

Sylvia pressed her lips tight, but finally decided to answer. "Her name is Pirjo Larsson. She's Finnish, married to a Swede, but speaks abominable Swedish. I found her through the recommendation of a friend of mine about two years ago. Only Finnish women can clean properly. Swedes are too lazy and Chileans and those types are too ignorant," she declared.

"How often does she clean your place?"

"Three times a week. Monday, Wednesday, and Friday."

"Where does she live?"

"Don't know. Out in Angered, I think. I have her phone number at home."

"Did your husband say anything else?"

"Well, he was supposed to go buy two open-faced submarine sandwiches for us to have the evening I . . . when I came home."

Again she bowed her head. Her shoulders shook a little, and for a brief moment Irene almost had the feeling that she was trying to stifle a fit of laughter. But the dry, hot sobs indicated grief. Irene decided this was enough for now.

She took a couple of steps toward Sylvia, but sensed that she shouldn't touch her.

"Thank you for answering my questions. I'll come by tomorrow. But I'll call first. If you'd like to talk to any of us involved in the investigation, just call the number on this card," Irene said.

She handed her a card with the number of her direct line written on it. When Sylvia didn't seem to take any notice, she stuck it carefully between her clasped hands, which were still resting on her knees.

As she turned to leave the room, Irene thought that a glow appeared in the eyes of the mummylike old woman in the next bed. Hatred. Seething hatred. But it could have been just a reflection from the lights in the corridor, since the door was open and a nurse came in with coffee.

SHE SPENT the time before the five o'clock meeting writing up reports about the day's inquiries. As yet there had been no formal interviews. Still, she felt pleased with the results. There was already a great deal of information, even though they had only been working on the case for twenty-four hours. This was the advantage of stepping into the investigation quickly. Were the murderer and motive lurking in the material already acquired, even though they couldn't yet see them? Or were they still light-years from the truth? As long as there weren't any concrete leads to follow, it was just as well to continue digging and scratching here and there. Something useful might always turn up.

She called home. Krister answered. He had just come in the door but told her that Katarina had already taken off for her judo training and Jenny was out walking Sammie.

"I'll talk to Jenny tonight and try to get a handle on this thing with the 'White Killers.' I'm reading about you in the evening paper right now. VON KNECHT MURDERED! all the headlines are shouting. It's obvious they stopped the presses all over the country and tore down the newspaper placards that were printed this morning."

Irene sighed. She always had a guilty conscience about Krister having to stay home most of the time. On the other hand, she was very glad that he was handling the discussion with Jenny.

Feeling stressed, she said, "We're going to have a meeting at five o'clock. I guess that means right now. I've got to run. Probably won't be home before nine. Kisses and hugs!"

She had stolen that last bit from a TV show. Cute.

Before she left for the conference room she grabbed a fresh notebook from her desk drawer. On the front she wrote "Von Knecht" with a black marker. She turned to the first page and printed neatly on the top line: "Pizza."

SHE WAS the last to arrive, but they hadn't started yet. She passed the pizza list around the table, and everyone who wanted one wrote his or her name and the kind of pizza. Light beer and salad were included. The list was sent out to a secretary who would phone in the order to be delivered to HQ at six o'clock.

Andersson went over what Pathology and the techs had put together during the day. The only thing new to Irene was that they hadn't managed to get hold of Ivan Viktors. Andersson had left a message in his mailbox and another one on his answering machine.

The inquiries that Tommy Persson, Hans Borg, and Fredrik Stridh made in the neighborhood were largely negative. The only positive thing, although somewhat questionable, was the statement from a retired teacher. She was eighty-one years old and almost blind. "But that's why my hearing is so sharp," she said. Stridh wasn't convinced, but he reported what she had told him.

"She claims that she heard the door to the farthest trash room close after the last sirens died out. That would mean about quarter to six, before the last ambulance arrived on the scene."

The superintendent interjected a question. "How does she know that it was the door to the farthest garbage room?"

"Her apartment is right next to it. So she lives directly across the courtyard, viewed from von Knecht's stairwell. But if what she says is true, it seems a little suspicious that the door was opened again almost immediately and she heard quick steps moving toward the courtyard door that leads to her stairwell. Not running, but sort of nervous-sounding. She assumed that the person who was hurrying wanted to get out of the rain. Not so strange, because it was pouring at the time. But she claims that she knows her neighbors by the sound of their footsteps. Her apartment is on the second floor, so she certainly has the opportunity to keep tabs. But she didn't recognize these footsteps. It wasn't someone from her building."

Jonny Blom groaned and rolled his eyes to the ceiling. Fredrik ignored him, but looked down at his notepad before he went on.

"She heard the courtyard door open and someone went up the steps to the ground-floor apartment, but then the footsteps didn't continue up the stairs but instead crossed the hall and went out the front door to the street. The door is heavy and closes with a thump, according to the old lady."

Andersson interrupted him with another question. "Did she seem confused or senile?"

"Well, she *is* ancient, after all. And I don't know if she hears as well as she claims. But she seemed pretty sure of what she was saying."

Anyone over fifty was a fossil in Stridh's view. Andersson gave a little sigh before he asked, "Did any of you check to see whether someone in the building was out taking a walk at that time?"

Stridh, Borg, and Persson had found no one who confessed to being out at the time in question who might have been the cause of the slamming doors or the footsteps in the courtyard.

Andersson said, "If this was our murderer, then it shows he was incredibly cold blooded. To wait in the building for fifteen minutes after the murder! On the other hand, at first everyone probably thought it was suicide. No one was looking for a killer. And if it's true that he went across the courtyard and straight through the entryway, then he would have come out on Kapellgatan. A whole block from the murder scene!"

Andersson wasn't as doubtful as Stridh. Experience had taught him that sedentary old people who kept watch on their neighborhood were invaluable witnesses.

Eagerly he said, "Assume that it actually was our killer. Under cover of rain and darkness he slips out into the courtyard. For some reason he slinks quickly into the garbage room and disposes of something. What? An idea is coming to mind. Any suggestions?"

Andersson looked around the room, but no one else came up with a guess. Triumphantly he exclaimed, "The rag! The rag with the Ajax on it! It wasn't found in the apartment. The only cleaning rags we found were in an unopened package in the broom closet. Now we've run into some bad luck, because we weren't on the alert this morning. The sanitation department came and picked up the garbage before we had a chance to look through the cans. And the only fingerprints on the door opening onto the courtyard belonged to Irene and to Henrik von Knecht. Someone wiped off the handle before Irene and von Knecht's son touched it."

The others gave Irene a quizzical look, but neither she nor the superintendent felt like explaining about the hide-and-seek game with the press the night before.

Instead Irene said, "According to Sylvia von Knecht the cleaning woman is Finnish; her name is Pirjo Larsson and she speaks terrible Swedish. We have to get her phone number, and then we can find her address. She lives somewhere out in Angered. Hannu, may I ask if you speak Finnish?"

Hannu Rauhala nodded.

"Would you please handle the interview with Pirjo Larsson?"

Another nod from Hannu.

Irene reported on the conversations she had had during the day. They all thought, just as she did, that quite a few interesting angles had developed, even though there was no motive yet or any plausible perpetrator.

Birgitta Moberg had managed to reach the Wahl couple in Provence by phone. Their youngest daughter, who was unmarried, was listed in the phone book; she had given Birgitta the number. She had called the couple, who had already heard that Richard von Knecht had been murdered, from one of their daughters. They told Birgitta that they had taken the car ferry to Kiel the previous Sunday evening. This morning they reached their farm about fifty kilometers outside Aix-en-Provence. They could only confirm what others who were at the party had said, that von Knecht was happy and in high spirits as usual, and that they didn't have the foggiest idea of a motive or murderer. *Unbelievable*, was their comment. She leafed through her notes.

"Waldemar Reuter was at his brokerage office. He didn't have time to talk to me today but promised to come here tomorrow morning at eight. He did say this much: He was shocked and found it impossible to comprehend why anyone would want to kill von Knecht. Seems to have been a regular model citizen, that Richard von Knecht," she said dejectedly.

There was a discreet knock on the door, and the secretary came in with a thick stack of faxes under her arm. Dryly she said, "Greetings from the fax room to Inspector Huss; the fax machine burned up! Do you know why?" With that she slammed the heap on the table in front of Irene.

She had to admit that her journalist contact at *Swedish Ladies' Journal* was a real find. Irene could see that, even after a cursory glance through the pile. Everything was neatly arranged in chronological order and stamped with the date.

Jonny reported on the investigative material he had been allowed to examine with his two colleagues in Financial. Von Knecht was mixed up in a tangle of suspected tax crimes that had to do with moving money out of the country for stock deals abroad. The material, gathered over a period of almost two years, had been left untouched, Jonny explained.

"These guys in Financial are trained to unravel financial crimes, but they work here at police headquarters, even though they're actually associated with the National Unit for Financial Crimes in Stockholm. So it's a government deal, really. But since their work often runs into a hitch on the prosecution side, they do some other investigative work here at Crime Police. Evidently there were suspicions of insider trading relating to the sale of a pharmaceutical company a couple of years ago. But it couldn't be proven. Von Knecht made a neat little profit of eleven million on that one. According to the financial guys, they think his offshore assets are larger than the ones he has in Sweden. But since foreign brokers handle those deals, they're hard to check up on. And in Sweden he's taxed on personal assets of a hundred and sixty-three million!"

The appreciative whistles and shouts in the room were interrupted by an angry buzz from the intercom.

"Hello! This is the duty officer! Will you please come down and get your damned pizzas? It stinks like a pizzeria in here!"

Fredrik Stridh and Birgitta Moberg volunteered. It occurred to Irene as they vanished out the door that she had seen them together quite a bit lately. Jonny Blom seemed to be thinking the same thing. He unconsciously pressed his lips together as he gazed after them with a gloomy expression. The others were busily rising and stretching their legs.

The pizzas were devoured quickly, right out of the boxes, using the plastic utensils that had been supplied. The local pizza maker knew what was required when he made deliveries to police headquarters.

The coffeemaker was turned on. Andersson leaned back in his chair, feeling full, bloated.

Just at that instant a powerful muffled explosion was heard. The pressure wave made the windowpanes bend inward and start to rattle ominously.

"Damn, one of the refineries on Hising Island must have blown up!"

Jonny meant it as a joke, but nobody laughed. It was an unpleasantly large *boom*, even if it wasn't the Shell Oil tank that had exploded.

Andersson shrugged his shoulders and tried to ignore the outside world.

"That explosion is someone else's problem. Well, we've heard a report from everyone—except for you, Hannu."

Hannu Rauhala looked straight at the superintendent when he began to speak. His voice was unexpectedly deep and his lilting Finnish accent sounded pleasantly soft. "I've been at the tax office—"

Jonny sat up in his chair and interrupted him, sounding agitated. "We don't need to do double work!" He sounded agitated. "I've already ferreted out everything of interest from Financial!"

Hannu's expression didn't change, and his voice didn't alter, but his eyes took on a colder ice-blue tinge.

"Richard von Knecht has another son."

In the tense silence that followed, it seemed as though the sirens from all the police cars and fire engines in Göteborg began wailing at once.

Chapter Six

"WHAT ARE YOU SAYING? And what the hell is going on in town?"

The color in Andersson's face rose considerably. He had thought they had a good grip on things. And suddenly all hell was breaking loose, both inside the department and out!

Hannu Rauhala kept his eyes riveted on the superintendent and continued, unmoved. "The tax authorities have copies of his personal file. Richard von Knecht has admitted paternity of a son, Bo Jonas, born July twenty-third, nineteen sixty-five, in the Katarina district in Stockholm. The mother is Mona Söder, November second, nineteen forty-one. It's all on von Knecht's death certificate."

"How did you get access to . . . Oh, the hell with it."

One look in those ice-blue eyes and Andersson decided to put off the question until later. Instead he said, "This is interesting. I wonder whether the wife and his son Henrik know about the existence of Jonas? Irene, since you're already in contact with both of them, you handle it. Hannu, you take Pirjo Larsson. We have to find out if she has a key to von Knecht's apartment. Ask her who may have visited him while she was there, or if she saw anything else that seemed odd. And the rag. Don't forget to ask her about the rag. Keep digging for information about Jonas and his mother. Maybe we'll need to enlist the help of our colleagues in Stockholm. What a damned racket those sirens are making. Has half of Göteborg blown sky-high?"

Angrily he pressed the intercom button for the duty officer. At first nobody answered his call. He had to try again.

"Yeah, Dispatch here," replied a calm male voice.

"What's happening in town?"

"A building on Berzeliigatan is on fire. Suspected bombing. Didn't you hear the explosion? It's barely a kilometer from here."

"Sounds like the boys at PO-One are going to be busy tonight!"

"No doubt. See you."

The superintendent looked crestfallen when the intercom clicked off. To cover his embarrassment, he continued briskly, "So now we know, but that's somebody else's headache. We have to concentrate on the von Knecht family. Go on, Hannu, do you have more info on the second son?"

Hannu shook his head. "Nope, but you can take it from here, right, Jonny?"

"The rest of the family's assets, last year's tax returns. Sylvia von Knecht's income was one hundred fifty thousand, personal net worth six hundred sixty-eight thousand. Henrik von Knecht's income was five hundred thousand, net worth four hundred fifty-three thousand. Charlotte von Knecht's income was seventy-two thousand and she has a net worth of zero."

"A pauper compared to Pappa von Knecht. And who isn't, compared to him?" Fredrik commented on Jonny's research. Casually he remarked, "Truth be told, Charlotte and I are in the same financial bracket."

The others laughed before taking a coffee break.

The meeting went on for another two hours. They went over and over various suggestions and hypotheses, but couldn't tell whether they were getting any closer to the truth. Or whether it might already have been approached without anyone realizing it.

Andersson stifled a yawn and decided to wrap up the meeting with a few concluding remarks. "Okay, see you all here at seven-thirty in the morning."

They had started packing up their notebooks, pens and pencils, coffee cups, and everything else essential to the investigation when there was another knock at the door. Without waiting for an answer, Officer Håkan Lund opened it, filling the entire doorway. He began with a greeting. "Peace. Thought I'd drop by with a report that might interest you."

The group watched in surprise as he strode to the end of the table. Once he was there, he started his report. "I just came from the fire on Berzeliigatan. An eyewitness heard a loud explosion and then the place went up in flames. The windows of all the nearby buildings were blown out. According to the same witness the explosion came from the third floor. And there . . ."

He paused melodramatically and gave his audience a look before he went on. "That's where Richard von Knecht had his office!"

You could have heard a pin drop; no one could think of a thing to say. Håkan Lund was obviously pleased with the effect of his news. He continued, "My shift was supposed to end at four, but we were held up by a big traffic accident near the Tingstad tunnel. Sleet and black ice. Five cars involved in a rear-ender. No injuries to speak of, but plenty of peripheral work with reports and directing traffic. Just as we were finishing, we got the call about the explosion on Berzeliigatan, corner of Sten Sturegatan. It was burning good by the time we arrived. There were three fire engines on site and a couple of patrol cars."

"Is the building a total loss?"

Lund gave Andersson, who had asked the question, a thoughtful look and replied, "Let me put it this way: On a fire scale of one to ten, where one is a match and ten is a quasar, this was a nine. An inferno. So yes, the entire building was gutted."

"God damn it!"

It wasn't the most intelligent comment the superintendent could have made, but it expressed precisely what everyone in the room was feeling. Lund resumed his report of the events.

"On the ground floor there's a hair salon. The hairdresser who was in the salon escaped to the street. She was busy cleaning up after the day's work. Fortunately, she only received minor injuries to her head and back. On the second floor there are two apartments. The residents of the larger one, a retired couple, managed to escape. They were in shock, their hearing was damaged, and they had a number of ugly burns. The tenant across the hall works as a desk clerk at the Sheraton and wasn't home when the place blew up. He arrived just as I was leaving. Evidently he heard about the fire on the news. On the third floor is— or *was* would be more correct—von Knecht's office. Apparently, it was a large apartment, according to the downstairs neighbors. By the way, von Knecht owned the whole building. The apartment next to his is currently vacant. It's a little two-room place that he rents out to companies that need an apartment for short-term periods."

Lund broke off, quickly went over and poured the cold dregs from the coffeemaker into a plastic cup, swished the coffee around in his mouth before swallowing, then smacked his lips contentedly and said, "Your mouth gets so dry from a fire. And from talking too."

No one responded, so he returned to his place and went on with his report.

"On the fourth floor of the building there's a photographer. He lives in the two-room space and has his studio in the larger apartment above von Knecht's office. The witnesses from the second floor, the retired couple, think he must be out of town at the moment. They haven't seen him in several days. He sometimes does fashion shoots abroad.

For his sake, let's hope he's away shooting beautiful women under the palms. Otherwise he's dead. Grilled. It'll be several hours before the smoke-eaters can go into the building."

Lund paused and looked quite stern and serious as he went on. "On the fifth floor they managed to rescue a young woman with the hook and ladder. She was in shock, of course, and refused to climb down the ladder. But the fireman grabbed her and more or less carried her down. When she reached the ground, she suddenly remembered that her boyfriend was asleep somewhere in the apartment. But it was too late. There was no chance of getting back inside. Her apartment was completely engulfed in flames and there was a big risk that the floor would cave in. The lady in the apartment next door had better luck. She came home from work in the middle of the fire-fighting work. She had evidently heard about the fire, but it was still a shock. She collapsed on the street and the ambulance had to take her to the ER. The sixth floor was empty. Work had just started on renovating it into an apartment that would take up the whole floor." .

"He seemed to have a penchant for that type of apartment building. How did you know that we were still here?" Birgitta Moberg had managed to muster enough nerve to make a comment and ask a question.

"Pure chance. Irene and I met after von Knecht's little air show yesterday. According to the evening papers, I see that he had some help with it. Interesting. Well, after we were relieved by the swing shift, I called in to Dispatch and asked if any of you were still in the building. According to them, you were sitting here devoting yourselves to orgies of pizza. So I thought I'd drop by and light a fire under the pot with some real red-hot stuff," Håkan Lund concluded with a satisfied smile.

"I think we all agree you've succeeded," Andersson said flatly. He tried to pull himself together enough to ask some sensible questions. It wasn't easy.

"How did you get hold of all this information, about von Knecht's office, the fact that he owned the building, who lives in the various apartments, and all that?"

"Didn't I tell you? The retired couple on the second floor. They were very well informed, real gold mines of inside information. Let's see . . ."

Lund fished around in the pockets of his new uniform jacket made of heavy leather. "Here's the note with their name and address. They're staying with their daughter in Mölndal for the time being. But they'll probably be in Mölndal Hospital for a few days."

"Thanks, Håkan. You're a gold mine yourself . . . well, you know what I mean." It wasn't the best-formulated remark, but Lund sensed the intended compliment, bowed deliberately, and said, "My pleasure. I'll be going now and leave you to your theories. Good night!"

With these words he sailed out the door, if a man who weighs a hundred kilos can be said to sail.

Silence settled over the room for a while. Andersson was the one who broke it. The color was rising in his face again as he energetically clapped his hands and exclaimed, "So now we're going to have to track the progress of the fire! Fredrik and Tommy, get over there. Try to sum up the situation. Report back to the rest of us at seven-thirty tomorrow morning. You can take off right now. Here's the note with the name and address of the retired couple's daughter."

The other six stayed for the better part of an hour but got nowhere. Finally Andersson said, "Okay, let's wind it up for tonight. See you at seven-thirty on the dot."

KRISTER WAS still up when Irene got home. It was almost eleven o'clock. Sammie was bouncing around, claiming that no human had paid attention to him all day. But his light, wheat-colored coat was glossy and newly brushed, and his food dish was washed and on the drainboard. He had nothing to complain about. As Irene flopped down in the easy chair in front of the TV, he tried to climb onto her lap. But eighteen kilos of soft-coated wheaten Irish terrier was too much to hold when she was trying to relax; he had to stay on the floor and sulk. A scratch behind the ears had to suffice.

Krister told her about his conversation with Jenny. It seemed to be her dream to play in a real band. And a used electric guitar would make it happen. The leader of the band could arrange to get a good one for a thousand kronor. They decided to think about it for a few more days. Maybe it would be a suitable Christmas present.

"But too expensive! We ought to have a fortune like von Knecht— more than a hundred and sixty million! He must have plenty of pensions and golden parachutes and that sort of thing too," Irene said glumly.

"Hey, old lady. What good did all his millions do him yesterday when he fell without any parachute?"

Sometimes Krister's Värmland earthiness was quite refreshing. As was his profession, which asserted itself now as he asked, "Would you like something to eat?"

"No thanks. The pizza feels like concrete in my stomach."

"What would milady prefer, then?"

"Whiskey. A big one."

"But of course, my darling. Chivas Regal, Jack Daniel's, or Famous Grouse?"

"Chivas."

With a laugh Krister got up and went out to the kitchen. He returned with two glasses and a can of Pripps pilsner. Irene looked disappointed.

"For once I feel the need for a good shot of booze to unwind. Not much. An ordinary whiskey will do," she complained.

"We could make punch in this can: five centiliters of O. P. Andersson and one deciliter of Amontillado. That's all we've got in the house. I'll go to the liquor store tomorrow and pick up a few bottles of wine for the holidays. I'm working late on Friday, but I can go early on Saturday. Of course, I know something else that might make you unwind. Just come with uncle, and you'll get some goodies . . ."

Sammie realized what was going on, lowered his tail, and slunk up the stairs to Jenny's room. He understood that a paltry scratch behind the ears was all he was going to get that evening.

THEY WERE all in place in the conference room at seven-thirty. Tommy Persson sat yawning, while Fredrik looked like he'd slept for eight hours instead of his usual four. And he was the one who had to give the report on the fire.

"Tommy and I were there by nine-thirty. We went around and questioned the people in the building across the street. They confirmed what Håkan had told us. The explosion came at precisely six-twenty P.M. The fire blazed up instantly, and it seems that it spread explosively. Could they have poured gasoline all over the apartment?"

"The neighbors should have smelled it," Jonny put in.

"Yes, you're right. But the firefighters are leaning that way. This morning they're going to go inside because that guy who was asleep in the apartment on the fifth floor is missing. Apparently he moved in with the woman the week before. I guess she hadn't gotten used to having him there. That's probably why she didn't remember him until it was too late. His name is Mattias Larsson, twenty-two years old. A student at the teachers' college."

Fredrik looked upset and started leafing through his papers before he went on. "Here it is! The photographer in the apartment above von Knecht's called Dispatch; they then contacted us. He saw the report on the fire on the late news. What a shock! Imagine, getting comfortable in an easy chair with a beer, turning on the hotel TV, and finding out that your home is burning down! He's working on an assignment up in Stockholm, he said. But he's going to come down today and will be in touch with us. His name is Bo-Ivar 'Bobo' Torsson. We thought we'd continue with our follow-up on the fire and see if it produces any connections to the murder."

The superintendent nodded. "Okay. You should also contact the retired couple when they're released from the hospital. They're going to be staying with their daughter in Mölndal. Of course there is a connection between von Knecht's murder and the bomb in his office. The question is why they had to blow up his office too. Did he have any employees, maybe a secretary?"

"I'll be talking to Sylvia von Knecht this morning. She should know," said Irene.

"Then why don't you take on Henrik von Knecht too? Tommy and Fredrik will follow up on the fire. Birgitta is supposed to meet Waldemar Reuter, the stockbroker, today."

"Yes, first thing this morning," Birgitta confirmed.

"I want to be with you at that interview. He must have been among the last to see von Knecht alive. Jonny, can you try to get hold of the opera singer, Ivan Viktors? We haven't heard back from him, despite the notes we've left and messages on his answering machine. Wait a minute, I have the note here somewhere . . ."

The superintendent rummaged around in his papers on the table. Finally, he exclaimed: "Here it is! Take it. And Hannu, keep digging up information on the illegitimate son in Stockholm. Although the most important thing right now is to get hold of Pirjo Larsson."

Hannu nodded and to everyone's surprise actually spoke. "She's not in the phone book."

"Okay, well . . . you'll figure it out somehow."

Andersson still wasn't quite sure that he wanted to know about Hannu's methods of gathering information. But they were effective.

Irene turned to Hannu and said, "Sylvia von Knecht said that she has Pirjo Larsson's phone number. I'll call her right after the meeting and set a time to meet, ask her for Pirjo's number, and give it to you right away."

Hannu nodded again. Andersson turned to Hans Borg, who was dozing in his chair, as usual. To wake him up, Andersson raised his voice and addressed his oldest inspector, "Hans, you'll have to drive back to the von Knecht neighborhood. Whatever hasn't burned down, that is. Find out if anybody saw anything on Kapellgatan, around twenty to six on the night of the murder. There's a parking garage across the street. Even if it was dark and crappy weather, somebody might have seen the killer if he went out through the street door."

Andersson paused, preparing to close the meeting. "We'll get together here this afternoon around five."

A knock on the door interrupted him. The secretary came in with a fax in her hand.

"Fresh fax from the pathologist," she said briskly.

Andersson took it from her. The others could see his bushy eyebrows arch up to his nonexistent hairline when he exclaimed, "Von Knecht had a blood alcohol level of point-one-one! He wasn't dead drunk, but clearly feeling no pain. That would have made it easier for the murderer."

BACK IN her office, Irene called Sylvia von Knecht. Hannu, who came sauntering after her, sat on a chair by the door.

Sylvia answered at once. When Irene identified herself, Sylvia flew into a rage, denouncing the entire Göteborg police force for turning her apartment upside down. She got a good head of steam going. From where he was sitting, Hannu could hear her saying shrilly, "And I can't get hold of Pirjo either! I've been calling her since seven o'clock. She has to come in today and help me clean up!"

Irene held the receiver a little way from her ear and gave Hannu a knowing glance before she put the receiver back and said in a friendly tone of voice, "So good of you to mention Pirjo. We would like to talk to her too. Could I get her phone number? Or perhaps the number of the cleaning firm, her employer?"

There was silence on the other end of the line. Finally Sylvia snapped, "It's not a crime to pay your cleaning woman under the table."

It most certainly is, Irene felt like saying, but knew this wouldn't be good psychology. Calmly she said, "No, of course not, Fru von . . . Sylvia, but I'd appreciate it if you could give me her phone number."

Reluctantly Sylvia gave her the number. Irene wrote it down on a slip of paper and handed it to Hannu. With a nod he disappeared down the corridor.

Only then did Sylvia mention the fire the night before. "So odd that the building on Berzeliigatan would burn down the day after Richard's death. But it's an old building, of course. There was probably a short circuit in the wiring. They had started tearing up the top floor. It was going to be a studio. I hope he had adequate insurance on his computers. I know the building was insured," she said.

Irene asked carefully, "Did he have any employees at his office?"

"No," Sylvia replied quickly. "He watched the whole world's stock exchanges on his computer screens. He didn't need a secretary to do that. His broker takes care of all the daily business with the stock trades. Richard was only there a few days a week."

Sylvia agreed to meet Irene at ten.

With a sigh Irene looked at the pile of gossip magazine faxes awaiting her. Procrastinating a bit, she called Henrik von Knecht and set a time to meet him. He would come down to HQ after one o'clock.

ANDERSSON FOLLOWED Birgitta Moberg into her office. Waldemar Reuter hadn't shown up yet, but it was only five past eight. Andersson liked working with Birgitta. She was quick witted, alert, young, and pretty. There was only one problem. She made the superintendent feel old and a little clumsy. She was in the swing of things, went out with friends, traveled abroad, and skied in the winter. She also had a scuba diving certificate and often went to the Red Sea or the Mediterranean.

Bosses were supposed to show interest in their subordinates; that's what they had said at the last manager development course, so Andersson began by asking, "Will you be diving in the Red Sea or skiing in the Alps this spring?"

"Neither, I'm afraid. I'm trying to save money. No vacations until next fall. Then I'm going to Australia for at least two months. Pack everything in a rucksack and bum around."

"By yourself?"

He felt foolish after he said it, but it was his spontaneous reaction.

She gave him an easy smile. "Of course. Guys just slow you down. If you take a guy along, you always have to worry about his needs. No, I want to experience things and be open to everything."

"Isn't it dangerous for a single woman to travel alone like that?"

Birgitta laughed. "As you know, it can be dangerous to go out on your balcony!"

Would he dare venture into the Australian outback? Never! Sleep under the stars with nocturnal predators stalking around? Snakes and spiders? He shuddered. And felt about as old as Methuselah.

"A trip like that must cost a lot of money. How do you manage to save up that much?"

"I have a cheap studio apartment out in Högsbo. My car is twelve years old and I repair and maintain it myself. But my seed money was actually a small inheritance from my grandmother."

There was a noise at the door, and Waldemar Reuter made his entrance. He waved at someone out in the corridor. Both detectives noticed that he was slurring his words when he said, "A thousand thanks, my dear lady. It was kind of you to escort me through the labyrinth of Göteborg Police Headquarters."

With a small lurch he turned around and fixed his bloodshot eyes on Birgitta. "Oh, good morning! Beauties abound in this building!"

He made a deep bow and belched audibly. His breath, which spread through the room, could have been sliced up and sold as well-aged Stilton. Reuter wasn't hung over, but he would be in a few hours. His round head seemed to be fastened directly to his globular body, without any neck visible in between. He actually appeared to be as wide as he was tall. His arms seemed to stick straight out from his body, but his attempt to keep his balance by using them as stabilizers may have contributed to this impression. His legs were short. His feet, clad in expensive shoes, were surprisingly small. He had a Burberry trench coat over one arm, which flapped and waved in the air when he flailed his arms. His suit was dark blue, made of a soft wool fabric with discreet shiny piping. For some reason his tie was draped under his lapel and not around the collar of his shirt. But at least he still had it on.

Birgitta grimaced with disgust behind Reuter's inclined back, but when he straightened up she flashed him a dazzling smile, asked him to take a seat in the visitor's chair, and introduced herself and the superintendent.

Waldemar Reuter blurted out, "Oh, hell, there's a guy in the room! I didn't even see you!" He gave Andersson a moist handshake and winked mischievously, casting a roguish glance toward Birgitta.

Was it an advantage that he was drunk? Perhaps. The best tactic would be to let Birgitta handle the interview. Reuter clearly viewed her as a little cutie pie, not as a cop. Andersson tried to make himself invisible in his corner, which was entirely unnecessary. Reuter had already forgotten his existence.

Birgitta asked amiably, "Would you like some coffee, Herr Reuter?"

"Call me Valle, sweetie! Everyone calls me Valle!"

"Coffee?"

"Yes, please."

Andersson was taken by surprise when Birgitta signaled to him to go get the coffee. But that was only proper. She was the one running the interview, after all. Though he did feel rather stupid as he walked over to the coffee vending machine. He bought three cups, which he regretted on his way back. It was hard to carry three at once.

Andersson set two of the cups on the desk. Valle Reuter was sobbing and took no notice of him. He crept back to his corner.

". . . my oldest friend. We had known each other forty-five years!" Reuter wiped his nose on the checked lining of his coat. With a well-feigned expression of sympathy Birgitta handed him a tissue.

"We understand that you were at the party last Saturday. Their thirtieth anniversary."

"But of course! Leila and I served as bridesmaid and groomsman at their wedding."

"Leila?"

"My ex-wife. We divorced five years ago. She didn't get a dime!"

Birgitta decided quickly to drop the subject of the ex-wife. Reuter's voice had turned aggressive and hate-filled. With good humor she asked, "Was it a nice party?"

"Party? What party?"

"At the von Knechts' last Saturday."

"Ah, the party! Excellent fun! Wonderful food and superb wines. With the appetizer they served an interesting white from South Africa, of all places! Neil Ellis, Sauvignon Blanc. Dry and peppery, fresh and round. A long finish. Slight aroma of pissant and spice shop. Excellent with the salmon tartare!"

To the superintendent's ears it sounded like total drivel, but since Birgitta seemed to be following it all right, he didn't interrupt.

Reuter sank farther into the fog, chattering on. "With the main course they served a fantastic French wine. Thank God that Richard doesn't subscribe to that boycott nonsense. A red, Bandol Cuvée Special 'ninety-two. A profound nose, concentrated, rich and fruity with a hint of licorice. The saddle of venison landed in good company, I must say."

Andersson thought it sounded disgusting. Licorice in your red wine! On the other hand, he didn't like red wine anyway. White once in a while, with shrimp. He preferred beer with a schnapps.

Birgitta asked, "Did you think Richard seemed the same as usual?"

"Absolutely! Happy and in high spirits, as always. We love parties, Richard and I. But now he won't be going to any more parties. Richard . . ."

Again Birgitta had to come to the rescue with a tissue. Reuter blew his nose loudly and stared at her, red-eyed. He took a deep breath before he went on. "My dear, I beg your pardon. I've been drinking all night long. In memory of Richard. My friendship with Richard. He's my best friend."

"How did you remember you were supposed to come here?"

"Mats Tengman came and got me. I asked him to do it yesterday. After you called, dear . . . what was your . . . oh yes, Birgitta. He's a fine boy, Mats Tengman. I handpicked him. My successor. My son is a doctor. He's going to specialize in pharmaceuticals, because he wants to work with people, not for money, as he says. My whole staff is first-rate. If you only knew what fine employees I have."

Another audible snort underlined his statement.

"When he dropped me off here, he saw how . . . distressed . . . I am, after everything that happened . . . with Richard. And then he said, 'Valle, I'll take care of the business. Take the day off and rest.' That's what Mats told me."

Andersson saw Birgitta discreetly jotting something on her notepad. Cautiously, she coaxed Valle to go on.

"Tell me about Tuesday, Valle."

"What about it?"

"Your lunch last Tuesday."

"We've been doing that for more than twenty years. Every Tuesday we've had lunch together. It started when Richard sold the shipping company. He was clairvoyant when it came to economic trends. If I'd dared to believe in his . . . then I'd be a very rich man today. But I've done all right for myself." He paused and stared blankly into space.

Birgitta prodded him with another question. "Which shipping company was it that he sold?"

"The one he inherited, of course! The family company! He got a good price. He invested in real estate, together with Peder Wahl. Do you know Peder?"

"I've spoken with him on the phone."

"He's a great guy. It's a shame that they live down south in Provence most of the time. I miss Peder. Tell him that next time you talk to him," Reuter said.

Birgitta glanced at Andersson and rolled her eyes. He made an encouraging gesture. It always helps to interview someone with a loose tongue. Birgitta continued valiantly. "Where did you eat last Tuesday?"

"We took a cab out to Johanneshus. An excellent inn out in Billdal. We wanted to go before the Christmas hysteria sets in. Then it gets too crowded."

"What time were you there?"

"Where?"

"At Johanneshus out in Billdal. The lunch with Richard."

"Oh, right, of course. The lunch."

Valle Reuter tried hard to concentrate.

"I think the cab must have arrived out there by one or one-thirty. Somewhere thereabouts. Ask Peter, the innkeeper."

Birgitta made another note. She certainly would inquire.

"So what did you have to eat?"

"Oh, *frutti di mare!* The appetizer was ice-cold oysters with lime. A not entirely compatible wine with it, from . . . let me see . . . from the States. Golden Hind Sauvignon Blanc. Not good with oysters. A blunder. An excellent wine with oysters is—"

"The entrée, Valle. Tell us about the entrée."

"Poached halibut with grated horseradish and melted butter. The potatoes weren't mashed . . . they were . . . now, what's it called? . . . Pressed! Pressed potatoes. We decided on the South African wine. Did I mention the wine we drank last Saturday? The white with the appetizer . . . oh yes, of course . . . it was from there too. A splendid wine. Bouchard Finlayson, Chardonnay. It was just fantastic. We ordered two bottles. With dessert, which was an ice cream mousse with Arctic raspberries, we snubbed the sweet wines of the Old World. Ordered a bottle of Mike Mossison Liqueur Muscat. An Australian. Very good choice. Very good."

Andersson was starting to get royally tired of goofy wines and weird food. Still, when she caught his eye appealing for help, he motioned to Birgitta to continue.

Her sigh was barely audible as she went on. "When did you finish the meal?"

"We rushed a bit. We left at three-thirty. By cab, of course. Sylvia was coming home that night, and Richard wanted to get back and check on things. And he had a slight cold. He was going to have a little whiskey and sit in the sauna. I like to do that too when I feel a cold coming on. But I say to hell with the sauna!"

Valle Reuter found this extraordinarily funny, and he began chuckling and wheezing in amusement. Neither Andersson nor Birgitta Moberg felt like laughing along with him. There was something sad and depressing about the little round man. Birgitta leaned across the desk and shouted, "Valle. Hello? Valle!"

Reuter wiped his eyes with the soggy tissue. But he managed to calm down.

"As you know, Richard was murdered. Who do you think did it? And why?"

Reuter straightened up and gave Birgitta a sharp look, which made her wonder for a moment whether he was more sober than he let on. Caustically he said, "Sylvia! It has to be Sylvia. She inherits the money. She's crazy about money. Miserly. And spiteful. If you only knew what she said to me." He put on a deeply injured expression.

"According to several witnesses she was down on the street just as he hit the ground," Birgitta stated dryly.

This brought back the worried furrows to Reuter's brow. But he said nothing, merely mumbled inaudibly.

"Is it the inheritance, all that money, that you think is the motive?"

"Sylvia. The money." He nodded to himself, looking extremely pleased with his own perspicacity.

"Valle, what did you and Richard do after you got out of the taxi?"

"We took the elevator upstairs. I got off on the second floor and Richard continued up to his place."

"Did you see him, or speak to him later?"

"No. That was the last time I saw Richard."

Andersson was afraid that Reuter was going to start crying again. But he didn't. He sat slumped in the chair like a punctured balloon, gave a big yawn, and blinked his red eyes. Andersson realized that he had to hurry up and ask his question. He stood and walked slowly toward Valle, who started and said in surprise, "Are you still here? What was your name again?"

"Sven Andersson. One last question before we call you a cab. Where were you last Tuesday evening and night? We knocked on your door, but you weren't home."

Valle pressed his lips together firmly. It was obvious that he had no intention of answering.

Patiently the superintendent continued, "It would be good if you would answer the question. You'd save us a lot of work. You were the last one to see Richard von Knecht alive. Besides the murderer." He put special emphasis on the last word.

Valle was on the same page, and he leaned forward and said conspiratorially, "The murderess! Sylvia."

"Don't you understand? You're a prime suspect!" Andersson exclaimed.

Valle looked deeply wounded. "Me? Kill my best friend? Never!"

"Then where were you?"

Birgitta had an idea. She played along with the conspiratorial mood by leaning over the desk and saying, in a slightly teasing tone, "Tell the truth, Valle—there's a woman involved, right?"

The little man fairly shone with joviality. "But of course, my dear. A woman's honor."

"You've known each other a long time, isn't that so?"

"Absolutely, three years . . . If you already know about her, why are you asking me?"

"I don't know her name." Again Valle looked displeased. He stared at Birgitta gloomily.

She challenged him. "Valle, you have to have an alibi."

"She doesn't want me to tell. She'll get mad at me."

"I'm sure she'll understand that since you have become involved in a homicide investigation through no fault of your own, you need an alibi. And she's the only one who can give you one."

Valle slumped down a bit more. After a long silence he muttered, "Gunnel . . . Gunnel Forsell."

"Where does she live?"

"Now listen, my dear, she doesn't want cops running around her place. Don't tell her I said anything or I'll never be able to go there again."

His tone of voice, along with the anxiety in his wide eyes, said it all. In his loneliness he'd found comfort with a prostitute.

Quietly Birgitta asked, "When did you leave for her place?"

"The usual time." He stopped and gave Birgitta an apologetic look. "I usually go visit her on Tuesday. At five-thirty. But I was a little early . . . she had a guest . . . but he left after a while, and then I could go in."

"At five-thirty?"

"A little before that, I think."

"How did you get there?"

"Taxi."

"When did you get home?"

Again he hesitated with his reply. "I usually spend the whole night." He gave Birgitta a defiant look.

"Where does she live?"

"On Stampgatan."

"When did you get back home?"

"Around ten. In the morning. Then I went down to the office."

A hooker who fixed breakfast. Neither of the officers had ever heard of such a thing. This had to be a very special arrangement. Something told Andersson that it was costing Reuter a small fortune. With great effort the stockbroker tried to get up. Finally he was on his feet, wobbling unsteadily. He gave a big yawn and said, "All right, now I want to go home. Thanks for the pleasant company, my dear. Don't forget to try Neil Ellis sometime. Perhaps we could . . . ?"

Birgitta smiled sweetly and picked up the phone to call a cab.

"BIRGITTA, CAN you go to the Johanneshus restaurant to verify the times? And to our pretty chicken on Stampgatan? Check if she's got a rap sheet," said Andersson.

"Hardly. I can smell a high-priced call girl a mile away. Fixing breakfast after a whole night's sleep! Small, loyal, wealthy clientele. No walking the streets. I'll try to get hold of her this morning; there's a better chance she won't be with a john so early," replied Birgitta.

"Ask her if she knew Richard von Knecht. Who knows? Maybe they were both clients of hers."

Reluctantly he went into the corridor. He had two meetings set up. The first was with Police Commissioner Bengt Bergström. The second was with the people assigned to take measurements for the new police uniforms. Everyone in the building had already been there, except Andersson. Would Reuter have babbled just as openly if he and Birgitta had been in uniform? Doubtful. After working plainclothes for thirty years, he was going to be forced to sign up for a uniform in his final years of service despite the fact that he had no intention of putting it on. But it wouldn't do any good, no matter what he said. Orders from on high. "The public must know that they are talking to a police officer"—that was the argument. No dispensations had been granted. His only means of protesting had been to avoid going to the fittings. But there was no longer any excuse.

Chapter Seven

IRENE HUSS ONLY HAD time to skim through the faxes from *Swedish Ladies' Journal*. She jotted down a few important dates and events on her notepad. The rest of the investigative group needed a report on the von Knecht family's past at five o'clock.

It was interesting to read old gossip now that she had personally met those involved. Her picture of Richard von Knecht had to be constructed solely from the clippings and from what she had seen and heard during the course of the investigation.

After his military service, young Richard was apparently sent to England for two years. In an article about a college party at which Princess Birgitta was a guest, she found a picture of Richard and the princess in the midst of the dancers. The caption read: "Princess Birgitta was dazzlingly happy in the company of stylish Richard von Knecht." In the brief article it said she "danced several times with young Richard von Knecht. He has just returned from studying economics at Oxford. His father Otto von Knecht, king of Göteborg's shipping magnates, must be pleased that his son will now begin his MBA studies at the Stockholm School of Economics."

From the picture she could see that the gossip columnist was right. Richard was definitely stylish. Tall and slender. His dark blond hair was most certainly too long for the fashion of the time. He wore it parted on the side, with an unruly shock of hair slipping forward in a thick wave over his left eye. But the most attractive thing about him was his smile—a smile that glinted in his eyes and radiated from his perfect teeth. A lovely mouth. A sexy face, no doubt about it. Not a pretty boy's face, but handsome. Masculine. How in the world could this man be Henrik's father? Everything about Richard that seemed alive and vibrant in a photo almost forty years old was no more than a vague physical resemblance in his son. Henrik possessed none of the joie de vivre evident in Richard. Had he ever? Curious despite herself, Irene continued leafing through the faxed pages. There were several pictures from parties and premieres where Richard was seen in the crowd. Always with some young lady on his arm. Seldom the same one twice in a row. In 1962 Richard attended a large Whitsuntide wedding and was photographed with a beautiful woman at his side. Irene didn't recognize her. The article said: "One of the young men from the princess's jet set, Richard von Knecht, converses with an enchanting young lady. Could he be telling her that he just passed his MBA exam and will start at Öberg's brokerage in the fall? When our reporter asked why he didn't start right away with his family's shipping company in Göteborg, Richard von Knecht replied that it's always useful to gather experience from other fields before you settle into one profession."

The following two and a half years he appeared in various society photos. But in January 1965 the magazine ran a whole spread with a huge headline: OTTO VON KNECHT DIES SUDDENLY. From the article it appeared that Richard's father suffered a cerebral hemorrhage on New Year's Day and died a week later, at the age of sixty-nine. Richard was called home to take the helm of the family shipping company. His mother appeared in some of the pictures, a rigid and severe-looking woman. From the text it was quite evident that she was the one running the shipping operation. Richard must have met Sylvia relatively soon after that. In a photo from the May Day Ball that year, Richard was seen dancing with a tiny, graceful blond woman. "Our new shipping magnate Richard von Knecht danced all night with the new star of the Grand Theater, Sylvia Montgomery, 22."

The tall Richard and the elfin Sylvia made a very handsome couple. They were magnificent at the elaborate wedding of Waldemar Reuter and his Leila on Whitsun Eve, a month later. Richard was elegantly attired in his white tie and tails, and Sylvia was innocently sexy in a bare-shouldered pink silk gown. The wedding took place in the old Örgryte Church. The bridal couple looked quite odd. He was half a head shorter than the bride, short and plump. According to the article, he worked in his family's brokerage firm. She was a brunette, startlingly pretty, and looked to be no more than twenty years old. Even though she was holding the bouquet in front of her stomach in the photo on the church steps, it was obvious that she was pregnant.

In late August Richard and Sylvia got engaged. Richard's mother was said to be "simply delighted." The wedding was set for November 18. Uh-oh! That was a bit rushed. The reason, of course, was Henrik. The pictures from the wedding were charming. Sylvia was a dream in heavy cream-white silk. No one could see the slightest sign that she was pregnant. Richard was more stylish than ever, and according to the captions "he had eyes only for his lovely bride." There were three photos that showed Richard dancing with three different women. Naturally the bridegroom had to dance with all the ladies present. But there was something that suggested things were other than they seemed, upon a closer examination of the pictures. Especially one of them, which showed him dancing close with a now flat-stomached Fru Leila Reuter. Richard's face was turned to the photographer. His eyes were closed, and his lips slightly parted. His lower body was pressed hard against his partner's. Damned if "he had eyes only for his lovely bride." It was perfectly obvious that it wasn't eye contact he was looking for.

Irene leaned back in her chair and stretched. When this wedding took place, Richard's son in Stockholm was already almost four months old. Did Sylvia know that he existed? This was an important question to ask at their upcoming meeting.

A clipping reported on their parental joy when Henrik was born in April 1966. He was a very sweet baby, just as they usually are. Richard looked straight into the camera and smiled broadly; Sylvia looked down at her child.

Then it was relatively calm on the gossip front for a while. Irene focused on two clippings from a couple of society parties. Richard was shown with the same woman in both, and it was not Sylvia. Her name was not given. The clippings were from September and October 1967.

Six years later, in July 1973, Richard's mother Elisabeth von Knecht died, at the age of sixty-five. "She lost her courageous battle with cancer," the magazine announced.

Less than a year later the sale of the family shipping company had been arranged. The price was kept confidential, but the article hinted that considerable sums were involved. After this, it was possible to track Richard's meteoric career as one of Sweden's biggest and most successful financiers.

Sylvia was glimpsed only now and then in an official capacity—a lunch with the king here and a Nobel Prize banquet there. Richard was seen often in photos from premieres and major sailing races. There were always women around him—but Sylvia was seldom among them. A distinct characteristic became evident with regard to Richard—a weakness for young, beautiful women. And he did nothing to hide it. This wouldn't be easy to discuss with Sylvia, but it was important. Perhaps a motive? Now there were two for Sylvia: money and infidelity. The problem was that it would have been impossible for her to murder

Richard. You can't be standing down on the street and at the same time shove someone off the sixth-floor balcony. Henrik was eliminated for the same reason. But did he have any motive? Yes, money. Lots of money.

She started turning the pages faster. She was running out of time. Suddenly her attention was caught by the headline: WILL HENRIK MAKE IT? PARENTS CONSTANTLY AT HIS SIDE. To her surprise Irene actually remembered the news story. But it had been nine years ago. Back then she had been employed full time as well as having two four-year-olds. This item had been pushed back into the recesses of her memory, just like so many others. She spread out the faxes on the desk and quickly read about how Henrik and one of his army buddies from his commando unit had fallen ill. The progression of the disease turned serious, especially for Henrik. One complication was that he'd come down with meningitis. At the time the article was written he had been in a coma for two weeks. Suddenly Irene noticed a discrepancy between the text and the accompanying photo. The text said that "the parents were keeping vigil," but in the photo only Sylvia was seen on her way in through the hospital entrance. Maybe they took turns keeping vigil? If she had the chance, she should try to ask Sylvia about it.

A week later the magazine reported that Henrik had come out of the coma. Both the doctors and parents were reticent about his condition. Richard had told the reporter that "Henrik will soon be his old self again!" After that there was no more news of Henrik in the gossip columns.

His father was seen, as before, at various society events. And even Sylvia began to be seen more often—not together with her husband, but in her capacity as a prominent choreographer. She staged several ballets at the Grand Theater, she worked with the Cullberg Ballet in a performance, and she was invited to be guest director of the Helsinki ballet company in the spring of 1991. But she returned home from Finland that same summer. The reason she cited was "homesickness," but between the lines could be discerned *professional differences*.

The only report of Henrik and Charlotte's wedding was a brief announcement with no photo. Irene almost missed it, under the heading HEARD AROUND TOWN. In the middle of the column it said: "Richard and Sylvia von Knecht's only son Henrik was married to Charlotte, née Croona, in a simple ceremony at the Copenhagen Town Hall on September 10. Present were the couple's parents and the bride's siblings." Irene checked the date in the top corner. A little more than three years ago. She leafed further, but could find nothing else about Henrik and Charlotte.

The last thing she had time to glance at was the report from Richard's sixtieth birthday celebration out on his private peninsula in Bohuslän province. In all there had been three hundred guests, including various royals, diverse celebrities, and the elite of the financial world and the social register. Irene only took time to look at the pictures; she would read the articles later. He was still good looking. His hair was flecked with gray, thick, with a shock still falling over one eye. He had put on a few kilos since the wedding pictures, but there was no sign of flab. His complexion looked deeply tanned against the white tuxedo. With a champagne glass raised to the camera he smiled his sensuously disarming smile. It was unchanged, just like the glint in his intense blue eyes. *Vitality, joie de vivre, sensuality* were the words that flew through Irene's mind. Not the more obvious ones: *money, power, influence.* Strange, because they were equally apropos when it came to Richard von Knecht.

A quick look at the clock revealed that she had fifteen minutes left until her meeting with Sylvia. It would be best to show up more or less on time. She stuffed the stack of faxes in her bottom desk drawer and slipped a notepad into her jacket pocket.

SYLVIA WAS still upset over the mess in the apartment. She grumbled at Irene, who represented the police in general and the technicians in particular. Irene let her rant, following in her wake into the magnificent living room. The curtains were still open, letting in the gray daylight. Irene went over to one of the high French doors and looked out. A narrow balcony no more than two meters wide ran along the entire room. The balustrade consisted of pink vase-shaped marble columns with lintels of black marble. The railing looked dangerously low. There were also no handles on the outside of the glass doors. This prompted Irene to dismiss her thoughts of a façade-climbing killer. It would be impossible to get in from the outside through the balcony doors. And people would have noticed him, since it would only have been a little past five o'clock. No, that theory was no good.

Her thoughts were interrupted by Sylvia's plaintive voice.

"Pirjo isn't answering the phone either, just one of her imbecile kids. Even when I speak Finnish to him he still can't tell me where Pirjo is. He claims he has the flu and that a Finnish policeman is coming to talk to them this afternoon."

"That's true. One of our inspectors speaks Finnish. He'll get in touch with Pirjo," said Irene.

"What's the point of that?"

"She and her daughter may have seen or heard something on Monday, when they were here cleaning. Does she usually bring her daughter along?"

"No, only if we've had a big party. And if the girl is free," replied Sylvia brusquely.

Irene looked around the huge room. Now she saw that the columns supporting the floor of the upper level were not made of solid marble at all, as she had thought two days earlier. They were wooden columns very skillfully painted with a marble finish. Naturally, real marble would have been too heavy. The walls were lined with groupings of antique furniture and beautiful cabinets. And what paintings! Irene felt like a lone privileged visitor to an art museum. Parallel to the row of balcony doors shone a dark dining table of mahogany, the longest she had ever seen. She saw a good opening for her conversation with Sylvia.

"What a lovely table. And so long! Is this where you sat on Saturday evening?"

"Yes, of course we were here," Sylvia said guardedly.

"How many were you?"

"Twenty. We didn't want to invite too many, just our closest friends. They had all attended our wedding. Except for Henrik and Charlotte, naturally."

That depends on how you look at it, in Henrik's case, Irene thought.

Sylvia went on, "Richard's sister and her husband couldn't come. They live in Florida. He was having an operation on his prostate or something. He's seventy-five."

"And how old is she?"

"Sixty-seven."

"Could you please tell me who was at the party?"

"Of course. Besides Richard and myself, there were Henrik and Charlotte, Sven and Ann-Marie Tosse, Peder and Ulla Wahl. They had come back to Sweden to see grandchild number four. They were here a whole week before the party. Their eldest daughter Ingrid and her husband came too. Ingrid was a flower girl at our wedding. She was five years old at the time, so sweet. She wasn't the one who has the new baby; it was the middle daughter Kerstin. She was only two when we got married, so she wasn't at the wedding. That's why I didn't invite her. Or the youngest daughter either. She's the same age as Henrik."

She stopped, looking confused. Irene realized that she had lost her train of thought. She had managed to jot down all the names Sylvia had mentioned and was pleased at the pause; it gave her a chance to catch up.

Irene took pity on her and said, "You've told me that your family, the Tosses, and the Wahl clan were present. What's Ingrid's last name?"

"Von Hjortz."

"Thank you. I'd like to get the phone numbers for all of them before I go."

Sylvia nodded and took a deep breath before resuming her guest list. "My mother, Ritva Montgomery. She's seventy-eight. My sister Arja came over with her from Helsinki. Then there was Valle Reuter—"

She broke off. A cloud of undisguised contempt passed over her face. Quickly she continued, "We were so pleased that Gustav Ceder and his wife, Lady Louise, could come. Her father is almost a hundred years old and on his deathbed. They came last Friday night and flew back to London at lunchtime on Sunday. We haven't seen them since their silver anniversary four years ago. They couldn't make it to Richard's sixtieth birthday, because that's when her father fell seriously ill, although he made a recovery . . ."

Suddenly she fell silent again, confused. Angrily she exclaimed, "God, how I'm going on! Now I've lost my train of thought again!"

She cast an imploring look at Irene, who humored her and said, "Valle Reuter and then Gustav Ceder with his noble wife Louise."

"Thank you. Our good friend Ivan Viktors, the opera singer, you know, was here too."

Irene vaguely recognized his name. Apparently he was someone she ought to know, since the superintendent had been so charmed when he heard of him. But Andersson was an opera fan, and Irene was not. The Beatles, Rod Stewart, and Tina Turner were more her taste.

"That leaves only Richard's two cousins and their husbands. They're the two daughters of Richard's aunt. They're our age and were, as I mentioned, at the wedding. Pleasant, but we don't see them very often. Both of them live in Stockholm. My mother-in-law was from Stockholm. I'll give you all the names and addresses you want," Sylvia said.

She turned on her heel and began gracefully ascending the stairs to the upper floor. Irene decided to follow. The thick runner effectively muted her brisk footsteps on the stairs. At the top Irene caught a glimpse of Sylvia heading through the doorway to the room that was someone's office. The desk and computer had led her and the superintendent to draw the erroneous conclusion that it was Richard's. The ballet poster, however, indicated that it must be Sylvia's. Richard had a whole apartment for his office, after all.

Irene quickly crossed the soft carpets in the hall and library. Sylvia gave a start when she realized she was no longer alone in the workroom. Irene was perplexed by this reaction, and by the expression on Sylvia's face. She looked as if she'd been caught red-handed.

As Irene later recalled this fleeting image, Sylvia leaned her forehead lightly against the frame of the photograph that hung on the wall next to the computer table. Irene took a few cautious steps into the room and looked at the picture. The photo itself was A4 letter sized, surrounded by a broad mat within a narrow silver frame.

The smile was the same. The glint in his eyes, the expression of joie de vivre. A markedly pulsating, sensual presence. But it wasn't Richard; it was Henrik. The short-cropped hair and the beret that sat nonchalantly—but certainly according to regulations—at an angle showed that the picture must have been taken when he was in the service. The commandos, the magazine article had reported.

Sylvia gave Irene a look brimming over with rage and hatred. Suddenly she started to cry. Her eyes wide, without blinking, she stood erect with her arms hanging loosely at her sides, without uttering a sound, but tears were streaming down her cheeks. Irene had an uncomfortable feeling of having witnessed something very personal. She felt the need to break the unpleasant scene which she had unintentionally provoked.

Contritely she said, "Forgive me, I must have misunderstood you, but I thought I was supposed to follow you up here and write down the addresses."

Sylvia didn't reply, but her smoldering fury subsided. Instead she began to shake violently. On impulse Irene went over, carefully put one hand on the woman's shoulder, and led her to the desk. She pulled out the chair and Sylvia sat heavily. She was still staring straight ahead. Almost inaudibly she whispered, "I usually talk to him."

"To Henrik?"

Sylvia nodded. Irene was slightly annoyed. It was obvious that they talked often. For one thing, they only lived a few kilometers apart, and for another, there were plenty of telephones in the apartment. But she had a vague, nagging feeling that she was on the wrong track. That wasn't what Sylvia meant. It had something to do with the brief scene with the photograph. Adoration?

Doubtfully she asked, "Do you mean that you talk to Henrik's picture?"

Sylvia continued staring stiffly into space as she nodded. The tears were still flowing, though not as copiously. Was Sylvia about to break down again? Maybe it had been too soon to send her home from the psych ward? Best to take it a little easy. Cautiously Irene asked, "Does he answer?"

Sylvia straightened up and said firmly, "*This* Henrik answers me!"

What did she mean? It felt as though they were walking on thin ice, ice that was cracking beneath them with each step. This was the widow of a murder victim, just released after a nervous breakdown. It was important to proceed carefully, since she still seemed unbalanced. Was Sylvia about to slip into psychosis? But at the same time it was important to nail down her meaning.

Tentatively Irene said, "You said *this* Henrik. Is there another Henrik besides your son?"

The question was phrased incorrectly. Irritated, Sylvia shrugged and snapped, "Of course it's Henrik. But the way he used to be!"

Then the penny finally dropped.

"You mean before he got sick? Before the meningitis?"

Sylvia gave her a mute, slow nod in reply.

"Is he very different since his illness?" Irene went on.

"Yes. He was in a coma for eighteen days. When he woke up he was completely changed. He had a hard time reading, difficulty walking, and often got headaches when there was too much noise. He withdrew from his old friends. Didn't think he could hang out with them anymore. Finally they stopped calling too. Just like Emelie."

Sylvia fell silent and a pained look passed over her face.

Irene asked in a low voice, "Who was Emelie?"

"His girlfriend. They had found an apartment and were going to move in together when he finished his military service. Much too early, I thought. But he loved her. Although she didn't love him. It was obvious during the time he was in the hospital. She found herself a new boyfriend, an old mutual friend from their childhood. A double betrayal. I think that's what finally broke him."

There was hatred in her gaze again. But she was talking—which, for Irene, was the main thing. She remembered the photo clipping, with Sylvia going into the hospital alone.

"How did you husband take it? Henrik's illness and all?" she asked cautiously.

Hatred flamed in her eyes again. It felt physical, like a slap in the face, but Irene understood that it wasn't directed at her. It was for Richard.

In a stifled voice Sylvia said, "He denied it was happening! Henrik wasn't sick! He would soon recover from his little ailment and be just the same as ever!"

"But he didn't."

"No."

"What happened?"

Sylvia's voice sounded infinitely weary. It seemed to cost her all the strength in the world to answer the question.

"Henrik worked hard at therapy and improved physically. But he was so different. He was no longer Henrik. The doctors said that there had been damage to his brain. It took almost three years before the dizziness and headaches went away. Gradually, Richard and Henrik slipped farther and farther apart. They had done so many things together before. Above all, Richard fretted that Henrik had suddenly lost interest in the stock market and business deals. He was furious when Henrik started to study art history at the university, specializing in the history of fashion. But after a while Richard changed his attitude. He was the one who suggested to Henrik that he start purchasing antiques directly for his clients. In time, Richard became one of his biggest customers. It brought them a little closer to each other again."

"But things were never the way they were before the meningitis."

"No."

Once again Sylvia, by bending her head forward, had let her platinum-blond hair close like a curtain in front of her face. Irene was undecided. Could she get any farther? Sylvia might appear strong willed and self-centered, but intuitively Irene understood that she was psychologically fragile. The remaining questions were extremely personal and intrusive. But they had to be asked, and preferably now. She would have to proceed cautiously, so she started by asking, "But when Henrik married Charlotte three years ago, he must have been feeling quite well, wasn't he?"

Not even a ripple in the platinum curtain. No reaction at all. But the worst questions were yet to come. Was it best to start neutrally, or perhaps begin with something positive?

"He seems to be getting along well with her now," said Irene. "And in the midst of your grief you have the joy of becoming a grandmother—"

Suddenly, Sylvia was all over her, like a wildcat, biting, kicking, and scratching with all her might, yelling, "It's not true! You're lying! You're lying!"

At first Irene was so surprised that she didn't defend herself and received a deep scratch on her neck. After that, she reacted from instinct. She easily blocked Sylvia's flailing arms. *Gedan-uchi-uke* was ingrained in the medulla oblongata of the former European women's champion. With her left hand Irene grabbed Sylvia's thin wrist and pulled her a little off balance, twisted her right arm up behind her back, and pressed lightly; with her right hand she gripped Sylvia's left forearm and then put her left arm under Sylvia's chin. Effectively locked, Irene pulled the woman's efforts against herself. Either because of the bodily contact or the lock hold, the air went out of Sylvia. She fainted.

Irene regained her composure, saying out loud, "This is crazy! I wonder what would have happened if I'd asked one of my sensitive questions?"

She picked up Sylvia's featherweight body and carried her into the bedroom. The thin little figure seemed to disappear in the down coverlet of the wide double bed. Naturally, Sylvia hadn't made the bed. No doubt Pirjo would have to do that when she arrived.

Irene raised Sylvia's legs straight up and massaged her calves. After about a minute she began to come around. She mumbled something and tried to sit up. Irene pressed her back down and talked to her soothingly, as if to a child. Sylvia moaned weakly.

"Henrik, I want Henrik."

Maybe that was a good idea. If Henrik came here, Sylvia would calm down. He and Irene might as well have their appointment here as down at headquarters.

"I'm going to call Henrik. Where can I find his number?"

"Press two and the pound sign."

Speed-dial numbers are practical. Irene went over to the phone on top of a small curved cabinet next to the bed.

Henrik picked up on the second ring. Irene told him who she was, and then couldn't figure out exactly what to say next. She was deliberately vague. "I'm at your mother's right now. She . . . had a slight breakdown. She wants you to come over."

"Certainly, I'll be right over. Mamma is quite unstable right now. Why did she break down?"

That was precisely the question Irene wanted to avoid.

"I tried to cheer her up with something positive. I congratulated her on becoming a grandmother . . . I thought she knew."

There was a long silence. Irene wondered whether Henrik had keeled over too. Finally he snapped, "God damn it!"

Click! He had hung up on her. Irene felt stupid. As if she had done something wrong. Had she? Guiltily, she thought about how she had restrained the hysterical Sylvia. Could she have done it some other way? Hardly.

When she turned back to the bed again, she saw that Sylvia was holding a medicine bottle in her left hand and was about to put her cupped right hand to her mouth. The top drawer of the nightstand was open. Instinctively, Irene bent over and grabbed the woman's right hand. Three small white tablets with a notch across the middle lay in her palm. There was no question of a suicidal dose.

Making an attempt to regain Sylvia's trust, she said in an overly cheerful voice, "Would you like some water to take the pills with?"

Sylvia nodded without looking at her. Irene pried loose her grip around the medicine bottle. She quickly read the label: STESOLID TABLETS, 5MG. When she put the bottle back in the drawer, she saw several more just like it. The technicians must have noted this so she closed the drawer.

She went out to the luxurious bathroom and ran some water into a toothbrush glass hanging in a gilt holder on the wall. The glass was cut crystal; and the faucets were gold plated. A large, wet terry-cloth bath towel had been tossed on the floor. Absentmindedly, she hung it up on the heated towel rack on the wall. Pirjo would have a lot to straighten up when she returned.

Sylvia lay staring up at the ceiling when Irene brought her the water glass. She raised herself up on one elbow to take the pills. Then she sank back, exhausted, on the comforter. With her eyes closed she whispered in a barely audible voice, "I didn't mean to hit you. I wasn't prepared. It's all been too much for me."

Irene didn't want to let Sylvia off quite yet. It was easy to be seized with sympathy for the small, fragile woman, but Irene had a strong feeling that there was much hidden beneath the surface that needed to be dug out. Why not the truth?

She decided to proceed more cautiously. In a voice overflowing with empathy she said, "You have to forgive me. I thought you knew that Charlotte is pregnant. They told me about it yesterday at police headquarters."

Sylvia kept her eyes shut. It was an effective way to block out Irene and her disagreeable prying.

Irene was at a loss; how was she going to make any headway? Then she remembered something. "The telephone list, the addresses and phone numbers of the guests last Saturday. Could I have the list?"

Reluctantly Sylvia raised her eyelids. Her eyes were furious and cold, just as hostile as her tone of voice. "I can't do it. You made me faint. My head is spinning and it feels like I have cotton in my ears. I feel terrible." She pressed her thin fingers against her temples and began to massage them.

To her own amazement Irene felt anger rising from the pit of her stomach, to her throat, to explode in her head. She tried to control herself, but it was no use. In a cold, neutral voice she said, "Now that you're lying down anyway, I might as well ask my next question. I've looked through a bunch of old newspaper clippings. Richard was seen remarkably often with various beautiful young women. How did you react to that?"

Sylvia stopped massaging her temples. Her eyes again blazed with rage, but her voice revealed nothing when she replied. "Those stupid bimbos were his hobby. He had strong . . . desires. I was always the most important woman in his life. He always came back to me when he began to lose interest in his latest conquest. It usually didn't take long. He would cower behind me when they started pressuring him, making demands. It's no use my denying it, because he never made any effort to hide anything. I just had to take it!" Finally, it was out. The bitterness.

Irene said benignly, "And what about you? I didn't see any similar photos of you."

Sylvia gave a harsh, scornful laugh before she replied. "We gave each other great freedom. Freedom for him, I should say."

She made a show of closing her eyes again, pressing her lips into a thin line. With a sigh Irene realized that it was time to change the subject and her tactics. She sat down on the edge of the bed. Her knees almost hit her in the chin when she sank down into the downy softness. "Sylvia," she entreated, "we're trying to investigate your husband's murder. We have no clue as to a motive or a suspect. You have to help us. We have to ask unpleasant questions so we can try to get at the truth."

Sylvia's blue-glazed eyelids twitched. But when she opened her eyes they were completely expressionless. She gazed vacantly at Irene.

"Who would be served by the truth?"

Irene was at a loss for words. But she had one question left that she had to ask. She took a deep breath and steeled herself for whatever might come.

"We've studied Richard's personal records, which means everything contained in his files. It's the sort of thing that parish ledgers used to protect in the past. Now the tax authorities use this sort of information and for that reason it's now in the public record."

Irene stopped, because she wasn't sure that that was completely accurate. But Sylvia's expression didn't change. She didn't want Sylvia to have time to think about it, so she continued quickly, "Did you know that Richard had admitted paternity of a son before you were married?"

Sylvia shut her eyes instantly. Her nostrils flared and she exhaled audibly before she replied tonelessly, "I'm not entirely surprised. There were some mysterious phone calls in the early days of our marriage. A woman who called and argued with Richard. I managed to overhear some of it. I gathered that it had to do with . . . a child."

There were decades of sorrow in those final sentences. Irene felt a tug of sympathy, but she decided to press a bit harder.

"He never told you anything about the child?"

"No."

"Does Henrik know anything?"

"Don't tell Henrik!"

"Unfortunately, he's going to find out anyway. If not before, then when it's time to read the will."

It happened like lightning. Sylvia was suddenly sitting, her slender legs hanging over the edge of the bed. Red patches of indignation burned on her cheeks, her eyes flashed with wrath, and the cool elfin features were transformed into those of a shrew.

"That despicable bastard inherit? Never! Over my dead body! I won't permit it! I'm going to call Tore right now . . . Never!"

She fell silent. Irene understood that she was referring to Tore Eiderstam. Unless she was a spiritualist, it would be impossible to contact the attorney. But someone must have taken over the firm, she supposed. She said as much to Sylvia, who looked bewildered.

"There are several attorneys in Tore's law office. I presume I'm permitted to call them? Damn it all! It was always Richard who kept track of our financial and legal affairs," she said helplessly.

She was interrupted by the doorbell. Irene went down and opened the front door. Henrik looked haggard but resolute. He gave her a curt nod and took the stairs two at a time to the top floor. Irene followed him, lost in thought. Sylvia's reactions were very odd. What should have evoked happy exclamations and chatter about the anticipated joys of being a grandmother had unleashed instead an absolute explosion of rage. She had responded readily, if bitterly, to the embarrassing topic of the other women in her husband's life. The other son was not entirely unexpected and provoked no reaction until she realized that he might have a right of inheritance. Maybe it would be a good idea to contact von Knecht's lawyers, even though they couldn't say anything before the will was read to the family.

In the bedroom, mother and son were sitting side by side on the edge of the bed. Sylvia flung her blond hair back with a spiteful snap of her head and said, "Henrik just told me the same thing you did. I must really be off balance, reacting the way I did."

It took a moment before Irene realized that this was not only an explanation, but also an apology. She nodded and smiled encouragingly, but got no response, from either mother or son. Henrik looked like he hadn't slept in several days. Irene began to feel thoroughly sick of the weird behavior of this family. Having to tiptoe around and be so careful when they were trying to investigate both a murder and a homicidal bombing!

She decided to get straight to the point with Henrik. Matter-of-factly she said, "Henrik, I just told your mother . . . Sylvia, that we have discovered information that your father has a son from a prior relationship."

Henrik's face remained expressionless. He blinked a couple of times, but said nothing.

"Did you know of the existence of your half brother?"

He shook his head gently, still without replying.

Sylvia said rancorously, "Apparently he's supposed to share in the inheritance! Never, I say! Never!"

Henrik gave her a weary look. "Mamma, there are laws for such things. Leave it to Pappa's lawyers."

No one said a word. Neither Sylvia nor Henrik had any questions about the newly discovered half brother. Wouldn't it have been natural to ask where he lived, how old he was? But maybe that's not what people did in a situation like this. Maybe the shock was too great. The silence was becoming embarrassing.

Irene cleared her throat and said, "Henrik, what do you think about the fire last night?"

"It might not have any connection with Pappa's death."

She could hear from his voice that he wasn't convinced himself. Irene continued. "Did either of you ever observe that Richard was being subjected to threats?"

They looked at each other, then back at Irene; both shook their heads. Irene went on, unperturbed. "Did he ever talk about anyone having hostile or vindictive feelings toward him? Perhaps related to business?"

Sylvia looked away, uninterested, and pretended to study a Chinese artwork above the bedstead. Irene had also noticed the risqué silk scroll painting. Her thought was that if a woman could twist her hips into the position assumed by the one in the picture, it would be like having sex with a female contortionist. Impulsively she stretched out her hand, pointed at the painting, and exclaimed, "Why did he collect sex pictures?"

Henrik gave her a cool look and replied haughtily, "Sex pictures? This is the finest collection of erotica in Sweden."

Sylvia jumped up from the bed. She waved a thin finger in front of Henrik's face and shouted, "No! She's right. Sex pictures are precisely what they are. They have to go. Get rid of them! I'm sick to death of them!"

She stopped and looked around the room, at all the pictures of naked or copulating people. Again the tears began quietly flowing down her cheeks. Softly she sobbed, "He was so proud of his collection. I hate them. Hate them all."

Henrik stood up and put his arm around his mother's shoulders.

"Mamma, I'll handle the sale. There's a big market in Europe. Especially in England. I imagine Christie's would be very interested. This collection is worth several million kronor, you know."

She nodded and sobbed aloud. "Yes, I know. I don't want to look at them anymore."

"I'll help you take them all down. We'll put them in my old room. Do you want to take down the Zorn, too?"

"All of them."

Irene felt a bit desperate. It was hard to get a grip on everything simmering beneath the surface. Clearly there was a lot of tension in the von Knecht family. But was it the reason for Richard's death? Or the bombing of his office? Since the friction seemed to be old and ingrown, it could hardly have anything to do with the events of the past few days. But it would be worth remembering what had been said and what had transpired today in the apartment. When one began to stir up the mud, clouds of old swamp gas arose. She had to keep at it, for the time being. Eventually something she could use would turn up. She moved on to her last questions.

"There are a few more details before I go. First of all, does Pirjo have a key to this apartment?"

Sylvia shook her head when she answered. "No. Either Richard or I would let her in."

"How many keys are there?"

"Three sets."

"So there are three different key rings?"

"Yes. Besides the door keys there are the keys to the seven deadbolt locks. The insurance company requires it. They also said we couldn't have handles on the outsides of the French doors. Or the balcony door upstairs."

"Do you know where all three key rings are right now?"

"Of course. I have my own keys in my handbag. The extra keys are in my desk drawer. I saw them this morning. Richard's key ring is where I found it yesterday, on his nightstand."

She pointed to the other side of the bed. A smaller key ring lay there, apparently holding car and garage keys. Next to it was a black leather key case. Irene unsnapped the case and counted six keys. She had a fleeting image of the tongue twister "Six shiny sardines stuffed in a shiny sardine can."

"How many of these keys are for the apartment?" asked Irene.

"Two. One to the Yale lock and one to the deadbolt."

"What are the other keys for?"

"Two are for the house on Kärringnäset, our house outside Marstrand. The other two must be for Richard's office."

"Are there any spare keys to the office?"

"Yes. They're on the spare-key ring in my desk drawer."

"There are no other sets of keys?"

Sylvia shook her head. "No. But speaking of keys, I remember that Richard was looking for his spare keys to the car and garage. Like the ones lying there on his nightstand," she said.

"When was that?"

"It must have been at least a week ago."

"Did he find them?"

"Not that I know of."

Irene made a note in her notebook. In order to clarify, she asked again, "The car keys here on the table are his regular set? Not the spare set?"

"Exactly."

Irene jotted down more notes. Evidently the spare keys to the car and garage were still missing. She quickly asked another question.

"Who cleaned Richard's office?"

"Pirjo did it sometimes. She would agree on a time with Richard, and he would let her in. Most often on Tuesdays or Thursdays. Those are the days she's not cleaning here. Occasionally she takes on other cleaning jobs, I understand."

A thought occurred to Irene. It was a long shot, but no idea could be ignored.

"What does Pirjo look like?"

"Rather chubby, and short. She must be a little over thirty, but looks like she's well over forty. Her hair is thin and blond, usually put up in a ponytail. She looks sloppy, but she's actually the best cleaning woman I've ever had. Alice, my friend who recommended her, said so too. But she smokes. If she quit she'd have more money for herself. I'm not paying her too little—she's smoking it all up!"

Irene got a feeling that there had recently been salary negotiations between Sylvia and Pirjo. An illegally employed cleaning woman hardly has much clout, even when she can plead her case in Finnish. With a sigh Irene had to abandon her little idea. There couldn't have been any hanky-panky between Richard and Pirjo. She had gleaned enough about his preferences to realize that he would hardly view a fat, worn-out cleaning woman as a sex object.

"My next question is for you, Henrik. Where can I get hold of Charlotte today?"

"At home. Why?"

"I need to ask her where she was last Tuesday evening, between five and six P.M. to be specific."

Henrik nodded and gave a curt, joyless laugh as he said, "If anybody has an alibi, it's her."

"And the two of you."

"And the two of us. She was out picking up her new car. At the Volkswagen Center on Mölndalsvägen."

Sylvia gave a start. "What? Has she bought another new car?"

"Calm down, Mamma. Her old Golf was in the shop most of the time. The electrical system was always shorting out!"

"But it wasn't even two years old!"

"We traded it in and got a good deal. Now she has a brand-new Golf. They're selling off this year's model at a five percent discount."

Sylvia looked sullen. "She could have bought my BMW. I can manage with Richard's Porsche," she said.

"Your BMW is three years old and has only thirty thousand kilometers on it. You'll get a good price when you sell it."

"But that's so much trouble. You have to place an ad, people have to come and look at it. It's so complicated when you're alone."

Henrik sighed. "Let a car dealer do it for you," he said patiently.

"No, they don't pay much if you're not buying a new car. By the way, maybe I'll sell the Porsche and keep the BMW. You can get more for a new Porsche."

Sylvia seemed to have slipped quickly into the role of a single woman. But all her problems were clearly of a financial or practical nature.

Irene cleared her throat to remind her that she was there. "I'll let you know when we've established more facts about the fire on Berzeliigatan. I should probably tell you that there are very strong indications that the fire was caused by a bomb. Since the newspapers will get that information this afternoon, I wanted to give it to you now."

At first Sylvia looked utterly baffled. But Irene was completely unprepared for the reaction that followed.

"A bomb! And you didn't tell me until now? There's a totally insane murderer on the loose. He might be out to get all of us!"

Henrik turned so pale that his skin took on a waxy yellow tinge. He looked as if he might pass out at any moment. Maybe, in addition to the complications from his old meningitis attack, he was ill.

"We need police protection! No, we demand it!"

Aimless and restless, Sylvia flitted around the room. Irene tried to be as reassuring as she could.

"Of course we'll have to investigate whether there is any overriding threat. But nothing that has come out so far points to this. Has anyone else in the family been threatened?"

Henrik just shook his head weakly, while Sylvia gesticulated wildly.

"No! Not yet! But we probably won't get any protection from the police before the whole family is murdered and blown to bits!"

That's what you call a tautology, Irene recalled from her philosophy lessons in high school. Was it the proximity to Hvitfeldt High School that was making things like that crawl out of the dust in the attic of her memory? Evidently Sylvia had forgotten her complaint about the boorish rampage of the police through her upper-crust neighborhood. Now she wanted them back. Irene felt that it was time to wind up the conversation and said in a friendly tone, "We'll stay in touch. Call me if anything turns up."

Irene again gave them each her card with her direct line noted. But experience had taught her that people always tended to lose such cards. She didn't need to look any farther than herself.

Henrik escorted her downstairs in mutual silence. Not until they reached the front door did he ask, "Is it all right if we drive up to Marstrand this weekend?"

Irene was caught off guard. She tried to think before she replied. "As far as we know, there is no threat to the rest of your family. It was your father who was murdered, and the bomb was at his office. Did anyone else in the family ever visit him there?"

Henrik gave a start, but then realized what Irene meant. "You mean, perhaps the bomb was intended for someone besides Pappa? No, it was probably meant for him. It is . . . was extremely rare for any of the family to visit his office."

"Did he really need an office? From what I understand, he had a brokerage firm that looked after his affairs," Irene asked tactfully.

Henrik bowed his head as if totally absorbed by the intricate pattern of the soft carpet. She was beginning to think he didn't intend to answer, when he muttered, "He needed somewhere he could have peace and quiet. That was Mamma and Pappa's old apartment. The one they lived in when they were newlyweds. I must have been two years old when they moved to this building. They kept the apartment, because Pappa needed an office even then. Later, he bought both this building and the one on Berzeliigatan. Along with a bunch of other property with Peder Wahl. But all the other property has been liquidated."

"How big was the office apartment?"

"Four rooms and a kitchen. Bathroom and toilet. About a hundred and thirty square meters."

"Getting back to your plans to go to Marstrand. Will both Charlotte and your mother be going?"

"No. Charlotte is going to her sister's in Kungsbacka. But Mamma needs to see to her horses. She has a stable up there. And I need to get away. Very early on Monday morning, at four A.M., I'm driving up to Stockholm. Lilla Bukowski's November auction is starting that day. I have a number of commissions there."

"May I ask how that works? Do you buy up specific rare items and then sell them to interested buyers?"

"No, I work as an agent, you might say. The buyers read through the auction catalogs and then they contact me. They tell me which items are of interest and the maximum price they're willing to pay. I charge an hourly rate and the client pays for travel and expenses. Often there are several buyers who go in together to cover my services, especially for jobs abroad. The cost of the trip and my expenses are the same, but they're shared by several people."

"It sounds like an expensive way to collect antiques," Irene observed.

Henrik shrugged. "My clients have a lot of money but not much time. And they know what they want and what it should cost."

"So you never buy with your own money?"

"Not when I'm buying on behalf of my clients. Sometimes I buy things for myself, of course. Like the Tang horse."

His face had almost returned to its normal color as he talked about his unusual profession. But Irene realized that he didn't view it as a job. A faint flush had appeared on his cheeks. She remembered his ardent lecture about the Haupt furniture and the carpet and all the rest. This was really a matter of passion and zeal. It would not be easy competition for the beautiful Charlotte. Her value resided in the moment. In fifty years her collector's value would be zero. The ideal man would be an archaeologist. In his eyes a woman would grow more interesting the older she got. And what about a collector of antiques, who only looks at the patina and future investment value? Irene felt grateful that she and Krister had purchased their household furnishings mostly from the local furniture warehouse, IKEA, in Kållered.

Real curiosity made her finally ask the question, "What in the world is a Tang horse?"

Amazement was reflected in his eyes, and she realized that this was something everyone was expected to know.

"A ceramic horse from the Tang period, of course! The Tang dynasty in China lasted from the beginning of the seventh century A.D. through the early years of the tenth century. The horse followed its owner in death, so we're talking about grave goods. When he was buried, the deceased was provided with everything he might need in his existence on the other side. Household implements, jewelry, whole staffs of servants, and entire armies have been found. During the Tang period everything was made of ceramics but earlier, humans were sacrificed. There is a clear similarity with—"

"Hold it! Wait!"

Both Irene and Henrik jumped at the unexpected sound of Sylvia's voice. She came running down the stairs from the upper floor. A little out of breath, she said, "Here are the addresses and phone numbers of the guests last Saturday. I have my whole contact list in the computer. All I had to do was print out the ones you wanted. Very efficient."

IRENE WENT via Berzeliigatan on her way back to headquarters. It was high time she had lunch. The hot dog stand on Heden was calling to her, with the best mashed potatoes in town. But first she wanted to see the remains of the building that had burned down. She caught sight of Tommy Persson talking to one of the arson technicians. There was a parking place right outside the barricades, and she pulled into it. A handicapped parking place, but it would be a while before anyone who lived here would be able to use it again. Most of the building was no longer habitable.

Apart from the acrid smell of smoke, an air of unreality hovered over the charred skeleton of the building. It didn't belong here in the prosperous downtown section of Göteborg. Maybe in Chechnya or Sarajevo.

Irene went over to Tommy. He gave her a cheerful greeting and introduced the arson investigator, Pelle, who nodded and raised his hands— encased in thick gloves—in greeting. He excused himself at once and tromped off in his heavy protective gear.

Tommy said somberly, "They found a completely charred body inside. It's behind the door to von Knecht's office. Apparently there was steel on the inside of the door, which protected the body from being totally cremated. The door was blown open by the explosion, and the poor guy crawled in behind it when he couldn't make it down the stairs. The heat must have been horrible."

Both of them shivered, and not just because of the cold. A pale sun was trying to break through the gray clouds. It would eventually succeed, because it was starting to clear up and turn colder. The temperature would probably fall below freezing later that night. Then the water on the ravaged building would freeze and form an armor of ice around it. There is nothing sorrier or more depressing than the sight of a damaged and mangled building, ruined by fire and water. If you know that a person died in the flames, the sight becomes a brooding threat. Irene felt slightly nauseated, but blamed it on her hunger and the suffocating smell of smoke.

Tommy turned around, nodded toward the corner at the brick building across the street, and said, "Do you see the tobacconist over there?"

Irene saw the little shop with a worn-out sign that stuck straight out from the very corner of the building. She nodded and murmured affirmatively.

"Guess who Fredrik and I found in there when we were going around knocking on doors?"

"No clue."

"Shorty Johannesson! And he's the one who runs the store!"

"You're kidding! I thought he'd been sent up forever and they'd thrown away the key."

"That would have been too good to be true. We checked. He was released this summer. He served six of his nine years."

If you live in Göteborg, you know that anyone with the nickname Shorty or Half-Pint is at least the height of an average basketball player. And if you live in Göteborg, you know who Lasse "Shorty" Johannesson is. On the list of the ten most dangerous criminals in recent years, he was right up there between Lars-Inge Svartenbrandt and Clark Olofsson.

Chapter Eight

TIME WAS TIGHT, BUT Irene managed to write down the most important points from her meeting with the von Knecht mother and son. She also called Charlotte von Knecht but got no answer. The Volkswagen Center on Mölndalsvägen was next in line on her phone list. After some paper shuffling the woman at the service desk managed to find the right file. Yes indeed, Charlotte von Knecht had picked up her new Golf last Tuesday, but she didn't know at what time. The salesman in charge was off on Thursdays and was impossible to reach before ten o'clock Friday morning. The woman grew more cooperative after Irene began to mutter about "interfering with a police investigation of a felony." With a lot of grumbling she finally gave Irene the salesman's home phone number. When Irene called she had to deal with a dashing answering machine that trumpeted, "Hello! You've reached Rob's home! I'm either out or doing something else right now, so I can't take your call. Leave your name and number after the beep and I'll give you a jingle a little later." Irene curtly left her name and her direct line to the department. She made a point of emphasizing her title.

THE USUAL procedure for ordering pizza was automatically initiated before the run-through could begin. Then the superintendent took the floor.

"It's been a hectic day. At the press conference today I announced that a bombing caused the fire on Berzeliigatan. The arson techs found the remnants of an explosive device in the hall of von Knecht's office apartment. It was practically like I'd set off a bomb under the reporters. They went crazy! Naturally they're making a connection between von Knecht's murder and the explosion last night. They've been hounding me all afternoon. Newspapers, radio, and all the TV channels in existence! The techs will be stopping by at any moment to report developments on their end. Svante Malm and the new guy, Ljunggren, promised to show up."

He looked around at his seven inspectors and quietly cleared his throat.

"Let's go around the table, one by one."

He gave Irene, to his right, an expectant look. The report on her survey of the gossip clippings from *Swedish Ladies' Journal* took time but was necessary. It gave a picture of Richard von Knecht's public life. The account of her conversation with Sylvia and Henrik also gave most of the inspectors a clearer picture of the family members. Irene summed up her own thoughts and conclusions.

"It's a regular soap opera. Both Sylvia and Henrik seem to be emotionally cool toward Richard. Not to mention that he felt the same about them. It wasn't a happy family. The motives are the classic ones: money, unfaithfulness. What contradicts the theory of murder within the family, of course, is the bomb. There's a chance that the murder and the bomb had nothing to do with each other. But actually I think that chance is microscopic," she said.

The others nodded in agreement. Irene concluded by telling them about Charlotte's still-unconfirmed car-buying alibi and the guest list from Saturday's party that Sylvia had given her.

Andersson looked pleased. "I myself had the great pleasure of eavesdropping on Birgitta's interview with Waldemar, alias Valle, Reuter. Tell us about it, Birgitta." His whole face lit up with a broad smile, but the smile was quickly extinguished when Birgitta began to speak.

"Valle Reuter is a very pathetic man. He has been a serious alcoholic for many years. I've been in contact with the president of his brokerage house, Mats Tengman. When I explained to him what it was all about he was quite candid. Valle is still part of the firm in name only. He owns it, but has no influence on the business end, and no one is more aware of this than Valle himself. He still has his office. He sometimes goes inside and locks the door, saying that he's extremely busy and is not to be disturbed. This usually means that he's hung over. But they have to keep him on. The president calls it 'social therapy.' Reuter doesn't have anywhere else to go. Except on Tuesdays, when Richard von Knecht was in the habit of having lunch with him. This was the high point of the week for Valle, Mats Tengman told me. But now we know that there were also other high points on Tuesdays . . . Valle was thoroughly loaded when he came here and he gave us a good deal of information. I checked with Johanneshus, where von Knecht and

Reuter ate lunch last Tuesday. The restaurant owner confirms the time. They arrived between one and one-thirty, left around three-thirty. The reason Valle Reuter wasn't home on the night of the murder was that he spent the night with his girlfriend of the past three years, Gunilla Forsell. He managed to remember the address, and I contacted her this morning. She wasn't particularly happy about the attention, to put it mildly. At first she refused to meet me. But I threatened to have her picked up by a squad car if she didn't show up voluntarily. Then she was more cooperative, because the neighbors in the fancy boarding-house on Stampgatan have no idea what little Fru Forsell does on the side. An extra job that pays more than her regular job. Guess what her day job is."

Birgitta looked around among her colleagues, who were following her report with interest. "Stripper," "day-care worker," "nurse" were some of the suggestions. Birgitta laughed and shook her head.

"Wrong, wrong! Librarian!"

Everyone around the table looked disappointed. None of them had imagined such a genuinely musty occupation. Jonny Blom whispered to Fredrik Stridh, "Ha, the driest bushes burn the best!"

Birgitta pretended not to hear him and continued. "I went over there at eleven. She turned out to be thirty-five years old and good looking—but no supermodel, if you know what I mean."

Jonny interrupted again. "No, I just don't get it. I'd better head over there and check her out!" He pretended to get up, grinning broadly at Birgitta.

She gave him an icy stare and said in a neutral tone, "It's no news that you don't get it. But the rest of us, of normal intelligence, will proceed. As I said, Gunnel was not happy to see me. But after a while she started to talk. She's been divorced for five years, no children. For ten years she's had a part-time job at the city library. She didn't think it would be so hard to find a full-time job after her divorce. But it turned out to be impossible. In these times of cutbacks, all the municipalities are reducing their library staffs. She couldn't make ends meet on a half-time salary, so the solution for her was four gentlemen on the side. All of them are older men. Valle is the only one who isn't married. She has Tuesdays, Thursdays, and weekends off from her library job, and that's when she devotes herself to the gentlemen. She didn't want to explain the arrangements, but apparently they have fixed days and times. On Tuesdays she has two visitors. Gentleman number one usually comes at twelve and leaves at two. 'Extended lunch,' he calls it.

Valle is gentleman number two and has a special agreement. He comes
at five-thirty, they have something to eat, talk, and watch TV. He's
always fairly loaded when he arrives, since by then he's already had
lunch with von Knecht. They usually go to bed around eleven. For the
most part he falls asleep right away, but sometimes he wants to have
a 'little massage,' as she called it. Then they sleep in her big queen-
sized bed. In the morning they have breakfast together, then she goes
to work and he toddles home."

Andersson couldn't help interjecting a question. "How much does
he have to pay for that?"

Birgitta looked at him with her clear brown eyes until he started to
blush. "She wouldn't say. But I can tell you this: She lives in a cozy
three-room apartment on Stampgatan. The art and furniture are first-
rate. She wears jewelry that could easily have financed my trip to
Australia, and she was impeccably and expensively dressed. When I
was leaving I saw a car key on the hall table. I asked what kind of car
she has. A Saab 900, she said, last year's model."

A meditative silence fell over the room. This wasn't your usual
type of prostitute, selling herself for a couple of hundred kronor on the
backseat of a car and quickly spending it on booze or dope. Everyone had heard of call girls and high-priced "escorts," but no one in
the room had ever actually encountered someone in that category. Not
until now.

Andersson wanted to proceed with the investigation and broke the
silence. "What did she say about Valle's visit on Tuesday?"

Birgitta smirked when she replied, "That must have been some enter-
taining day! It's precisely for that reason that Gunnel was quite sure
of the times. On Tuesday, gentleman number one didn't show up at
twelve like he normally does. She assumed that he was sick or tied up.
But at four-thirty he rang the doorbell and demanded his weekly screw.
That's a good deal of money for Gunnel. She said that if he hurried it
would be fine. And it would have been, if Valle hadn't come staggering to her door just before five on that particular Tuesday. She couldn't
have him yelling out in the stairwell, so she had to let him into her
living room and prop him up with a stiff drink while she finished off
gentleman number one. Then she had to pilot him out so that the two
gentlemen wouldn't see each other. According to Gunnel, all four of
them think they're 'the one and only' for her."

"Could Valle Reuter have paid her to give him an alibi?" Irene
interposed.

"No, I don't think so. Their stories fit pretty well. Neither of them was overly eager to talk. No, it doesn't seem made up. But . . ." Birgitta fell silent and smiled slyly before she went on, "in exchange for a promise that we leave her in peace with her 'gentlemen,' I got the name of Tuesday's gentleman number one!"

"Hot damn!" said Andersson, looking impressed.

"I called him at his office and explained what it was all about. He was not eager to cooperate, but faced with the threat of a formal request to come down here to make an official statement, he gave in. He confirms Gunnel's and Valle's stories."

She looked up from her notes and stretched her shoulder muscles before she went on. "If I have to draw any conclusions, then it would be that Valle Reuter is no murderer. Which I never believed for a moment anyway."

The look she gave Andersson was challenging, and he hurried to agree. "No. You don't murder your best and only friend. He has no motive and isn't the killer type. As I said, I listened to Birgitta's interview with Valle. Speaking of conversations, that photographer, Bobo Torsson, called me just before the meeting. He's thinking of staying another night in Stockholm. He's taking the train tomorrow and will come straight here after lunch. One of you will have to talk to him. I have to go and get fitted for that damned uniform."

Jonny looked surprised. "But wasn't that what you were doing earlier today?"

"Yes, but they only had pants in children's sizes. By the way, did you get hold of Ivan Viktors?"

"Yes, by phone. He called around three and said that he had just returned from Copenhagen. It was evidently on the TV news in Denmark, because he already knew what had happened. I guess you have to be sure to wash your hair and change your shirt every day now, so you look fresh on screen."

He licked the palm of his hand and stroked it lightly over his hair. Birgitta snorted, but before she managed to make any derisive comment, the boss headed her off.

"I'll handle all contact with the media. Refer them to me. That's easiest. I don't have much hair to wash."

The superintendent imitated Jonny's gesture over his own pate. Irene snorted, trying to stifle her amusement.

Jonny pursed his lips and assumed a professional tone. "Ivan Viktors is coming here tomorrow morning at ten."

"So you can be the one to talk to him. Anything else?"

"Yes, I had a look at the house up in Marstrand. On the map, that is. It's located on a peninsula north of Marstrand called Kärringnäset. It includes the peninsula itself and property a bit inland. The total we're talking about is fifteen hectares. On the map you can see a big stable and paddocks. And down by the sea there are two cabins, each about a hundred square meters. I saw that the boundary of the plot was marked with a sturdy fence or maybe a wall. Next to the stable, right next to the road, down toward the von Knecht palace, there's a house labeled the 'caretaker's residence.' Then I got the phone number of the summer residence and was connected to the caretaker, Lennart Svensson. He and his wife take care of the horses and property. The wife evidently cleans the big house. He's fifty-seven and has worked for the von Knechts for fifteen years. Before that he was in the military. He told me that von Knecht's parents owned this land. After they both died, Richard tore down the old house and built a giant mansion."

Irene waved her hand. "Good that you're talking about Marstrand, Jonny. Henrik asked me if it was okay for him and Sylvia to go up there this weekend. I said I didn't think there would be any problem."

Jonny leaned across the table and said in surprise, "Sylvia? Don't you mean Charlotte?"

"No, Charlotte is going to her sister's in Kungsbacka."

"Ha! Now you see that Henrik and Sylvia have an incestuous relationship! They did away with Richard and the next in line is the lovely Charlotte. She needs a bodyguard! I'll volunteer!"

"And who stuck a quarter in you? Such a shame that the two of them were standing five stories below when he was shoved off the balcony." Just at the right moment the intercom beeped and a voice reported that the pizzas were ready to pick up down at the front desk.

"THIS PIZZA habit is getting a little monotonous. I'm going to make a radical change in diet. Next time I'll have a kabob." Tommy Persson groaned and unbuttoned the top button of his jeans. He leaned back in his chair and drank his light beer in big gulps. It was his turn to report on the day's activities. He stifled a yawn with the back of his hand before he began.

"Fredrik already told you what it was like last night on Berzeliigatan. The damage to the adjacent property is quite extensive. All the windows on the neighboring buildings were blown out. The only one that survived, strangely enough, was the shop window of the tobacconist's on the corner. Irene already knows who owns it, but the rest of you don't. Any guesses?"

Jonny grumbled, "A lot of damned guessing here today!"

Tommy ignored him. "Our own Lasse 'Shorty' Johannesson!"

Even Jonny shut up.

The color rose in the superintendent's cheeks, and his eyes gleamed with excitement. "The worst possible hooligan right at our doorstep! Literally. That might mean something. Damn it, it's got to mean something!"

He was unconsciously rubbing his hands together. Impatiently he signaled Tommy to continue.

"The arson techs can just barely get up to the third floor. Higher than that it's too risky. As luck would have it—well, depending on how you look at it—the guy's body was found behind the door to von Knecht's office. Apparently he barely managed to make it that far and crept behind the door for protection. He was horribly burned. The pathologist is looking at him now. Poor devil," Tommy said glumly.

He paused briefly. Then he went on with his report about the legwork in the neighboring buildings. No one had noticed anything suspicious. Everyone had heard the powerful explosion and felt the blast wave. The techs had found parts of a large homemade bomb in the entryway to von Knecht's office. Pelle, the arson tech, had found some lumps of plastic around the site of the bomb. According to him, they were probably remnants of gasoline cans. Whoever placed the bomb there wanted to make sure that everything would burn up. The techs would report tomorrow with more details about the bomb.

Andersson was still looking flushed when he said, "Tommy, you and Fredrik check out Lasse 'Shorty.' Find out when he got out. This might be a lead. Hans, did you get hold of anyone who saw anything at the parking garage Tuesday night?"

Hans Borg shook his head. "I went through the building a second time. I concentrated on the apartments facing Kapellgatan, but there was nothing. From two o'clock until four-thirty I talked to people who came to get their cars from the parking garage. No one saw a thing. A teacher from Ascheberg High School loaned me a notepad and a felt-tip pen. So now there's a note inside the entrance of the garage asking for anyone who saw anything unusual on the night of the murder to contact us."

"There's not much more we can do. Maybe we should show up around five-thirty in the evening. Someone who may have observed something might put in an appearance at that time. No, now I know what we should do. Tomorrow we'll launch an intensive drive in the parking garage. We'll start at six in the morning and keep it up till seven in the evening. Everyone who parks in the garage will be quizzed about anything they noticed Tuesday night. If that doesn't produce anything, we'll have to call this approach a dud. But I think it's unlikely that the killer would have walked away in the pouring rain after the murder. I still think he had a car. Jonny and Hans, I'm giving this assignment to you," Andersson said firmly.

Neither of the designated officers looked particularly enthusiastic about it, but they realized there was some logic to their superintendent's reasoning.

"All right, only Hannu is left. Did you get hold of Pirjo?"

"No, just the kids. I drove out there this afternoon. They live near Angered Square. Two rooms and a kitchen."

"Not much room for five people."

"Four. Göte Larsson took off. The kids haven't seen him in two years. Maybe he's at sea. He's a sailor."

"But he and Pirjo are still married?"

"Yep. The little boys, Juha and Timo, were at home. They have the flu. Pirjo hasn't been heard from since Wednesday afternoon."

"So who's taking care of the boys?"

"Marjatta. She's thirteen and is used to taking care of her brothers."

"Does Pirjo usually disappear like this?"

"No, it's never happened before. Marjatta says there isn't any other man. I checked with the Angered Police and called all the emergency rooms. Not a thing. We should probably report her missing."

"Yes, we probably should. You'll have to look for her, Hannu. It definitely seems strange. Why should the von Knechts' cleaning woman disappear at the same time he's murdered and his office is bombed? She must have seen something last Monday when she was there cleaning. By the way, wasn't her daughter with her?"

"Yes, she was."

"Thirteen, you said?"

"Right."

Andersson thought about it. He turned again to Hannu. "Did she hear or see anything of interest last Monday?"

"No. But her Finnish is hard to understand."

"Are there different kinds of Finnish?"

"Yes, Pirjo and the kids come from northern Karelia. From Joensuu. I'm from Övertorneå. Different dialects, almost a different language."

He was interrupted by a knock on the door. The techs had arrived, and there was a short pause while they greeted everyone and chairs were found for them. They'd already eaten, so they declined the remnants of pizza that Irene and Birgitta offered them. They did want coffee though.

After everyone had settled down, Hannu continued, unperturbed. "Pirjo doesn't take a newspaper or listen to the Swedish news. She didn't know that von Knecht was dead. She went to the von Knechts' place, as she does every Wednesday. There she was met by the techs, heard about the murder, and went home. According to the boys she got home at eleven-thirty. She doesn't have a car, but always takes the bus or street-car. Marjatta came home from school at three-thirty. Pirjo made dinner. After five she said she had to go out and do some extra cleaning, but she didn't say where. She hasn't been seen or heard from since."

There was a moment's silence in the room. It was as though everyone had to catch their breath after this unexpectedly long speech from Hannu. Andersson was the first to recover. He asked, "Do you know how long Pirjo and the kids have lived in Sweden?"

"Three years."

"And Pirjo has never disappeared like this before?"

"No."

Andersson looked genuinely worried. What did Pirjo's disappearance mean? Was it a coincidence? Had she gone underground voluntarily? Was she threatened? From pure instinct the superintendent felt that this had something to do with the von Knecht case. He slammed his hand on the table.

"Hannu, you'll have to pull out all the stops. We have to get hold of Pirjo! Damn it, she can't just disappear like this, with three kids to take care of! She must have seen something last Monday. Lean on her daughter a little more."

He reflected for a moment, but couldn't think of anything else to do to find Pirjo.

"Now we've got a homicide, a bombing, and a missing person to investigate. And we don't know if there's any connection or if they're all sheer coincidences. But I have a feeling they're related," he said grimly.

He took a deep breath, got up, and paced back and forth at the end of the table. Moving around usually cleared his mind. Just now his head felt chaotic.

"Getting back to von Knecht's murder. Hannu, did you get hold of the illegitimate son and his mom?"

"Since I was in Angered, I asked a pal from the academy for help. A detective from Stockholm. He'll call us tomorrow."

"Can't he call you at home tonight?"

"No. I haven't gotten a phone put in yet."

"You mean you just moved to Göteborg, and not merely to General Investigations?"

"That's right."

Everyone was waiting for more, but nothing came. When Andersson realized this, he moved on.

"Irene, you still have to talk to the car dealer tomorrow. You might as well wait for the call from Stockholm too. Then Hannu can get going right away with the search for Pirjo."

Irene gave Hannu a questioning look. He nodded, and the shadow of a smile passed over his face. He was actually quite a handsome guy. And no wedding ring. But about as forthcoming as a sphinx. She quickly put a question to him.

"What's your pal's name in Stockholm?"

"Veiko Fors. Detective Inspector."

Andersson was very near asking whether there was a secret Finnish information network within the police corps, but reason prevailed. It's not good to have every question answered. Instead he turned to Birgitta.

"Birgitta, you help Hannu search for Pirjo. It's a top priority. Do we have a description?"

Hannu nodded. "About a hundred and fifty-five centimeters tall. Her daughter doesn't know how much she weighs, but says she's fat. Blond, shoulder-length hair. Thirty-two years old. She cleans part time at a newspaper kiosk. She's on welfare. I talked to the welfare office since they needed to know that Pirjo has disappeared. They promised to keep an eye on the kids."

Fredrik raised his hand politely, wanting to ask a question.

"So she has plenty of money then? I mean, welfare plus legal and illegal wages, the whole thing?"

Hannu leafed through his notebook, found what he was looking for, and rattled off: "Half-time wages as cleaning woman, forty-three hundred kronor, plus welfare and rent and subsidies for the children. After taxes, forty-one hundred and ten kronor a month, which has to cover the rest of the rent, food, and clothes for four people. The welfare office had all the figures. She needs the illegal jobs."

Irene looked pensive and asked to speak. "I wonder how many hours a week she worked for the von Knechts? Even if it was three days, I think it was only a matter of a few hours at a time. Should I check it out?"

"Yes, call your dear little friend Sylvia and ask her."

Andersson chuckled, pleased with his joke. Irene had a guilty conscience. Was it so obvious how much she disliked Sylvia? At the same time she felt she understood the woman to some degree and maybe even had a certain sympathy for her. It couldn't have been much fun being Richard von Knecht's wife.

Andersson slapped his palm on his knee. "No, now I want a coffee break before Malm and Ljunggren take over with their hot technical clues."

He got up and went over to the coffee machine. A third pot had just finished brewing. The night was still young.

SVANTE MALM started talking as soon as he took his last sip of coffee and stuffed a pinch of snuff under the left side of his top lip.

"Today we started to sort out all the fingerprints. We found a total of twenty-two different sets. Thirteen are identified. Colleagues from the various locations where Saturday's guests reside are helping us take their fingerprints so they won't have to come all the way in to Göteborg. Hannu gave me prints from Pirjo's daughter, and he also took Pirjo's prints from the alarm clock by her bed. In von Knecht's apartment there were no prints on the light switches in the hall, kitchen, and pantry, the bedroom on the top floor, the bathroom, or the light panel at the foot of the stairs leading to the top floor. These were all carefully wiped off. As were the door handles to the balcony and the outer door and the handle of the cleaver. On the other switch plates there are plenty of prints, mostly from Richard and Sylvia von Knecht. As well as a good number from Pirjo and her daughter. They were there on Monday to do the cleaning. Even the controls on the washing machine were wiped off."

"Strange. Why would he wipe those off?" Andersson, who asked the question, looked baffled.

Irene replied quickly, "Maybe there's a simple explanation. Perhaps it wasn't von Knecht who put the wash in the machine, but our killer. Could I change the subject from the fingerprints and ask what kind of medicine bottles Sylvia von Knecht has in her drawer in the nightstand?"

Malm leafed through his papers. "Here it is. Four bottles of Stesolid, five milligrams. One was almost empty, the others unopened. Two bottles of Sobril, fifteen milligrams. One just started, the other unopened. One bottle of Rohypnol, one milligram, which was almost used up."

Fredrik looked at a loss and asked, "What sort of medicines are those?"

"Stesolid and Sobril are sedatives. Rohypnol is a soporific. The prescriptions were written by three different doctors. I'm no doctor or expert, but it's obvious that there's a drug abuse problem here," said Svante Malm.

The upshot of the rest of the technician's report was that they hadn't found anything noteworthy. Strands of hair and textile fibers had been cataloged, but since the apartment was extremely well cleaned they hadn't found large quantities. Some hairs had already been identified as belonging to guests on Saturday night. Malm asked Hannu to take a hair from Pirjo's hairbrush, and to ask Marjatta for a few of hers. There was a good chance that the hairs found in the pantry in front of the cleaning closet belonged to the mother and daughter. Saturday's guests from Stockholm and Helsinki had to be contacted. He wound up his report, "The double bed upstairs had just been changed. Clean towels in the bathroom, but not in the sauna. There we found the towel that von Knecht had used."

Irene thought about this. Finally she said aloud, "I don't know how it is with you guys when you're home with a cold, but I know how it is with my husband. He almost never gets sick, but if he gets the slightest cold he acts like he's about to die. Used tissues all over the nightstand. Water glasses, bouillon cups, and snacks. Cough drop wrappers, newspapers, and other reading material all over the floor. Especially once he starts feeling better. But we haven't found any sign of a mess from Richard von Knecht. It was clinically clean. I mean, he was home alone with a cold for a day after Pirjo and her daughter cleaned up after the party. He didn't leave the apartment until one o'clock on Tuesday when he went out to Johanneshus with Valle Reuter."

A thoughtful silence descended over the gathering. After a bit of self-examination most of them nodded in agreement.

Jonny snorted. "It doesn't get like that at my place. My wife keeps it clean."

"Precisely! She picks up after you. That's exactly what I think happened with Richard too! He comes home to a shining clean apartment after his lunch with Valle. The bed is newly made, the towels changed, and the washing machine is running. No doubt the rooms he has been in for the past twenty-four hours have been vacuumed. The vacuum bag! Svante, did you find anything in it?"

"No. Just changed. Completely empty."

"Then it's possible that both the bag and the trash were dumped in the trash room. If it was the murderer who was in there. So far none of the other residents has admitted to being in the trash room at that time."

Andersson had to interrupt. "But von Knecht must have noticed that it had been cleaned again. It stank of Ajax when we came in the door several hours later!"

"Yes, he must have been prepared for it. Used to it."

The implications of this caused yet another thoughtful silence to descend.

"You mean that the killer cleaned the place before the murder?" Andersson looked dubious.

Irene shrugged. "Not necessarily the killer. But perhaps. At any rate someone wanted to remove all traces of being in the apartment. The careful cleaning that was done couldn't have been done after the murder. It must have taken a couple of hours."

Andersson was so excited that his ears were glowing. He exploded, "That can't be right! Nobody would let someone in to erase all traces that he had been in the apartment. And then go out and eat a huge lunch—? Then home to his lovely sauna and whiskey and calmly let himself be knocked on the head by the party concerned! Anyway, there were no signs that two people had taken a sauna and spent a cozy time together." He stopped to catch his breath.

Tommy Persson saw his chance to interject, "Wait a minute. I think Irene is on the right track. Could it be like this: Von Knecht let Pirjo in to clean! After what?"

Jonny lit up. "An orgy! That's obvious. His wife was away, after all."

Birgitta couldn't pass up the opportunity. "Don't judge everyone else by your own behavior!"

Andersson's ears began to pale a little; he looked from Tommy to Irene. "Pirjo? Sure, why not? One idea is no more nuts than any other. But it doesn't really fit. Why should she come back the day after she did a major cleaning? On the other hand, it explains why von Knecht was alone when he came home. She had already left. Hannu and Birgitta, you have to find Pirjo!"

Hannu made a calming gesture. Irene remembered something else she wanted to ask about.

"Svante, were there any sandwiches in the refrigerator? Sylvia told me that Richard was going to buy two sub sandwiches for supper."

"No, it was almost empty. A little cheese and some eggs. A few beers and pickled herring. No fresh food."

"I see. He told Sylvia on the phone when they spoke on Tuesday that he was going to bring home two subs, but I guess he forgot. They vanished in the alcohol and eucalyptus vapors," she surmised dryly.

Malm nodded and went on, "If we move on to the fire site on Berzelii-gatan, there is no doubt that it was caused by a firebomb. I spoke with arson investigator Pelle Svensson and he says there are definite traces of a large bomb. From what they've found so far, it seems to have been a devilish variant, a thick iron pipe filled with plastique. Apparently det cord was connected between the bomb and the gasoline cans."

"How was the bomb detonated?"

"Pelle promised to let me know about that tomorrow. The proof hadn't been secured yet, but he has a theory. That's all he would tell me."

"And the body that was found?"

"We don't know much about the man yet. Stridner promised to look at him early tomorrow morning. They told me at Pathology that she's busy with a scientific symposium in forensic medicine. And the other pathologists are there too."

Now it was Birgitta's turn to ask a question. "What's det cord?"

"Detonator cord. Most people who've been in the military know about it. Let me put it this way: If you wind this fuse around an ordinary pine tree and trigger the detonator, the fuse explodes and splits the trunk. Explosive fuse, you might call it."

He sat down. A general surge of ideas and questions resulted, but they didn't seem to be getting much farther. At nine o'clock the superintendent decided to adjourn.

"Okay. Let's go home and get some shut-eye. We need to be clear headed all day tomorrow. You all know what you have to do tomorrow?"

They muttered and nodded.

"I'll be here all day from seven to . . . as long as necessary in the evening. As soon as you find out something, give me a call. We'll all meet here at eight on Monday morning. Weekend duty on Saturday is assigned to Tommy. Backup will be . . . Irene. Sunday duty, Hans. Backup will be . . . me."

That was fine with her, Irene realized. Then she'd have Sunday off. On Saturday night she and Krister would have a real cozy evening. Great. Suddenly she noticed how tired she was.

EXCEPT FOR Sammie's happy snuffling and small yips, it was completely quiet in the house, even though it was only shortly after ten. The dog's coat was getting shaggy; it was time to have him groomed. But it would have to wait until this investigation was over. Or at least until things calmed down. She felt a pang of guilty conscience. Sammie was a lovely dog, but nobody really had time for him anymore. Everyone had taken on too many work, school, and leisure-time activities. He had his doggy pals, of course, at the dog-sitter's. To compensate him a little and to soothe her guilty conscience, she took him out on an evening walk.

From the street she saw that there was a light on in Katarina's room. She was lying on her bed reading or else she had fallen asleep with the light on. Before she went to bed, Irene would have to go in and turn it off.

Actually Krister's schedule was ideal. He always worked late on Thursdays, until midnight. Then either Friday or Saturday was a late night too. Every third weekend he had both Saturday and Sunday off. When the twins were little, her mother had taken over when his schedule and her overtime conflicted. But now the girls were big and Grandma hadn't needed to come over as often during the past three years. The passage of time works for the benefit of parents of small children.

She walked along smiling to herself, lost in her thoughts. That's why she was totally unprepared when Sammie suddenly barked and hurled himself at a figure slipping into the deep shadows next to the garage.

Chapter Nine

"GOOD MORNING, SWEETIE. YOU look like a disaster zone."

"Thank you, dear. That's just the sort of comment that makes my day!"

Irene angrily snatched the bath towel he was about to dry himself off with and flicked the towel into the spray of the shower. A little revenge is still revenge, even if it's childish. Krister laughed annoyingly.

"Okay, okay. So it's one of those mornings. About time for your period?"

That did it. "No, but I've worked more than fifty hours in four days! And yesterday Jenny made a point of seeing that I threw in the towel for good!"

"Did we get off on a towel thing for some reason?"

"Oh, go jump in the lake!"

Mad as a hornet she climbed into the shower. When she turned around she saw Krister take her towel and walk out the door, whistling. Now she was the one with no towel. There was no justice in the world. "Just one of those days." Or was it "things"? Was it Frank Sinatra who sang that song? Didn't make a damned bit of difference which old fart it was. It was a rotten day even before it got started.

She felt a little better after the shower, but still spoiling for a fight. Krister wasn't the main adversary, but he'd get his. First she had to take on Jenny.

Her other daughter was sitting at the breakfast table.

"Where's Jenny?" Irene asked.

"She says she's sick," said Katarina, who was absorbed in the front page of GP. Holding the newspaper open in front of her face, she asked, "Mamma, were you there when they found the guy who burned up?"

Krister was in a teasing mood. "If he was burned up, they couldn't have found him, could they?"

"Ha ha. Very funny. Don't be such a konk," was his daughter's comment.

Krister looked deflated. Irene rejoiced to the depths of her black soul at his confusion. He obviously didn't know what a "konk" was, but didn't want to ask Katarina and then reveal that he wasn't up on the latest teenage slang. He raised an inquisitive eyebrow at Irene, who merely smiled sweetly. With her fangs bared.

She turned to Katarina. "No, I never saw the guy who died in the fire. Thank God! What do you mean, Jenny's sick?"

"You'll have to ask her. Not me. I'm fine!" Katarina gave her a fierce glare. "Just one of those . . ."

Irene sighed. And decided to change her tactics. It wasn't good to be at odds with the whole world. In a weary tone she said, "It must have been last night that gave me the willies. I went out for a walk with Sammie right after ten. I don't think we were out for more than half an hour. When I came around the garage Sammie jumped at somebody slipping behind the corner. I almost had a heart attack, I was so scared! It was Jenny. If I hadn't had the dog with me, I never would have seen her. But of course he knew her scent from far away."

Krister turned at once to Katarina. "What was she doing out at ten-thirty on a school night? Katarina!"

She was staring hard at the newspaper and pretending not to hear. But two pairs of staring parental eyes are hard to ignore. Finally she had to answer, "She was out playing. With the band," she said sullenly.

Irene sighed again. "Yes, that's what she told me too. But she has a big hickey on her neck. And she won't say who gave it to her."

Katarina sprang up, flinging the paper away. "That's her own damned business!" Furious, she stomped out of the kitchen.

Krister's playful teasing mood vanished instantly. He gave Irene a serious look. "Forgive me, but I didn't know anything about this. You were all asleep when I came home at midnight."

"Exhaustion. Exhaustion pure and simple."

"Irene, I'll go up and talk to Jenny. Eat your breakfast in peace and quiet."

With a sob in her throat she threw her arms around him. She felt a deep gratitude to fate or to whoever it might be who had given her such a wonderful husband. She herself was a whining wife and bad mother who couldn't handle a job, husband, home, and children. And a dog, she was reminded when Sammie's ruffled mustaches appeared in the doorway.

"HELLO! DOES anyone know where Hannu Rauhala is? He's got a call from Stockholm."

Irene gave a start. Stockholm! It must be the inspector Hannu knew. She dashed for the intercom.

"Hello! Irene here. Switch it over to me. Hannu asked me to handle this matter."

Not exactly true, but she didn't have time to be entirely truthful. While she was trying to pull off her jacket, the phone started ringing insistently. Breathlessly she lunged for the receiver, with one arm still in her sleeve.

"Inspector Irene Huss."

"Hi, Veiko Fors, Stockholm Crime Police. I'm looking for Hannu."

"I know. We're both working on this case. We're understaffed so Hannu asked me to take your call today. He's out searching for a material witness who disappeared."

"If Hannu is on the job, you'll have that witness pretty soon."

There wasn't a trace of Finnish intonation in Veiko Fors's voice. He actually sounded like a guy from the south side of Stockholm.

"Yes, he's a dynamo, all right. The von Knecht case has just been expanded, as you may have seen in the papers," Irene said.

"Yes, it looks like you've got shit by the boxful. But that doesn't mean I haven't got plenty too."

"Shit by the boxful?"

"Exactly. Jonas Söder is an artist, lives on Fjällgatan. It's impossible to get hold of him. I called several times and even drove over there and rang the bell on my way home last night. Zip. Mona Söder also drew a blank. I got hold of the old lady's home phone number and she answered at around five. But when I introduced myself and started to explain that we needed to talk to her and Jonas regarding the von Knecht homicide, she totally flipped out! Refused to talk to me. Says she'll only come down to talk to somebody who's in charge of the investigation. So I'm bouncing her back to you in G-borg. Sorry!"

Irene wrote down the address and phone number of Jonas and Mona Söder. Veiko also had Mona's number at work. He told her that Mona Söder was listed in the phone book as "personnel director."

Dejectedly she hung up the phone. How would she solve this? There was no time to think about it, because the phone rang again.

"Inspector Irene Huss."

"Hi there! Robert Skytter here!"

The name didn't mean a thing to her, but she recognized the trumpeting tone. The car dealer from Volkswagen. His youthful voice sounded like a commercial for energizing cereal flakes or some ginseng preparation. Maybe she ought to buy a bottle of ginseng. Did it come in a five-kilo size? A new trumpet blast shocked her out of her reveries.

"Hello! Are you still there?"

"What? Yes. I was busy with something else. Excuse me. Listen, Robert, I called you about the fact that Charlotte von Knecht was down there picking up her new car Tuesday evening. Is that correct?"

"That's right!"

"When did she arrive?"

"Well, after four, maybe closer to four-thirty."

"What time did she leave?"

There was a brief pause. There wasn't the same self-confident zing in his voice when he replied. "Don't know for sure. Right after five, I should think."

"Not *before* five?"

"No, I'm quite sure of that. I remember hearing the five o'clock news on the radio."

"Weren't you selling a car? How did you have time to listen to the radio?"

"Well, we were taking a test drive in Charlotte's new car. She was feeling a little insecure about driving it. I was giving her some advice."

"Didn't she have a Golf before?"

"Yes, but this one is much newer. More features. For instance, a more powerful engine, hundred and fifteen horsepower—"

"Thanks, but I already have a car. By the way, how old are you?"

Now there was a long pause. "What does that have to do . . . twenty-two."

"Married or living with someone?"

"Neither. How about yourself? Are you trying to pick me up or . . . ?"

Her response caught her by surprise, but she couldn't stop it. The laughter surged up from her chest and exploded from her lips. She had to put down the phone. She leaned over the desk as tears of laughter made even more spots on the already soiled blotter on the desk. She ended up with a cramp in her diaphragm. With a powerful effort she pulled herself together, wiped her nose and the corners of her eyes with her sleeve, and picked up the receiver.

"Hello, excuse me, Robert. But it was just too funny. I could almost be your mother. If I'd only started in time."

"That's cool. I'm glad I can make somebody happy. Although I do prefer mature women."

"Like Charlotte?"

"Charlotte is really something special. And fun. Nice as hell."

"And you're sure you heard the five o'clock news while you were in the car?"

"Yes. Even though I wasn't sitting in the car then. I had just gotten out. Charlotte wanted to see how to remove the spare tire. The car door was open, so we heard the news. Charlotte said something like, 'Is it five o'clock already?' Well, then we checked to see if she had all her papers and everything. Then she left."

"So it would have been about ten after five. Or more correctly, seventeen-ten."

"Yes, it must have been."

"Thanks, Robert. Please forgive the laughing fit, but you really made my day."

"No problem. Drop by if you ever need a good car."

Well, damned if a faint clearing on the horizon didn't herald a clear day. A little sun never hurt. It hadn't been seen in almost two weeks. Irene felt renewed energy flowing through her body. Wasn't that called "comic relief"? Screw the ginseng; a little flirting on the phone works wonders with ladies approaching forty.

Andersson was sitting in his office. When Irene knocked lightly on the door frame he jumped in his chair.

"Jesus, you scared me!"

"Sitting there trying to think? It smells like something's burning." Irene sniffed the air.

He gave her a weary look. "How do you manage to be so cheerful in the morning? And *smells like burning* is the right expression. The fire on Berzeliigatan doesn't seem to fit in with von Knecht's murder. Yet it was incredibly convenient. And now the cleaning woman has disappeared."

"I spoke to Hannu's pal in Stockholm, Veiko Fors."

"So how were things going for him?"

"Nothing yet. He had shit by the boxful."

"Shit by the boxful . . . are you nuts?"

Irene laughed and even got Andersson to smile a little.

"Those were his exact words. Stockholm slang, you know. The shit is that Jonas Söder can't be found. He's apparently an artist. His mamma went crazy when Veiko Fors said he wanted to talk to both of them regarding von Knecht's murder. She refuses to speak to anyone but the detective in charge of the investigation."

Andersson looked out his overgrown window thoughtfully. The poor lily hanging in its macramé holder had given up the ghost long ago. He sat in silence for a long time. Without looking at Irene, he said pensively, "Besides myself, there's only you and Jonny here right now. Jonny is talking to Ivan Viktors. They may have already started by now. How are you doing?"

"I thought I'd call Sylvia von Knecht in a while and ask how many hours a week Pirjo works for them. Otherwise, I just talked to the car dealer in Mölndal. He gives Charlotte an alibi up to about ten minutes past five."

"Then she couldn't have made it downtown and hoisted her father-in-law over the balcony railing. It's also hard to believe that Charlotte is particularly skilled at bomb making."

"Something tells me she can't even cook a meal."

It was meant as a joke, but she could hear her own cattiness. In her mind Rob's cheerful voice exclaimed: *Who needs to know how to cook with steering wheels like that . . . wow!*

Andersson didn't seem to notice the comment about Charlotte's deficiencies in the domestic arena. He was busy with his own thoughts and plans. "And then Jonny and Hans have to watch the parking garage. Tommy and Fredrik are checking Berzeliigatan. Birgitta has to talk to the photographer, Bobo Torsson, and help Hannu look for Pirjo Larsson. And I have to talk to Yvonne Stridner. Richard von Knecht is finished being examined, you might say. What else is there? Oh yes, I have to try on some pants."

At the last sentence a shadow came over his face. He took a deep breath. "No, it'll have to be you, Irene—you're going to have to take care of the mother and son in Stockholm."

"That's fine. I have Veiko Fors's phone number. But first I'm going to call Sylvia."

THE PHONE rang about a dozen times before Sylvia's slurred voice was heard at the other end of the line. *Have you overdosed now, little Sylvia?* thought Irene. But she didn't say it. Instead she chirped in her softest voice, "Good morning, Sylvia. Pardon me for waking you. It's Inspector Irene Huss."

An incoherent mumble and grumbling was her reply. Irene hastily plunged ahead, "I'm calling on behalf of Superintendent Andersson.

We're searching for Pirjo Larsson. She's been missing since last Wednesday afternoon. You still haven't heard from her?"

"No-o-o. Not . . . gone . . . I think she lives in Angered," Sylvia mumbled.

"We know that. But she's been missing from her apartment and left her three children alone since last Wednesday."

"Oh . . . that's odd." It sounded as though she was starting to wake up. "So who's going to clean our apartment then?"

She was awake now. Irene stifled a sigh and continued undeterred, "We were wondering how many hours a week Pirjo works for you."

There was silence for half an eternity. Finally came a dejected, "Fifteen hours."

"Divided over three days? Monday, Wednesday, and Friday? Is that correct?"

"Yes."

"How much do you pay Pirjo?"

"I can't see that that's any of your business!"

Irene tried to sound as convincing as possible. "Yes it is, actually. We're investigating Pirjo's financial situation." That sounded good. But it didn't impress Sylvia.

She snapped, "According to her it's not nearly enough!"

"Does Pirjo want a raise?"

"Yes."

"What does she get per month?"

Again silence. Finally Sylvia said, resigned, "Eighteen hundred."

"And she wants?. . ."

"Two thousand five hundred! Insane!"

"How much will she get?"

"No raise at all! I was utterly shocked!"

Anger made her sound like she was completely alert now. Irene decided to wrap it up on a more neutral subject. "I heard from Henrik that you're going up to Marstrand over the weekend."

"That's right. Nothing wrong with that, I hope." Her tone said that even if there was, she planned to ignore them.

"Not at all. I just wanted to mention that if anything should turn up, or if you need to contact us, give us a call. The investigative group is always here."

"Do you work around the clock?"

"No, not really. We have a duty schedule."

Guardedly they wished each other a nice weekend and hung up. She needed a quick cup of coffee before she called Mona Söder.

"SWEDISH DATA, good morning. How can I help you?" The voice was professional and friendly.

"I'm looking for Personnel Director Mona Söder."

"Just a moment, please."

Click, click. A soft whirring to indicate that the signals were actually going through. A smoky and pleasant female voice answered.

"Mona Söder."

"Good morning. My name is Irene Huss. Detective inspector with the Göteborg Police. I'm working on the investigation of the murder of Richard von Knecht."

Mona Söder took a deep breath. "I don't want to get involved! Not now . . . not the way things stand right now. We don't want to have anything to do with him. Are we under suspicion for something?"

"As you no doubt are aware, this is a homicide investigation. We're going over all the facts about the victim. We discovered that you and Richard von Knecht had a son together in July nineteen sixty-five."

Quiet sobbing was heard on the line. But only briefly, before Mona Söder sniffed loudly and steadied her voice. "Could we meet in person?"

"Meet? You're in Stockholm!"

"Yes, I know. But this is important for your investigation. You have to come up here!" It sounded like both an appeal and a command.

"Can't we do it on the phone?"

"Absolutely not! It's very important that you come here, because you have to see with your own eyes."

"I'll have to talk to my supervisor. The Göteborg Police are on an austerity program, like everyone else."

"Call me as soon as you know. See you later!"

Irene hung up the phone, impressed. It was obvious that Mona Söder was a woman who was used to telling people what to do.

"WHERE DID you get that idea? Going up to Stockholm! What is it the woman can't say on the phone?"

"She said she had to show me something. According to her it was very important for the investigation."

"Show you? Very important?" Andersson put his hands behind his back, a habit from his days on the beat, and paced aimlessly back and forth in the room. Suddenly he stopped in front of Irene, who happened to be sitting in the visitor's chair. Resolutely he said, "You have to go. It's the first time in this investigation that anyone has said they have something important to contribute. Check on the train times. Write up a travel requisition, and I'll make sure you won't have to front the money for too long. Okay?"

"That should work. But I have to take care of a few practical things first. Jenny is sick at home. Nothing serious, just a cold. Krister is working late tonight. Katarina has to practice for a judo match on Sunday. I'll call my mother. Just hope she has time. Since she retired, she's almost never home. You know how it is, 'When you're a happy retired person . . .'" She sang the last part loudly and off-key.

"Thank you, but I'm actually quite musical. Get going on your trip to Stockholm instead of torturing me," said Andersson.

"MONA SÖDER, here."

"Inspector Irene Huss again."

"Yes, hi. When are you coming?"

That stopped Irene short, but she managed to pull herself together. "I'm taking the X-two-thousand at eleven-oh-five. Arriving in Stockholm just after fourteen hundred."

"Good. I'll meet you at Five Small Houses at three P.M."

"Where are the 'Five Small Houses'? Is that where you work?" Something about prefab housing came vaguely to mind.

Mona Söder laughed, a warm and pleasant laugh. "No, I work at a computer company. Five Small Houses is a cozy restaurant in Old Town. I'll buy," she said.

As if they were old friends. To her surprise Irene discovered that eating a late lunch with Mona Söder seemed like a fun idea. Although being treated might be construed as bribing an official . . . There was a risk, so it was probably better to go Dutch.

"Do you know your way around Stockholm?" asked Mona.

"Yes, I lived there for a year, when I was at the police academy out in Ulriksdal. I lived on Tomtebogatan downtown."

"Go over to Österlånggatan and walk down a few blocks. The restaurant is on Nygränd, one of the cross streets down toward the water."

"I'm sure it'll be easy to find."

They assured each other that it would be nice to meet in just five hours. Irene glanced at the clock. One more hour before the train left.

Her mother had promised to drive out to stay with Jenny and Katarina that afternoon. Krister had been informed.

Had she forgotten anything? Nothing that she could think of. She stuck her head in the superintendent's door to say good-bye, but he wasn't there.

SINCE THE major renovation a few years ago, Göteborg's Central Station is quite a beautiful place to visit. The dark, polished woodwork of the walls, benches, and pillars creates a turn-of-the-twentieth-century atmosphere. But the crowded flow of travelers, the stoned junkies, and the winos asleep on the benches are the same as always. The ticket line is the same too, even if nowadays it's computerized with little paper numbers and digital displays above each ticket window. A glass door separates those waiting patiently for tickets from the people in the waiting rooms and on the platforms.

It took Irene almost half an hour to buy her round-trip ticket. She had to dash out into the biting wind and run full speed for the shiny, silvery blue Intercity train.

It was the first time she had been on an Intercity train. Even before she sat down she knew that she was out of place. She wasn't wearing a suit or high-heeled shoes, and she carried no briefcase or laptop. In her black jeans, her down-filled poplin jacket, and her red wool sweater she felt like a total misfit. A woman in a masculine-looking gray pin-striped suit, complementing her pageboy haircut, looked at Irene disapprovingly over the edge of her reading glasses when Irene sat down facing her on the other side of the aisle. The only baggage Irene was carrying was a yellow plastic bag from the newsstand with snacks and newspapers. Since she didn't even own a handbag and never had, most of what she needed in her daily life she kept in her jacket pockets. They bulged unaesthetically. She decided to pretend there was a fax machine in her right pocket and a palm computer in the left.

She gave the woman in the suit a radiant smile and sat down. That's the most effective way to startle people: They think you're crazy and instantly avert their eyes. She demonstratively opened up GT and read about the attempts of her investigative group to solve the von Knecht case. The papers still didn't know about Pirjo Larsson's disappearance or the fact that von Knecht had another son. It was his mother she was going to eat lunch with, after traveling more than five hundred kilometers.

Within fifteen minutes the detective inspector was asleep under her newspaper.

THERE WAS a desert in her mouth. That wasn't the only thing that proved she had been snoring. The woman in the suit across from her was smirking maliciously. Irene decided that the two of them were enemies, so she fired off another smile. The gray-toned woman pursed her lips and lost herself deeper in her three-ring binder. It was almost one o'clock. Irene needed a cup of coffee and some food. She opened her newly purchased can of Coca-Cola and ate a Heath bar. The important thing was to save room for lunch. It was beginning to feel quite exhilarating to be taking the train up to the capital like this, unexpectedly. At the same time she had to admit that she was starting to feel a little curious. What was it that Mona Söder wanted to show her that was supposed to be so important to the investigation? Could the solution to the von Knecht case be in Stockholm? She just hoped that she would be able to make it back on the next X2000 train at eight-thirty that evening.

IT WAS no problem getting to Old Town on the subway. Despite the biting cold wind, a pale winter sun peeked through the clouds now and then. After wandering through the narrow lanes and stopping in a few small boutiques, she headed for Nygränd and Five Small Houses. Funny name for a restaurant, since it unquestionably was located in only one house. But a careful look would reveal that there were actually five different house façades next to each other. They varied somewhat in design and were painted different colors.

The lovely warmth of the restaurant enveloped her when she walked in through the heavy old wooden door. A middle-aged hostess gave her a friendly nod. On a sudden impulse Irene asked why the restaurant was called Five Small Houses. The hostess didn't seem surprised at the question; many people had probably wondered the same thing over the years.

In a friendly voice she recited, "The restaurant extends, as the name indicates, through five small houses. It includes the ground floor and basement of all of them and even the second floor of some. As you can see over there, the archway and stairs mark the transition between the houses. There have been small inns in these houses ever since the seventeenth century. Even illegal pubs. Sometimes the premises were used as coal cellars. At the beginning of the nineteenth century the houses were converted to small apartments. Actors and ballerinas once lived here. They're all retired now, but several of them have been back to look at their old place, which is now a restaurant again, and has been for many years."

"How interesting. Thank you so much for taking the time to tell me about it. I can practically feel the poet Bellman breathing down my neck."

The pleasant hostess laughed. "Let's hope you're spared Carl Michael Bellman's breath. Something tells me it might spoil your appetite. Where would you like to sit?"

"I'm supposed to meet Mona Söder here at three o'clock."

"She's already arrived. Please follow me."

She guided Irene between the tables with blinding white tablecloths down the stairs and through small archways. Irene was soon quite lost. And she usually had such a good sense of direction! In the far corner of a room at the very back of the house a woman was sitting alone. Irene's eyes had adjusted to the scant light in the vaulted room, but it was still hard to see what the woman in the dim corner looked like. When Irene approached she slowly rose to her feet. Mona Söder was only a few centimeters shorter than Irene. She was stocky but not at all fat. *Power*, that was the word that came to mind as Irene shook hands with Mona and said hello. She didn't have a sparkling, vital energy of the type that took your breath away, but rather a calm, sure, authoritative power. Irene did not doubt for a second that Mona must be an extraordinary boss.

Mona Söder gestured graciously toward the chair across the table. "Please have a seat, Irene. I hope you forgive me, but I've already ordered for us. Is grilled Baltic herring all right, followed by plum cake with vanilla ice cream for dessert?"

"That sounds fantastic."

Irene had only eaten grilled Baltic herring once before. *Burned herring with mashed potatoes* was what she would call it.

Mona turned to the waiter who had soundlessly materialized at their table. "We'd like two large porters and two shots of Aalborg Aquavit."

Irene gave a start. That was enough of someone else making decisions for her. "No thanks. I'd like a large pilsner, no schnapps for me," she said quickly.

A little furrow appeared on Mona's brow, but she only shrugged and waved away the young man with their orders. She gave a hard, curt laugh.

"Don't think I sit and drink schnapps every day for lunch. But sometimes it seems like a good buzz is the only thing that keeps me on my feet. Today's one of those days. You'll soon find out why. But let's eat first, before we get down to business."

The herring was heavenly. Irene found herself practically shoveling in the excellent food. They drank a *skål* to Old Town, with Aalborg and Pripps pilsner, respectively. Mona was easygoing and unpretentious in her conversation. There were no embarrassing moments, although there were long pauses.

They had just polished off the fabulous plum cake and were drinking a second cup of coffee. Mona had ordered a cognac, but Irene declined. Mona could really hold her liquor. The slight tension across her shoulders may have relaxed a bit, but there was no change in her speech or gestures. Irene concluded that she was used to drinking a good deal. Mona took out a pack of cigarillos from her fashionable handbag, which perfectly matched her light gray jacket of soft wool. Under it she wore a white silk blouse with a straight black skirt. Comfortable gray pumps with a low heel completed the picture of a woman with style, power, and money. The heavy gold chains around her neck further emphasized this impression. She wore no rings.

Mona offered the cigarillo pack to Irene, who declined, and then carefully lit hers, exhaling with pleasure and sending a cloud up toward the ceiling. Squinting slightly through the smoke, she looked around. They were alone in the room. Voices could be heard from the rooms in front as well as the vaulted room, but in here there were none. Pensively, she began her story.

"We met in the spring of 'sixty-four, Richard and I. He blew in like a whirlwind one April evening, as Strindberg writes in *The People of Hemsö*. I was twenty-two and he was twenty-eight. I had been attending social work college for a year but I didn't feel at home in Stockholm. If you're born and raised up north in Härnösand, Stockholm is a real culture shock. Some people thrive and have a blast. Others just get homesick. Like I did."

Only now did Irene notice the slight lilt of the Ångermanland accent in Mona's speech. At first she had just heard a nicely enunciated, cultivated Swedish, but the hint of Norrland was there like a pleasant undertone.

"But I had nothing to go back to. Pappa died in a sawmill accident when I was fifteen. Mamma met another man. They got married and she moved to Umeå with him and my two younger sisters. I stayed behind in Härnösand, paying for room and board with Mamma's cousin and her husband while I finished up high school. In a fit of boldness I answered a classified ad: 'Young lady with a talent for languages wanted for office position.' In Stockholm. I almost fainted when they called and told me I could start in August. I found a room in a boardinghouse run by an old lady on Birger Jarlsgatan. A sad little room in back off the courtyard. But it was cheap and suited my modest salary."

Mona broke off for a coughing fit. She took a sip of lukewarm coffee to clear her throat. After a deep, greedy drag on her cigarillo, she went on. "The job was pure shit work. After a year I had had enough, and I applied to the social work college. Everybody was going there in those days! With my grades it was no problem, I got in. After just one semester I realized that sitting in a welfare office was not what I wanted to do either. Bringing salvation to tattered lives would have to be left to others. I didn't feel I was the type who could really get involved. I had enough problems of my own."

She fell silent and downed the last of her cognac. Irene was fascinated. It was hard to imagine this worldly and obviously authoritative woman as a lonely, uncertain student in the big city. But she must have been hard nosed even then, since she didn't stay at the office job long.

"My fellow students were Communists on the far left who wanted to change the world. The Social Democrats were viewed as a bourgeois party. Imagine, how the pendulum always swings back!"

She laughed heartily and stubbed out her cigarillo in the little glass ashtray.

"I followed the administrative path and have always worked as a civil servant. First a few years in Södertälje municipality. But I started in the private sector in the late seventies. The past ten years I've been the personnel director of a computer firm."

She coughed again and rinsed out her mouth with the last drops of coffee.

"My life. That's all there is to it. The only things that ever happened are Richard and Jonas. So, back to Richard."

Again she fell silent. Her hand trembled a little as she ran her fingers through her short, well-coifed steel-gray hair. Their waiter appeared in the doorway, and to Irene's surprise Mona whistled softly to him. When he came over to their table, Mona said, without taking her eyes off Irene, "Two cognacs."

Irene tried to object but Mona silenced her by placing her hand over hers.

"Richard and I met on a glorious April evening at Mosebacke in southern Stockholm. As you can hear, the ghost of Strindberg is back. There was spring in the air even though it wasn't very warm yet. I was wandering around aimlessly, feeling lonely. I had just broken up with a boy at school. I was fed up with him and all the other boys. I was sitting on a bench, trying to think of nothing at all. Suddenly a man sat down next to me. I was scared to death, and it was quite obvious. We started talking and the time just whirled away. He was simply effervescent with . . . the joy of life. Yes, that's the phrase I associate most with Richard. Joie de vivre. Jonas has that in common with his father. I had never ever experienced anything like it before!"

Mona paused to light another cigarillo.

"I realized that he was older than I was. So urbane! I was dazzled and very impressed. Of course I was attractive in those days, but no man had ever looked at me the way Richard did. He thought everything I said sounded intelligent. Everything he said sounded exciting and exotic to my ears. We talked and talked for several hours. Then we went back to his apartment on Fjällgatan. We split a bottle of wine and made love for three days and three nights. And I stayed there the rest of April and May. I still had my room on Birger Jarlsgatan, but I was hardly ever there. In June and July he went down to Göteborg. He had to help his father with the shipping company and was taking a combined vacation and leave of absence, he said. Later I found out that her name was Madeleine. They had a hot romance, although she was married. But I, who didn't read any weekly magazines or have any close girlfriends to gossip with, I had no clue. It wasn't until early September that I heard from him again. And I was idiotically happy. Didn't ask a thing, didn't want any answers. Just made love and made love. In late November I realized that I was pregnant. I wasn't overjoyed, but I thought it would all work out. Richard did have a great job and made plenty of money. I would have to take a year off from my studies. Then we would get a nanny. And before that we'd get married. Or so I thought. Richard never let on what he thought about getting stuck with me and with a kid on the way! Getting married was the last thing he wanted to do. At least to me. But he didn't say a thing; he was just as charming and tender to me as before. He did start working late more often, though. He said he needed money now that the child was coming. And I wanted to believe it was true."

She broke off and gave Irene a sharp look before she went on. "It probably doesn't sound too smart to your ears. What a dope I was! But you have to realize that I'm talking about a different person. The girl I'm telling you about no longer exists. She's been gone for years. But once she was a real person. With tears and laughter and love. She could love unconditionally. And she still believed that people were basically good. You get thick skinned from fighting and losing too many battles."

Irene saw the reflections from the candle flame glittering in Mona's tears. Several years as an interrogation leader had taught her that the biggest mistake at such a moment would be to say anything. The person being interviewed has a need to talk things out.

As if she had read Irene's mind, Mona continued in a more businesslike tone of voice. "What I'm telling you now I've never told anyone but Jonas. It doesn't concern anyone else. But since Richard has been murdered, everything has to be completely aboveboard. I want to explain how everything was and why neither Jonas nor I have anything to do with the murder."

She was embellishing her speech with many more sweeping gestures now than she had at the beginning of the conversation. It was the result of equal parts fervor and cognac.

"Anyway. It was getting on toward Christmas. Richard said he had to go down to Göteborg. I had moved into his apartment in the middle of December and given up my room on Birger Jarlsgatan. When I realized that he didn't intend to take me with him to meet his family, I finally staged the big scene that I should have attempted much earlier. We argued for several hours. More precisely, I argued for several hours and said what was in my heart. I was so young and had never heard of the concept 'fear of confrontation,' but after a while I noticed that he wasn't defending himself. I would attack and he would sidestep without any particular finesse. He was quite simply not used to arguing! Nobody could argue with the gorgeous, charming, rich, and talented Richard von Knecht! And that's how it had been his whole life. Free of any conflict. If things got unpleasant, he would just slip away discreetly. If any unappetizing remains were left behind, there was always someone who could be hired to sweep them away."

Mona was now so agitated that she grabbed Irene's untouched cognac. Irene didn't say a word; she hadn't intended to drink it. Mona needed it more than she did.

"His father suffered a timely embolism and Richard was granted permission from the brokerage firm to leave his job and go down to take over the family empire. You know, of course, that his father was a shipowner. Richard left for Göteborg in early January. I was entering my second trimester. Abortion had not yet been legalized, nor did I consider it. Deep inside I believed that he would come back to me. And the child. He couldn't ignore his child, could he? Good Lord, I was so naive!"

There was no mistaking the bitterness in Mona's voice. She downed half the cognac in the snifter in one gulp.

"He paid the rent for six months in advance before he left. I stayed in the apartment and tended to my studies. I didn't hear a word from him the whole time. I started using my meager student loan to buy the weekly magazines. There was a lot about him: 'The crown prince becomes the new shipping king,' 'Most eligible bachelor.' I don't remember everything I read. In May I saw pictures from a ball in Göteborg. That's when he met Sylvia."

She paused and finished off the cognac.

"Then I finally woke up from my coma. The baby inside me was kicking. I felt responsible for this tiny being. And suddenly I realized that I was utterly alone and would have to fight. The new Mona began to take shape. I started calling him, both at home and at the office. I could hear from his voice that he was scared shitless. He didn't want either his mamma or the delicate little ballerina to find out about his escapades here in Stockholm. Suddenly I had the advantage. And I intended to use it. He paid another six months' rent. To shut me up, of course. I took it easy and lay low that summer. On July twenty-third Jonas was born. The instant he was put in my arms I knew that for his sake I would be able to fight. He's the most amazing thing that's ever happened to me."

Her voice broke a little and she fell silent. When she resumed her story there was a diamond sharpness in her tone.

"I began to demand my rights. And Jonas's right to a father. After many heated arguments on the phone Richard promised to come up to Stockholm and 'fix everything,' as he put it. Instead he sent his lawyer, Tore Eiderstam. He threatened that Richard would deny all knowledge of me. Deny paternity. But I stood my ground. When he realized that I didn't intend to back down, he started threatening me. I would never get a job, Richard and Tore would see to that. Then I threatened to go to the tabloids with my story. We went back and forth like this for several days. Suddenly one day Tore switched tactics. He said that he and Richard weren't going to bother with me any longer. They proposed a settlement. Richard would admit to being Jonas's father. He would put the apartment in my name and pay the rent until Jonas was twenty, plus child support of five hundred kronor per month. Remember that the rent in those days was four hundred kronor. A new car cost about eight thousand. A single mother who wasn't even half finished with her studies had no choice. I accepted. In return I promised not to tell Jonas who his father was until his twentieth birthday. A week later I read in the papers about Richard's engagement to Sylvia and their impending wedding. That's when the old Mona disappeared for good."

Mona hid her face in her hands. Irene cautiously inserted a question. "Did you and Richard have any contact over the years?"

"No, never. He didn't even send presents to Jonas on Christmas or his birthday. And that had to be the worst thing. Seeing the boy's excited anticipation before holidays. And then his wordless disappointment. After a while he didn't care anymore. On his twentieth birthday I told him the same story I just told you. He just shrugged his shoulders and said, 'My father never cared about me, why should I care about him?'"

She fumbled in her handbag and took out a tissue. She tried to control herself, but the tears blurred her voice.

"Jonas has always been such a fantastic person, even when he was little. Always happy and kind. He was born with artistic talent. He drew and painted before he could talk. There was never any discussion that he would be anything but an artist. I let him keep the apartment on Fjällgatan. I bought a condo on Lidingö when he was nineteen and had started at the Art Academy. We've always been very close. Even after he met Chester, who became like a son to me too. We lost him last summer. And now Jonas is going to disappear too!"

Mona was sobbing uncontrollably now. Out of the corner of her eye Irene could see the waiter fluttering nervously over by the doorway. She tried to calm Mona down, and after a while she succeeded. Mona sniffled and dried away her tears. She gazed steadily at Irene and her voice was totally under control when she went on.

"They got AIDS. Who infected them or whether both of them had HIV when they met, we don't know. It doesn't matter. But Chester died six months ago and Jonas is dying. That's what I want you to see. You have to meet Jonas. So that you will never suspect that he had the least thing to do with his father's death!"

MONA INSISTED she was going to drive her Audi, but Irene was intractable. If she was going along to meet Jonas, she didn't want to ride with a driver who risked arrest for drunk driving. Mona gave in. She knew that Irene was right. They got into the car, which smelled like it was brand new. The odometer showed thirty-two hundred kilometers.

Irene sighed blissfully. "What a wonderful car!"

Mona sounded quite pleased when she said, "I picked it up last week. I don't allow smoking in this car! My old one was only three years old, but it stank like a tar factory. At home I only smoke out on the balcony."

"So where are we going? Where does Jonas live, I mean?"

"At his private hospital. We like to joke about it. 'Jonas Söder at Söder Hospital.'"

Mona fell silent and stared out at the evening darkness, which was not really dark. In a big city there is never any real darkness, just another sort of light. Artificial. It creates hard contrasts and deep, frightening shadows.

"God, how sick I am of Stockholm!" Mona said. "Why did I stay here? I long to go home to Norrland, to the soft twilight and the night. The silence."

"Härnösand isn't really all that rural. And it's cold as hell in Norrland."

"The outside temperature, yes. But not between people."

Irene didn't really follow the reasoning, but decided not to dwell on it. It was time she made some progress with respect to the purpose for her visit to Stockholm. Calmly she said, "Why is it so important that I meet Jonas?"

Mona took a deep breath before she answered. "You have to see how sick he is. He's getting large doses of morphine now. You can't tell him that Richard was murdered. I haven't told him. He hasn't heard any news or read a newspaper in several weeks. He's got enough to do with dying."

She started to sob again but then pulled herself together. "The reason it's important for you to come tonight is that the nursing staff working the swing shift is the same one that was working last Tuesday night." Mona had turned her head and was staring hard at Irene from the side. Slowly she said, "You have to ask them if I was there last Tuesday. Jonas has been there for almost three weeks and I've come every evening, right after work."

"What time?"

"Around six. I normally stay with him until about eleven. By then he's usually asleep."

"And you haven't missed a single evening or come late?"

"No."

Mona turned her head and stared with unseeing eyes straight into the headlights of the oncoming cars. "When you're convinced that what

I'm saying is the truth, I want to ask that Jonas and I be protected from the media. We have nothing to do with Richard's life or his death. We just want to be left in peace."

This last sentence contained enormous resignation and sorrow. But Irene felt that there was more that needed explaining.

"Is that the only reason?"

"No. You're not stupid. And neither are the other detectives working on the investigation. Jonas will inherit from his father. And when Jonas dies, I'll inherit from him. That's why it's important that you convince yourself of our innocence. You have to ask the nursing staff. There mustn't be any doubt. We need peace and quiet so he can die."

"But what if there's a will? Can Jonas really inherit then?"

"A child always has the right to his lawful share of the inheritance, which is half of the estate. And by law Jonas is counted as a stepchild. Stepchildren always have the right to demand their share of the inheritance when their parents die."

"Sounds like you've read up on the subject."

"Of course. I looked it up right away in *Everyday Jurisprudence* when I read in the papers that Richard was dead. This was bound to come up eventually, but I repressed it. Neither Jonas nor I need his money. In the eyes of the police, though, we must be suspects. I realized this when the papers started talking about murder. But we want nothing to do with his money. He has never shared in our lives, or we in his. Except for the generous support payments. He bought his way out. And for our part that was certainly the best thing that could have happened. We had no financial worries while I finished my studies. Or later, when Jonas was growing up. The salaries of social workers have never been huge, but thanks to Richard's support my school loans were modest. I paid them off long ago. And I got out of living with Richard. That was my best revenge against Sylvia. And I didn't have to lift a finger."

She gave a curt, joyless laugh. "I had no reason to kill Richard. Besides Jonas, he's the only man I ever loved, but he has been dead to me for thirty years. And I intend to donate Jonas's inheritance from Richard to Noah's Ark, the AIDS support organization."

For the rest of the way they sat in silence, each absorbed in her own thoughts.

ON THE way up in the elevator, Mona told Irene that Jonas was in a special ward for AIDS patients. There were eight beds. Jonas's condition had declined so drastically that he now had a private room.

Unsentimentally she said, "We had decided that he would be allowed to die at home on Fjällgatan. But it didn't work. Sometimes he's completely incontinent and can't hold his urine or excrement. We couldn't handle things at home. Both of us were thankful that he was allowed to come here. We thought that he'd only have to come in for a few days to be rehydrated a little. But he can no longer keep food or fluids down. He has to be on an IV all the time. That's not something I can take care of. Thank the good Lord that the national health-care system is still functioning!"

They went in through the glass doors to the ward. As they approached the door marked STAFF, Mona slowed, smiled wanly, and whispered, "He's in the first room on the left, just past the staff room."

Mona quickened her step and opened a door a few meters down the hall.

Irene could hear hard-rock music streaming out the door. She recognized the sound; the glam-rock band Kiss, playing "Heaven on Fire." She entered the staff room and found two nurses, dressed in blue scrubs. One of them was young and blond. When he stood up Irene saw that he was close to two meters tall. His female colleague was middle aged and plump. She said in a friendly voice, "Hello. Are you looking for someone?"

"Well, yes. I'm a friend of Mona Söder. We're visiting Jonas. Mona hasn't arrived yet, has she? Isn't she always here in the evenings?"

Good grief! Why was she lying? But she knew she wanted to help exclude Mona from the von Knecht case.

The nurse nodded and smiled. "Every evening. Why do you ask?"

Irene managed an apologetic and helpless smile. "I tried to call her Tuesday evening. Here. But no one answered Jonas's phone. I got the direct number from Mona. So that's why I thought maybe she wasn't here last Tuesday?. . ."

"Oh yes, she was here. We were working Tuesday night. Maybe she pulled out the jack if Jonas was sleeping."

"Yes, maybe that's what happened. I just wanted to mention that Jonas's phone might not be working right . . . But I suppose it's fine. Sorry to disturb you."

With an apologetic smile Irene backed out into the corridor. The nurses gave her a friendly nod, turned back to each other, and continued their interrupted conversation.

It was as easy as that. She was without doubt a natural-born liar. Once you start down that path, you might as well keep following it. She quickly slunk out through the glass doors and went over to a pay phone she had seen near the elevator. She fed in some coins and took out the crumpled note with the number of Swedish Data. Maybe there wouldn't be anyone at the switchboard on a Friday evening just before six o'clock?

"Swedish Data, good afternoon."

Irene sighed with relief before she spoke.

"Good evening, I'm looking for Personnel Director Mona Söder."

"She's gone for the day."

"Will she be in on Monday?"

"Just a moment . . . No, she has three weeks' vacation."

"Oh, that's too bad! I was looking for her on Tuesday, but didn't get hold of her. Was she off that day too?"

"Off? No, you must be mistaken. She was here all day on Tuesday. She hasn't had any time off all week. May I tell her who is calling?"

"Birgitta Andersson. I'll call her again in three weeks. It's not urgent. Have a nice weekend!"

SHE OPENED the door to Jonas's room. The volume of the music had been turned down. She recognized this artist and song too: Freddie Mercury, "Mr. Bad Guy." Impulsively she said to Jonas, "This isn't really one of his best songs. Or albums either, for that matter."

He seemed not to hear, but after a moment he opened his eyelids a bit. "No, this album was never a big hit," he replied weakly. He coughed violently, and his whole torso shook.

Irene had steeled herself for the sight of Jonas. She was afraid she would see a trembling skeleton, stinking of his own excrement, bald, and covered with pustules and sores. But he was a handsome man. Thin, but indisputably like the pictures she had seen of Richard von Knecht as a young man. His dark blond hair was cropped short. He had opened his eyes now, and she could see that they were a bright, intense blue, despite the spiderweb of morphine overlaying his consciousness. He fixed his gaze on her and the smile he gave her was amazingly alert.

"You must be Irene. Mamma told me about you."

A mild coughing fit interrupted him again. Irene took care to raise an inquisitive eyebrow at Mona. She shook her head. So she hadn't told him that Irene was a cop. What had she said? Mona picked up on her query and said in a natural tone of voice, "Yes, it was a good thing you came to work at Swedish Data. I wound up with both a skilled colleague and a good friend."

Another born liar, apparently. Wanting to signal reassurance, Irene replied, "I'm sorry to be late. But I checked with the staff. Evidently there was nothing wrong with the phone on Tuesday when I tried to call you here. You must have pulled out the jack while Jonas was asleep."

Mona looked extremely relieved. But her voice betrayed nothing when she answered, "Yes, I must have."

"It didn't matter anyway. We took care of things and found a temp."

Irene turned to Jonas as she spoke but he didn't seem in the least interested. He was looking up at the IV. The yellow fluid in the little bottle was almost gone. The big bag hanging next to it was filled with a clear liquid. There was a lot of text printed on it. Apparently it contained a great number of important and useful components. With a deft hand Mona turned off the drip from the little bottle by pulling out the red plastic wheel in the drip regulator. The tubes went down to a drip tap that was fastened by adhesive tape to Jonas's collarbone. Irene shuddered when she realized that the catheter went directly through the skin on his neck. The insertion point was covered with a thick compress.

Jonas looked at her again and asked, "Do you like Freddie Mercury?"

"Not so much as a solo artist. He was best when he was with Queen."

Jonas nodded. He gave Irene a mocking look. "We have a lot in common, Freddie and I. We're gay. On our death certificates posterity will be able to read the cause of our death. AIDS. And that we died too young."

He was seized by a powerful fit of coughing. When he again tried to fix his gaze on her, Irene saw that his eyes were glazing over. He had probably just received a dose of morphine, which was beginning to take effect. He breathed with difficulty and tried to speak carefully to avoid coughing.

"Mamma, help me with the oxygen," he managed to say.

The oxygen hose was hanging over the bedpost. Mona slipped it expertly and carefully over his head. It looked like a transparent halter. Mona placed a cannula with two tips under his nostrils. Without hesitation she turned on the regulator on the wall. The oxygen meter on the wall came to life as a faint rushing sound came from the hose.

Then Irene noticed the painting. Two big yellow butterflies with black markings on their wings hovered over a vast landscape, a shimmering stream in the valley and blue-tinged mountains in the distance. In the foreground there were beautiful meadow blossoms. The blue of the forget-me-nots was dominant, but there were also splashes of white and pink flowers that she recognized but couldn't name. They came so close to the observer that it felt as if she were lying on her stomach among the meadow flowers and peeking over the edge down into the long valley, up toward the two gaudy butterflies. The sky was not blue, but a silvery white circle above the mountains dispersed a strong light that became a warm pink at the outer edges. It was not the sun and not the moon. It was the Light.

"What do you see?"

Jonas's question made her jump.

"The painting . . . it's wonderful!"

She smiled at Jonas and her gaze was pulled down into his. Down there she saw the contrasting picture. Darkness, despair, dread, and loneliness. But also a great calm. The knowledge that everything is one. If he hadn't possessed the contrasting image, he never would have been able to depict the Light.

"It's me and Chester. The swallowtail butterflies. I painted it the week after he died. I finished it in twenty-four hours, but then I collapsed. It was blood poisoning," he said in a clear voice. He looked at her with eyes wide open. All haziness seemed to have vanished.

"The top butterfly is Chester. He's already in the tunnel of light. On the beach by the river of Life lies his congealed blood."

Only then did Irene notice that the beach had a pale pinkish brown tone. Closest to the waterline there was a sharper bloodred line. In the left corner the bloodred color was repeated until the flowers took over.

"In the left corner you see my blood. It's running out. Running out . . . of the picture." He coughed and breathed more heavily.

"The butterfly flying below is me. I'm still tied to the earth, which is symbolized by the flowers. But I'm on my way. Upward."

He was silent for a long time. Irene was fascinated by the painting. It was big, surely two square meters. Despite the fact that the interpretation he had given her should have made her sad, the picture prompted no feelings of sorrow whatsoever. On the contrary, she felt a joy of life and a sense of optimism flowing toward her.

"You have to understand, Irene, that I look forward to dying. Not because I want an end to my suffering, because I don't have much pain anymore. But I have no dignity left. I shit myself and have to use a catheter and diaper. I can't even jerk off. I feel anxious when I have shortness of breath and because I can't walk anymore. But I don't want to end it. Life is a gift. All the way to whatever you are given."

It was much too long a speech. The coughing fit that followed seemed as if it would never end. The shaking of his emaciated body made Irene felt powerless. Mona put her arm around his shoulders to support him.

She spoke softly and soothingly, as all mothers do when they comfort a sick child. Although this child was a grown man. Who was dying.

Jonas nodded off for a while. Mona and Irene looked at the other painting that was in the room. It hung on the wall facing Jonas's bed so that he could easily see it. It was a portrait of a dark-skinned man. In the background was a saxophone, music scores, and notes. There was a gold sheen over the entire picture, from the saxophone to a faint misty gold over the man's mouth and eyes. Irene turned to Mona and asked, "Who is the man in the picture?"

"Chester. Chester Johnson, jazz musician. He became my son-in-law in April. They were married at home, because Chester was too sick to go to the city hall. Jonas was going through a slightly better period just then. But since Chester passed away he just hasn't wanted to go on. Except when he painted the butterflies."

Jonas woke up and cleared his throat. He started talking again in a weak, slightly slurred voice.

"I'm curious. It's a journey we all have to make. But not alone. Just as in the painting, Chester will be with me. He's leading me and holding my hand if I get scared. He's been with me several times the past few days. But he did the right thing. It's better to die in the summertime. It's warmer and more beautiful, with all the flowers. People won't have to freeze their feet off at the cemetery the way they will at my funeral. Poor planning on my part. On the other hand, there might be a lot of snow and then it would be beautiful with the flowers against the snow. Although it will be cold in the grave."

His chest heaved violently, rattling ominously. He took a few deep breaths and closed his eyes. His strength was gone and soon he fell asleep. Mona signaled that they should go out into the corridor.

"It's almost seven o'clock. Can you catch the train back to Göteborg? Otherwise you're welcome to stay with me."

"Thanks, but I'll make it. The train goes at eight-thirty."

"Shall I drive you?"

"No thanks, I'll call a cab."

There was a brief silence between them. Simultaneously they both took a step toward each other and exchanged a quick and awkward hug. Embarrassed, they muttered "I'll be talking to you" and "Call if something happens." Irene hurried off to the elevator. A painful lump sat in her throat, and her eyes were blurred with tears.

NATURALLY SHE was there. Just as grayly correct as on the trip to Stockholm. She sat a few rows farther back, with the same binder on her knee. Irene had a quick vision of the gray woman spending her days sitting on X2000, traveling back and forth, back and forth, back and . . . Irene couldn't stop herself. Just before she sat down she flashed a movie-star smile at the Gray Lady. In return she received a wildly startled look, filled with naked terror. A look that revealed recognition that she was locked in an Intercity train with a total madwoman, with no possibility of getting off!

After fifteen minutes the detective inspector fell into a restless and dream-filled sleep. Somewhere in the dark the terror was approaching. Before her she saw Jenny and Katarina. Unfazed, they walked straight toward the threatening darkness. She tried to call out and warn them, but found herself completely mute. Since no sound came out when she screamed, she tried to run and catch them. But something was holding on to her feet. Behind the girls' backs, darkness closed in and soon hid them completely.

With sobs of fear pounding in her chest, she woke up with a start, only to find that she had gotten her right foot stuck between the seats in front of her.

Chapter Ten

AS SUPERINTENDENT ANDERSSON EMERGED from the commissioner's room he just caught a glimpse of Irene disappearing into the elevator, on her way to Central Station and Stockholm. He had a sudden impulse to call her back. It would have been nice to have a chance to go in her place. Bengt Bergström's order to "keep him continuously informed" was aggravating. No, a trip to Stockholm would have done him good. Speaking of doing him good . . . with a sigh he realized that Irene couldn't try on pants in his place. He would just have to stay where he was.

To cheer himself up a little he decided to go and visit Ivan Viktors. It's not every day you meet your idols on the job, so you should take advantage of the opportunity. He knocked on the door and was greeted by Jonny's annoyed voice.

"Now what is it? Can't you see I'm busy . . . Oh, pardon me! This is the superintendent." He addressed the latter remark to a man with silver-gray hair and a distinguished appearance. When he stood up to shake hands, he was almost a head taller than Andersson.

"Superintendent Sven Andersson, how do you do?"

"How do you do? Ivan Viktors."

His voice was deep and well modulated, naturally. His smile was warm and genuine. Andersson made an apologetic gesture.

"I was just passing by and thought I'd say hello."

Ivan Viktors leaned toward the superintendent and said in a low, conspiratorial voice, "Inspector Blom is about to narrow in on my mysterious activities."

Jonny's ears turned red, and he quickly read aloud from his notes: "'Took the afternoon train up to Stockholm last Sunday. Visited an older brother at the Caroline Hospital.' What's he in for?"

"Compound fracture of the femur and concussion. He was operated on a week ago. Old men shouldn't run across the street after the light turns red and think they can make it!"

Viktors tried to sound easy going, but Andersson heard an under-tone of anxiety. He quickly asked, "Is it serious?"

"Not anymore. He's recovering, thank you."

Jonny again looked down at his papers and went on reading aloud: "'Monday morning at nine o'clock V. met a pupil. They practiced until four P.M. Broke off only for lunch at noon.'"

"V? Is that me?" Ivan Viktors gave an effervescent laugh that to Andersson's ears sounded like a pitch perfect A major.

Jonny grew peevish and gave the opera singer a gritted-teeth look. "I always abbreviate names in my reports! The name of the pupil is Claes Winer. I've got his phone number and address and will call and check later."

Andersson nodded and saw Ivan Viktors watching Jonny with a smile. Nothing in the man's behavior seemed tense or uncertain. On the contrary, with his self-confident elegance he did not seem a bit per-turbed by the dreariness of police headquarters; he seemed to fit right in and feel at home, which he no doubt did everywhere. Andersson reminded himself that skilled opera singers are also good actors.

Viktors turned directly to Andersson. "That's how far Inspector Blom and I had gotten before you came in. On Tuesday morning I flew directly from Stockholm to Copenhagen. I had a delicious lunch with some old friends from the Royal Theater. They had contacted me regarding their production of Wagner's *Flying Dutchman*. The young man who's going to sing my old starring role is having problems find-ing his way in the songs, so to speak. And it *is* very difficult to sing. I can recall—"

"What hotel did you stay at?" The fact that Inspector Blom didn't give a damn about all the flying Dutchmen in the world was clear from his tone of voice.

"Hotel? Oh yes, the Admiral."

"And in Stockholm?"

For a split second Viktors lost his worldly self-assurance. But it passed so quickly that afterward Andersson wasn't sure if he had seen correctly.

"Stockholm? My brother's apartment, of course. He has a wonder-ful place on Strandvägen. The penthouse."

Jonny Blom fired off his questions in an angry staccato. "Does he live alone?"

"Yes. And no. He's divorced, but now is keeping company with a judge from Sunne district court. She commutes back and forth every week. My brother has a son from his marriage who has three charming little girls whom I call my grandchildren. Unfortunately my wife and I never had children. So I won't be having any grandchildren of my own."

The superintendent gave a start. He was all too familiar with that situation. Strangely enough it wasn't until recent years that he had felt any longing for children and grandchildren. But he did have his niece's children as surrogate grandkids. It was a good situation, since he only had to meet them three times a year at most. Maybe Ivan Viktors felt the same way.

Jonny looked really pissed off. At first Andersson couldn't figure out why. After a while he understood that it wasn't just Viktors's annoy-ing attitude, but also his own presence that was bothering Jonny. The superintendent admitted to himself that maybe the man had a point. Despite his blunt and insensitive manner, Jonny was actually very good at questioning people. Especially the tougher hoodlums. Right now the inspector was glowering at Ivan Viktors, while his brain was running at high speed. Finally he decided where to strike the next blow. Brusquely he said, "Were you alone in the apartment?"

Viktors was quite clearly shaken out of his complacency. His face turned red and he looked close to having a pulmonary hemorrhage. Quickly he pulled himself together and made a brave attempt to feign indignation.

"What do you mean? That must be obvious," he said superciliously.

Jonny sensed the presence of a lie. He had an idea and leaned across the desk. His voice was hard edged and insinuating when he said, "So it's not true that your brother's girlfriend was also staying overnight at the apartment?"

Boom! Andersson saw at once how Viktors regained his confidence. It had wavered for a second, but now he was obviously again on solid ground. With his best patronizing and theatrical tone of voice and look-ing deeply insulted, he said, "My good inspector! My brother is sixty-nine years old and his partner is sixty-three! She is a highly respected lawyer and serves as a judge. The reason she commutes is because she will be retiring in two years and likes living in Sunne so much that she doesn't want to leave her job there. Now she's working Monday through Thursday. She comes home late Thursday evening and drives back on Sunday night. No, you know what? We didn't see each other at all that night."

"Do you have a key to the apartment?"

Viktors took a deep breath. His look said, *What an idiot!*

"Naturally my brother gave me a key. He's still in the hospital; all you have to do is call and check. Please do, here's the number."

He pulled out his wallet from the breast pocket of his suit coat and took out a little yellow note, which he handed to Jonny Blom. Without thanking him or looking at the note, Jonny stared him straight in the eye.

"Was there anyone else at the apartment on Sunday night?"

"No. And if there were, I can't see what business it is of yours. You're investigating what happened to Richard, aren't you? Not what I was doing in Stockholm last Sunday night. And at that time Richard was alive and in the best of health. He died on Tuesday, after all. And I was in Copenhagen at the time."

Sulkily Jonny looked down at his papers. He felt that he had missed something, but didn't know if it was of any importance to the investigation. Andersson agreed with him, but also wasn't sure what it was that had passed through the room. Just a hunch. Jonny continued persistently, "What were you doing Tuesday night?"

Again a light sigh from Viktors. His gaze held a trace of pity. "At six-thirty I ate dinner at one of the best restaurants in Copenhagen, St. Gertrud's Cloister."

"Alone?"

"No. There were at least ten of us. All from the theater. I'd be happy to give you their names."

"Thank you, two would be sufficient."

Andersson felt that it was high time for him to break in for a while. If nothing else, it would give Jonny a chance to figure out what it was that had fluttered past them. Viktors wrote two names on the back of the yellow note with his brother's phone number on it. Andersson cleared his throat softly before he said, "Going a little farther back in time, what did you think of the von Knechts' party last Saturday?"

Surprised, Viktors looked up from the note he was writing. He looked like he was thinking it over.

"Well . . . what can I say? As a matter of principle I don't believe that people should wage war. The Thirty Years' War, you know. Ha ha. It was fun to see old friends. I hadn't seen Gustav and Louise in at least ten years."

"Was the mood good?"

"It certainly was! Top-notch, as they say. Excellent food and drink. Although the young people seemed a little subdued."

"The young people? Do you mean Henrik and Charlotte?"

"Yes."

"But Richard and the rest were the same as usual?"

"Yes. Richard, Valle Reuter, and Peder Wahl sat and talked about wine for half the evening. They reminded me of druids, sitting and trumping each other with exciting decoctions. 'Taste this one, my good man! You'll be in seventh heaven!' And then we sang a bunch of wine-drinking songs."

"You're not a wine connoisseur?"

"Ha! Next you'll be writing down in the minutes of the interview, 'V. not a wine connoisseur'! No, not like those other three. For them it's almost a sport. Actually borders on religion. What country, what valley did the grapes grow in? What type of grape? What vintage? I've never had time for that. Sven Tosse and I like to joke about it and say that at least we can tell the difference between a forty-five-krona wine and a two-hundred-krona wine. Then Valle cringes so hard he starts shaking. 'Fie on you two! That's blasphemy!' he says."

His imitation of the fat little Valle Reuter was extraordinarily skillful. Andersson caught himself laughing out loud. Jonny looked even grumpier, if possible, and said sourly, "There's nothing more you have to say about the murder of Richard von Knecht?"

Both Viktors and Andersson were stopped short in their merriment. Viktors gave Jonny a chilly look.

"No," he said curtly.

"Will you be home in Särö in case we need to contact you again?"

"Up until Sunday evening. Then I have to go to Copenhagen again. I'll be back next Wednesday."

Andersson thought that Viktors was pleasant, but he realized that he had let himself be entranced by the man's charm. There was something there, but it slipped away like quicksilver as soon as he tried to get a grip on it. Ivan Viktors headed for the door, turned around, and made a deep bow.

"Good-bye, gentlemen!"

"Good-bye."

Andersson tried to ingratiate himself with Viktors as the stately man vanished out the door. When he had closed the door, Andersson turned to Jonny and said, "You noticed it too, didn't you?"

"Yes. That devil weaseled out of it. What kind of hanky-panky was he up to on Sunday night?"

"Maybe it's like he said, of no importance to the case. But it doesn't seem that way. Maybe he was with some hooker."

"Quite possible."

Suddenly Andersson froze and his eyes took on a glassy, faraway stare. Jonny sat quietly. He knew that when the chief looked like that, he was getting an idea. Anyone who didn't know this might think he was about to have an epileptic fit. Excitedly Andersson said, "Maybe he met Sylvia von Knecht! She was in Stockholm last Sunday night!"

"But not alone. Her mother and sister were with her. They were at the theater," Jonny reminded them.

"Yes, that's what she said. Check that out with the sister and mother. Ask them what they did in Stockholm on Sunday evening. It's a shot in the dark, but they've paid off before."

Jonny's resigned sigh revealed what he thought about the possibility. But since he didn't have any better idea, he started searching for the addresses on his computer.

"When are you supposed to relieve Borg at the parking garage?" Andersson asked.

"Twelve-thirty. He'll take an hour for lunch, then come back and take over until four. Then I'll go over there again, and both of us will stay until seven."

"Okay. If anything comes up, call me on my direct line. Tomorrow I'll be here. Eight o'clock Monday morning we'll have a big meeting to go over everything. Hopefully by then we'll know more about the fire on Berzeliigatan. And where Shorty fits into the picture. Maybe he didn't have anything to do with it. Although if there's mischief going on in Shorty's turf, he's probably mixed up in it!"

"That's not really his thing, though. Drug abuse, firearms, bank robbery, yes. Arson homicide, hit men, bombs—I doubt it. It takes planning and intelligence, and that's not typical for Shorty," Jonny offered.

The superintendent pouted a little and screwed up his eyebrows, but it was no use. He had to agree with Jonny. Irritated, he exclaimed, "There's some shit in here stinking up the place! I know the smell, but I can't find the source. And I don't know who's responsible. But someone's walking around with shit on his shoes, that's for sure!"

Amazingly poetic for Andersson. Jonny knew what he meant and agreed. He'd been a cop long enough to recognize something unpleasant when it popped up. This whole case was unpleasant. Like the superintendent said—it stank.

EXACTLY FORTY-EIGHT hours earlier Andersson had walked through the doors to Pathology, just as he was doing now. Yvonne

Stridner didn't know he was coming in person this time either. She expected him simply to call her. But the pale sunshine had prompted an impulse to get outside for a while. It seems reasonable to ask why someone who longs for a little sunshine gets into a car and drives through downtown Göteborg breathing nothing but exhaust. But he knew the answer. He wanted to get out of the four walls of police headquarters. Sometimes they stifled him. Not that the walls at Pathology were any less stifling, but they would do as a change of scene.

Stridner wasn't in her office. No matter how much he hated the idea, he was going to have to go into the autopsy room. With a gurgling feeling of discomfort in his stomach region, he was already regretting his little outing.

She stood dressed in a green paper smock and something that looked like a shower cap of the same material, talking to a young man who was also dressed in scrubs. Slowly she pulled off her rubber gloves as she coldly observed the graduate student.

"If you don't finish up the course on forensic medicine I don't comprehend how your previous autopsies could be approved. You're a typical slacker. Others have to do the job, while you stand next to them and 'assist.' That means handing them instruments and looking the other way. Leaving the room when it starts getting disgusting. Don't you understand that pathology is the basis of all medicine? If you don't know what it looks like both inside and outside a person who's been struck by a particular illness or trauma, you'll never be able to figure out what's happening! What stage is the illness in? How is it developing? What's happening to the patient? And if the patient is dead, what happened, and why did it happen? If this doesn't interest you, I think you ought to seriously consider whether you're at all suited for the medical profession! I'm flunking you!"

The young man hadn't said a word during the dressing-down. Without a word he turned on his heel and rushed out. He apparently didn't notice the superintendent, who saw the expression in the student's eyes. An experienced detective can read murder in someone's eyes when he sees it.

Stridner noticed Andersson and nodded curtly. She gave him a stern look, and the superintendent had the strong feeling that he had also flunked.

"The standards for graduates are getting worse and worse. They're slackers. They think all they have to do is read a few pages in a textbook to make it! No desire whatsoever to do a little extra," fumed the professor.

She snorted audibly and fixed Andersson with her gaze. The feeling that The Last Judgment was approaching grew stronger.

"And you police officers! Can't even tell the difference between girls and boys."

Astonished, he stared at the angry redheaded pathologist. Lamely he stammered, "That . . . that's something we can usually handle."

"Not this time."

With determined steps she strode across the room to an autopsy table. His stomach turned over when he realized what she was about to do. She whipped off the sheet. The body was severely charred. Arms and legs were bent in the typical defensive position since the intense heat had contracted the musculature. A faint smell of roasted meat penetrated the other odors in the autopsy room.

"Late yesterday afternoon this body was brought in. Your guys told our duty officer that it was the body of a young man, just over twenty years old," Stridner said.

"Yes, that's right. Mattias Karlsson—"

"Wrong! The body I just finished the postmortem on this morning belongs to a middle-aged woman. Apparently thirty-five to forty-five years old. Height about one-point-five-five meters. Weight is hard to determine, but she was stocky. Bad teeth. She has had a child. European."

The superintendent stared at the charred corpse. For a moment he felt dizzy, but it quickly passed.

"Finnish," he managed to say.

Andersson heard his voice croaking. Stridner gave him a sharp look and snapped, "Finnish? That's possible. Are you missing someone Finnish?"

"You can say that again! Pirjo Larsson, thirty-two years old. The description matches so far. She was von Knecht's cleaning woman. What the hell is she doing here?"

"Well, she didn't come here herself. You should be asking what she was doing there!"

There was no answer to that. He glared, but he had to agree with her. What was Pirjo doing in von Knecht's office when the bomb went off?

She pulled up the sheet and said, "I'm going to wash up. You can wait in my office."

He obediently slouched off.

"FINISHING UP Richard first, I can say that the identification is quite clear. The forensic odontologists didn't doubt it for a second. The teeth matched perfectly. I've also checked the fracture of the right tibia. I managed to dig up thirty-five-year-old X rays taken after a skiing accident in St. Anton. Uncomplicated healing."

She waved some large X rays in the air. Andersson had a hard time trying to look interested when his thoughts were hovering around another body. How was he going to get hold of Hannu? He'd have to borrow a phone.

"Excuse me. May I borrow your phone? I have two inspectors running all over town looking for the woman lying under the sheet out there."

She nodded and gestured to the phone on her desk. Andersson got hold of a secretary who promised to track down Hannu Rauhala and Birgitta Moberg. She would call them back to headquarters at once for an urgent meeting with him.

Now he could pay better attention to Stridner's continuing report. It had been proven beyond all doubt that it really was von Knecht who was crushed on the sidewalk on Tuesday evening. Seventy-two hours ago. Since then, he felt like he had aged three years.

Stridner's pedagogical voice snapped him out of his reverie. "There were no other signs of violence other than the contusion on the back of his neck and the cut across the back of his hand. Other injuries resulted from the height of the fall. Oh, that's right—I did do one slightly unnecessary thing. Just to satisfy my curiosity. Today I got preliminary results on the PAD I requested. There is a clear fat buildup in the liver. Our good Richard had apparently been drinking quite a bit lately."

"Does that surprise you?"

"Yes. He was always careful of his appearance and stayed in good shape. He was precise about how much food and drink he consumed. I never saw or heard that he was highly intoxicated at any party during the years we knew each other. But of course, that was fifteen years ago."

"What does that indicate?"

She sucked in her lower lip and seemed to ponder this a long time before she replied. "Hard to say. Most commonly people take to the bottle when they have problems they can't solve. Especially men."

Andersson guiltily thought of the strong beer he drank every evening, but decided quickly that he wasn't an alcoholic. At his age it was good to relax in the evening with a beer or two. Or three. And it helped him sleep well. Although it did have some side effects. Unconsciously, he tried to suck in his stomach. Glumly, he looked at the pathologist and summarized the situation.

"So we have a healthy sixty-year-old man fresh out of the sauna. Physically in good shape, but with recent signs of increased alcohol intake. Blood alcohol content one-point-one. In his stomach a good lunch is being digested. At five-thirty one rainy and blustery November evening he goes out on his balcony, despite his great fear of heights. There he is struck on the back of the head, cut on the hand, and shoved over the balcony railing. And not a trace of the murderer! And you found nothing else on his body?"

The last sounded like a reproach. And it was. She shook her head, but stopped and cocked it to one side. She had a mischievous gleam in her eye.

"Well, maybe. The little charmer didn't have so bad a cold that he wasn't able to have sex the day before he died. It's not a hundred percent certain, but I'm actually quite convinced that he did have it. Intercourse, that is."

"The day before? Tell me about it!"

"On the tip of his penis, on the glans itself, I found a shallow cut four millimeters long. I've seen such things before. They occur during intercourse when the man gets a hair caught in between. The interesting thing is that the wound was no more than a day old. Of course a man can get a hair inside his foreskin without having sex, but that usually doesn't cause injury. He would notice the hair before that happened. But during high arousal he usually doesn't, as we know."

Andersson nodded and said meditatively, "So on Monday or Tuesday he got laid in the marital bed. But not with his wife, since Sylvia was in Stockholm. Someone else. Who could it have been?"

"Now we're talking about your job again, not mine," said Stridner.

She smiled wanly and seemed pleased at the effect her discovery had on him. Possibly the flushed coloration of his face indicated that his blood pressure was getting a little too high.

"Are you taking medication for your hypertension?" she asked.

"My hyper . . . What the hell does that have to do with von Knecht and Pirjo Larsson?"

When he realized what he had done, his blood ran cold. He had yelled at pathology professor Yvonne Stridner! That wasn't good.

Her voice was low and absolutely ice cold when she replied, "Nothing. Except that you could have a cerebral hemorrhage and never solve Richard's murder or find out what happened to the Finn. Was her name Pirjo?"

"Yes. Pirjo Larsson. Please forgive me for yelling. There's a lot going on right now."

"All the more reason to check your blood pressure and tend to your medication. That's all the time I have for you right now."

She turned on her computer screen and started to type, without looking at him.

Disgraced! He always felt stupid and disgraced when he was with Stridner. Everything was on her terms. He was like one of the poor graduate students. They had his full sympathy.

"Thanks a lot. See you later," he said lamely.

Without looking up from her screen she muttered, "'Bye."

So busy with her important work. He felt anger rising up inside him as he walked toward the exit. His temples were pounding, and he guiltily recalled that he hadn't taken his blood pressure pill this morning. Maybe he should go to the health service and get his pressure checked. Still, it was a little late for that. Whew, who has time for this? That silly doctor. What did she know about blood pressure? Look at the state of the patients who came in contact with her. In their case there was no longer any blood pressure to talk about!

Invigorated by telling off Stridner in his mind, he got into his car and drove back to headquarters. It was lunchtime but he wasn't at all hungry. The smell of grilled meat was still lingering in his nostrils.

BIRGITTA MOBERG was in her office. She was surprised when she heard that Andersson had been looking for her. That's not why she had returned to headquarters; she was there to eat lunch before her meeting with Bobo Torsson. Should they go to the cafeteria together? No, not a good idea.

He motioned to her to come into his office. Without interrupting even once, she listened attentively to his account of what had happened at Pathology. He left out the discussion about his blood pressure since that was no one else's concern.

Her brown eyes, usually so lively, now looked sad. "It sounds like it actually is Pirjo. Her poor kids, left all alone," she said.

"What about their stepfather, Larsson?"

"Hannu got hold of him on the phone this morning. Göte Larsson, forty-seven years old. He's moved down to Malmö. Evidently he lives with a Polish woman in Rosengård. He's working on a Polish freighter right now. Claims that he hasn't set foot in Göteborg in two years."

"Hmm. Welfare will have to look for her relatives in Finland. No, you go on and eat, I'll wait for Hannu. At one o'clock I'll be busy for a while, but we'll meet here at two-thirty."

"Okay. I'll try to figure out who von Knecht's sex partner might have been. Valle Reuter's little girlfriend Gunnel denied all knowledge of Richard. And I believe her. She was as open as you could want about her gentlemen. No, it has to be someone else. Maybe he got himself a call girl. Too bad he took a sauna and shower."

With a wave she vanished down the hall toward the lunchroom. Andersson sat there a long time staring thoughtfully into space. Not one usable idea occurred to him. He kept on seeing the image of Pirjo's charred body. In his ear Stridner's voice rang, *You should be asking what she was doing there!*

HE PUT a note on Hannu's desk. The last line read, "Urgent & important info re Pirjo L.," to underscore the importance of talking to each other.

He returned to his office after a tiresome and sweaty fitting for the uniform pants. Hannu was sitting with a notebook on his lap, looking out his dirt-streaked window. Were the pale, sparse sun breaks also tempting him to go out into the city? His ice-blue eyes revealed nothing of his longing or any other feelings when they turned toward Andersson. They were calm and alert.

Hannu also listened without interrupting. He just nodded a few times. Clearly the pieces fit together for him. The superintendent envied him. He himself thought that everything seemed like one big mess. If only he could get hold of the right string and start to unravel the tangle. But in the present situation they had to sniff around for a while longer and dig where they smelled the most shit. Routine police work, in other words.

The superintendent asked, "What have you found out about Pirjo besides what we already know? Birgitta told me that Pirjo's old man is in Malmö now, so we can skip him for the time being. What we need is something that can explain where she fits into the picture when it comes to the bomb on Berzeliigatan."

"I found her in our records. She's been up twice for shoplifting. Suspended sentence each time. The first time she took some ski overalls at Obs department store, the second time Falun sausage and a box of macaroni at ICA on Angered Square," Hannu reported.

"Nothing else?"

"No."

"She doesn't sound like a terrorist bomber. Interesting that she has a rap sheet; it means she had some criminal inclination, at least. Have you asked our colleagues in Helsinki whether they have anything on her in their records?"

"I have. They'll get back to me this afternoon."

"One of your pals in the Helsinki police force?"

Andersson could have bitten off his tongue. But at the same time he was so damned curious about this reticent man. Why? Because he was an old snoop, he chastised himself. Still, the question had been asked. And would get the answer it deserved.

"Yep."

Calmly Hannu turned to a page in his notebook. Without looking up he began to summarize, "On Monday Pirjo and Marjatta cleaned von Knecht's apartment. During the night Juha and Timo took sick; they got the flu. Pirjo cleaned the Press Bureau office on Tuesday afternoon. Wednesday morning Pirjo took the bus to the von Knechts' but had to return home. She told the kids that von Knecht was dead. In the afternoon she cooked dinner. Just after five she told her daughter that she 'had to go out and do some extra cleaning.' Then she disappeared in a cloud of smoke. Literally."

Andersson felt a slight shiver at the back of his neck. He nodded to conceal it and said, "What was she doing at Berzeliigatan?"

The icy blue eyes regarded him for an instant before the answer came. "Cleaning."

Their eyes met. Both shook their heads simultaneously. His voice heavy and emphatic, as if he were afraid that the meager little idea he had come up with would slip his mind if he dressed it in precise words, Andersson said, "No. She knew that von Knecht was dead. She had two sick kids at home. It was almost six-thirty when the building blew up. No, she didn't go there to clean, but to steal."

"Right."

It was silent again. Both saw the problem. It was Hannu who voiced it. "The key."

"According to Irene, Sylvia von Knecht said that all the keys she knew of were in place at the apartment on Molinsgatan."

"That she knew of," echoed Rauhala.

When he heard his own words repeated, Andersson also understood the solution. Excitedly he said, "There must have been a set of keys that Sylvia didn't know about! But how did Pirjo get hold of them?"

"Stole them. Or was given them."

"Stole them?"

"When she cleaned von Knecht's place on Monday. He might have left them out."

"Maybe. But was given them?"

"Because she was supposed to clean the office."

The superintendent understood. Sylvia had told Irene that whenever Richard wanted to have his office cleaned, he would ask Pirjo to come over. He nodded.

"You've got a point there. Then he must have given Pirjo the 'secret' set of keys. That explains why she had a key and also why Sylvia didn't miss it. You don't miss something you don't know about. I think we've come up with something!"

He was almost going to slap Hannu on the back, but at the last moment he thought better of it. He managed to mask the sweeping gesture of his right arm by stroking his bald pate and running his fingers through the sparse fringe of hair.

"*Ahem*, yes. We'll have to ask Tommy and Fredrik what turned up today in the arson investigation. We have to establish that it's really Pirjo lying there in Pathology. Can you talk to her daughter and find out what dentist Pirjo went to? If she went to one, that is."

He remembered what Stridner had said about the victim's poor teeth. Hannu gave the superintendent a somber look.

"I'm not saying anything to the kids until we know for sure it's Pirjo."

"No, it's probably a good idea to wait until we're sure," Andersson agreed. But inside he was convinced that Pirjo had been found.

"So it wasn't her on Tuesday."

"What on Tuesday?"

Hannu gave him a patient look. "It wasn't Pirjo who cleaned von Knecht's place on Tuesday while he was having lunch. It must have been the killer. Pirjo was cleaning the Press Bureau."

Andersson suddenly realized that he was staring at the man across from him. His respect for the weather-beaten man with the icy eyes and the pale blond hair rose another notch. With a slight feeling of shame he recalled how close he had come to accusing him of being the leak to the evening paper. He quickly pushed these thoughts aside and said, "Have you checked that she wasn't anywhere else, that the Press Bureau was the only place she cleaned on Tuesday afternoon?"

"I have."

The superintendent fell into thought for a while. The situation had changed in an instant when they found Pirjo's body at the fire site.

"You have to keep looking around for facts about Pirjo. Above all we need somebody who can question the children. Will you have a chance to do it tomorrow? We have to follow this lead while it's hot," Andersson concluded.

His choice of words was unfortunate. The smell of burned meat was still in his nose. He knew that it was his imagination, but also knew that lunch would have to wait for a while longer.

Hannu closed his notebook with a brief nod. "Right."

AROUND THREE Andersson began to get hungry and went down to the lunchroom. He bought coffee, two dried-up open-faced cheese sandwiches in plastic, and a marzipan tart. It was an uninspired choice, but it filled his stomach. With the steaming cup of coffee in front of him on the table, he leaned back and tried to relax for a while. Plainclothes and uniformed colleagues filed past his table. Some just greeted him; others stopped and exchanged a few words. Most simply walked on by. Suddenly he became aware that someone had stopped behind him. When he turned his head he saw Birgitta Moberg.

"Hi, have a seat," he said.

"No thanks. I'm too damned mad to sit down!"

Now he noticed that she was standing with her arms akimbo and her legs rigid and planted wide apart. Her voice was like a viper's hiss. Even though according to his ex-wife he was about as sensitive as a sawhorse when it came to women's feelings, he could see that she was furious. Some colleagues at nearby tables stared at them in astonishment. Andersson thought it very unpleasant. Imagine if they thought she was mad at him. She wasn't, was she? Uncertainly he asked, "Do you think we should go up to the department and talk?"

"Yes."

She spun around on her heel and strode out the door. With a disappointed sigh the superintendent had to abandon his coffee. *It's important to listen to the personnel when they bring you their problems* was something that had been clearly emphasized in that idiotic course he had been forced to take a few years earlier.

"THAT ARROGANT bastard! What a . . . prick!"

"Who, me?"

"No! Bobo Torsson!"

The superintendent's first reaction was relief, the second surprise. Cautiously he asked, "Did he annoy you in some way?"

She exploded completely. With tears gushing from her eyes, she screamed, "Annoy! He shoved me up against the wall, grabbed my crotch, and bit me on the breast! I think I'm going to report him!"

Andersson was totally speechless. It didn't help matters when Jonny's irritating voice was heard from the doorway. "So, little Birgitta has been discovered by the big-time fashion photographer! You probably showed him what you had to offer, eh?"

He stood nonchalantly leaning against the doorjamb with a smug grin on his face. Andersson had time to think: *That guy has a God damn big mouth.*

Then the second explosion came. Half choking with rage, Birgitta snarled, "This is what I had to offer!"

Birgitta shot across the room like an arrow. Jonny reacted too slowly and never saw her knee as she drove it into his crotch. With a muffled moan he collapsed with both hands pressed between his legs. Birgitta said triumphantly, "Personal best! Two guys with blue balls in less than half an hour!"

With her back straight and head held high she climbed over Jonny's collapsed form and marched out to the corridor. Then Andersson woke up.

"Birgitta! You're not going anywhere! What the fuck are you playing at? Fighting like little kids! Two police officers!"

Slowly she turned, her face blotched with tears. It was hard to hear what she said, since her voice was quavering so much with emotion. "You don't understand. I have never in my life been assaulted that way! Maybe as a woman, but never as a professional!"

Andersson's head started pounding. Jonny was still moaning on the floor but had begun to pull himself up to a sitting position, using the doorjamb as a brace. Some colleagues from General Investigations stopped outside in the corridor, curious. Andersson took a couple of steps across the room and slammed the door with a *bang*.

"Now sit down! Both of you! This can go to Internal Affairs if you're not careful!"

Jonny hissed, "That's fine, I'm going to report her. God damn whore!"

Andersson saw Birgitta turn pale as wax. For a moment he thought she was going to faint. When she spoke again her lips barely moved. "I've had enough. That was the last straw!"

She directed her gaze toward Andersson. Usually her brown eyes gleamed and laughed, but now they were like molten lead.

"Ever since I started here I've been forced to take it from that idiot. First he tried to grope me, but when I quite clearly explained what I thought of such behavior, the taunting started. That I've got 'round heels.' An easy lay. You heard it yourself just now: *'God damn whore.'* I have to put up with 'playful' slaps on my butt. I got an interdepartmental envelope that's full of pictures of huge balls and lesbian couples cut out of porno magazines. I've always known that Jonny was behind it, but couldn't prove it," she said tonelessly.

"Why didn't you say anything to me?" Andersson asked in astonishment.

She gave him a weary, crooked smile. "And what would you have done?"

"Well, I . . ."

He fell silent, confused. What would he have done? Irritation rose again inside him. There were always problems when women were involved! It was better at the beginning of his career—in the days when female officers only did paperwork and office jobs, and there hadn't been very many of them. Back then there were only guys out in the field, which was practical. You didn't have to take into account female oversensitivity when it came to dirty jokes and taunts. No, having women on the force was hard. The worst thing was that there were more and more of them. If they chose a male profession, then they had to accept the conditions and the lingo! Although clippings from porno magazines was probably an extreme case . . .

She was still standing with a lifeless expression on her face, waiting for his answer. Andersson had an unpleasant feeling of complicity, but in what? Birgitta gave him the answer.

"Sexual harassment. That's what it is. Finally you just get fed up with it. It's a given that you have to take it from your colleagues. But I'll be damned if I'm going to take it from trash like Torsson!"

Suddenly the superintendent felt old and tired. This was beyond his capacity to handle. Jonny was on his feet over by the door, and the look he gave Birgitta blazed with fury.

With a pounding headache Andersson got up and put out another chair by the desk. For safety's sake he set the two visitors' chairs at either end of his desk. With a weary gesture he signaled for the two combatants to sit down. Reluctantly they sat down across from each other. Neither looked at the other.

Andersson said severely, "We can't have stuff like this going on in the department. Okay?"

Neither of them replied. He continued resolutely, "Jonny, you have to stop at once with all the stupid jokes and clippings. And you, Birgitta, have to be careful about attacking people. Even if it's only men. Imagine if Bobo Torsson reports you for police brutality! One more incident like this and I'll see to it that you're transferred to the stockroom. And that goes for you too, Jonny!"

It wasn't good, but it was the best he could come up with. He needed more coffee. And a headache tablet. There was a roll of antacids in the desk drawer. But he had to clear this up first. Wearily he turned to Jonny.

"What was it you wanted when you came in here?"

First Jonny looked as if he didn't intend to answer, and sat sulking. But discipline prevailed, and he said with restrained rage, "I've been in contact with Sylvia von Knecht's mother and sister. They corroborate Sylvia's alibi. They went to the theater, and afterward they had a late supper. So she wasn't the one that Viktor spent his Sunday evening with. And now I think I'll drive over to the parking garage on Kapellgatan. And I never sent any porno clippings in an interdepartmental envelope to Birgitta!"

With great effort he gathered up his remaining dignity and tried not to limp as he went out the door.

The air went out of Birgitta again, and she rested her head heavily in her hands. Andersson worried that she was going to start crying again; he had always found it unpleasant when women cried. A bit too quickly he said, "I'm going to get us a couple of coffees from the vending machine. Then you can report on what happened with that scumbag Torsson. After we drink our coffee."

He added the last remark hastily when he thought her shoulders were beginning to shake again.

"HE ARRIVED at three o'clock. Tall, thin, and tan from a tanning salon. Bleached blond streaks in his hair. Armani sport coat and worn blue jeans. According to his Social Security record he's thirty-seven years old, but he works hard at looking ten years younger. When he was shown into my office he sailed in with the words, 'I'll admit everything if you not only interrogate me but seduce me too!' And then he started laughing like a madman. He stank of stale booze but he's on something else. A tentative guess is amphetamines. Maybe cocaine.

He rubbed his index finger under his nose several times as he sat and babbled. He could have snorted some snow before he came to see me. He was exhilarated and restless at the same time. Couldn't sit still on his chair, kept jumping up and down. Toward the end of the conversation, after about half an hour, he started to sweat profusely. Then I asked him if he was feeling bad. That's when . . . he jumped on me. 'I'll show you how bad I feel!' he yelled, and when I got up he pulled me close and lifted me up against the wall. And grabbed me between my legs and . . . bit me on my right breast."

Birgitta broke off and was fighting hard not to start crying again. Andersson looked very worried when he leaned over the desk. In a sympathetic voice he asked, "Was it a hard bite? Did it leave marks?"

She gave a sob and nodded.

"Good! I mean, it wasn't good that he bit you. But if there are marks we'll have to see about getting them photographed. And a doctor will have to examine you and sign a statement. Go on."

"At first he didn't seem to notice the pain when I kneed him in the groin. I had to press my fingers into his eyes to get him to let go. He started to laugh like a crazy person again. Then he collapsed with his hand in his crotch. For a long time he didn't make a sound. I was ready for another attack, but the air had gone out of him. Finally he got up and whispered, 'I'm going to mark you. I know your name. Even your own mother won't recognize you!' And then he disappeared out the door. Good Lord! I sat there shaking like an aspen leaf in my chair. Then I got mad. Maybe I was mostly afraid, but it turned to rage. That's when I knew that I had to talk to somebody. Well, I found you in the lunchroom and you know the rest."

Andersson nodded and thought for a moment. He called the secretary and asked her to make an emergency appointment with the doctor for Birgitta. He emphasized in particular the importance of photo documentation.

When that was taken care of, he turned again to his inspector. She seemed to have recovered her spirits. She even gave him a wan smile.

To encourage her he said, "I'm sure we have time to go over what Torsson told you. First of all, where does he live?"

"You won't believe it. He told me he was living with his cousin. Right across from the building that burned down on Berzeliigatan. His cousin is the owner of a small tobacco shop."

"Lasse 'Shorty' Johannesson! Is this a joke or what?"

"No. Bobo Torsson and Shorty are actually cousins. Their mothers are sisters. Unfortunately it wasn't until the end that this came up. I didn't have time to dig any go deeper, because that was just before he . . . flipped out."

Andersson didn't care anymore that Birgitta was in the room. He excused himself, pulled out his desk drawer, and took out the tube of antacids. He stepped out in the corridor and went into the men's room. There he took a plastic cup from the vending machine and dissolved two tablets. While he waited for them to stop fizzing, he caught sight of his face in the mirror.

Old. For the first time in his life he thought he looked old. Ancient. Ready to die. No, not yet. But well on the way. Florid, hair thin, with his eyes embedded in wrinkles and folds. You could sum him up in three words: *bald, fat, ugly.* It was no use to have the blues about the inexorable passage of time. He was mostly to blame. Physical training had never interested him. A little gardening and fishing now and then was what he called enough exercise. He gulped down the contents of the plastic cup and cast another self-critical glance in the mirror. Unfortunately, antacids are no youth elixir. He looked just as old and tired as before. Was it the conversation with Birgitta that had triggered this paranoia about his age? That sweet, lively girl, who was so attractive that men couldn't contain themselves but bit her on the breast and sent her pornographic clippings. He slowed his steps and thought about how she must feel right now. Distressed, violated, and furious. Afraid. There was a real reason for fear if Shorty was in the picture. The pounding in his temples hadn't let up yet; it was too soon after taking the medicine. The minute he thought about Torsson and Shorty, von Knecht and Pirjo, the roaring that started in the convolutions of his brain made his headache worse.

Birgitta was sitting just as he had left her. All energy seemed to have gone out of her, and she looked tired. Tonelessly she continued where she had left off. "Torsson went up to Stockholm last Friday night. He took the train, says he's a little afraid of flying. He spent the weekend with two 'old buddies,' both photographers. I have their names and addresses. These three are supposed to do a big job together. A catalog of next year's fall and winter fashions. This is apparently supposed to start in January. They were meeting to plan their strategy. From what I understood of his babble, they drank like pigs the whole weekend. He rattled off a bunch of pub names where they spent their evenings and nights. Café Opera, Gino, and other places like that. And then that repulsive laugh."

"You're positive? He was obviously on narcotics?"

"No doubt about it! High as a kite. The strange thing is that he didn't stay with either of his buddies, but at the Hotel Lydmar the whole time. According to him it's a jazz club and the coolest hotel in Stockholm. I assume he was making this up, because a jazz club can't really be a hotel at the same time, can it?"

"In Stockholm anything is possible."

"Could be. I'll look into it. Evidently he had barely checked in to his hotel room when he and the other guys went on a bender all weekend. With no sleep. That's why I'm starting to lean toward amphetamines."

"Sounds quite probable."

"During the week they apparently tried to work, and according to Torsson they got some fantastic 'visions' of the job's setup. A biennale, he said! Isn't that some sort of big art exhibition that's held every other year? At any rate, the partying eventually took its toll. On Wednesday evening they ate dinner somewhere, but after that Torsson felt the need to go back to the hotel and sleep. He bought a big bottle of beer, took it up to his room, and sat down in front of the TV to unwind. He watched his home and photo studio burn down on the late news. First he called up Shorty on his cell phone. Apparently Shorty was the one who told Torsson to contact us, because he didn't know what had happened either. That's when I started to ask about his dealings with Shorty and found out that that's where he's been living. And that they're cousins. And after that . . . that was when he jumped on me."

The intercom beeped shrilly. The secretary informed them that Birgitta had to be at the doctor's as soon as possible.

"Okay. Take off now. Go straight home afterward and get a good rest. We'll try to find Bobo Torsson and arrest him for assault on a civil servant," said Andersson soothingly.

He stood up from his chair and went over to her. He almost patted her reassuringly on the shoulder, but her rigid neck and stiff back made him reconsider. Uncertainly he continued, "That stuff with Jonny, we can forget that for now. I'll talk to him. He probably doesn't mean any harm with his jokes. And I'm sure he understands that you were upset and angry after what happened with Torsson—"

He cut himself off when she turned to look at him. Her face was completely blank and expressionless. Her eyes were again pools of molten lead. Her voice sounded hoarse and quavering when she said, "You still don't get it."

Stiffly and mechanically she got up. Without looking at him she vanished down the corridor. He didn't understand this female nonsense! That thing with Jonny, anyway. He could understand that she would be mad and scared when Bobo Torsson attacked her. On the other hand, he had no idea what else he was supposed to understand.

What a day. And it wasn't over yet. The only positive thing was that his headache was starting to ease.

Chapter Eleven

THE SOBS WERE SEARING her throat. She tried to call but Jenny and Katarina couldn't hear her. Their liquid laughter faded away in the air. They whirled away, higher and higher toward the shimmering mother-of-pearl sky. She tried to fly after them, but the thousands of meadow flowers held her back in the warm earth with their soft, invisible hands. In vain she tried to brace her feet against the ground to push herself off. But her toenails only dug deeper and molten metal ran in her veins. "Good God, don't let them be sucked into the tunnel!" She cried and pleaded until she realized that there wasn't any light tunnel, only a crevice between the pearly pink clouds, through which the friendly light blue summer sky appeared.

With a jolt Irene awoke and sat up in bed. Sammie grunted reproachfully. He was lying comfortably with his head across her shins. No wonder her feet had gone to sleep and felt heavy as lead. He wasn't allowed to be on the bed but always crept up in the early morning. At that point there was little risk that anyone would feel like arguing with him. It was five-thirty, and she had slept for almost five hours. Now she was wide awake. That was the risk of sleeping several hours on the train.

Krister was snoring heavily next to her. He didn't have to be at work until nine. With a thrill of joy she remembered that tonight they were going to have a cozy evening together. She would peel potatoes and make the salad. Maybe open a bottle of wine. He would create something delicious at the stove and graciously accept her applause. She had nothing against applauding, as long as she got out of making dinner. She lay back down, tried to push the dog aside, but he just rolled around on his back with his paws in the air and pretended to be asleep. Which he soon was. Dog and master began to snore to the beat of a schottische. With a sigh she realized she might as well get up.

THE DREAM had been clear as glass. She remembered all the details as sharp as a knife. You didn't have to be a trained dream analyst to understand its meaning. Was she really so distressed about the twins becoming independent? She was filled with a sense of powerlessness, the feeling that she could no longer protect them against every danger. Something she had read or heard occurred to her: "You can never teach your children to grow up based on your own experiences. As a parent you can only try to hide your sorrow and worry. Try to offer careful guidance when things go awry. Be available."

She felt a pang in her heart and grimaced at the dense November darkness outside her windshield. Even though the road was almost deserted, she drove below the speed limit, not her usual habit. Why was she having such a hard time shaking off that dream? Could it be because she had seen so much misery during her years as a cop? Youths, mercilessly kicked out of society, who died violent deaths and were mourned by few or none. They were victims of poverty, unemployment and hopelessness, the wrong friends, and drugs. Or else they happened to be in the wrong place at the wrong time. Like John. She shivered at the memory of one of her most trying experiences as a cop.

She and Tommy had been loaned out to the Kungälv Police to assist in the investigation of the murder of John, age fourteen. It had happened in August, in unusually warm and fine weather. John and a friend had gone to Ingetorps Lake to go camping. In the evening four skinheads showed up. At least two of them were seriously drunk. The only one of them who actually knew John was a fifteen-year-old who went to the same school and had been following and bullying him for a long time. The other three had never seen John before. In the next two hours the four skinheads played a grim game of cat and mouse. Sometimes they were "nice" and sometimes they abused John and his friend. They threw John in the lake, but when he started to swim away they forced his friend to yell, "Please, John, come back. They're going to beat me!" He went back and thus saved his friend's life. Then he himself was kicked unconscious and thrown into the lake. As he drowned, they rolled cigarettes and stood talking on the beach.

She suddenly realized that she was clenching her teeth so hard that her jaws ached. Her grip on the steering wheel was so hard her fingers were cramping. Memory refused to loosen its grip: the sniggering skinheads during the trial who seemed unmoved as they whispered and rustled their papers. The attorneys who talked about leniency for the young killers: They could be damaged for life. The fact that they had already taken an even younger life suddenly didn't seem so important. The parents' unspeakable despair. The mother's bitter whisper outside the courtroom: "They plead for leniency for the defendants, but not for the victim. There's no sense of respect or morality."

Irene swung into the parking garage at police headquarters, turned off the engine, but remained sitting in her car. The projection of her memories was still playing against the windshield of her car. The pictures that the prosecutor showed of John's mangled body: The boy had injuries over his entire body, but the perps had mostly aimed for his face. His head was swollen, eyes glued shut, and his lips split. His head and neck were a grotesque violet-black color from internal bleeding. After this senseless lethal beating, he was unrecognizable.

Many of the spectators couldn't stand it, but left the courtroom crying. The despairing father had had enough. He stood up and screamed at the four unmoved skinheads, "Look at him now, for God's sake!"

Several of them raised their heads, but didn't look at the slide screen. The fifteen-year-old stared straight ahead with an ice-cold expression. None of them batted an eye when the prosecutor related how they had gone about the murder.

She had seen primal instincts reverberating through the parents. Revenge! Revenge! But was there any justice in a case like this? Over the years she had often asked herself that question, but never found a satisfactory answer. Maybe there wasn't any.

Why were these painful memories coming up just now? Evidently it was because of the CD she had stepped on as she sneaked in through the front door around midnight. The disc had fallen out of Jenny's open school bag. First she stuffed it back in the bag, but a subconscious signal made her pull it out again. Yes, she had seen correctly in the weak light of the hall lamp. There was a swastika on the cover. The group's name seemed to be "Swastika." It took great self-control to quell the impulse to rush into Jenny's room and ask what this meant! She peeked in through the doorway as she always did and saw her little girl sound asleep, with her golden blond hair spread over the pillow. It would have to wait until this evening. Or tomorrow. This evening was their night for cocooning, they had decided.

A glance at the dashboard told her that it was almost seven. Time to go up and write a report on yesterday's trip to Stockholm. It was not going to be easy.

THE REPORT was as good as done when Tommy Persson and Hannu Rauhala arrived simultaneously. They each took a cup of coffee and sat down for a run-through of yesterday's events. Before they started the superintendent showed up. He looked worn out, with red eyes and a grayish complexion, but no one commented on his appearance. They had been awaiting his arrival, with plastic cup, from the coffee vending machine. It was crowded around Irene's desk. Naturally there was a big coffee stain on the first page of the report, but she could print out another one later. Everything was saved on the diskette marked VON KNECHT.

Andersson started by telling them about his suspicion that the charred body at Pathology belonged to Pirjo. After a dejected silence Irene asked, "But what about the body of that guy?"

It was Tommy who answered. "Evidently he's on one of the upper floors. The arson techs haven't dared search up there yet, but they'll get to it this weekend. Pelle said it's quite certain that it was a 'devil bomb.' Whoever built it wanted to make sure it was done right. There wasn't anything left undamaged in the whole building. Except von Knecht's safe, which is cemented inside the wall and awkward to get at. Pelle mentioned taking a skylift over there. By the way, I haven't been able to interview the elderly couple on the second floor. They were bandaged up at Mölndal Hospital on Wednesday, stayed overnight, and then were released to stay with their daughter. But on Thursday morning the man had to be admitted again. Heart attack. He's in CIC in very serious condition. His wife has collapsed. The daughter is very upset and asked me to wait to talk to her mother until Monday."

Hannu asked, "CIC?"

"Cardiac intensive care. I'm keeping in touch with the retired couple, because I suspect they may have heard or seen something that has to do with the bomb. To make a bomb that big, a lot of equipment would have had to be dragged in. The gasoline containers in particular should have been noticed."

Andersson cleared his throat. "Are there any witnesses who noticed anything suspicious in recent days?"

"No, and that's strange. Nobody can think of any mysterious person or remember hearing anything odd. There's only one statement that sounds interesting. An elderly man in the building next door to von Knecht's, address on Sten Sturegatan, has his bedroom window on the second floor facing the courtyard. Outside the window there are some rented parking places, one of which is von Knecht's. According to this gentleman, von Knecht parked his Porsche in that parking space just before one in the morning on Saturday."

"On Friday night, you mean?"

"Right. And he's positive. It was the Porsche. There aren't that many Porsche Targas around, now that the happy-go-lucky eighties are over for most people. I called up Sylvia von Knecht yesterday afternoon and asked if that could be right. According to her it's absolutely impossible. Apparently there was a preanniversary get-together on Friday night. Nobody went to bed before one-thirty in the morning, except Sylvia's old mother. Even if she didn't like her son-in-law, I don't think the old lady would take the Porsche and zip down to Berzeliigatan to rig up a bomb. And clearly no one else from the preparty did either. Sylvia got mad as hell at me when I asked if Richard was drunk on Friday night. Finally it came out that he was obviously plastered."

Andersson remembered what Stridner had told him at yesterday's meeting. It seemed that von Knecht drank a good deal toward the end of his life. To establish the chronology he asked, "He was with the others until one-thirty?"

"Yes."

There was a long silence as all four of them tried to figure out some angle. Anyway, it was obvious. Irene was the one who took it up for discussion.

"The car. The Porsche. How could it be on Berzeliigatan that night? Where was it parked earlier in the evening?"

"I asked Sylvia where the car was now. According to her, it's in a locked garage on Molinsgatan. Just like her own car, a BMW," Tommy replied.

"So it hasn't been stolen, but was put back in its garage. Is it certain that it was von Knecht's Porsche and not someone else's?"

Tommy shrugged his shoulders. "The old guy on Sten Sturegatan claimed it was von Knecht's," he said curtly.

Again a thoughtful silence descended over the meeting. Finally the superintendent slapped the palm of his hand on the table, which put another coffee stain on Irene's report, and exclaimed, "It's some damned phantom sneaking around, going through locked doors, and taking locked cars. And putting them back! Without leaving a trace. Up in smoke!"

Hannu caught his eye. "More keys."

Andersson fell silent and took on an absentminded look of concentration. The others also realized that it was the only explanation. Irene said enthusiastically, "Of course that's it! There has to be an extra key to the car and the garage. By the way, Sylvia said that Richard had been searching for the spare key to the Porsche the week before he died.

On the same key ring there's a key to the garage. There must also be another set of keys to the doors in von Knecht's building on Molinsgatan and the building on Berzeliigatan. But Sylvia told me that there were only three sets of keys to the two apartments. I saw them myself; she has all three key rings at home in her apartment."

Andersson looked at Irene after her input. Thoughtfully he said, "Sylvia certainly didn't know about any more keys. He had a whole bunch of secrets, our fine Herr von Knecht. There must be another set of keys. Which the killer is now walking around with. Plus the spare keys to the Porsche and the garage."

As the words sank in, Irene understood the threat. "That means that Sylvia shouldn't be staying in the apartment before the locks are changed," she said. ·

"Precisely." Andersson made a calming gesture. "But we can lie low over the weekend. She's at Marstrand with Henrik, after all. As long as the murderer doesn't have keys to that house too."

Irene gave a start and exclaimed, "Wait a minute. There *were* keys to the Marstrand house on the key rings! We can't lie low. We have to warn her."

An anxious furrow creased Andersson's brow. "Irene, try to get hold of her right away."

She nodded and felt a slight uneasiness inside. Sylvia might be in danger. An obvious question popped up, demanding an answer. "But who would have access to a whole set of keys to von Knecht's various houses and cars?" she wondered.

All of them tried to figure out an answer. Finally Hannu said, "Richard von Knecht."

At first Andersson was visibly irritated, but he had to admit the logic of Hannu's conclusion. "And who would he give the keys to?"

Nobody had a good answer, and they dropped the subject after a while.

Irene reported on her trip to Stockholm. Her colleagues had plenty of comments about her excursion: Was it really necessary to spend a lot of taxpayers' money going up to Stockholm? Did Mona Söder stand to inherit? Why couldn't she have said all that on the phone? Could Mona have flown down to Göteborg on Tuesday afternoon and back the same evening? Or driven it in her fast new car?

With a dismissive gesture Irene tried to answer the questions one by one. "It was actually not so dumb of her to demand that I come up and see Jonas with my own eyes. Jonas is dying, and she has been by his side every evening. Now she's on vacation, so she can stay with him around the clock. I've checked with the hospital staff and they say she was there on Tuesday evening. According to the switchboard at her job she was there all day Tuesday. The Audi has only gone thirty-two hundred kilometers. I'm actually quite convinced of her innocence. We don't have to waste more resources by checking up on her and Jonas. They just want to be left in peace. To your question, Hannu: Yes, Mona will inherit Jonas's share of Richard von Knecht's estate, that's the law. But she doesn't need his money and doesn't want anything to do with the von Knecht family. Can we keep her and Jonas out of the official reports to the media?"

She addressed this question to Andersson in an almost entreating tone of voice. He looked at her, surprised, but then nodded briefly.

"We'll have to trust your intuition for the time being, until something turns up. From what I understand, Jonas isn't going anywhere. And his mother isn't either," he said crassly.

Energetically he slapped his palm on the table again, so that his cup fell over and the last drops of coffee trickled across Irene's report. With a sigh she acknowledged that she would have to print out a whole new one. Andersson didn't notice, but turned to Tommy.

"Tommy, what have you found out about Shorty?"

"Fredrik and I split up the job. I concentrated on the buildings around Berzeliigatan. Fredrik took Shorty. I didn't see a trace of him all afternoon. But if I know Fredrik, there will be a complete report. First thing Monday morning, if not sooner."

Andersson suddenly looked like he had an idea and interrupted Tommy. "There's an interesting thing that Birgitta ferreted out yesterday during her interview with Bobo Torsson."

He stopped, recalling the heated exchange between Jonny and Birgitta the day before. He decided not to tell the others about it. Instead he gave a lively account of Birgitta's interview of Torsson. The attack on Birgitta's more intimate body parts made those present especially indignant. But when the superintendent fired off his final remark, they gave him an almost distrustful look. As if he must be lying.

". . . and finally it came out that Torsson is living with Shorty right now. He and Shorty are cousins!"

He was pleased with the effect of his words. At the same time he had to admit that it didn't simplify matters in the least that the chic doper fashion photographer and the notorious hoodlum were close relatives. He sighed heavily and said for the thousandth time in the past few days, "What a mess! Does any of it make sense, or are we running around chasing our phantom along a bunch of unrelated sidetracks?"

"I think it seems normal for a homicide investigation. We spend ninety percent of our time on leads that don't have a thing to do with the case. Routine jobs, following a lot of leads, checking witnesses' statements, verifying times and the like. No, I think it's the same as always," said Tommy.

He rolled his eyes to heaven and the others laughed. They all knew very well that this was no routine case.

Andersson turned to Hannu. "What have you found out about Pirjo?"

"Dental X rays. She was in emergency at the community dental clinic in Angered six months ago, had a toothache. They pulled it. She didn't want a root canal."

Andersson leaned toward him excitedly and asked, "Where are the X rays now?"

"Pathology."

"Good! Then we'll find out soon whether it's really Pirjo lying there. Although it most likely *is* her. Anything else?"

"Yes. I got word from Helsinki. She was arrested for illegal distilling and bootlegging along with her ex-husband. The boys' father. He was sentenced to one year. In prison he was stabbed by another inmate after a fight over a gambling debt. He died. There's nothing about Marjatta except 'father unknown.'"

"Did Pirjo do time?"

"No. She got a suspended sentence, because of the kids. Less than a year later she married Göte Larsson and moved to Sweden."

"So that was three years ago?"

"Yep."

"And now he's in Malmö living with a Polish woman."

"Right."

They remained seated and continued to discuss things without getting much further. Just as Andersson stood up to go to his office, the door opened and a uniformed officer stuck in his head. It was Hans Stefansson from PO1. He greeted them cheerfully. "Hi! Just wanted to tell you, Andersson, that we haven't found Bobo Torsson. Shorty told us to go to hell when we wanted to enter his apartment and look for him. Should we get a search warrant?"

Involuntarily Andersson's whole face took on a disapproving expression. Irene knew why. Then he would have to contact the prosecutor in charge, Inez Collin. But he had to relinquish his personal distaste. He nodded.

"Okay. Hang on a minute, and I'll try to fix one," he said.

Tommy looked surprised and asked, "Why does Torsson have to be brought in so soon?"

"Assault and battery on a civil servant. He voiced a serious threat to Birgitta. I would feel better if I had some hold over little Bobo. And for him to know it. Remember, Shorty is his cousin. There's a risk he'll send some of his friends. There's always some creep who owes a guy like that a favor. Why not take on the pleasure of beating up a cop? Especially a female one!"

His facial color had risen and he looked very serious. He gazed meditatively at his inspectors and went on, "One of you has to go on the patrol that picks up Torsson. Even if you don't find him at the apartment, you can always get a sense of the lay of the land. Tommy, will you take it?"

"Yep."

"Remember to proceed cautiously. Shorty has shot at cops before."

Irene couldn't help asking, "Why is one of society's worst enemies set up in a little tobacco shop?"

"A legitimate question; unfortunately, I don't have a good answer. But mark my words: If he's on the scene, something fishy is going on!"

The superintendent looked very stern and determined. No one contradicted him.

WHEN THE others had left the room, Irene started to look for the phone number to Marstrand. She managed to find the number of the caretaker, just as Jonny Blom had.

A female voice answered. "Svensson."

"Good day, this is Detective Inspector Irene Huss. I'm actually looking for Sylvia von Knecht. Can you connect me?"

"I can take a message. She and my husband are out exercising the horses right now. They won't be back for at least an hour."

"Would it be possible to talk to Henrik von Knecht?"

"Unfortunately, I can only switch the call to the big house. The smaller houses don't have phone lines."

"Do you happen to have his cell phone number?"

"No, sorry."

In a friendly voice the caretaker's wife promised to give the message to Fru von Knecht.

Annoyed, Irene slammed down the receiver. Strangely enough, Henrik's cell phone number wasn't in the phone book either. Lacking anything better to do, she got started on all the material lying on her desk. She zealously sorted, wrote reports, and filed various witness statements. She jumped in her chair when the phone rang. With a quick glance at the clock, she saw that almost two hours had passed since she started looking for Sylvia.

"Inspector Irene Huss."

"Sylvia von Knecht. Anita Svensson said you had asked for me. What is it regarding?"

Irene could hear from her voice that it would be fine to skip the pleasantries and chitchat. She assumed an authoritative tone. "We have indications that there seems to have been a fourth set of keys. Do you know anything about this?"

"No, I already told you! There are no other sets of keys except for the three I showed you."

Irene chose her words with some care before she went on. "We have reason to believe that there are. And that the murderer has access to these keys. Plus the spare keys to the garage and the Porsche."

There was a long pause. Irene could hear that Sylvia was breathing fast on the other end of the line. Finally she said, still in a dismissive tone, "What makes you think there are more keys?"

Irene referred to the statement that the Porsche had been seen on Berzeliigatan on Friday night. Sylvia herself had stated that it couldn't possibly have been Richard who was driving. So someone had keys to both the garage on Molinsgatan and to the car. This someone also had access to keys to the locked street doors, both on Molinsgatan and Berzeliigatan. The garbage room doors and the doors onto the courtyard were locked in both neighborhoods. Despite this the murderer had passed unhindered through these doors and stairways. So there had to be additional keys. In conclusion Irene said, "I want to remind you that you said there were keys on your own and Richard's key rings that fit the house outside Marstrand. Is that correct?"

"Yes."

Her voice sounded thin and afraid. She had grasped what Irene was getting at. Shakily Sylvia said, "You mean that the murderer might be able to come here! And would be able to get in, because he has the keys?"

Now the panic in her voice was blatant. Irene assumed a soothing tone when she replied, "From what we can tell, there is some risk of that. It can't be ruled out. Are you alone in the big house?"

"Yes. Henrik is down in his cabin."

"Can you ask him to sleep in the house with you tonight? Or can you stay down there with him?"

There was a long silence. Finally she heard Sylvia's voice, sounding much steadier and stronger. "I'll take care of the horses up here. Then I'll drive to a friend's house. Henrik can drive home to his own place; the murderer wouldn't have any of his keys, would he?"

"Probably not. Can you tell me where you're going?"

"I can't see that it's any of your business!"

The familiar feeling that arose whenever Irene talked to Sylvia now reappeared. Her patience ran out and the adrenaline started pumping in her arteries. Softly and pedagogically, as if she were dealing with an unruly child, she said, "Sylvia, we suspect a dangerous killer is behind the events of the past few days. Try to understand that we're not snooping into your private life. We're trying to protect you."

"Then catch the murderer!"

Click!

Astonishment changed to anger as Irene sat staring stupidly at the receiver. God damned bitch, didn't she realize! Irene stopped her angry torrent of words. An idea popped up in the back of her mind. She picked it out, scrutinized it, and gave it her approval. Decisively she stood up and went in to see the superintendent.

"IT'S ACTUALLY not such a dumb idea. Go ahead. If anything comes of it, call me. I'll probably be here until six. Otherwise I'll be home all evening. Tomorrow I thought I'd try to get home a little earlier. I'm going to dinner at my niece's place—Marianne, you know."

Irene nodded. She was well aware of Marianne and her two small boys, even though they had never met.

"Have they found Torsson yet?"

"No. He's gone underground; he must know that things are getting hot. You can't just bite a police officer with impunity on the ti . . . on the breast!"

Irene managed to conceal her smile in a light cough. The superintendent, struck by newly acquired respect for the fair sex, was amusing.

It was just before noon, no time to lose. Her lunch would have to be a hot dog on the way.

HIGHWAY E6 is almost ten kilometers longer, but it's faster than driving on narrow city streets. The wind was blowing; gray clouds had drawn the damp hems of their skirts low over Hisingen. Traffic was heavy. Apparently all the residents of the suburbs were headed for Göteborg to shop, look at the Christmas displays, and eat hamburgers with their kids at McDonald's. Suddenly Irene realized how hungry she was. She braked quickly at the first gas station that had a hot dog stand. But it wasn't easy to eat while she was driving. The last bit of sausage slipped out of the bun and landed in her lap. The mustard showed up well on black jeans. She borrowed some words from her boss's vocabulary. She almost missed the exit north of Kungälv, but at the last moment saw it and turned off.

The road out toward Marstrand is extremely beautiful, and she usually gave it the attention it deserved. On this gray November day, though, she was focused on driving as fast as she could while she kept an eye out for her colleagues from the Traffic Division.

She had memorized the route before she left Göteborg. Holta Church flashed by. She knew that there would soon be a side road and that she should take it toward Tjuvkil. Then she was no longer sure, so she pulled off the road and took out the map.

Just as she was about to start off again, she caught sight of a car coming toward her at high speed. A hunch, or rather an instinct, made her hold the map up in front of her face and peek over the edge.

It was a red BMW. And Sylvia von Knecht was driving. She didn't even deign to give the old dark blue Saab a look. On the other hand, Irene saw her clearly. She sat with her eyes fixed on the road ahead, on the edge of her seat and with her back erect.

Calmly, Irene put the car in gear and made an elegant and illegal U-turn. She tried to keep one or two cars between her and Sylvia. It was easy to follow her since there was still a lot of traffic.

Sylvia took the same way back toward Göteborg. But at Olskroksmotet she headed toward the western part of town on Västerleden. Was she going out to Västra Frölunda? Apparently not, because she drove past Frölunda Square and the exit Irene usually took when she was going home to her row-house neighborhood.

Askim, Hovås, Skintebo. Now Irene knew where they were heading. She increased the distance between her and the red BMW. Sylvia passed the exit sign for Kullavik, continued a few kilometers, and turned off toward Särö.

Ivan Viktors. He was the one she planned to spend the night with. The superintendent hadn't been far wrong when he suspected that Sylvia and Viktors had spent Sunday evening together. But Sylvia had been with her mother and sister the entire evening. And Viktors had visited his brother in the hospital. Where was the gap in the chronology? The answer was as simple as it was logical. They had concentrated on the wrong evening. It wasn't Sunday evening, but Monday evening that Sylvia and Ivan Viktors had spent together.

She was so full of this revelation that everything nearly went to hell as she almost ran straight into the back of the BMW, which had stopped to turn off toward Särö Västerskog. Quickly, she turned the wheel and whipped by on the left side. It was her good fortune that there were no oncoming cars. Everything happened so fast that Sylvia probably didn't have time to notice who had thundered past her. Irene swung into a passing turnout a little farther ahead. In her rearview mirror she could see Sylvia driving at a leisurely pace toward King Gustav V's favorite tennis courts. Irene performed another illegal maneuver but wasn't in much of a hurry to head toward the small cluster of turn-of-the-twentieth-century houses.

During the eighties large villas had been built on the meadows in front of the nature preserve, but along the narrow old country road there were several grand old patrician villas. The red BMW stood outside a big redbrick house with pinnacles and towers and a somewhat overgrown garden. Irene drove on about a hundred meters farther before she parked her car and got out. With her chin tucked down, her collar turned up against the wind, and Katarina's black baseball cap on her head, Irene would not be easy to recognize, in case Sylvia happened to look out the window. There was a greater risk that she would recognize Irene's jacket. But she probably didn't burden her memory with such soiled attire.

Usually, the lovely preserve was full of people strolling around. In the summer swimming was popular at the sandy beach. But on a damp Saturday afternoon in late November there were no crowds. Irene was completely alone. She kept close to the bushy vegetation along the shoulder of the road and tried to blend into nature. When she reached the hedge that surrounded the garden of the redbrick house, she had to duck down quickly and pretend to tie her shoelace.

Sylvia was loading Viktors down with suitcases and bags from the trunk of the BMW. Was she thinking of moving in? From the amount of baggage it looked like it. She had almost as much as Irene used to pack for the whole family's three-week vacation at her husband's parents' summerhouse up in Värmland. It was too windy for her to hear what they were saying to each other. But judging by Sylvia's body language, she was very excited. She gesticulated as she talked, tossing out the baggage with great energy and making swift, abrupt movements. To top it off she went up to Viktors, wrapped her arms around his waist, and leaned her head against his broad opera singer's chest. He glanced around quickly and for a moment Irene thought he was looking straight through her peephole in the lilac hedge. Evidently, he didn't see her. With an impatient movement he broke free of Sylvia's embrace. Carrying all the gear, he started walking toward the solid oak front door. It closed heavily behind them.

BACK AT headquarters, Irene found out that not much had happened. Torsson seemed to have been swallowed up by the earth. Shorty claimed that he had no idea where his cousin was. Andersson was very pleased with Irene's investigative efforts. He was especially happy that he had been right about Sylvia and Ivan Viktors. He clapped his hand to his chest and beamed like the sun.

"Male intuition, understand? Male intuition!"

Irene tactfully refrained from pointing out whose intuition had led to the disclosure.

Andersson went on, "Fredrik called just before you arrived. From lunchtime until midnight yesterday he kept Shorty's smoke shop under surveillance. A person who may have been Bobo Torsson entered the street door to the stairwell of Shorty's apartment building at three-thirty yesterday afternoon. The same man left after about an hour. In his hand he was carrying a large bag. Based on my description of Torsson, which I got secondhand from Birgitta Moberg, Fredrik thinks it was him. Now I've spoken with both Hannu and Fredrik. They're continuing the surveillance of Shorty over the weekend. Not because I think Torsson is so damned stupid that he'd show up on Berzeliigatan again, but you never know. It might be good to see what Shorty's up to as well."

Irene teased him, "Male intuition?"

"Nope. Cop intuition," said the superintendent.

Both laughed. Andersson turned serious then. "Speaking of cop intuition . . . because Torsson threatened Birgitta, I've asked her not to stay at her apartment this weekend. She must have been feeling jumpy, because she complied. Really. She's staying with her mother in Alingsås for a few days."

"You're afraid that Shorty and Torsson might be our phantoms?"

"Well . . . no . . . but I don't want them tramping around in this shit. They're stirring things up!"

From many years of working with Andersson, she knew what he was getting at. Maybe Shorty and Bobo Torsson didn't have a thing to do with the von Knecht case. They were troubling elements, though, and the police couldn't just ignore them. Shorty was too well known to the force for that. Suddenly, she had an idea.

"What if I tried to ferret out something useful on Bobo Torsson?"

"There should be something on him. Birgitta is stone certain that he was high as a kite. Go check with Narcotics, see what they've got."

The only person she could find in the International Narcotics Division was unknown to her, a relative rookie. He muttered that he had tons of things to do, but promised to get back to her on Monday morning. There wasn't much else she could do just now. She wrote a report about her surveillance of Sylvia von Knecht and decided to go home. It was almost five, and she was tired, but pleased with her day. And she looked forward to the rest of the evening.

A WONDERFUL feeling of excited anticipation rippled through her as Irene turned into their parking lot. She almost ran over Jenny, who was on her way out of the row-house courtyard. Quickly, she parked the car and went over to her daughter. Irene gave Jenny a hug. She noticed her reserve, but decided not to mention it. Cheerfully she said, "Hi, pal! Where are you off to?"

"Out."

"Yes, I can see that. Where to?"

Jenny sighed heavily. "To the rec center. We have to practice."

"The band? White Killers?"

"Yeah."

"Aren't you going to stay home with us tonight? We're going to have a special evening and—"

"You're going to drink wine and eat dinner! What's so special about that? I want to be with my friends!"

"But Katarina—"

"She went to Uddevalla with the judo crowd."

"Uddevalla?"

"Did you forget the tournament that's going on there tomorrow? Admit you forgot it!"

"Well, yes . . ."

She had indeed. The von Knecht case had taken up all her mental energy this week. Still, that was no excuse for forgetting that Katarina was competing in the junior Swedish championship in judo. But she hadn't forgotten the hickey on Jenny's neck. As nonchalantly as possible she asked, "Is that guy coming, what's-his-name?"

"Markus."

Right into the trap! Jenny was furious when she realized she had let the cat out of the bag. "Lay off, will you? Do you think I'm one of your crooks to be interrogated, or what?" she screeched in rage.

Irene was worried the neighbors would begin to wonder. Tactfully she said, "Not at all. Do want us to pick you up?"

"No!"

"Then don't come home later than midnight. On the dot! Are a bunch of you going together?"

"Yeah. I'm supposed to pick up Pia."

That was a relief. Pia lived a few buildings down, in their neighborhood. She was a good, responsible girl, Irene thought. The rec center was about a kilometer away, so it wouldn't be far for them to walk. But Markus was waiting for her there. Irene realized there wasn't anything she could do about it. It made her uneasy, through. A little too quickly she said, "Have a great time. If you need anything, give us a call."

"Yeah. 'Bye!"

Impatiently, Jenny slipped out of her mother's attempt to give her another hug. She vanished into the November darkness. The same forlorn feeling that Irene had experienced in her dream seized her without warning. It took all the self-control she could muster to resist the impulse to run after her little daughter.

THE HOUSE already smelled lovely inside. Her mood and spirits brightened instantly.

"Hello, dear. Child-free tonight!"

Krister stuck his head out the kitchen doorway. His kiss tasted of the sea and he smelled like garlic.

"Oh, don't tell me!" Irene sighed, delighted. "You're making crab au gratin!"

"I have to take the opportunity when we're alone. Although I split a small crab. It's only for an appetizer."

"And the entrée is something with garlic."

"Mmmm. Roast lamb fillet marinated in oil and garlic, with sliced potatoes and puree of parsnips. A tomato salad with onions and olives will also be served. With the appetizer we'll be drinking the usual Freixenet champagne, then a red wine with the lamb: Baron de Ley, Reserva nineteen eighty-seven. Rioja. What do you say?"

"Save your wife from death by hunger! When do we eat?"

"You've got time for a shower."

NEWLY SHOWERED and feeling fresh, wearing a new sky-blue polo shirt that was exactly the same color as her eyes, Irene enjoyed the glorious repast. They observed one of the few absolute rules they had in their marriage: no talk about work until after dinner. Instead of dessert they drank coffee with a piece of chocolate, sitting on the sofa in the living room.

She dug her bare toes into the soft Gabbeh rug and sighed with contentment. Was it permitted to feel this good? Sammie came squirming under the coffee table and tried to lick her toes. He preferred them sweaty and warm, but right out of the shower would do. Irene laughed, "No, Sammie, stop it! I know you want a little attention. When was he out last?"

"It's probably quite a while ago, I'm afraid. We could take a walk later, after we digest our food. It's only ten o'clock."

Krister put his arm around her and she snuggled up to him. He sniffed at her newly washed hair.

"Irene. The restaurant owner wants me to increase my hours and work full time. There's a lot of pressure at Glady's right now even with two of us working shifts. They need one of us to work full time. Sverker is sixty-three now, and he doesn't want to give up his partial pension. It has to be me."

"Well, if that's something you want to do . . ."

"It wouldn't be such a bad idea. I've worked thirty-hour weeks since the girls were little. It's about time we thought about putting something into the General Supplemental Pension. That is if there's anything to think about. Although it's been very nice working part time."

"That's the only reason it worked out at all. Plus a little help from Mamma. But the girls are big now. They don't need us the same way anymore."

The last remark sounded false and hollow even to her own ears, but he didn't seem to notice.

"Precisely. They're independent. Jenny has her music, Katarina her judo. And we have each other."

He gave her a big hug. She felt warm inside and blessed by life.

Sammie started whimpering over by the door. One more minute and despite his training, he'd be forced to pee.

IT WAS icy out, cold and clear. Irene put her arm under Krister's. It was great to get outside; she felt drowsy from the food and wine. They walked along the illuminated walkway and bike path. It led all the way down to the swimming beach, less than two kilometers ahead. They would pass the rec center, and Irene felt a stab of guilty conscience. Was she about to spy on Jenny? No, they were just passing by with the dog. But she had to be honest with herself and admit that the unknown Markus seemed like a troubling element.

Two young people came walking toward them. When they came closer, Irene saw that one was Pia. The other wasn't Jenny, but another classmate.

Irene greeted them. "Hi, Pia. Is Jenny still at the rec center?"

"Hi. Jenny? No, she hasn't been there."

The girls walked on by. Irene didn't move. She noticed that her grip on Krister's arm was much too hard, but she couldn't loosen it. She felt a desperate need for support. The dreamlike feeling of wanting to scream, but not being able to, constricted her throat. She could only whisper, "Where is she? Good God, where is she?"

"Now, now, don't get upset. She must be around here somewhere. Probably with that boy," said Krister. He meant to calm her, but his words pushed Irene's worry to the verge of panic.

"We don't even know his last name, just Markus!"

Silently they turned toward home. The gloriously cozy mood was gone, replaced by a terror as black as the November night all around them.

Their cluster of row houses came into view just as Irene saw two skinheads coming toward them. Involuntarily she thought of her memories that had been replayed early that morning. She was glad to have the dog with her.

A few meters before they would pass each other, one of the skinheads stopped abruptly. Sammie began to pull on his leash and bark. Astonished, Irene heard that he didn't sound angry, but glad and eager. The skinhead, who stopped abruptly, then spoke, saying in a quavering voice, "Hi, Mamma and Pappa."

Chapter Twelve

SOME MONDAY MORNINGS WERE more "Monday" than others. Feeling tired and heavy-headed, Irene Huss entered her office at police headquarters just before seven-thirty. The night had been largely sleepless.

Tommy Persson came through the doors at the same moment and started pulling off his old leather jacket. He greeted her hastily, "'Morning!"

"Hi, Tommy," said Irene, grumpily.

Tommy gave her a searching look. It wasn't necessary to have known Irene for seventeen years to see that something was wrong. He waved his hands dismissively.

"Don't tell me! Krister took off with that delicious little blond waitress!"

Irene reluctantly managed a smile before she sighed, "No, but Jenny shaved off her hair. She's a skinhead, but 'only because she likes the music.' We had a fight, spent all day yesterday arguing and pleading. But it just made her more stubborn. She's a skinhead because her boyfriend is. And because they play in the same skinhead band. Oh Tommy, she doesn't understand!"

Irene sank down on her desk chair and hid her face in her hands. Neither of them said a word. When she finally removed her hands she glanced up at him. She had never seen him look so serious. In a sharp voice he said, "She has to understand. If she's shaved off her hair and claims that she's a skinhead, she'll also have to take the consequences. You can't be a little bit skinhead. You have to make it clear to her what the shaved head stands for!"

"We tried! But whenever we mention Nazism and racism, she denies that the Holocaust ever happened. And according to her we're racists ourselves. It's true that both Krister and I have griped about certain immigrants who come here and live off our taxes. And as a cop I've seen a lot of felonies committed by immigrants."

"But how do you think these young criminal immigrants are supposed to have any feeling of solidarity with Swedish society? They're consistently locked out of everything! They live in suburban ghettos, they're outsiders at school and outsiders in terms of the language. Many of them can't speak either Swedish or their native language correctly. And they're outsiders in the job market too. If an employer sees that someone has a name he can't pronounce, that person isn't even called for an interview. It doesn't matter how good an education he has. Under-the-table cleaning jobs are the only thing they seem to be good for in Sweden!"

"Like Pirjo Larsson.

"Like Pirjo. The only thing that gives many immigrant kids a sense of security and belonging is the gang. We've both seen what a lot of these gangs get up to. We don't see the ones who aren't criminals, just the ones who are. I'm never astonished by what kids are doing. I'm just terrified at what kind of society we're creating for our kids. And now I'm thinking about our *own* kids! It's our kids who are shaving their heads. It's our kids who get into fights with immigrant kids. Often they're injured, and sometimes, somebody dies. Our kids don't feel any sense of belonging in Swedish society either; they just cling to ready-made, cheap solutions. 'March with us, for a pure Aryan society!' 'Throw out all the niggers and Northern Europe will become the eternally happy thousand-year Reich! Sieg Heil!' And so our kids put on their boots and go marching off to Hell!"

Speechless, she stared at him. She had never heard him react so powerfully. To her he was even-keeled Tommy, the calm, secure father of three and also her oldest friend from the police academy. He was so worked up that he was pacing around their little office and stomping as he gave Hitler salutes to underscore his meaning.

"And because they're our kids," Tommy went on, "we have to take responsibility. We can't abdicate it! You have two kids, I have three. But those skinheads who will be gathering around statues of King Karl the Twelfth all over the country in a few days are our kids too!"

She felt confused and tired, wanted to protest, but her weary brain couldn't formulate her thoughts. She made a vague attempt anyway. "I don't think that just because Jenny shaved her head, all skinheads are kids like mine."

"If you deny that, you also deny the society that has hired you to protect it! These skinheads are part of Swedish society. We all have a responsibility. But above all, they're a symptom of our society's ills."

"A symptom?"

"Of alienation! Swedish society forces people outside! And once you're outside you're damned well never going to be let back in!"

"But why do you think young people are voluntarily choosing to join groups of outsiders?"

"Young people have always done that. In our day we wore FNL buttons and Palestinian scarves; we talked about solidarity with the Third World and all that stuff. Many of us were swept along with the Green Wave, the ecology movement. We had correct opinions and views!"

"But everybody was politically Red in the seventies!"

"Young people were, sure. We belonged to the progressive youth generation. We weren't like *them*—I mean our parents. No, we stood for something different, something better. The only correct path for the future."

"Is what we're seeing with neo-Nazis and skinheads the same thing? Is that what you think?"

"Yep. They've given up trying to get into our restrictive society before they even make an attempt. It's better to give up voluntarily than to be locked out. So they feel solidarity with groups of outsiders. They look for strength in the group. It's easy to blend in and acquire an identity, since all of them look the same in their boots, military clothes, and bald heads. They inspire fear in other people by their very appearance. Young people learn prefabricated arguments and seek support from them. Their leaders make such a cocksure impression when they stand up and scream their slogans with electric guitars and heavy drums thundering in the background. How beautiful to avoid thinking for yourself! Just march along!"

Why was Tommy so agitated and impassioned? Irene was astonished but didn't get the chance to ask him, since the intercom beeped and called them to "morning prayers." Tommy took a deep breath and appeared to made a quick decision. He blurted out, "It's been a while since I've seen Jenny. I think you should invite me over tomorrow or the next day."

Irene was confused by his abrupt change of subject, but said at once, "You know you're welcome anytime. As always! Krister and I have been talking about a little Lucia party, and of course you and Agneta will—"

"That'll be cool. Although that's not what I was thinking of," said Tommy. His voice was very serious.

Irene also understood that he wasn't talking about a pleasant evening. Right off she made up her mind and said, "Let's make it Wednesday night. Krister can fix dinner for us. I know what you think of my cooking."

"It's just as high-class as my own, although mine is a tiny bit better. Wednesday will be fine. Make sure Jenny's home."

Just as Irene was about to enter the conference room, a secretary showed up and handed her a brown interdepartmental envelope. With a quick glance she noticed the name "Bo-Ivan Torsson" in the text.

Superintendent Andersson cleared his throat and called for silence. "Okay. We're all here. The techs are coming later. They're working on a car bomb that went off this morning. Have you all heard about that?"

The majority of the group looked surprised and shook their heads. Apparently the explosion was the top story on the seven-thirty news, but most of them had been busy getting ready for "morning prayers" at the time.

Andersson went on, "Damned strange. A car exploded in the parking lot at Delsjön golf course at six o'clock this morning. Nobody was in the vicinity except for the driver of the car, who was much too close. He was literally vaporized to atoms! The theory is that some kind of terrorist set off the bomb by mistake. IRA or Hamas or something. Or maybe old shit from the former Yugoslavia. I remember what a hell of a mess we had with Ustasha in the seventies . . . Well, someone else will have to take care of that investigation. Now let's go over what we've found out since Friday."

He continued by informing them that the charred body in Pathology was probably Pirjo's. They would have definite word that afternoon, when the forensic odontologist looked at the X rays and compared them with the corpse's teeth. He provoked even greater interest when he mentioned the cut on the head of von Knecht's penis. Stridner's assumption that he had had sex the day before he died prompted many questions and speculations. Irene recounted that she had checked out Jonas and Mona Söder. Without going into detail, she said that they should be left out of the investigation for the time being. Their alibis for Tuesday were impeccable. She quickly moved on to the theory that there was an extra set of keys to the two apartments, but also emphasized that so far it was only a theory; it would be important to follow up on what had happened to Richard von Knecht's spare-key ring for the Porsche and the garage. She recounted Saturday's conversation with Sylvia and the subsequent surveillance. When she revealed that it was Ivan Viktors who was the "boyfriend," Jonny couldn't hold himself back. Maliciously he hooted,

"I knew it! There was something that smarmy customer was hiding. He may be a celebrity and a stuck-up fart, but we've got him now!"

Irene was unusually grumpy on this Monday morning of all Mondays. She couldn't hold back her acid comment, "Got him for what? That he's screwing Sylvia von Knecht? There's no law against that. They're both grown-ups, that's for sure."

Jonny scowled at her but couldn't come up with any deadly repartee. Instead he told the others about Friday's interview with Viktors. Then he went over what he and Hans Borg had found out during the stakeout of the parking garage on Kapellgatan on Friday. It didn't take long. The results were zip.

Andersson shrugged. "Okay, that was a dud. We'll skip the parking garage for now. Evidently, in the crappy weather, our killer was on foot. Birgitta, tell us about our charming photographer, Bobo."

Birgitta told the story of what had happened on Friday afternoon, without giving a single hint about her own feelings. Relieved, Andersson saw that she seemed to be her normal self again. He hoped he wouldn't have to get any more involved in what had happened between her and Jonny later that day. Damned unpleasant.

The only thing Fredrik and Hannu had to report was that Bobo hadn't shown up on Berzeliigatan over the weekend. After comparing his description with Birgitta's account of his appearance and clothing during the interview, they were positive that he was the one who had picked up a large bag on Friday afternoon. The search of Shorty's apartment had apparently been a regular circus. Tommy tried to stay in the background to record whether there was anything of interest in the apartment. It was a large two-room place, but filthy and messy like the crash pad it probably was. Shorty was totally infuriated at the encroachment by the police, and got himself so worked up that he started smashing his own furniture. He didn't threaten the police directly, but watching the way he slammed his own fist straight through the seat of a chair was "a tad unsettling," as Tommy put it.

"Actually we should have had a narcotics dog with us. But we were looking for Bobo Torsson, not drugs. And he wasn't in the apartment. We had to go back to basics. Shorty didn't know where Bobo was, but he told us repeatedly where he thought we ought to go. I wouldn't want to run into him alone on a dark night."

No one else looked particularly fond of the idea either. They all agreed with the superintendent that the presence of Shorty and Bobo in the investigation was troubling.

Birgitta interjected a question, "Did he seem to be on drugs?"

"Quite possible. But that guy is notorious for his bad temper, so it's hard to say for sure," said Tommy.

"Could there be some connection between von Knecht and those rotten eggs? Could our respectable millionaire have been on drugs too?" It was Birgitta who posed this question, and all of them took time to think about it.

Finally Jonny replied, "Nothing we have discovered so far indicates it. Like all big businessmen he had a little shit on his fingers, but it was mostly irregularities with foreign stock deals. Not the kind of thing Bobo and Shorty are into. No, the only point of contact is Berzeliigatan. The fact that they lived close to each other, Torsson above von Knecht's apartment and Shorty across the street."

Fredrik took over. "We checked out Shorty. He was released from Kumla prison in August, after serving six of his eight years. He was convicted of a felony narcotics offense, felony assault, and attempted murder. 'Good social prognosis, because Lasse Johannesson has been allowed to take over an apartment and small business from an elderly relative,' it says in the documents. This elderly relative is an unmarried aunt of Bobo and Shorty. She had a cerebral embolism in June this year and lies paralyzed in Vasa Hospital. Apparently she's doing better, but she can't take care of herself in the apartment on Berzeliigatan. The old woman is supposed to get a place at a nursing home. According to Kumla it was Bobo Torsson who arranged all the practical matters involving the takeover of the apartment and the business. Everything was ready and waiting when Shorty got out."

Irene remembered the interdepartmental envelope she had received before the morning meeting. After quickly glancing through the text, she asked to speak. "Last Saturday I asked Narcotics for any information they might have about Bobo Torsson. This morning I got a report from them. He's been convicted three times for possession of narcotics. Each time he was caught in raids on various clubs and discos. The first time was 1983, the second time 1985, and the third time 1989. He got suspended sentences the first two times, since he only had small amounts on him. In 1989 he was sentenced to four months in prison. He was nabbed at the same club where Shorty was so dramatically apprehended! Torsson was in the crowd when the police stormed in, and he had ten grams of cocaine on him. A little too much for his personal use, the court thought. Shorty and another big drug kingpin, Tony Larsson, were in the club's office and didn't even manage to hide the drugs that were in a bag on the desk. They were literally caught with their fingers in the cookie jar. Both of them had snorted cocaine and were extremely loaded. Both were armed. A violent shootout followed. Tony was shot in the shoulder by one of our colleagues, which provoked great discussion in the media," Irene concluded her hasty summation.

Andersson broke the silence that followed.

"So-o-o, Bobo was already mixed up in Shorty's circle back then. Of course, both of them have continued to do drugs the whole time, although Shorty has been more visible. He's more brutal and loves weapons and bang-bang! Naturally, he's been sent up numerous times. But the slippery Bobo Torsson has maintained a lower profile. 'Fashion photographer'—I don't think so! He's been moving in the right inner circles, and it was easy for him to deal undisturbed. Something tells me that it's time to call in the Narcs."

They all nodded in agreement. First of all, it would take a load off their own already overworked investigative group, but above all the narcotic investigators knew so much more about current conditions inside Göteborg's drug scene.

Satisfied with this decision, the superintendent said, "Let's take ten minutes for a coffee break while we wait for Pelle, the arson tech."

Gratefully, they all took advantage of the chance to stretch their legs and try to spark some life into their weary brain cells with a little caffeine. Some poisons are required by the body in order to function better, Mona Söder had said. Irene had a vague notion that she was turning into a caffeine addict. But in that case it should probably be viewed as an old dependence, since she had been drinking her daily dose of at least ten cups of coffee for more than ten years now. With slightly shaky hands she downed cups number four and five for the day.

WHEN ANDERSSON emerged from the rest room, Birgitta Moberg was standing a few meters away. He could tell that she was waiting for him. She walked right up to him and said, "Could I have a few words with you? I'll make it fast."

His stomach knotted. Was she going to start harping again on the fact that Jonny had sexually harassed her? Reluctantly, he ushered her into his office. Without any hemming and hawing, she got right to the point.

"It was a good idea you suggested on Friday, that I should stay at Mamma's over the weekend. I didn't want to say anything in the meeting, but it was probably Bobo Torsson who came by and rang my doorbell several times this weekend."

"Are you sure?"

"No, not at all! That's why I wanted to cool it and not say anything in front of the others. As you know, I have a studio apartment in Högsbo. My closest neighbor on the same floor is a sweet little old lady. She's eighty-three, but sharp as a tack. It was late before I got home last night. It was almost eleven-thirty. When I put my key in the lock my little neighbor opened her door. She had stayed up waiting for me and was very upset. We have an intercom at the street door. If you don't have your key, you have to ring someone from the street and ask them to open it. Sometimes kids ring as a prank, but what happened on Saturday and Sunday went well beyond the usual. Someone stood there and pressed all the doorbells at once out of sheer rage. When my neighbors answered their intercoms they got an earful of swearing and abusive language! My neighbor heard several times that the voice wanted to get hold of 'that fucking whore who calls herself a cop.' She quite correctly drew the conclusion that it had something to do with me, since I'm the only cop in the building. This occurred around seven on Saturday morning and at nine on Sunday night."

"Did anyone see the 'voice'?"

"No, that's just it. He drove his car right up to the front door. Above it there's a little roof to protect you from the rain and snow. I live on the third floor. That's why my neighbor never managed to see more than a brief glimpse of a man climbing into his car and screeching off down the street. He was tall and thin. The car was big and red, she was sure of that."

"And now you want us to check whether Torsson has a red car?"

"Right."

"Why couldn't you mention this in the conference room?"

She avoided looking at him directly and shifted her gaze around the room before she replied. "Because there's someone in our department who's tall and thin and has a red Volvo."

He knew at once who she meant, and he wished he could break out in a hearty yet indulgent laugh and give her a reassuring pat on the shoulder. But the laugh froze in his throat because he couldn't rule it out as completely impossible.

"Jonny. You mean Jonny," he said glumly.

"Yes."

There was a long silence. Finally she took a deep breath and said, "That's why I'm staying with Mamma for a while longer. But you're the only one I'm telling. Nobody else. You have the address."

She turned on her heel and strode out. He nodded to the closed door.

THE ARSON technician and the others had already taken their seats when the superintendent came in. He pretended not to notice their inquiring glances, but signaled to Pelle to get started.

Pelle began by telling them that the theory about the devil bomb was stronger than ever. It had been a real charge with explosives in an iron pipe, blasting cap, pentyl fuse, and gasoline containers, just as he originally suspected. The bomb was placed on top of a bureau in the entryway to von Knecht's office. The reason they knew this was partially due to Sylvia von Knecht. Before she drove up to Marstrand on Friday night, she had helped Pelle make a rough sketch of the apartment and its furnishings.

Tommy raised his hand before he asked his question. "A bomb like that, is it hard to make? Does it take a long time?"

"For someone who knows how, it goes pretty fast. No more than an hour. The problem is getting hold of all the components. You can't just go into Domus department store and buy blasting caps, plastique explosive, and pentyl fuses. The other stuff is easier to get hold of. To continue with what happened Wednesday night, I have to explain more about the detonator mechanism. The outer door to the office apartment was really solid. It opened outward. A thin steel wire was stretched between the handle on the door and a pin on the spring of the blasting cap. When the door was pulled open by the person we first thought was a young man, but we now know was a woman, the pin was pulled out and the spring struck the blasting cap. *Boom!* We know the result. It's only thanks to the solid outer door that there was anything left of the body at all. She was flung backward and was probably knocked unconscious instantly. The reason she was lying in a semiprone position when we found her is probably because she slipped down when the door swung back. We found this in the outer door."

You could hear a pin drop when the arson technician pulled a thick plastic bag from his pocket. There was a blackened key ring inside.

"And yesterday I found this, at the spot where the body was found."

Like a magician he pulled another bag out of his pocket. It also contained a key ring, but it was much smaller with only three keys on it. He shook the smaller ring.

"Two of these are car keys. To a Porsche. The third fits a garage door on Molinsgatan, where the von Knecht family keeps their cars."

They all felt the draft as the phantom passed by. His breath stank of death and ashes when he laughed right in their faces.

Andersson's eyes were popping out of their sockets like red Ping-Pong balls. His face was turning purple and his breathing was labored as he wheezed. Nobody moved. They all prayed silently that the superintendent wouldn't have a stroke.

Pelle was disconcerted. He could sense the charged atmosphere, but he wasn't quite sure what the cause was. So he kept silent and waited for Andersson's comments on the discovery of the keys.

Andersson tried hard to pull himself together. It wasn't easy, since even he realized that all the hypotheses and theories he had been working on had dissolved at a single blow. Finally he wheezed resolutely, "Somebody is screwing with us. Have you managed to indentify where the other keys on the ring go?" He asked even though, inside, he already knew the answer.

The arson tech nodded. "Yes. Two of them are to the office door on Berzeliigatan. Two are to von Knecht's apartment on Molinsgatan, and the last two are to the summerhouse at Marstrand. Three are deadbolt keys and three are a normal Yale type. Each door has a Yale lock and a deadbolt."

"We've always said that both these sets of keys had to be somewhere. And now they've both been found at the same impossible place, for Christ's sake!"

Andersson put into words what everyone was feeling. The arson tech looked bewildered, but decided to go on with his report. He turned a page in his notebook and continued, "The problem right now is to get into a safe that's set inside the wall. It's not that large, but it's in a tricky location, since there's no floor to stand on. We're trying to do it by standing on a skylift. We'll have to drill around the safe and try to lift it out with a standalone."

Several of the group said simultaneously, "A what?"

Pelle grinned and explained, "A standalone. To put it simply, it's a big forklift truck on which you can raise the lifting fork very high while the truck stands 'alone' on the ground, so to speak."

A weighty silence descended. It was Irene who finally broke it.

"So the situation is apparently as follows: Pirjo had the keys to von Knecht's two apartments and to his car. Why in the world would he give her these keys? Sylvia told me that Pirjo didn't have any keys, that she was always let in to the apartments by someone in the family. And as far as the car is concerned, I wonder whether Pirjo even had a driver's license. We'll have to check on that. We know she didn't have a car. She always took the bus or streetcar. If the car keys were lying where we found Pirjo's body, did it mean that she had the keys on her? In her pocket, for instance?"

"Yes," the technician said, "unless someone dropped the keys outside the door and they wound up underneath . . . what was her name? . . . Pirjo, when she was knocked unconscious by the blast. But it doesn't seem very likely."

The superintendent recalled what Hannu had said a couple of days earlier and put in, "How could she have gotten the keys?"

Irene tried to think clearly before she replied. "On Monday she was at Molinsgatan with her daughter. She could have taken them then. In that case, I wonder where she found them. After all, Sylvia von Knecht denied the existence of a fourth key ring. Although then the question is, why did she wait until Wednesday evening? Why not Monday or Tuesday evening?"

"Her kids got sick and had a high fever," said Hannu.

"You might be right about that. A mother has plenty to do when her kids get the flu. And two of Pirjo's kids had it. But Marjatta was home and could take care of her sick brothers when Pirjo was away for a few hours. On the other hand, maybe they were so sick that they took priority over her little break-in."

None of them thought that really jibed with the picture they had of Pirjo. Tommy thought out loud, "It doesn't make sense. On Monday evening Pirjo could have been quite sure that Richard von Knecht wouldn't be at his office apartment. He had a cold, which she had seen for herself when she was there cleaning that day. On Tuesday evening she wouldn't have been as sure. No, from a logical standpoint she should have chosen Monday evening. Keep in mind that she didn't know von Knecht was dead until Wednesday morning!"

Irene nodded agreement and went on, "Maybe she stole the keys, but she chickened out. Not until she found out that von Knecht was dead did she think it was risk-free. Sylvia told me that Pirjo thought her pay was too low. Maybe she was thinking of taking some items and selling them, because she needed money. Although I doubt that Pirjo knew where to go to sell antiques and art. Richard von Knecht didn't surround himself with off-the-shelf items."

Fredrik had a suggestion. "Could it have been a put-up job? Let's say that somebody knows that von Knecht has a particularly valuable item in his apartment, so he asks Pirjo to steal the keys. And then to go into the apartment and steal the thing."

After not saying a word for a long time, Birgitta broke her silence. "Imagine if someone gave the keys to Pirjo so, unsuspecting, she would go over there and trigger the bomb."

Irene felt an icy chill even though the air in the room was heavy and stuffy. Slowly she said, "It would be terrible to deliberately send a mother of three to certain death. And to risk the lives of the other renters in the building."

Andersson couldn't drop the matter of the keys, but kept on working at it. "But what about the car keys! Explain those God damn car keys! Why give the keys to a Porsche to someone who probably can't drive?"

Nobody had a good explanation, so he continued, "Do we have any witness who saw Pirjo arrive at Berzeliigatan?"

Tommy tried to hide his embarrassment when he answered the question. "No, we didn't know we were supposed to ask if anyone had seen a fat little woman arrive at the building. The whole time we assumed it was a time bomb, with the perpetrator sitting in safety far from the site. I'm going to meet the woman who has the hair salon on the ground floor today, and the woman who lives with her daughter in Mölndal. I'll probably have to wait a while to talk to her husband."

"Okay," Andersson said. "That will be your assignment for today. Hannu, you check on whether Pirjo had a driver's license. See if you can get anything else out of the daughter. Keep in touch with Pathology and contact me as soon as the forensic odontologists are done with their examination."

He looked around and his gaze fell on Hans Borg, who true to habit was sitting dozing in his chair.

"Borg!"

Everyone in the room jumped, especially Borg.

"Wake up! You have to go out and do some legwork. Go around to all the key makers downtown and try to find out where and when the keys were made. I want to know everything about those keys! Also find out whether this is the only spare key to the car and the garage."

Borg nodded and stifled a yawn.

"Fredrik and Jonny, you go and stake out Shorty, at least until we nab Bobo Torsson. Is anyone on Berzeliigatan right now?"

Fredrik nodded. "An old lady from General Investigations, Eva Nyström. Hannu arranged for her."

Irene's first reaction was surprise and then indignation. Eva Nyström was the same age she was. *Old lady, my foot!*

Andersson gave Hannu an approving nod. "Fredrik and Jonny, take over from Eva Nyström and organize the search. So far it's been quiet down there at the smoke shop, but I have a hunch that some kind of monkey business might be going on. Irene, you've already been in contact with the Narcs. You and I will go over there in an official capacity and inform them about our dear cousins. In other words, tell them we need help to figure out what those two are up to! Birgitta, dig into all the files we have on Bobo and Shorty. Somewhere there's got to be a clue to where Torsson might be hiding out. We'll all meet back here at seven-thirty tomorrow morning."

THINGS DID not go smoothly between Superintendent Andersson and Assistant Superintendent Annika Nilsén in the International Narcotics Division. In vain she tried to explain that they didn't have any personnel to spare for what in her eyes wasn't a lead for Narcotics, but part of the investigation into the von Knecht case.

The superintendent, puffing up his cheeks, gave her a riveting glare, explaining without trying to conceal his anger that this was a matter of homicide, homicidal arson, and assault on a police officer. And since it all had to do with a known criminal who was previously mixed up in narcotics cases along with his small-time drug addict pal and cousin, it was definitely a matter for Narcotics!

An expression of infinite indulgence and patience came over Annika Nilsén's weary face. "If all the crimes involving drugs and drug addicts were automatically assigned to us, you could rename the entire Göteborg Police Headquarters 'the Narcs,'" she said quietly.

This wasn't completely true, but close enough. Andersson knew it, but still was so furious that he looked like he was going to fling himself at the poor assistant superintendent. Into this charged atmosphere came the same young colleague who had helped Irene over the weekend with the information on Bobo Torsson.

Irene turned to him with a happy smile. "Well, hi there! And thanks for the help with Torsson."

"Oh, don't mention it."

She extended her hand and he shook it without hesitation. A dry, warm handshake. Irene had found the person she needed.

"Irene Huss. I think I forgot to ask for your name."

"Jimmy Olsson. Assistant."

With a radiant smile and a gleam in her eyes, Irene leaned toward Annika Nilsén and turned on her most charming manner. At least she hoped so as she chirped, "I'm sure you've already thought of the fact that Jimmy here knows a little about what we're investigating. I wonder if you would possibly consider lending him to us?"

The assistant superintendent, puzzled, ran her fingers through her salt-and-pepper pageboy haircut. "I suppose it would be all right," she said vaguely.

A quick glance at Andersson revealed that he wanted something more concrete. Two or three inspectors would do. Annika Nilsén saw her chance. She stretched a little in her unbecoming navy-blue jacket and looked at Jimmy Olsson.

"Have you ever been in the Violent Crimes Division?" she asked.

"Well, as a rookie I was in the Criminal Department for eight weeks. In the Burglary Division, not Violent Crimes."

"Then this is an excellent opportunity for you to broaden your knowledge and network of contacts. You will assist Violent Crimes in the von Knecht case. But I want you back again!"

With this last remark she jokingly shook her finger at him while giving Irene a knowing smile. It was her way of telling them that Jimmy was a very good choice. And nobody could come and say that Narcotics never helped out!

IRENE SPENT a few hours bringing Jimmy up to speed. She had no complaints about his interest. He hung on every word she said. It couldn't be denied that she envied him his enthusiasm faced with this intricate mystery. His puppylike eagerness was surely due to his youth, but his questions were intelligent. Her instinct had been correct. These days, the more complicated things got, the more tired she felt. But she remembered how it had been the first few years. The excitement, the aroused hunting instincts, and the feeling of triumph when the case was solved. Of course she still had these feelings, but noticeably attenuated. Far too many cases had not left behind the sweetness of victory, but rather a bitter aftertaste. You become jaded and cynical in this profession, she thought in her darker moments. But she didn't want to become either jaded or cynical! You had to go on, keep moving forward. You couldn't stop and dig yourself a hole. The job she had chosen was not without its dangers, but she had never wanted to do anything else and had always enjoyed her work. The past few years she had begun to notice an insidious feeling that hadn't existed before. Only recently had she been able to identify it. Terror. Terror of people's indifference to the human values of others and terror of the ever-increasing violence.

She must have sighed out loud, because Jimmy Olsson glanced up in surprise from the papers on the desk. In front of him lay the sketches of Marstrand. Not because it was necessary, but because he was interested. To cover her sigh she said, "Well, it's high time we got something to eat. I wonder what delicacies the cafeteria has to offer today."

Jimmy made an eloquent grimace. They decided to take a quick break in town and try to find a decent "special of the day."

On the way out they stopped by Birgitta Moberg's office. She was deeply ensconced in her papers and data files, but agreed to accompany them. It was almost one o'clock, and her stomach was rumbling.

THEY HURRIED along, their shoulders hunched against the biting wind. The sky was overcast, and rain was threatening. The wind tore angrily at the branches of the newly erected Christmas tree in Drottning Square. It didn't succeed in eliciting any great Christmas spirit in the passersby. Everyone was huddled up and wanted only to get indoors. Only three dumb cops would come up with the idea of trudging more than a kilometer in this kind of weather, just to have lunch. But both Irene and Birgitta had the same need to put some distance between themselves and headquarters, to be able to relax. It wasn't anything they had discussed, just a shared feeling. And all the rookie Jimmy had to do was tag along. Even if he had any opinion about their lunch excursion, he didn't feel it was his place to say anything. He held his tongue, like the smart young police assistant he was.

They plodded across Brunnsparken and along the Great Harbor Canal. There were white geese on the canal; the water level was high. This usually presaged a storm. With a feeling of salvation from hunger and cold they walked through the doors to the Golden Days. An abundance of shining, polished wood and red plush, a dark and cozy English pub atmosphere enveloped them. It seemed totally natural to order beer by the pint.

They gorged at the salad bar and ate creamed hash. It was getting on toward two o'clock. They were almost alone in the restaurant. Not until the coffee arrived did they begin discussing their ongoing research. After offering cigarettes to the other two, who declined, Birgitta lit one for herself. Irene was surprised; she thought Birgitta had quit smoking. After gracefully blowing a smoke ring, Birgitta told them, "I have a little idea about where we could look for Bobo Torsson. While reading through Shorty's thick file, I found a report about his arrest, along with two pals, following an armed bank robbery in Kungsbacka in nineteen eighty-two. They got around eight hundred thousand, but their luck ran out during the getaway. The driver was a nervous guy, barely eighteen, who drove the stolen car onto a traffic island and crashed into a signpost. There was no time to arrange for a new car, so they chugged off in their damaged car. At the old northern turnoff to Kungsbacka there's a big kiosk. That's where they turned in and forced a newspaper deliveryman to hand over his car. But it took time. There was a classic car chase along the coast, with our colleagues from Kungsbacka hot on the tail of the Honda. At Billdal Church they ran into a police roadblock, and the chase was over. But at the end of the report our colleague writes something interesting. He mentions that Shorty was mad as hell at the poor eighteen-year-old and screamed, 'How the hell could you miss the turnoff?' In the interrogation our colleagues put extra pressure on the kid. Finally he spilled the beans and told them he was supposed to turn down a little cow path before Lindås, but he was so jumpy he just stomped on the gas and missed the turnoff that led to their planned hideout, a cottage belonging to Shorty's grandparents, where both his mother and Bobo's mother had grown up. Today it's a summerhouse."

Irene leaned across the table and said excitedly, "That's one more point of contact between Bobo and Shorty! Do their mothers use it as a summerhouse?"

"Not Shorty's mother—she died five years ago. His father is unknown, according to the file. I know a little more about Bobo's parents: they're divorced. The mother is remarried and lives in Vänersborg. I just tracked down her address today and asked our colleagues up there to check it out, so that little Bobo won't hide out at his mamma's place. But she said she didn't know where he was living. She was extremely upset. Claimed that the whole thing had to be a mistake: her Bobo was the most conscientious boy you could imagine. I don't know where his father is. He's a set designer who took early retirement, but I can't find either an address or phone number for him."

Jimmy raised his eyebrows and said, "Sounds like a great place to hide out. With Daddy, I mean."

"Well, he's sixty-three and was pensioned off early because of mental problems ten years ago. A serious alcoholic. According to what I found out, he's homeless."

There was a moment of reflection. Finally Irene said, "I think Billdal might be worth investigating. It's the closest thing to a lead we have. Jimmy and I will drive out there and scout about. You'll have to hold down the fort and keep looking for possible hideouts for Torsson."

"That sounds good. By now I'm so familiar with Bobo's and Shorty's files that I'm probably the best qualified to keep on trying to track him down," said Birgitta.

They quickly paid the check and ran out into the rain that had just started to fall. The planets were favorable today. The number seven streetcar came just as they reached the stop. They took it to Lilla Stampgatan. From there it was still a way to police headquarters. Soaking wet, they went through the doors, leaving small puddles behind them like a trail of bread crumbs leading to the elevator.

THEY TOOK out maps of the area mentioned in the report from the 1982 arrest. It took a while before they located the cottage. The "cow path" that the eighteen-year-old had missed was no more; a large rowhouse development had grown up where it had been. All the streets were redrawn. And at first they were searching much too close to the coast. But finally Irene succeeded in finding the little property, less than a hectare in size, on the border of the Sandsjöbacka nature preserve. In the report the cottage was called "Solhem," and its location was marked on the detailed map.

Irene exclaimed, "What a fantastic setup! Not a house within sight of the farm. Perfect for someone who wants to hide out. Dense forest toward the nature preserve, hills on the north side, and open fields to the south and west. And no buildings in any direction."

She stopped and continued with less enthusiasm, "There will be problems. How can we reach the house without being seen?"

Jimmy and Irene bent their heads over the map. Irene finally found a possible route.

"We'll have to drive in via the Lindås interchange and then take the back roads toward Sandsjöbacka until we can't go any farther. There are some small residential areas, but we'll have to park out of view. We don't want anyone getting worried and calling the police. Somewhere around here I think would be good. We'll have to stay in the woods and head along the edge of the forest to the north."

She made an "X" with her index fingernail on the map and Jimmy nodded, Yes.

His eyes followed the line that Irene drew with her fingernail. He was vibrating with excitement, although he was unaware of it. But it had an effect on Irene, who felt like an army commander before a battle. Yet she knew it was one thing to go over the route on the map and another thing entirely to stumble across rugged terrain in the rain and the dark.

Birgitta asked, "Do you have a chance to put on dry clothes before you take off? If you have to stand still outdoors to keep watch you'll be frozen stiff."

She gave their wet jeans and shoes a critical look. Irene remembered the box with her jogging outfit in the car and said, "I have my workout clothes in the car."

"You can't go roaming around the woods in judo pajamas!"

"No, not the judo clothes. A jogging suit. Tommy and I were going jogging Tuesday evening. But Tuesday was a washout, as you know. Jimmy, do you have any dry clothes?"

"Oh, I'll be all right. But I have to go get a cool gadget we might need."

He vanished out the door. Irene went down to her car. It was very windy, and the ice-cold rain whipped at her face. It was dark as night. Maybe it wasn't necessary to drive out to Billdal in this sort of weather. *Now, now*—that was just thinking of her own comfort, because the cottage did seem like a credible option. And credible options had to be examined. If for no other reason than to be dropped so the investigation could proceed.

Up in Birgitta's office Jimmy was showing off his gadget. It looked like the result of a fusion between a diver's face mask, a little tube telescope, and a gas mask. His whole face radiated enchantment as he demonstrated all the features.

"You can see them as clear as day! When people look in your direction you can't believe they can't see you!"

"What in the world is that?" Birgitta wondered.

"A night-vision telescope, actually an electronic light amplifier. It can amplify the existing light up to ten thousand times."

It was high time they got going, so Irene interrupted, "I'm putting on dry socks and my jogging pants under my jeans. Do you want to borrow my sweater?"

At first he looked dubious, but after glancing out the window at the rain being flung against the panes by the fierce wind, he nodded.

Birgitta turned energetic and practical. It was actually her plan they were following. "It's quarter past three now. We have to allow at least half an hour for you to drive out to Billdal in weather like this. How far do you have to walk through the woods?" she asked.

Irene measured on the map before she answered. "About five or six hundred meters. It's dark, the terrain is unfamiliar, and the weather is bad. Add on another fifteen minutes."

"You won't be in place until four at the earliest. When and how do we contact each other?"

Irene thought for a moment. "I'll take my cell phone but turn it off. I wouldn't want it to start ringing at an unlucky moment. Let's say this: I'll call you at five o'clock on the dot. If you don't hear anything within half an hour after that, send backup."

Jimmy gave her an astonished look and said, "Don't you think the two of us can take care of one guy?"

"Sure, Bobo we can take care of, but his cousin and his playmates might be on the way. Keep in mind that we're just doing recon. If Bobo is alone we'll take him. But if there are other people there, we'll withdraw discreetly and wait for the cavalry. Shorty's friends are always heavily armed. These guys feel naked without something heavier than an Uzi."

For anyone who's ever been in Narcotics, this wasn't news. Jimmy looked thoughtful. Finally he nodded at Irene and said, "Should we take Sigge along?"

Birgitta was only listening with half an ear, but reacted to the name. She asked, "There's nobody in the group named Sigge. Do you mean Tommy?"

"No. SIG Sauer, nicknamed Sigge. Our service weapons!"

They laughed, which relieved the tension a bit. Was their hunting instinct coming to life? Jimmy's visible enthusiasm at going out on a manhunt was infectious. Imagine if it turned out to be an anticlimax. He would be incredibly disappointed. Irene nodded. "Sure, we'll take our Sigges."

They stopped by the weapons case, got out their pistols, and loaded them with nine-millimeter ammunition. The SIG Sauer is a powerful weapon, far superior to the old peashooter—the Walther 7.65— that Irene had once used in training. But Jimmy had never had to retrain. The Sigge was his weapon, the one he was trained to use. A bit nonchalant, he loaded the pistol and stuffed it in his holster. Irene wasn't used to the holster since she seldom went armed. But she and everyone else had to use one when they went out with a Sigge. The weapon is heavy and can't be stuck in a jacket pocket, no more than a Walther can. From a purely practical standpoint, it's impossible to keep a gun in your pocket. There's no room in a pants pocket, and it's too heavy for a jacket pocket. An investigator who goes around in a jacket with one pocket hanging down to his knees might as well put a rotating blue light on top of his head. The holster is essential. The advantages of the SIG Sauer compared to the Walther are a larger caliber and a more powerful effect. The drawbacks are its weight and the sluggishness of the spring when cocking the weapon. It requires a good deal of strength to handle this pistol, a heavy weapon for the heavy boys. Simply put, the Sigge is macho. Irene preferred the Walther. Even though, according to Tommy, you had to aim the barrel down when you fired it so that the bullet would roll out.

THEY BUMPED along the country roads toward Sandsjöbacka. The wind took hold of the car and shook it angrily. The rain poured down. It was impossible to see where they were. They had to orient themselves by the road signs they passed. Irene drove and Jimmy read the map in the flickering light of his flashlight. He folded up the map and said, "We should park somewhere around here."

She almost missed the small forest road, had to brake sharply and back up. She parked the car precariously close to a big ditch in which water was gushing wildly. But there was probably no danger, because they wouldn't be staying long; they'd be back before the ditch overflowed. Irene took the map and checked their route one last time.

"We have to follow this gravel road to the end. Then we'll pass some small houses, I think summer cabins. Then we go into the trees and follow the edge of the woods about four hundred meters."

Jimmy nodded, and again she sensed his exuberance.

They started walking, the beams of their flashlights pointing down. There were no streetlights here. In order to see where the road went and to avoid stepping into hollows and pits, they had to use their flashlights. They could only hope that the howling storm and dense forest would hide them.

At the end of the road were two small summer cabins. There was a light on in one of them, but they couldn't see anyone inside or hear anything. To the left Irene discovered a big pile of lumber. She cautiously shone her flashlight around it and for a fraction of a second had a hard time comprehending what she saw. The beam fell on a big black motorcycle, half concealed behind the stack of boards. A Harley-Davidson chopper. On the back was a big Tour-Pak, on which a sign said in English: THIS BIKE BELONGS TO A HELL'S ANGEL — IF YOU DON'T

BELIEVE IT, JUST TRY TO MESS WITH MY BIKE! This hog could be left unlocked even in the most notorious slums. It would be completely safe. Most people have some instinct for self-preservation.

Like lightning Irene turned off her flashlight, and Jimmy did the same a fraction of a second later. They stood motionless and listened to the darkness. There was no sound from the houses. Carefully they crept past and moved as quietly as they could into the woods. For the first time they were thankful for the furious storm roaring in the treetops. It became an ally when they stepped awkwardly on fallen twigs or tripped over treacherous roots and slippery rocks. Finally they could no longer see the light from the cabin and dared to stop and turn on their flashlights.

Jimmy looked pale and grim. The rain had plastered his short hair flat to his head. Irene was grateful that she had put on Katarina's baseball cap before they left the car. He sounded excited when he whispered, "Holy shit, what does this mean? A Hell's Angels' nest! Out here in the woods!"

He was obviously shaken. She was too, but tried not to show it.

"I guess they rent one of the cabins during the winter," she said, feigning nonchalance.

She turned around and continued stumbling onward. But she had a hard time concentrating on what lay before them. What they had just left behind felt like an unpleasant threat. Even if it could hardly have anything to do with Shorty and Bobo's cottage, Hell's Angels could never be ignored. Finally she forced herself to focus her attention on what lay ahead. A faint light winked among the trees. Jimmy took her arm and silently mapped out a route at an angle along the edge of the woods. They were completely agreed. A high cairn of stones rose at the side of the clearing and would give them perfect cover, while also allowing them to get up a bit higher and have a better view.

Their fingers were numb from the cold. When they tried to climb up the cairn, Irene lost her grip and slid down. Her knee was banged up and her palms were torn, but her body was so stiff from the cold that she hardly noticed. When she climbed back, Jimmy was already crouched down, gazing through his night-vision telescope. Irene was grateful he had brought it along. Without it they would have had to crawl all the way up to the house. Now they could stay about fifty meters away. She peered into the distance toward the point of light and saw that it was an outside lamp attached to a little building that looked like a barn. Faint light was coming from some small windows.

Jimmy lay motionless so long that she started to grow impatient. She also wanted to look through the funny gadget. But his tense whisper when he handed the telescope to her filled her with foreboding. "You won't believe it. Look at the outer edge of the circle of light coming from the outside lamp."

The bill of her cap was in the way, so she turned it resolutely backward. It prevented the ice-cold rain from running down her neck.

Fumbling, she put the telescope up to her eye, strapped it on, and saw instantly what he meant. A large motorcycle stood parked by the wall of the barn. When she pointed the telescope toward one of the small illuminated windows, she could see a big fat man with long curly hair. He stood talking and gesticulating to someone hidden from view. Even though no one could hear them, she whispered, "I can only see one guy, fat with long hair. But it isn't Bobo Torsson. Did you see anybody else?"

"No. Just Fatso. And the bike! Did you see it? Hell's Angels again!"

"It's not the same one we saw at the summer cabin?"

"No, this one doesn't have a Tour-Pak on the back."

He was right. This one had two smaller boxes on each side of the rear wheel. The fat, longhaired man walked around talking to his invisible audience. For a split second Irene thought she saw the head of a much shorter person, but it happened so fast that she wasn't sure. She whispered to Jimmy without taking the telescope from her eye, "I think there are at least two of them. But what are they up to?"

"No idea."

A movement on the far right edge of her vision made her point the telescope in that direction. Excitedly she whispered, "Somebody is coming out of the house next door! That must be the house they actually live in. It's not Bobo Torsson. This one's a longhaired guy dressed in leather too, but tall and thin."

"Funny that he doesn't turn on the outside light. I can't see anybody."

"You can't?"

Irene put down the telescope and looked toward the house. It was dark. Only the lights in the barn were visible. The man was walking in the dark. He was invisible to anyone without night-vision equipment. She put the telescope up to her eyes, only to see the thin man disappear behind the barn. She quickly aimed it at the barn window. The big man stopped short and turned with his back to the window. She understood that the other one was talking now, because suddenly the massive man was quite motionless and seemed to be listening intently. She almost dropped the telescope out of sheer fright when he suddenly turned on his heel and gazed out the window. Reason told her that he couldn't see them, but the expression on his face said it all. Fear drove its stiff fingers into her body and she couldn't even hide it from Jimmy. Her voice almost cracked when she whispered with frozen lips, "Jimmy, they know we're here!"

"That's impossible. How could they . . . ?"

The thought struck them both simultaneously. The summer cabins. The motorcycle behind the pile of lumber. They had been seen.

Irene asked, "What time is it?"

He pulled up the sleeve of his jacket and looked at the glowing watch face. "Ten past five. It's time to get out of here."

They crawled down from the cairn. Irene started to pull her cell phone from her pocket. She turned it on but slipped it back into her pocket. Her subconscious had heard a sound, but her conscious mind registered it too late. The forest around her exploded like a shooting star in a thousandth of a second, then closed around her in impenetrable darkness.

HER HEAD was swinging from side to side and she couldn't do anything about it. Powerless, she tried to raise herself to throw up, but realized groggily that it was impossible. Her head was hanging down. A strong smell of leather and sweat stung her nostrils and increased her nausea. Instinctively she kept her body limp, as she desperately tried to fight against the dizziness and reenter consciousness. After a while she realized that a hefty man in leather, a Hell's Angel, was carrying her slung over his shoulder, like a butcher carries a dead carcass. His long wet hair slapped against the side of her face. Cautiously she tried opening her eyelids. She heard panting and labored breathing to her left. There were at least two other people, and it dawned on her that they were carrying something between them. Jimmy. Was he alive? Good God, make him be alive! Never before in her life had she experienced such a pure and unadulterated fear of death. She didn't have to pretend that she was incapable of movement. She was totally paralyzed.

A crystal-clear voice suddenly spoke through the panic inside her. To her surprise she recognized the voice of her old judo trainer, dead almost ten years now. Despite his forty years in Sweden, he had retained a very pronounced American accent. In his dry, calm voice he said, "Don't let them know that you're awake. Play possum. *Sonomama.* Remember *ukemi-waza.* Keep your head in so you don't hit it. *Mokuso.*"

Mokuso? Why should she meditate now, of all times? Then she understood. She needed to go outside her body to release herself from the paralyzing fear. And her body would have to take care of itself for a while; it would still be unconscious. She looked into her whirling brain, found the Point, and was sucked softly up into Yawara and the Light.

HALF OF her face lay in mud and ice-cold water. One of her nostrils bubbled when she breathed, but she didn't move her head. Her body had remembered *ukemi-waza* and fallen into a semiprone position. She sensed that there were several people around her. It took an incredible effort of will to concentrate on what they were saying and still pretend that she was unconscious.

"What the hell are we going to do with them? Who are these fucks?"

"SIG Sauer. And the telescope and phone. Great equipment. I think they're cops. Why the hell did you have to hit them so hard? We could have gotten something out of the girl at least."

"Don't tell the guys that it was a chick! She's tall as hell and she had a cap on."

"Fuck them, God damn it!"

The last voice came as a shock to Irene. A young girl. In a confused moment Irene imagined that it was one of her own daughters. The illusion passed and she managed to lie still.

"Shut up, you whore! If we're going to fuck anybody, it's you!"

Irene could hear at least three different laughs. Maybe four.

"Should we take them inside? It's pissing wet out here."

"Take them to the barn."

It took all the will in the world for her to hang limply between two Hell's Angels. They dragged her rather than carried her, and she banged her hip on the high threshold. She let her head hang down and tried not to allow even a quiver of her eyelids. She could hear the thud when they dropped Jimmy next to her. Presumably he was alive, since they took the trouble to bring him inside. Here it was dry but the floor was ice cold. To her horror she couldn't conceal the cold shivers that ran through her body. Stopping the occasional tremor was beyond her control, but she still pretended to be unconscious.

"Wake them up."

A swift kick in the side. She couldn't hold back a whimper, so she masked it with a low mumble. Dull thuds were heard as they kicked Jimmy, but not a sound came from him. After another kick she felt it was time to change the scenario. Whimpering, she moved her head and mumbled something incoherent.

"The broad is coming to!"

Twitch the eyelids, look confused and groggy. Be careful to survey the surroundings. Four leather-clad guys and a little blond girl, also in leathers. Jimmy lay next to her, less than a meter away. He was unrecognizable, covered with mud, his face swollen. At least he was alive. His chest heaved up and down.

"What were you and the shithead doing here on our property?"

It was the tall, thin one who was aggressively leaning over Irene. Safer not to lie. Not too much. She was very dizzy and had a hard time finding the words, but she did her best. She slurred, "We were on a stakeout . . . narcotics . . . police."

She closed her eyes and pretended to pass out again. Then the telephone rang. Squinting through half-closed eyes she saw the fat leader, bewildered, looking at the phone he was holding in his right hand. The thin one snatched it from him and unfolded it.

They could all hear a worried female voice say, "Irene? It's Birgitta. What's going on?"

At first he cast a dubious glance at Irene, but suddenly he raised the phone to his mouth.

"Fuck you!" he yelled.

Then he folded it up and broke into a contented grin. "That'll give the bitch something to think about!" he said happily.

The leader reared back and took a powerful swing. The blow from his fist landed squarely on the other man's chin. From Irene's perspective it looked as if he jumped straight up in the air and simply vanished. But from the thud that followed she knew that he had landed against the door.

The powerful leader massaged his knuckles as he screamed, "You stupid fuck! If a cop's phone rings, you ought to know there's another fucking cop on the other end!"

Another one of the gang could be counted out. At least for a while.

"Shit! She said it was the Narcs! God damn it!"

The fat one went over and stuck a heavy motorcycle boot into the left side of her ribs. There was a dry crack—at least one rib had gone. There was nothing feigned about the moan that came from her lips.

"Answer, you fucking slut! How long have you known about this place?"

"Don't remember . . . got a tip . . . a tip."

"Was it that shithead Bobo who tipped you? Answer!"

At first she was so surprised that she almost opened her eyes. There it was! A connection! But she quickly regained her composure. "Don't know . . . I didn't . . . answer."

"Did the tip come by phone?"

"Yeah."

"When?"

Good heavens! When? When would be logical? She had to trust her intuition.

"This morning."

The leader took a deep breath before he screamed furiously, "That fucking asshole! He split with the bread. Then he sets the cops on us while we sit here with our pants down! I knew we couldn't trust that miserable shit!"

He paused to ponder the new facts that Irene had served up to him. It seemed to ring true to him.

"You should be damned glad that we don't have a lot of time. But . . ." He turned to his pals. Even the thin one was now up on wobbly legs, staggering toward them. A malicious grin slid across his flabby face when the leader continued, "What does a Hell's Angel do with the fucking cops? Right! Like this!"

All four of them lined up in a row. They pulled down the zippers on their leather pants, pulled out their dicks, and started to piss, on Irene and Jimmy. The little blond laughed so hard she howled, slapped her knees, and had to lean against the wall.

It's nothing dangerous. It's only urine. This can't be happening! We won't die of it. Good God, let it be over soon. Silently Irene repeated this incantation to keep her hysteria in check. The stench of the hot piss on her face made her start to vomit.

Then it was over. The light was switched off and they went out, laughing. Before he slammed the door, the leader turned and said, "Don't you dare open the door if you want to live. Besides I'm putting on the padlock."

The way Irene was feeling, she wouldn't be able to move for quite a while. Her first reaction when the door closed behind the gang was an incredible sense of relief. They were gone. She could hear the heavy motorcycles in the sea of mud outside. They had been parked along the front of the barn.

Suddenly, she was aware that it was completely quiet outside. With all her senses on full alert, she sat up. Her rib hurt but she hardly noticed it. Carefully she stood. Stooping, half crawling, she moved over to the window by the door. Cautiously, she peered out from a corner of the broken windowpane.

The lamp attached to the wall outside cast a faint circle of light, and at the very edge she could discern the contours of four motorcycles and the gleam of leather overalls. On command they all started their machines at once. Three of them drove off, but the fourth lingered. Irene could see him make a throwing motion with his arm before he too took off. He had tossed something in through the broken window and instinctively she wanted to take cover. But several years of experience as a goalie on the police women's handball team now served her well. The little ball was surprisingly heavy. A Hell's Angel had thrown it, so it must be a hand grenade. The deep grooves in it confirmed what her intuition had told her. Without a conscious thought she flung it back out the window.

The hot pressure wave of the explosion seared her face. A magnesium-white light set fire to the darkness and arced out in all directions. The blinding light sucked away all sensory impressions and left her for a second in a cold, dark vacuum. The blast deafened her. Soon the total silence was replaced by a powerful pain and a shrill whistling sound that tore at her ears. Spots danced before her eyes in all the colors of the rainbow. Her field of vision was constricted from the sides, and a new wave of nausea rose up from her diaphragm. Her sight vanished; she was blind. The uncontrolled shaking returned, but it wasn't because of the cold. She sank down with her back to the wall. Whimpering, she slowly began to move toward where she thought the door was. Finally she felt the dry planks of the old stable door under her lacerated fingertips. She got it open by flinging herself desperately against the wood with her full weight, breaking off the rotten hasp. She staggered out into the rain and sank down on her knees, sat back on her heels, let her hands rest lightly on the tops of her thighs, and closed her eyes. She went into *Mokuso* while the rain rinsed away the piss.

That was the position they found her in.

Chapter Thirteen

SHE HADN'T BEEN IN the hospital since she had the twins. At first she protested at being kept overnight, but a determined and motherly nurse explained to her calmly and objectively, "You've had a blow to the back of your neck, which could cause bleeding and breathing paralysis. You could die before you got back to the hospital! And we don't want that. Here we can check you during the night and see right away if any complications arise. Agreed?"

A little upset, Irene agreed. She had a sharp pain in her neck all of a sudden. She carefully lifted the ice pack and touched the swollen area. As big as a small hen's egg. Sore. She was feeling dizzy and a bit nauseated. Most of all, she was tired and wanted to sleep. But it would have to wait. After a hot shower she had to put on a clean hospital gown, which was about as sexy as a garbage bag. Doctors and nurses ran in and out of the room. They talked to her to check that she wasn't about to slip into unconsciousness, took her blood pressure, and shone flashlights into her eyes to check the size of her pupils. When she ventured to ask a pimply youth why, he replied glibly, "If one pupil gets bigger than the other, it's all over!"

Fortified with this information, she decided to surrender. If only she could be left in peace! But it took several hours before she was allowed, exhausted, to sink into a light and restless slumber. She was constantly awakened by people who came in to check something or other.

Before this, Sven Andersson and Tommy Persson had been in to talk to her. Neither of them could hide his concern or relief. Tommy gave her a big hug. She shrieked, but excused herself, "Sorry, Tommy, but I'm black and blue all over. Look!"

Like a little kid she exhibited a bruised shoulder and hip, abraded hands and knees. She ended by saying, "The doctor thought that my rib down here is crushed but not broken. I have to take it easy for a while. How's Jimmy doing?"

Tommy replied somberly, "He's awake, but he took much harder blows to the skull than you did. How did that happen? Did they see that you were a girl, or what?"

"No, hardly! My baseball cap cushioned the blow. I had turned it backward so that the bill lay over my turned-up jacket collar. They probably didn't see it in the dark. He also took a few kicks to the head when we were inside the barn," Irene said glumly.

A busy time followed when she had to try to remember everything that happened and what was said. The superintendent was obviously interested when she told him that Bobo's name had been mentioned.

"'He split with the bread. Then he sets the cops on us while we sit here with our pants down!' The fat guy said something like that."

She had a feeling that Andersson was about to explode with secrets he was holding on to, but he was stopped by Tommy's sharp look. Who cared? She'd find out soon enough. Sleep. To be allowed to go to sleep and not have to think. Then the twins and Krister came in, in a flurry of tears and hugs. The motherly nurse who was evidently her personal Guardian Angel had promised them ten minutes, even though the doctor had advised against all visits and strong emotions. Irene tried to sound tough. "Ha! Strong emotions! After what I've been through today, I'd consider anything under seven-point-five on the Richter scale peaceful!"

Andersson winked at Krister. "She's getting better."

Irene saw Tommy give Jenny's head, clad in a cap, a long look. When Krister carefully hugged Irene and kissed her on the cheek, she whispered in his ear, "On Wednesday Tommy is coming to dinner. See that Jenny is home."

Krister looked astonished, but just nodded. Katarina gave her parents a suspicious look.

"What are you whispering about?" she asked.

"About how happy I am to have you all here. And that I'm coming home tomorrow."

Krister smiled, but the worried furrow in his brow was unusually deep.

"The nurse said that you probably can go home tomorrow. I'll come and get you. I'm taking the whole day off. I've switched with Sverker. And by then they'll probably have the car out of the ditch."

"The ditch? The car?"

"It sank into the dune by the ditch where you parked it. But the tow truck will pull it out. Everything's under control. Sammie sends plenty of licks. And we do too."

There was more hugging and kissing, and then the Guardian Angel came and shooed them all out. Exhaustion flooded over Irene; she wanted only to sink down into the depths and rest. But her sleep was shallow and restless.

BEFORE IRENE left the hospital she had to see to Jimmy Olsson. Krister had brought her some clean clothes; she was greatly relieved that she wouldn't have to pay a visit in her hospital gown. Jimmy was in the same ward. The Guardian Angel showed her to the right room.

She knocked softly and opened the door a crack. Jimmy looked like a cartoon character, but the situation was anything but funny, and Irene felt her throat tighten with sympathy. She limped into the room. Jimmy was awake, and his one visible eye lit up when he saw her. The other was hidden behind a compress. His head was wrapped in an elastic bandage, which held a plastic splint in place. There was an IV in his left arm. What she could see of his face was swollen and purple. But his voice sounded happy.

"Hello, Irene!"

"Hello yourself."

She placed her hand over his uninjured left hand and patted it a little in awkward encouragement. She had a big lump in her throat that refused to be dislodged. She managed to say in a light voice, "Now you know what it's like to go on a stakeout with someone from Violent Crimes. Talk about expanding your horizons and your contact network. A close contact with Hell's Angels!"

He started to laugh, just as she had hoped. "Damn! It hurts when I laugh," he said with a grimace.

Contritely, she patted his hand again and asked, "How's the concussion?"

"It's okay. Now I'll have something to blame in the future. But seriously, I don't feel too bad. Just a headache. I'll probably have to stay here a few days. Do you know if anything happened out in Billdal?"

"No. All I know is they had to pull my car out of the ditch. But it went okay. If I can, I'll go downtown and look at mug shots this afternoon."

"Of Hell's Angels?"

"Exactly. Can't say that I'm looking forward to seeing their lovely mugs again, but I've got to bring them in!"

"Wait for me, because I've got some scores to settle too."

Now a red flame glowed in the depths of his one visible eye. The effect was weird against the surrounding purple swelling. She understood him. There was a black depth within her from which voices whispered, *Revenge! Murder! Retribution!* Forbidden and meaningless thoughts. She straightened up and forced a smile.

"I'll come back tomorrow and tell you what's going on with the investigation. Take care of yourself."

AT HOME there were wild scenes of joy with Sammie, and he was also given a brief stroll to pee while Krister fixed lunch. She was allowed to pick anything she wanted. It was pasta with Gorgonzola sauce and a tomato and basil salad. They spoke about everything except yesterday's events. She couldn't face it. The black hole was too big, the voices too insistent. Krister understood and talked about other things.

"What was that about Tommy having dinner here tomorrow?"

"He had such a strong reaction when I told him about Jenny. He wants to talk to her. He went on and on about it being everyone's responsibility and that all skinheads are our children. Krister, I think we should let him take this up with Jenny! It can't do any harm, anyway. He's the only cop I know who works actively for Amnesty International. He's so involved."

He nodded, noticing that she was eating unusually little. He secretly scrutinized her. Normally she pulsated with energy, but now her vitality and power seemed diminished. They had known each other for sixteen years, but he had never seen her like this before.

The telephone rang. It was Sven Andersson. He wondered how she was feeling and whether she was able to come down to headquarters.

"I'll drive you, dear. Then call me when you're ready to come home and I'll pick you up," said Krister. It would be good for her to have something else to think about. Although sitting and looking at photos of the ones who had beat her up less than twenty-four hours earlier was probably not the best distraction, of course.

THE SUPERINTENDENT and Tommy were waiting for her. Before them on the table lay closed folders of criminal records. Andersson patted one and said, "We'll talk first. A lot has happened in the past twenty-four hours. Especially for you. How are you doing?"

"Well, so-so," Irene replied. "I was lucky. It's worse for Jimmy."

"I talked to the hospital an hour ago. He has to stay there at least another night. But we have to talk about this damned mess of an investigation. As I said, a lot has happened. We've got Narcotics involved with Billdal. First they give us a lousy little assistant, and then the whole division comes and takes over!"

"Sven, please. Don't call Jimmy 'a lousy little assistant.'"

"Hmm. It turns out that International has had a motorcycle gang on the west side of Göteborg under surveillance for several months. They're suspected of smuggling in large quantities of narcotics via Holland and Denmark. These scumbags are connected to the Hell's Angels, the gang that you and Jimmy ran into. They call themselves . . . 'Ded skvadron n-o one.'"

She understood that he meant "Death Squadron No. 1." Without laughing she said, "I wonder if they can spell it. What did the Narcs find out at the cottage in Billdal?"

Tommy took over. "Actually quite a bit. The grenade you talked about yesterday left a small crater. The door of the cottage was broken in. We found some pizza boxes and empty beer cans in the kitchen. In the little bedroom there was a bed, and on it was a brand-new down sleeping bag. On the floor was a plastic box and a receipt from Allsport on Södra Vägen dated last Friday. Today we checked with the staff at the sporting goods store and it turned out that Bobo Torsson bought it."

"Excellent! But you'll have to excuse someone who was just hit hard on the head—what does this all mean? Von Knecht? Pirjo and the murder bomb? Shorty, Bobo, and Hell's Angels?"

Both the superintendent and Tommy stared at her for a long time. Finally Tommy said, "And it gets even messier. We knew about it yesterday, but didn't want to tell you. We didn't want to upset you. Bobo Torsson is dead."

"Torsson is dead? Keep going, before I fall over!"

"Remember the car bomb in the parking lot at the Delsjön golf course early yesterday morning?"

Was it really only yesterday? It felt like several years ago, but she nodded to show that she was following. She began to understand the reason for Andersson's restrained agitation when he'd come to see her at the hospital.

Tommy said dramatically, "The techs found parts of a body, including a finger. The fingerprint shows that it was Bobo Torsson who was blown sky-high! And the car turned out to be Torsson's."

She wondered vaguely why the superintendent quickly interjected, "A red Toyota Corolla."

"Give me strength!" was Irene's only, but spontaneous, comment.

Andersson took over and nodded in assent. "Yeah, that's what I said too. 'Holy shit,' I said. How are we going to make any sense of this? But now the Narcs have agreed to join the investigation. Which in all honesty is lucky for us, because this is starting to get out of control!"

"What kind of bomb was it?" Irene asked.

Tommy gave her a rundown of the details. "A pipe bomb. In a briefcase that exploded when the briefcase was opened. The iron pipe was the same type used on Berzeliigatan, but much smaller. Svante thinks the type of pipe is interesting. They're old threaded drainpipes of different diameters. Modern ones are made of plastic, so they're no good for making bombs."

"Do we know what Bobo was cooking up with the Hell's Angels?"

"No. On Friday he bought a sleeping bag and headed out to the summer cottage. He probably knew we wanted to talk to him about the attack on Birgitta. We don't know what he was up to on Saturday and Sunday. But on Monday morning, at six o'clock on the dot, he was blown to bits by a bomb in his car!"

Irene looked just as confused as she felt when she asked, "Fatso thought that Bobo had split with the bread! *What bread*, I have to ask. Then he got the idea that Bobo had squealed and set us on the trail out to Billdal. While they 'sat and waited with their pants down,' as he expressed it. What did he mean by that?"

Tommy shrugged his shoulders. "Good questions. I don't have any good answers. We know that the biker gang hadn't been at Bobo's cottage for very long. At most a few hours. On the other hand, we found plenty of traces of them in the summer cabins a few hundred meters away. They obviously stayed there a few days. We're still looking into things, although now Narcotics has taken over. But we do know one thing: how they knew that you were on the way."

"I'd really like to know that!"

"They had set up an electric eye by the road, hidden in the lumber pile. When you crossed the beam an alarm went off inside the house."

"But why?"

"My theory is that they wanted to be forewarned in case anyone showed up, because they were busy with things that absolutely could not be seen by strangers. Actually, I can't imagine any activity of theirs that outsiders might see. Except when they ride around in big gangs on their choppers and look generally terrifying."

So it hadn't done them any good to turn off their flashlights and stumble blindly through the dark. Again the feeling of total helplessness came over her. She tried to control it and said matter-of-factly, "So we could have been struck down when we got to the summer cabins. Why weren't we?"

"They must have wanted to know who you were."

"I think I need some coffee before I look my Hell's Angels in the eyes. Even if it's only in mug shots."

Irene and Tommy went to get three cups of coffee from the vending machine. Mainly to put off confronting the photos. Suddenly an idea occurred to her.

"Tommy, have you questioned Shorty about this?"

"Have I! Ask Andersson!"

His cheerful response provoked premonitions that were verified by the superintendent.

"That idiot is nuts! We took him in last night, three guys from Narcotics and Fredrik Stridh from our group. We had known for three hours Bobo Torsson had been blown up in the car at the golf course. When the guys rang Shorty's doorbell he tore open the door as if he'd been standing there holding the knob! He yelled something like 'You fucking photo queer . . .' and then he shut up. Then that idiot started throwing punches! Since he was high on something, he mostly hit thin air. Which was damned lucky for our guys. Finally they got him on the floor and cuffed him. But they had a hell of a time getting him to the car! Right after we visited you in the hospital, I went to question the honorable tobacco dealer."

Andersson paused and took a big gulp of his coffee. It wasn't very fortifying, but he needed it before he could continue. "He refused to talk. Sat there staring into thin air. Finally I thought I'd better shake him up a little. 'Listen, you scumbag, do you know that Bobo's dead?' I said. He just kept on staring. After at least two minutes, when I had repeated that Bobo was dead several times, the devil seized hold of him! He jumped me and tried to get me in a choke hold! Howling like a wounded gorilla! Luckily Tommy was with me in the interrogation room, along with Bertil from Narcotics. And a few more came rushing in. That was the end of the interview last night. This morning we tried again, with strange results."

"What kind of strange results?" asked Irene.

"At nine-thirty this morning Tommy and I went to see him in the interrogation room. There sits Shorty Johannesson, public enemy number one, neat and dapper, newly showered and shaved. When we come in the shithead says, 'Forgive me for yesterday, superintendent. But it was such a shock when you said that Bobo was dead. I couldn't believe it.' And he gives me the most angelic look in the world. I was completely at a loss. I probably said, 'That's quite all right' or something of the sort. Then he says, 'Pardon me, but how did Bobo die?' And without thinking I told him about the bomb in the briefcase and all that. After that Shorty never opened his mouth."

"Didn't say a thing?"

"Not a damned word! We kept at him for several hours—nothing."

"That's weird."

"Weird? You can bet your . . . boots!"

He changed the end of the sentence abruptly after a curt knock was followed by the door opening. Prosecutor Inez Collin made her entrance and filled the small room with her authority and the scent of Chloë. She was slim and almost as tall as Irene. Her long blond hair was worn in a tight French roll. The hairdo and the high-heeled pumps with the dark gray suit made her look even taller. Her makeup was discreet, but the bright red silk blouse and her manicured nails were the same color. She smiled and said, "Hello. Excuse me for interrupting, but there's a little problem with Lasse Johannesson."

Andersson nodded and said courteously, "Hello. There's always been a problem with Lasse Johannesson."

"No doubt. It has to do with his arrest. From what I understand, there are no grounds for requesting detention of Johannesson, correct?"

"It's not so damned . . . not so easy to detain somebody when you don't know what crime he's committed. Just that he's done something!"

"Correct. But admit that there would be problems if we began taking away the freedom of everyone who fulfilled that criterion. Unfortunately I couldn't get away this morning when you were questioning Johannesson. I just went to talk with him. He didn't answer. The only thing he said was, 'You can't keep me here. I haven't committed any crime.' My question is: Has he?"

"But it's obvious that he has!"

"Then what? Do we have proof of any crime? Are there any grounds for detention?"

Andersson's face slowly began to assume that unbecoming tomato-red shade. Controlling himself, he said, "He and his cousin Bobo Torsson were up to some monkey business!"

"What was it?"

"We don't know! Something with the Hell's Angels out in Billdal. Drug deals!"

Inez Collin raised one discreetly penciled eyebrow and asked, "Do we know whether Johannesson had anything to do with the motorcycle gang? Any evidence?"

"Bobo did."

"But you don't know whether Johannesson had any contact with them. No evidence, that is."

"He was partial owner of the cottage! Along with Torsson!"

"That's not much evidence. I'm waiting with the detention order. We'll try to hold him for five days. 'Interfering with a criminal investigation' or 'risk of removal of evidence,' or the like. But if any legal representative starts yelling, I'll have a hard time justifying it. Within ninety-six hours I want hard evidence of a crime committed by Lasse Johannesson. Otherwise we'll have to release him. We have to try to keep in daily contact for a while now. I'm also dealing with the investigation of the bomb that killed Bo-Ivar Torsson. The top brass thought it would be practical. Now I won't disturb you any longer. Excuse me for interrupting."

She turned to go. At the door she stopped and turned back to the superintendent.

"Speaking of the top brass, Chief Bergström was chuckling about how well informed he was about the von Knecht case. I pressed him a bit to find out how that could be. It came out that he had asked you 'to please submit ongoing confidential reports.' I told him that all 'confidential reports' from here on have to come through me. Just so you know. See you later!"

She swept out leaving a cloud of Chloë.

Tommy sniffed the air and sighed, "What a woman!"

"Oh yes!"

The superintendent sounded as if he agreed, but Irene could tell that their reasons were not the same. To hell with it; the point now was not to delay any longer. Reluctantly, she slid over the first folder and started to page through it. But the pictures began to blur before her eyes and without being able to stop herself she asked, "How long do you have?"

"What? Time? As long as you need," the superintendent said generously.

Irene sounded like she was a crying for help. "No! Not the photo ID! How much time do you have from when the pin on a hand grenade is pulled until it detonates?"

The silence was intense and unpleasant. Finally Andersson said, "Don't think about it. Everything turned out all right."

"No! It did not turn out all right! I've been blown to bits! In my soul!"

Andersson gave her an uncertain look. Was she having a breakdown? Maybe women couldn't stand such rough stuff. But Irene was a hardened cop who had been through plenty of trying situations. He had never seen this kind of reaction from her before. At a loss, he said, "What do you mean? Why?"

"Why? The feeling of being totally at the mercy of these shitbags! The helplessness! Knocked unconscious and disarmed, then attempted murder with a hand grenade! Pissed on and degraded! And we couldn't do a thing. No, I did do one thing. I threw the grenade out the window. And that's what keeps going through my mind. What would have happened if I'd missed? Imagine if I hadn't grabbed it right away. Imagine if it had rolled away into the room. I know the answer to those questions, but I can't let go of one thing: How long have you got?"

Tommy stood up and went over to Irene. To Andersson's astonishment he bent over and put his arms around her. He leaned his head on hers and said, "Four seconds. He threw the grenade as soon as he pulled the pin, without holding on to it. They were in a hurry, he was probably stressed. That's why you made it. The throw must have taken at least half a second. Subtract that from the original four and a half. You had four seconds max."

"If he hadn't thrown it right away I wouldn't have made it!"

"No, Irene. You wouldn't have made it."

Tommy was still holding her, but she felt no comfort and warmth. An icy cold seeped up out of the black depths, and the voices echoed: *You wouldn't have made it! You would have died. Both of you ought to be dead! Nobody can make it in less than four seconds. Four seconds!*

Andersson fidgeted uncomfortably. "Stop thinking about what didn't happen. Don't get hung up on it; we have to go on with the investigation. Damn it, Irene, you're a hero who saved Jimmy's life! And your own. That's the sort of thing you get a medal for."

He stood up. Tommy had let go of her. The superintendent aimed a clumsy little pat at her sore shoulder. She flinched but said nothing.

Tommy looked thoughtfully at his boss and said, "Sven, you were pals with Olle 'Armstrong' Olsson, weren't you?"

"I sure was. We were partners for ten years on patrol. Then I went to inspector training and wound up with the Crime Police, while he went into the Canine Unit. He loved his animals—"

He broke off and looked at Tommy for a long time. "I know what you're getting at," he said curtly. He cleared his throat and turned to

Irene. "Irene, this happened twenty years ago. My old pal Armstrong worked in the Canine Unit. Hell of a talented guy. He was called Armstrong because he loved jazz. But that's not important. Olle and his dog were called to a burglary alarm at Obs, out in Hisings Backa. It's a big department store, so Olle took the dog off the leash, as usual. The dog picked up a scent and ran off. There was a shot and when Olle without thinking rushed after the dog, he saw the animal lying on the floor bleeding. He stopped short, with his pistol drawn. Then he felt a gun barrel shoved into the back of his neck and heard the old cliché, 'Drop the gun!' He did as he was told. There were two thieves. One of them took his pistol and then they took off."

The superintendent stopped and his expression turned grim. The words seemed to come from far away when he went on. "That's all that happened. Except that the dog died and Olle left the force."

He fell silent and Irene reluctantly felt that she wanted to know more. So she asked, "Quit the force? What did he do then?"

"Got divorced, moved to Örebro, and became a car salesman. He remarried a few years later."

"Do you ever see him?"

"No. We exchange Christmas cards. It must be fifteen years since we last saw each other."

Tommy eagerly leaned toward Irene. "It's shattering to be disarmed and have to surrender. That's true for everybody, no matter who you are. So don't feel like you're nuts or anything. It's a natural reaction."

Irene was still looking at Andersson when she asked, "Why didn't the rest of you help him?"

He gave her a surprised look. "Help him? What do you mean?"

"Help him to stay on as a cop."

"But what the . . . he had a breakdown! What were we supposed to do? He didn't want to do it anymore!"

"That's just what I mean. Why didn't you help him so he'd want to come back?"

"He didn't want any help! We're not psychologists, you know!"

"No. But pals."

He was speechless and glared at her angrily. What the hell had gotten into all the broads in this department? It didn't make sense to continue this discussion. He tried to pull himself together and smooth it over. "I was only trying to say that we understand that it's tough to be subjected to . . . something like you were subjected to. And you have pals and colleagues around you who are supporting you. You know that. Let's get those fucking assholes identified so we can bring them in!"

He turned to Tommy and motioned toward the door. "We'll go another round with Shorty. We'll have to take turns, try to wear him out. One of us will be back in a while, Irene. Hopefully you'll have some luck finding someone you recognize."

Andersson opened up the first folder and tapped urgently on the photos on the first page. Irene sighed but reluctantly started to turn the pages.

Within an hour she had identified Fatso and the Thin Man.

SWEATY AND mad, Andersson came steaming into the room where Irene sat with two plastic photo sleeves before her on the desk. Her arms hung heavily at her sides and her gaze was directed at the dead lily in a pot hanging in the window. Outside it was dark; there was nothing to see. She nodded lamely at the two plastic sleeves on the desk. Her voice sounded toneless when she said, "Those two. The thin one is Paul John Svensson, born 'sixty-four, and Fatso is Glenn 'Hoffa' Strömberg, born 'fifty-nine. He's called Hoffa because he's vice president of the Hell's Angels. Paul Svensson has no rank. But a thick rap sheet. Just like Hoffa."

"We're making progress on one front at least! That damned Shorty is driving me nuts! All he says is, 'I haven't committed any crime. You have to release me.' But mostly he just sits there in silence and grins."

He slammed his fist into the palm of his hand. It must have hurt, because he didn't do it again. Having let off steam, he sat in his desk chair, picked up the two plastic sleeves and scrutinized them. Pleased, he said, "Couple of ugly dudes. You couldn't find the other two?"

She shook her head. "No. Now that I think about it, they didn't say anything the whole time. Weird. I'm almost positive it was one of them who threw the grenade," she said thoughtfully.

"You didn't see any photo that reminded you of them?"

"No. Although I can't really remember what they looked like. But Fatso and the Thin Man are etched into my brain. Paul John, born 'sixty-four. You think his mama dug the Beatles?"

There was a light knock at the door and Birgitta Moberg came in. She greeted Irene cheerfully, asked how she felt, and was generally sympathetic. Until her gaze fell on the photos. She snatched them up and laughed. "So little Paul shows up here too!"

Her colleagues looked astonished. Andersson recovered first. "Do you know this scumbag?"

"Not personally. But on paper. This is the guy who drove up on the traffic island in the aborted bank robbery in Kungsbacka."

"In nineteen eighty-two? With Shorty!" Irene exclaimed.

"Precisely. And the one who missed the turnoff to . . ." She gave Irene a knowing glance. Both said in unison, ". . . the cottage in Billdal!"

The superintendent grabbed the plastic sleeve again. He stared irately at the cards, as if he were trying to hypnotize them into a confession. Angrily he hissed, "Now it stinks like shit again! This is a point of contact, a lead! We have to get the truth out of Shorty!"

"Confront him with this point of contact. Maybe he doesn't think we can connect him to the Hell's Angels," Birgitta suggested.

"The worst thing is that we can't! Not yet. We have to let Narcotics know. They're out at Billdal questioning people in the vicinity to find possible witnesses who might have seen Shorty together with the swine from the Hell's Angels. If we could just get hold of somebody, then the prosecutor can write a detention order. I want Shorty put under strict watch!"

"But we've been doing that since last Friday. According to our guys, he's only been in the shop and around the neighborhood on Berzelii-gatan. No trips out to Billdal," Birgitta pointed out.

"That's true. But he might have had telephone contact with them," the superintendent ventured.

Birgitta had a hard time holding back a sigh when she replied, "It's not something we can prove. There's no phone at the cottage. No, we have to develop proof that Shorty is mixed up in all this. Otherwise we have to let him go on Friday."

The other two knew she was right. Irene realized how terribly tired she was.

"I think I have to call Krister now. It's almost five-thirty and my poor pummeled body and brain are crying for bed."

Chapter Fourteen

KRISTER CAME TO PICK up Irene at headquarters. For a short time she managed to doze off in the car despite everything, but that was all the sleep she got. When they arrived home the girls swarmed over her with questions. Her answers were evasive. Finally she pleaded that she was too tired, just to get away from the topic. She went to bed before the ten o'clock news. She didn't feel at all sleepy, but it was a way to flee from what she still couldn't face talking about. Krister sensed this and crept in quietly next to her an hour later. He held her for a long time. She felt his warm body against hers. Normally, that would awaken desire and longing but now not even his warmth could thaw out the cold inside her. When he eventually rolled over into his side of the bed and fell asleep, she started sweating. It was impossible to lie still. The bottom sheet felt like a damp rope under her, and every muscle and joint in her body ached. Around four she gave up. Her brain was replaying the scenes from the barn, both those that really happened and those that could have. The scornful voices shrouded her brain in a thick gray spiderweb. It was impossible to find the Point, so the Light remained unattainable. There was an impenetrable obstacle in the way and she knew its components: terror and anxiety.

During the slowly crawling hours of the night she realized how impossible it is to run away from yourself. The black hole was about to swallow her up. She had to go into it and drive out the whispering voices. She had to fight her inner enemy. She was her own *uke*.

IN THE big dark blue police bag Irene packed a thermos of coffee, three sandwiches, clean underwear, and a clean *gi*. The last item was important. No old, irrelevant smells could be allowed to distract her. The fresh sweat in her workout clothes would tell her what it cost to drive out her demons.

The bells in the German Church tolled five o'clock as she parked outside the gym by the Harbor Canal. It was dark and quiet. There was little traffic, and she heard the lonely, distant squeaking of a streetcar. She found the right key and unlocked the door.

She was met by the familiar smell of sweaty workout clothes and liniment, which sent a vague thrill of joy down her spine. A good sign. With determined steps she went into the locker room and changed, comforted by the rough cotton suit and black belt.

The dojo lay plunged in deep darkness. The windows up high on the walls let in a sparse glow from the streetlights outside. She had left the door to the locker room ajar so a little more light could come in. She didn't turn on the ceiling light in the dojo itself but went at once to the middle of the mat and sat down on her heels, with her hands resting loosely on her thighs and her gaze straight ahead. When she felt *Mokuso* approaching, she closed her eyes and looked inward. It was empty and dark. The voices were whispering, but she could no longer hear as clearly what they were saying. She approached the Point, where Bruce's calm voice with his American accent could be heard through the hiss of the demons. His voice flowed into her and she heard him say encouragingly, "Okay, baby. Your fantastic *kata*, when you made black belt, third *dan*."

She felt sorrow and grief for him, surprised at the strength of her feelings. What she thought she had gotten over was still there. *Mokuso* became deeper, and she continued to seek the Point. Her breath began to make contact; suddenly she felt filled with an effervescent warm power. She became weightless and was borne by the power up toward the Light. The power flushed through her sore muscles and joints, cleaning away fatigue and pain.

As if in a trance she stood, still with her eyes closed. At first she moved slowly, but as the rhythm of the *kata* seized her the movements became faster and stronger. She opened her eyes and saw *uke*—a semitransparent foggy form with long hair down the back of leather jacket and a scornful grin.

To a spectator it looked like ballet with incredibly advanced choreography. A knowledgeable viewer would see a skilled judo master who at a furious pace went through *Sandan-kata*, combinations with *uke*, *tski*, and *geri-waza*. An initiate would also wonder why she didn't have an opponent. But she did have an opponent. Furiously she struck at *uke*. At first his laughter sounded derisive, but she had the Power and was filled by her proximity to the Light.

Exhausted, she sank down on the mat. Sweat was running down her whole body. She sensed its salty taste in her mouth and felt it trickling between her breasts and buttocks. Her rib cage heaved and she felt some discomfort from her crushed rib. But the Power and the Light flowed through her and so pain did not yet bother her.

Slowly the Power ebbed and she rolled over and looked up at the ceiling. Would the black hole open and the voices start whispering again?

All was silent. Only the Light remained, pulsating in her diaphragm, and she felt the stillness and peace. She had made it through.

IRENE FOUND them inside the conference room. It was just before eight o'clock, but she wasn't the last to arrive. Jonny Blom was missing but expected at any minute. He had called to say he had a flat tire outside Åby. Superintendent Andersson began to speak.

"We'll start without Jonny. Great to see that you've recovered, Irene. Damned if a good night's sleep isn't the best medicine!"

"I feel better. Just black and blue and stiff. And I didn't get much sleep. Later this afternoon I'll drive over to visit Jimmy, and then I'll go home," she replied firmly.

Andersson raised his eyebrow. He didn't comment. "Okay. First I have to report that the body of the guy who was burned to death on Berzeliigatan has been found. They removed it with the help of the telescopic boom. Narcotics wants to have a meeting tomorrow at one. Evidently they have a bunch of investigations going simultaneously, but it seems as though some threads are connected with this Hell's Angels crap. Hans, you had some luck with the keys?"

Borg nodded and tried without great success to stifle a yawn. In a tired voice he said, "Mister Minit at the Domus department store on Avenyn made a complete set of keys for Richard von Knecht in early August of this year. He ordered them himself and waited while they were made. That's why the guy who made the keys remembered that it was von Knecht. He stood there for quite a while, plus he is . . . or was . . . a celebrity. But he didn't have any extra key made for the garage or the car. Of course, he must have had a spare key to the Porsche. It's not even a year old. He must have gotten a spare key with a Porsche! You know what one of those costs?"

Andersson sighed. "More than you or I will ever be able to afford. We have to find out more about these damned keys. Irene, get hold of Sylvia von Knecht and ask her why she thinks Richard would have an extra set of keys made. We know that he had a spare-key ring for the Porsche and the garage. He was looking for it the week before he was murdered. Maybe Henrik von Knecht knows more about it."

Irene gave a slight nod when she replied, "Could be. But he left for Stockholm early yesterday morning to buy antiques at various auctions."

Andersson laughed and said with a wink, "Hope he makes some finds. He could use some newer furniture."

In the midst of the general merriment Jonny showed up. Bright red in the face, he rushed in and sat on a free chair. Out of breath he puffed, "Excuse me. I had a flat and the damned spare tire was flat too! A nice guy gave me a lift to a gas station so I could pump it up. He drove me back too."

"Don't you check your tire once in a while? I do at regular intervals. About every other month," said Hans Borg.

For once Borg was interested. Cars were his passion.

Jonny made an irritated gesture and replied, "Phooey. It's just one of those things that's always there. Sometimes you remember to check, but most of the time you forget. Who's interested in spare tires?"

Irene gave a start. She said pensively, "Charlotte von Knecht is."

"Is what?" asked Jonny.

"Interested in spare tires. According to the car dealer Robert Skytter, the spare tire was the last thing they checked on her new Golf before she drove off."

"Okay, I get it. Someone cares. But I have a lot of other things to think about. It doesn't seem important to check the air in the spare tire until the day you need it. And then it's too late!"

That matched Irene's own relationship with her spare tire. Charlotte didn't give the impression that she was the orderly type who checked everything in advance. She probably batted her heavenly eyelashes when things got screwed up. And some gentleman would come hurrying to the beauty's rescue. Were there a few sour grapes to these thoughts? Maybe, but life had taught Irene that it wasn't the practical girls in the woolen pants and rubber boots who awakened a male's protective instincts. It was the small defenseless creatures in high-heeled pumps and chiffon skirts who prompted men to fling their capes across puddles. For her part she never wore high heels. And the only chiffon skirt she had ever owned was quickly confiscated by the twins to play dress-up.

Andersson asked, "Fredrik and Jonny, you haven't discovered any activity at Shorty's over the weekend that would indicate contacts with Billdal?"

Each shook his head in reply. Disappointed, the superintendent snapped, "On Friday we have to be able to give Inez Collin some reason for the detention order! Jonny, you'll have to try to question Shorty today. Birgitta, have you found anything else interesting on Bobo or Shorty?"

"That's pretty hard to do where Bobo's concerned. He, his apartment, and his photo studio have all been blown to bits. I have to make do with what little there is. We have only those three arrests that I mentioned earlier. The assumption, of course, is that he's been using drugs for years. Narcotics thinks he was mostly dealing, but he probably was using a lot himself. We base that conclusion on his behavior," said Birgitta.

She paused and a dark shadow passed over her face. But it vanished quickly and she went on, "Today I'm going up to Vänersborg to talk to Bobo's mother. She was extremely upset when she heard that Bobo is dead. But when I called her today to set a time for us to meet, she asked if I thought it would take a long time before she got the insurance money!"

Insurance money? Who had said something about insurance money before? Irene couldn't remember, but thought it was Sylvia. Quick note in her notebook: "S. v. K. Changed lock? Insurance money?"

The superintendent nodded and looked pensive. "Has anybody tried to get hold of his father?"

"No. He's a homeless wino. I haven't spent much time on him," said Birgitta.

"Hannu, this sounds like a job for you."

Hannu nodded. Andersson asked him, "Did you find out if Pirjo had a driver's license?"

"I did. She never had one."

"Did you ask the daughter if she knew anything about the keys?"

"Yes, Pirjo didn't have any. Richard von Knecht loaned her his keys whenever they went down to the garbage room. All the doors to the courtyard are locked."

"So you have to have a key even to get out of the courtyard?"

"Right."

"That confirms my belief that our murderer had the spare-key ring. But how did Pirjo get hold of it?"

"Maybe on Wednesday," Hannu said.

Andersson regarded the department's "exotic" element. Slowly he nodded. "She came to the apartment on Wednesday morning. You mean that she could have pinched it at an unguarded moment. That's not impossible. Hans, you're in charge of the keys; ask the techs if there's any chance that Pirjo entered the apartment on Wednesday. And ask them if they saw a key ring lying around anywhere."

"Which techs were there on Wednesday morning?"

"Ljunggren and Åhlén."

Borg nodded but didn't jot down anything on his clean, blank pad. Irene asked Hannu, "Do Pirjo's kids know that she's dead?"

"Yes. They were told yesterday. Welfare has them now."

His voice was somber, and she understood that he was at least as affected by the fate of the poor children as she was.

Birgitta cleared her throat; her expression became stubborn. Harshly she said, "I still think Pirjo was lured by someone to Berzeliigatan. Maybe with the prospect that she would have a free hand to steal now that Richard von Knecht was dead."

No one said anything, but several nodded in agreement.

"But why was it so important for the office on Berzeliigatan to be blown up?" asked Irene.

That was another question that no one could answer.

Tommy Persson waved his hand in the air. "Late last night I got hold of the hairdresser on the ground floor of the building. Her partner was in bed at home with a cold, so she was alone in the salon on Wednesday night. She saw Pirjo arrive! When I described Pirjo's appearance, she was positive that she had seen her minutes before the explosion."

The superintendent interrupted him. "Why didn't she call and tell us about it?"

"According to her, she was so shocked by the fire that she forgot. By the way, she didn't see or hear anything out of the ordinary on Wednesday. When I asked whether she'd seen any unusual visitors on the days before the fire, she said something quite remarkable: 'There was always a bunch of funny characters going upstairs to that photographer. He's quite well known, of course, but I don't like him much.' Remember, she didn't know that the victim out at Delsjön was Bobo Torsson. I didn't tell her either. When I asked why she didn't like Torsson, it came out that he had been over to her salon, offering her a future as a photo model if she just did as he said. He promised her fame and fortune. But that is one tough dame, and she told him to get lost. The interesting thing is that he had asked both her and her partner whether they wanted to buy any dope. He said he could get hold of whatever they wanted."

Tommy paused, broke his Marie biscuit into three pieces, and stuffed them one after the other into his mouth. He washed each piece down with a sip of coffee. After he finished this ritual he went on, "My interview with the woman who lived below von Knecht's office confirms many of the hairdresser's statements. It was a brief conversation. Her husband is very sick because of his heart attack. She told me many strange people were always coming and going to Bobo's place. And some wild parties had kept the entire building awake until the wee hours. I asked in more detail about Friday night, whether they had heard anything from von Knecht's apartment around one o'clock. At first she couldn't remember, but after a while she recalled that she woke up that night because someone was going up and down the stairs. At least three times, she said. But she couldn't say for sure whether she had heard anything in particular from von Knecht's apartment."

The superintendent listened intently. Finally things were starting to move on Berzeliigatan. Eagerly he said, "That confirms what we already know. He was dealing. But what a careless devil, to invite people into his own building! Was that why it was so important to blow up the place? What was it that had to be destroyed, that we weren't supposed to see? Dope? Dope-processing equipment?"

A pensive silence followed the superintendent's last remark. Hannu straightened up in his chair and said, "No. Dope processing smells. It seems the bomb was sitting there primed for almost four days. It was von Knecht who was supposed to be blown up."

"But on Wednesday he had already been dead for twenty-four hours!"

"But not on Friday night. He was alive then. When the bomb was made."

The color began to rise in Andersson's cheeks and he stared glassy-eyed at Hannu. "So we're talking about two different murder attempts on von Knecht!"

"That's right."

"Would that mean that we have two murderers?"

"Maybe."

"So the bomb murderer was beaten to the punch by the one who hurled von Knecht off the balcony!"

Irene looked at Hannu thoughtfully. Circumspectly she said, "There might be something to this argument. Killer number one rigs up the bomb at Berzeliigatan on Friday night and then goes and waits for von Knecht to arrive and blow himself up. But von Knecht catches a cold and doesn't go there on either Monday or Tuesday. On Tuesday he eats lunch with Valle Reuter. And on Tuesday night he's murdered by number two! Without having set foot in the office apartment for several days! But the person who made the bomb knows that it's there, ready to explode as soon as somebody opens the door. There isn't any back way into the apartment, so he can't go in and disarm the bomb."

"How did he fasten the wire to the trip mechanism on the handle of the outer door?" Birgitta wondered.

"He must have stood on the outside and threaded the thin wire through using a long hook. It must have been nerve-wracking and not something he wanted to repeat. It would be far too risky. What does he do now? Well, he sends over an insignificant insect like a Finnish cleaning woman," Irene replied grimly.

"So the guy who made the bomb doesn't know that Pirjo has three kids?"

"Or else he doesn't care."

Again the cold presence of calculated evil gave Irene a nasty shiver down her spine. She saw both Tommy and Birgitta unconsciously hunching their shoulders. Jonny was unusually silent. She glanced at him and saw that he seemed to be brooding. As if he heard her thoughts, he asked to speak. "I'm sitting here thinking. Who and why? What can we say about Shorty? He's a notorious hooligan, he knows at least one and possibly more Hell's Angels, and he has been dealing drugs together with his cousin Bobo. He could certainly make one of these devil bombs. There's probably a do-it-yourself recipe on the Internet!"

The superintendent agreed enthusiastically. "Shorty? Yes, he could be the common denominator. But why? Why would he murder von Knecht?"

"Maybe it was the other one who murdered von Knecht! Hannu did say there could be two people."

"The other one . . . stop right there . . . Then why did the second killer murder von Knecht?"

The silence was answer enough. Andersson sighed heavily. "The damned truth is that in the von Knecht case we're just treading water! We know a lot about the family and their relatives and friends, but we have no motive for the murder. No answer to the question 'Why?' And where does Shorty come into the von Knecht picture? Was it Shorty who blew up his cousin? Hardly, since he didn't seem to know about Bobo's murder when he was brought in for questioning. I think we're heading off on the wrong track. The Hell's Angels, Bobo, and Shorty are a whole different case that we have to solve together with Narcotics. But in the von Knecht case we need a new angle. Let's check all observations and witness statements one more time. If it really was Shorty who tossed von Knecht, somebody must have seen him. That guy doesn't just melt into a crowd!"

Irene began to feel the churning sense of emptiness that always appears in a case that isn't solved quickly. Check and double-check all the witness statements. And check again, if you don't find anything new. A routine job. But that's the way you solve crimes.

Fredrik started preparing for his presentation. He opened his notebook and coughed lightly before he began. "No one in the neighborhood says they noticed anyone suspicious on Tuesday evening. It was rainy and dark, of course, but it was only around five-thirty. No reports that anyone saw Shorty. He would have looked pretty disreputable in that neighborhood. Two meters tall and just as wide! Of course he looks disreputable wherever he is. But maybe we should ask around in the building one more time. Plus we can check up on whether Bobo was seen. He was almost as tall, but thin. Also somebody that people ought to remember."

The superintendent nodded absentmindedly and sighed. "All right, go ahead and ask. Although I don't think it'll produce anything. But we should check. Maybe Bobo or Shorty threw von Knecht off the balcony. But there's not a shred of evidence that Shorty had any contact with Richard von Knecht, or that they had ever met. And not a single rumor about drug deals around von Knecht. I find it hard to believe that Shorty and Bobo had started speculating in stocks!"

"You've got a point, Chief. But maybe we can pick up some new leads on Friday. Now that they've cleaned up the site, they can go into the building and start drilling von Knecht's safe out of the wall. It's hard because there's a cellar under the building that they have to prop up from below. Otherwise they can't bring in the telescopic boom and the standalone forklift. That's heavy equipment and they don't want it to fall into the cellar. It'll probably take a day or two," Fredrik concluded his report.

"Okay. Tommy, Fredrik, and Jonny will have to plan a strategy and question Shorty. Grill him! Skip the von Knecht stuff for now and concentrate on drugs and the Hell's Angels. Birgitta, you haven't found any connection between Shorty and that vice president . . . what the hell kind of titles do these idiots give each other?"

"Vice President Glenn 'Hoffa' Strömberg. No, I haven't found anything yet. As for titles, they have all sorts of different ranks. There's one who's responsible for weapons, another who makes sure that there's always food and booze in the clubhouse, and so forth. Lowest in the hierarchy are the girls. They have no rank at all," Birgitta said dryly.

Jonny sniggered and said, "A well-ordered society, where the chicks know their proper place and function!"

Andersson shot him a dark look, so he didn't continue his exegesis of the social structure within the Hell's Angels. Somewhere inside the superintendent a vague uneasiness arose that the old lady in Birgitta's building could just as well have seen Jonny's Volvo as Bobo's Toyota. He firmly pushed those thoughts aside.

Birgitta clenched her jaws but ignored Jonny's comment and continued unfazed, "We'll find out more from the Narcs tomorrow. But I have to see if I can find the link between Shorty and Hoffa."

Resolutely Andersson slapped his palm on the table. "All right, now we're moving! If you find anything of interest, I'll be here until this evening."

They got up and went off to their respective tasks. Irene drew Tommy aside.

"Please come to dinner at six. Jenny will be home. And it's perfectly safe since Krister's in charge of the grub."

IRENE WAS surprised that Sylvia von Knecht was home and answered the telephone. But Ivan Viktors had said that he was going back to Copenhagen on Sunday evening. Sylvia must not have wanted to stay alone out in Särö. Without any great enthusiasm, Sylvia agreed to let her come over and ask some questions at eleven.

Irene tried to start her report on what had happened in Billdal, but it was slow going. She called Krister and agreed to pick him up after she visited Jimmy. She drank the rest of the coffee in the thermos and looked outside. There was a break in the rain, and a pale sun seeped through the clouds. Six degrees Celsius. A regular heat wave, compared to the temperatures in recent weeks. She quickly decided to take a walk up to Molinsgatan. It would take exactly the half hour that was left until eleven if she walked slowly. She put on her leather jacket and went out.

TRAFFIC WAS heavy and the air thick with exhaust. The big soccer fields at Heden lay soggy and abandoned. She crossed Södra Vägen and strolled up Kristinelundsgatan. A glance in the display windows of the exclusive boutiques reminded her that she had to buy a new jacket. She had already thrown out the one that had been pissed on in Billdal without even trying to have it cleaned. The leather one she had on now was too worn. Up on Kungsportsavenyn she stopped and

looked in the window of KappAhl while she discreetly buttoned up
her jacket. The last part of the way she cut across Vasaparken. Behind
the university she saw a gang of youths. The tall boy in the middle of
the group was black. Thick Rasta dreadlocks stuck out all around his
head. Her heart skipped a beat. Was there some kind of abuse going
on? But all was total harmony. Coolly and completely openly, the Rastaman handed over small plastic bags in exchange for wrinkled and sweaty
bills from the youths. Ecstasy for the weekend's rave, no doubt.

What was the difference between Bobo Torsson's and the Rastaman's
dope dealing? The environment, she decided. Smoky nightclubs and
trendy, hip spots don't change the fact that it's dope being bought and
sold. And that the buyers are drug-dependent, though they all vehemently deny it. She looked at the kids with sorrow. Some tried it out
of curiosity, got scared, and stopped. But many of them would end up
addicted. Some would manage despite great pressure to break loose from
their dependence. But all of them would be forced to live with the consequences of their addiction.

She memorized the appearance of the tall dealer so she could report
him when she returned to headquarters. The Narcs' street-dealer squad
probably knew who he was.

SYLVIA VON Knecht was haggard. For the first time she looked her
age. She was walking around in an enormous gray wool sweater, knit
in a pretty cable pattern, and actually wearing blue jeans, which greatly
surprised Irene. Apparently she still hadn't managed to clean up after
the technical examination of the apartment. Everything looked the
same as it had when Irene was there before. Big flower bouquets with
cards of condolence were placed randomly in the apartment. The heavy
floral scent seemed to presage the upcoming funeral. The pleasant fragrance had a rank undertone; the water needed to be changed.

They went upstairs to the airy library and sat down on the leather
sofa. Sylvia nervously bit a torn nail. She raised her face, which bore
no makeup, and looking at Irene said in a thin voice, "Can you imagine? I miss him so much! Every time the phone rings or someone laughs
down on the street, I think it's him. Sometimes I imagine he's going
to walk through the door and laugh, pleased that he was able to fool
everyone. I'm wearing his sweater. It smells like . . . him."

She sobbed and her curtain of hair fell across her face. Irene didn't
quite know how to approach the whole subject. How did things actually stand with Ivan Viktors? She decided to start with the keys.

"We found the key ring. And Pirjo," she said by way of introduction.

The newspapers would be informed at the press conference later that afternoon that the victim on Berzeliigatan was Pirjo. They hadn't mentioned it earlier, for "technical investigative reasons."

Sylvia started and said sharply, "You found the key ring? Who had it?"

"It was sitting in the door at Berzeliigatan. The door to the office apartment."

"Well, I never! Here I changed the lock on the apartment and spent more than two thousand kronor for nothing! Why couldn't you have told me about this earlier? Thank God I didn't bother changing them up at Kärringnäset!"

"We weren't completely sure that they were the right keys . . . for technical investigative reasons."

"And Pirjo! Where has that slob been hiding? I want her to come over here right away!"

"Sorry. She's dead. She was blown up in the explosion on Berzeliigatan a week ago."

It was cruel and brutally frank, but Irene wanted to see how Sylvia would react.

"You . . . you're lying . . . it can't be . . ."

The effect was not pretty. Sylvia shrank, shriveling up right before her eyes. Once again Sylvia's hot-tempered and slightly hysterical manner had provoked Irene to venture too far out on thin ice. Trying to smooth things over, she said, "It took several days for the identification. She was so badly burned. We got hold of the dental X rays and thanks to—"

"What was she doing at Berzeliigatan?"

Sylvia's voice sounded slightly hollow and her eyes reflected outright terror. She was scared. That hadn't been evident when her husband was murdered. But now she was scared to death, on the verge of panic. Irene tried to sound calm but still authoritative.

"We don't know. It's one of the questions I was thinking of asking you. First and foremost, we'd like to know where she got hold of the spare keys. If I understood you correctly, you didn't know about this spare-key ring?"

"No, I didn't know about any spare-key ring. Except for the one we have here."

"We've discovered that the keys were made late this summer. Richard went to Mister Minit on Avenyn to have them made."

Sylvia was breathing heavily. Her eyes glistened. She avoided looking at Irene now. Irene was even more convinced that Sylvia knew something or had her suspicions.

"I don't know anything about those keys," said Sylvia firmly. Her voice sounded steadier, but she had to press her hands together hard to prevent them from shaking.

Irene felt that she couldn't let Sylvia go yet. There was something here. She decided to press her a little more and reformulated her question. "So you don't have any idea what he wanted the keys for, or if he gave them to anyone else?"

"No."

She was lying. She was lying! But Irene didn't dare go out on the ice again. Not yet.

"The bomb that blew up the building detonated when Pirjo opened the outer door to your husband's office. She opened the door using the key ring. We found her behind the door," she said in a neutral tone.

"But the papers talked about a missing young man!"

"That's correct. He was found yesterday, a little farther up in the remains of the building. Two people died in the fire."

Sylvia got up from the sofa and started pacing aimlessly around the room. She wrung her hands and sighed quietly. She was incredibly shaken, Irene could see that. But why? If she knew who had the keys, why wouldn't she speak? Irene tried again.

"You don't have the slightest suspicion who might have received those keys?"

"No, I told you that!"

The ice was creaking and cracking. Best to look for less dangerous areas.

"Did you know any of the other tenants in the building on Berzeliigatan?"

She shook her head in reply.

"Do you recognize the name Bo-Ivar, or Bobo, Torsson?"

Sylvia frowned and actually seemed to think about it.

"The name sounds familiar. Wait . . . he was the photographer who rented the apartment above Richard's. He's one of Charlotte's old acquaintances."

Irene was so dumbfounded that she almost lost her composure. But she managed to assume a nearly neutral tone of voice when she asked, "An old acquaintance? What do you mean?"

"She worked for him as a photo model. It didn't amount to much, that modeling. Nothing Charlotte undertakes is ever successful."

"Did Torsson already have his photo studio on Berzeliigatan when Charlotte was working for him?"

"No. She recommended him to Richard. Richard thought it would be practical to have the same tenant in both apartments."

"When was this?"

"Don't know. Maybe three years ago." Sylvia wrapped her arms around herself, hunching up her shoulders as if she were freezing. But she seemed distracted when the topic of Bobo Torsson was discussed. Her thoughts were already moving in some other direction.

Irene tried again. "Does the name Lasse 'Shorty' Johannesson mean anything to you?"

"No."

"A huge guy around thirty-five."

"No."

Absentmindedly, Sylvia gathered up some fallen petals from a purple chrysanthemum that had dropped onto the dusty coffee table. Irritated, she swept the pile up and then seemed to forget both the petals and Irene at the same moment. Her shining eyes didn't seem to notice her surroundings as she sat gazing into her own abysses. Irene would have given a lot to know what she saw. But a glance at Sylvia's face made her less sure that she wanted to see it herself. The discussion about the key ring had made Sylvia retreat within herself. Irene had to get her to come out again. What might tempt her to start talking? A vague hunch told Irene that money could always get Sylvia to talk. Wasn't that what Valle Reuter had said?

"Well, Sylvia, that insurance you once told me about . . ."

She left the sentence unfinished on purpose to see if Sylvia would bite. At first she seemed not to have heard, but after a while she turned her head and gave Irene an unexpectedly sharp look.

"Insurance? Did I mention the insurance to you?"

"Yes, when we spoke on the telephone the first time. When you were in the psychiatric ward."

"I don't remember that. Maybe I did. They put me on a lot of medication, and I have very dim memories of those first few days."

She took a deep breath and to Irene's relief sat down in one corner of the angular sofa. She kicked off her Birkenstocks and, tucking her legs beneath her, started chewing on her chipped nail again. In a normal tone she said, "The insurance. That was probably the only thing Richard ever did for Henrik's and my benefit. He explained to me that it's a sort of retirement annuity. After he turned sixty, he could retire anytime he wanted and draw an annual income of a million kronor for ten years. But it's also life insurance. If Richard died, Henrik and I would receive the same sum over ten years, to be divided between us."

"So the insurance falls due with a survivors' benefit?"

"The same as most retirement annuities."

Henrik and Sylvia would each receive half a million per year over the next ten years. People have been murdered for less. Added to the rest of the fortune, maybe Valle Reuter was on the right track. If only mother and son hadn't been down on the street, surrounded by witnesses, when Richard fell. Irene decided to proceed cautiously.

"But the rest of your husband's assets and fortune, who inherits all of that?"

Now Sylvia was utterly calm. She looked a bit like a small Siamese cat that has just swallowed a goldfish.

"I do. But it's extremely complicated. The lawyers are busy making sense of it all. They say it could take a long time. But the insurance money will start being paid out next month, with this month's payment retroactive."

It had to be a hallucination, but Irene thought she heard a whirring sound as the wheels turned in her brain. The key ring was forbidden territory, but the money and Bobo Torsson had gone well. Should she continue with Bobo?

"Bobo Torsson is also dead. You may have read in today's paper that he was murdered early Monday morning. He was blown up in his car."

Sylvia gave her an uninterested look. "Blown up? No. I'm not reading the papers very carefully right now. I can't face it. I have enough to think about with everything that's happened."

"Do you know if Bobo and Charlotte were still seeing each other?"

"No idea. Charlotte likes to go out and be part of the hip scene."

"Does Henrik accompany her when she goes out and gets into the swing of things?"

Uh-oh, the ice was cracking again. Sylvia put her feet down on the carpet and gave Irene a measured look. Abruptly she said, "Henrik does not enjoy going out. Not after his illness, which I told you about."

Suddenly Irene was struck by an idea. "It was meningitis that Henrik suffered as a result, wasn't it?"

"Yes."

"As a result of what?"

"A childhood illness."

"Which childhood illness?"

"The mumps."

There was nothing left of the little contented kitten, only a sorrowful mother huddled in the corner of the sofa. Something clicked in Irene's mind. One of her male colleagues at the police academy got the mumps while they were attending Ulriksdal. Both his testicles were also affected, and they swelled up so grotesquely that he couldn't walk. Unfortunately his name was Paul, and he was always called "Paul Fig-Ball" after that. At a party he later confided to Irene and Tommy that there was a great risk that he was now sterile. Apparently it wasn't an unusual complication in adult men who got the mumps. Had this also happened to Henrik? It was a long shot, but she decided to try.

"It's common for adult males to become sterile after having the mumps. Were Henrik's testicles affected?"

Sylvia's eyes widened with terror. With a horrible crash the ice shattered and she fell through. She hid her face in her hands and began to cry hysterically.

It took twenty minutes before she calmed down enough for Irene to consider her somewhat stable. But Sylvia refused to answer any more questions and stubbornly repeated, "You have to go now! I'm due at the seamstress at one o'clock to try on my dress for the funeral. Go! Go!"

IRENE HAD a lot to think about as she sat in a mediocre pizzeria a few blocks down the street gnawing on the "daily special." It consisted of a serving of tough lasagne, along with some pitiful cabbage strips in vinegar. The ice water was lukewarm and the coffee looked like Sammie's bathwater. Not even Irene could manage to drink it. But it didn't really matter, because questions and facts were tumbling through her head. Sylvia was scared stiff when the spare keys were mentioned. She knew, or had an idea, who might have taken them. Or had they been given to someone? Why wouldn't Sylvia talk about it? Charlotte von Knecht and Bobo Torsson were old friends and had worked together. She initiated the contact between him and her father-in-law, and then Torsson was able to rent the two apartments. Did they still see each other? Did it have any significance for the investigation? Was this the point of contact they had been looking for? Irene had a hard time believing it. Not in her wildest fantasy could she picture Bobo Torsson knocking down Richard von Knecht and throwing him off the balcony, fabricating the bomb on Berzeliigatan, and then blowing himself to kingdom come. The last maybe by mistake. It wasn't even logical, since it didn't answer the question of why.

Why would Bobo murder Richard von Knecht? Why would he destroy his own home and studio? Not to mention himself! Picturing Charlotte in any of these roles was even harder. She certainly wasn't a bomb maker. But the fact that Bobo and Charlotte knew each other was interesting. Were they still friends? More than friends? It seemed to be time to have a talk with young Fru von Knecht. Henrik von Knecht had gotten the mumps as an adult, and subsequently meningitis. Had the mumps spread to his testicles? If so, was he sterile? Viewed in the light of this latest information, she thought that many of Sylvia's odd reactions over the past few days became more understandable. If you know that your son is sterile, would you be glad to hear that your daughter-in-law is pregnant? And the follow-up question was possibly even more interesting: In that case, who was the father of Charlotte's child? Why did Henrik react as he did? According to his own statement he was prepared to try to keep his shaky marriage together, "For the sake of the child and the survival of the family." That didn't make sense. Either he thought he was the father of the child, or else he didn't care. But if he was sterile he must know it! And if he didn't care, would he then be prepared to continue working on his relationship with Charlotte?

She was aroused from her musings by a voice in her ear.

"'Scuse. Lady want more coffee?" A short, dark waiter was giving her a friendly smile and holding out the glass coffeepot. To her dismay she realized that in her distraction she had actually been sipping the coffee slop.

JIMMY'S FACE brightened with joy when she came in with a bag of goodies and a stack of newspapers. He looked about like he did the day before, only a little darker purple in complexion. The IV was gone and he was sitting in a high-backed vinyl armchair over by the window. There was room for one more patient in the room, but that bed was still empty.

"Hi Jimmy! You look like an LSD hallucination," Irene said cheerfully.

"Thank you. That's just what I needed to hear."

He laughed heartily and they chatted about neutral topics. Irene gave him the latest news on the investigative front. He was exceedingly interested in the information about the traces of narcotics in the summer cabins.

"We've been investigating part of the motorcycle gang for a long time. Death Squadron Number One is especially interesting. They've been full members of the Hell's Angels for several years. The gangs ride around Europe and visit each other. It takes a lot before two lowly customs agents down in Helsingborg will start rummaging through twenty Hell's Angels packs when they've been visiting their brothers in Denmark or Holland. We also know that they smuggle narcotics in other ways."

"Why do they deal drugs?"

"Big business. Hardly any of the members have a job. They need plenty of money for daily living, new choppers and spare parts, clubhouses and weapons. They have enough weapons to start a revolution! And many of them are drug users themselves. So dope for their own use too. They say they belong to 'the extreme percentage—the sociopaths, for whom no laws apply.'"

He fell silent and both of them had the same thought. It was Jimmy who expressed it. "Sometimes I think, *They could have done whatever they wanted to me.* I was completely defenseless. And a defenseless cop! So sometimes I wonder why they didn't finish us off."

Once more Irene saw the glow of the explosion and she felt the hot pressure wave against her face. She could only whisper, "They thought about it. They tried."

Softly, she began to tell him as objectively as possible. Sometimes she had to pause to wipe away her tears, but she wanted him to know the exact course of events. He was the only one who could understand her feelings, since he had been there. While she was speaking, she noticed that the last emotional knots were loosening and she felt a sense of calm rising inside her. A troubling thought occurred to her: Had she transferred her anxiety to Jimmy? Not once during the entire account did he interrupt her. His one visible eye did not waver from her face. But his comment when she was done calmed her.

"What luck that you were the one who was awake and not me! I was always lousy at throwing balls. My best events have always been the high jump and the hundred meters. Those wouldn't have helped us much!"

He laughed heartily again and offered her some of the candy from the bag. Mentally he seemed unscathed, but his physical damage was much worse.

"A crack in one of the bones in my forearm. Do you know what it's called? You don't? Radius fissure. You learn a bunch of useful stuff when you're in the hospital. Although you have to be healthy to deal with it. Today I spent two hours on my back in Radiology waiting for a skull

X ray. To check that there's no bleeding between the brain membranes. Then you get a . . . what was it called? Wait, I wrote it down."

He got up and shuffled over to his bedside table. With a shock Irene realized that his injuries were even worse than she'd thought.

"Jimmy, what happened to your legs?"

He turned and grimaced. "Violent blows or kicks to my lower back. I have to get it X-rayed tomorrow. They suspect a fracture of one of the tail vertebrae. It hurts like hell to walk or sit. That's why I'm going to lie down now. You have to come over here. Ah, here's the note!"

Triumphantly he waved a little scrap of paper torn from a notepad.

"Computer tomography. No, that's the examination! A machine they stuff you inside. But you don't feel anything. What they're afraid I might contract is called subdural hematoma. It can appear several years later, say the doctors. That's why I can't go home before Friday. Damn it!"

He said the last when he had to lift his legs onto the bed. With a sigh he went on, "Then I'll probably be on the disabled list for a while. Although I'll try to get home care."

The last he said with a wink and a knowing look toward the door. A young nurse with a waist-long blond braid came in. She nodded to Irene and gave Jimmy a gleaming smile. There was a light blush on her cheeks, and her eyes indicated that she wouldn't be particularly hard to convince. She chirped at Jimmy, "X-ray preparations. Just a little micro-enema. I'll come back in a while and help you with the enema, if you want."

"Now you're talking, baby," Jimmy said in English. "No, all kidding aside, I can handle it myself."

She laughed and left a little yellow plastic tube with a long nozzle on his nightstand. With another bright smile she vanished into the corridor.

Irene stood up and said, "Well, I'll leave you to your anal orgies. If I can't stop by tomorrow, I'll call you."

"Calling is good enough. Although it's more fun when you come by."

He waved with his good hand.

Chapter Fifteen

AT SIX O'CLOCK ON the dot, Tommy Persson rang the doorbell of the Huss residence. Sammie was the first in line to bid him welcome. Since Tommy was one of his favorite guests, it took a while before all the jumping and licking were over.

Conspiratorially, Irene whispered, "The twins are in their room. I said that you're a grass widower today and that I invited you to dinner. They bought it without comment."

"Good. How's Jimmy Olsson doing?"

She gave him a detailed description of the young officer's health status; Tommy thought it didn't sound good. If you're married to a nurse, you're always learning something about diseases and their treatment.

Since they never talked shop when they were around their families, Irene wanted to know the latest news from HQ before dinner. "How did the interview with Shorty go today?"

Tommy hesitated before he replied. "Not so great. But Jonny actually managed to annoy him so much that he got mad and said something interesting. Jonny finally yelled, 'Don't you get it? You're under suspicion for taking part in everything that happened, as long as you refuse to speak! We're looking for your cousin's murderer!' Then Shorty leaned toward him and snarled, 'I don't have to look. That fuck'll be sorry!' And then he went back to imitating a clam. We pressured him like mad for several hours. But he's used to it and it doesn't bother him in the least. We didn't get one more syllable out of him. Andersson and Jonny will have a go at him this evening."

"Interesting. I also got a hot tip. Bobo and Charlotte von Knecht are old acquaintances. She worked as a photo model for him. She was the one who helped him rent the apartments on Berzeliigatan about three years ago."

"You've got to be kidding! Although that's a point of contact with Bobo, not Shorty. I don't think she knows Shorty."

"Maybe. I'm thinking of driving over unannounced to question the lady in more detail tomorrow morning. Want to come along?"

"Sounds just as good as haranguing Shorty. Jonny and Andersson can deal with him."

An aroma of fried onions that got their stomach juices flowing came wafting into the entryway. Krister stuck his head out the open kitchen door and teasingly shook his spatula at them. "What are you two whispering about?"

"Professional secrets, just professional secrets. For instance, how hard you can hit somebody with a baton without leaving bruises," his wife replied saucily.

"Great topic of conversation. Come and devote yourself to the hamburgers instead."

Irene called the twins. Heavy rock rhythms were thumping upstairs. Neither of them seemed to hear her. She went up and opened the door to Jenny's room.

They were curled up on Jenny's bed. Jenny was tossing her head in time to the music, while Katarina looked warier. Jenny became aware of her mother's presence and jumped up to turn off the CD player. But Irene had heard the last line of the song: "We're gonna clean this country and throw the Jew pigs in the sea. Clean it! Clean it!" Sung with hoarse rock voices, throbbing heavy-metal guitars, and pulsating drums.

Jenny was caught off guard, but collected herself and immediately assumed a defensive position. She said quickly, "It's not the words I like, but the music!"

Irene looked at her daughter's shaved head and angrily clenched fists. A feeling of powerlessness descended like a paralyzing blanket over her thoughts, and she couldn't think of a single appropriate remark. Instead she said with exaggerated good cheer, "Come on now and eat. It's one of your favorites, Jenny, hamburgers and onions."

"Did Pappa make his pickles?"

"Of course! And since Tommy is here, there'll be dessert in the middle of the week."

"What is it?"

"Apple cake with vanilla ice cream."

Without showing any great enthusiasm, Jenny shrugged her shoulders. "Okay."

The year before she would have been the first one down the stairs and seated at the table. Now she shambled after Irene and Katarina and sat down last. Tommy gave her a cheerful hello, his gaze lingering so long on Jenny's scalp that she was embarrassed. But he didn't comment on her sudden hair loss.

Pleasant conversation accompanied the dinner. No talk of murder, bombs, motorcycle gangs, dope, or fruitless interrogations with professional crooks. Irene felt safe and relaxed together with her family and her best friend.

When it was time for coffee, Tommy suggested that they go sit in the living room. He smiled at the twins and said, "I feel like telling you an absolutely true story from real life."

They sat down on the sofa and armchairs around the coffee table. Through the glass top the warm-toned Gabbeh rug was visible, and Irene thought it went very well with the framed Miró print on the wall. At Tommy's request they turned out all the lights and lit all the candles they could find.

The mood was cozy when Tommy began his story.

"This is both an exciting and very sad story. It begins in Berlin in nineteen thirty-two. The National Socialists, under the leadership of the great agitator Adolf Hitler, are about to take over all of Germany. The people are delighted and see Hitler as their great savior, freeing them from unemployment, poverty, and social injustice. Not to mention his skill at playing on their feelings that an unjust peace had been imposed after the First World War. There was a splendid breeding ground for Nazi ideas in Germany in the thirties. From nineteen thirty-three on the National Socialist Party was the only one permitted. Who would call for democracy, when a whole people rose up and marched in step? Books that were viewed as harmful to the national state were burned and authors were banned from writing. Only music approved by the state could be played. Movies and radio programs had to be censored before they could be broadcast. The schools put ideology on their curriculum, and the teachers who didn't submit were purged. The Jews also had to be purged. The explanation was that they were active in a worldwide conspiracy that threatened everyone. All Jews had to wear a yellow star on their clothes. Gradually, systems were set up to transport them to huge death camps along with gypsies, Danes, homosexuals, Communists, Norwegians, Russians, Poles, Englishmen—"

"There were never any concentration camps! That's just propaganda!" Jenny's face was red with rage, visible even in the soft candlelight.

"Is that right? Who is spreading this propaganda, then?"

"It's the . . . Communists!"

"Who are the Communists of today that are so stubbornly holding on to this lie?"

"It's the . . . Soviet Union!"

"There isn't anything called the Soviet Union anymore. No, Jenny, the people who were in these camps can tell you all about it. There aren't many left alive today, but the ones who are still here can testify that it's no lie. They speak for millions of people who never got out of the concentration camps alive. But even in their homelands there are groups today who deny what happened. It must be a bitter feeling for the Norwegian and Danish resistance fighters, who today are more than seventy years old, to listen to young neo-Nazis denying their horrendous experiences and the death of their friends."

Tommy took a gulp of his coffee before he went on.

"But all this flourished at a later stage of Nazi Germany's development. Back to Berlin in nineteen thirty-two. The National Socialists quickly gained strength. In the late twenties they had founded the Hitler Youth, a movement that aimed to make young people from the age of ten into trusted warriors for the Reich and the party. One dark January night a gang of five Hitler Jugend boys in their late teens was on the way to a meeting. They walked by a school and just as they passed by, a girl came out the gate. She was thirteen years old and her name was Rachel. The boys knew that she was Jewish and that her father was a bookseller. They forced her back into the schoolyard. There they took turns raping her. Four of them held her down while the fifth raped her. They kept on doing it until she started bleeding heavily. Then they got scared and left her lying there. Her father found her a couple of hours later. She lay as the boys had left her. Her eyes were fixed on the black night sky, and she didn't respond when they said her name. Rachel would never respond again."

Tommy fell silent and looked at his audience. Irene understood his intentions in telling the story and resisted the impulse to ask him to finish. Katarina looked like she was going to throw up. Jenny sat with a stony expression on her face, but Irene knew her daughter and could see from her nervously plucking fingers that she was extremely moved. Tommy took another deep breath and continued.

"You might think that since Rachel bled so heavily, she wouldn't have become pregnant. But she did. Her father was in despair. His name was Jacob Uhr. He was widowed at an early age and had come from Poland when Rachel was little, to build a future for himself and his daughter in Berlin. He worked for his unmarried uncle in the bookstore. When the uncle died several years later, he left the bookstore to Jacob. The store wasn't prosperous, but Jacob could support himself and his daughter comfortably. Until the rape occurred. Doctors came and went. Rachel lay in a coma as a result of shock and had to be cared for like a baby. Finally Jacob could no longer afford to pay the doctor bills and had to nurse Rachel himself as best he could. By then he knew that she was pregnant. A Jewish neighbor woman promised to help with the delivery."

Katarina was so agitated that her voice broke when she asked, "But why didn't the father report the boys?"

Tommy's tone of voice was unchanged. "He did, right after the rape occurred. The police just smirked and winked knowingly at each other. And nothing happened. Nobody was interested in even looking for five purebred Aryans who had raped a lowly Jewish girl. Jacob Uhr should have been grateful that his miserable lineage was infused with a little noble Aryan blood."

Jenny was pale as a corpse now, and her eyes looked unnaturally large in her hairless skull. She didn't take her eyes off Tommy.

"Rachel turned fourteen. Two weeks later the labor pains started. For the next three days the thin little girl lay there trying to push out the baby. Jacob had help from the neighbor woman, who was used to assisting at childbirths. She was the one who saw when Rachel died. Jacob refused at first to accept it, but she screamed, 'Now it's a matter of seconds!' She stuck her hands into Rachel's womb and with the blood streaming down her forearms pulled out the little baby in a torrent of blood. At first Jacob didn't want to look at the miracle that had cost his only daughter her life. But the midwife was a resolute woman. She bathed the screaming little mite, wrapped her up, and placed the infant in Jacob's arms. Then she said, 'Jacob Uhr. This little child is without guilt. Your daughter died that night in the schoolyard, and she never came back to us. But the child is alive and healthy. You have received her as a gift from God, instead of Rachel who was taken from you. The little girl shall be called Sonya, after me!'

"Then Jacob looked down into the baby's dark sapphire-blue eyes. The little one had stopped crying and looked steadily at her grandfather. And in his heart a light was lit for the little life and he whispered quietly, so that only she could hear: 'You will live. You will have a better life!'"

"Damn! What a damned shitty story you're making up!"

Jenny had jumped up from her seat, and her eyes glittered with tears and rage. Tommy looked at her calmly. Without a word he pulled out a thin, worn book with a brown leather cover from the pocket of his jacket. At first Irene thought it looked like an old diary. When Tommy held it up to the light, she could clearly see an elegant monogram in the lower right corner of the cover. The gilt had flaked off, but you could make out the letters J. U. Calmly he said, "You can read it yourself. This is Jacob Uhr's diary."

He held it out to Jenny. She instantly put her hands behind her back. She looked at the little book as if it were a cobra ready to strike. Tommy didn't take his eyes off her as he again spoke. "To make a long story short, with the help of the midwife Sonya, the little Sonya survived. A year later Jacob managed to get out of Germany. He found a job in a bookstore here in Göteborg that was also owned by a Jew. When he married a Swedish woman—Britta, a stubborn fisherman's widow from the island of Hönö—he fell into disfavor with his employer."

"Hönö! That's where your summerhouse is! Is that where you heard this story?" Katarina seemed relieved to begin to divine an explanation for the awful things she had heard this evening.

Tommy smiled and went on, "Part of it. Both Jacob and this woman were more than forty years old when they met. She once had a son, but he drowned in the same shipwreck as his father, during a storm in the North Sea. So little Sonya became like a daughter for Jacob and his wife. But the Jews in Göteborg threw him out of their congregation. Jacob had never been a particularly religious Jew, so he converted to Christianity. Little Sonya was confirmed in the Swedish Lutheran Church. She had blue eyes and wonderfully shiny red hair. She was teased about it, but not because she was Jewish. Nobody knew about that; she didn't even know herself. She knew nothing about her ancestry, but thought she was Jacob and Britta's child. Jacob had told her only that he came from Poland, but not that he was a Jew. He never mentioned the time in Germany or what happened there. Britta knew, of course, but she didn't say anything to Sonya either. She didn't find out anything until Jacob and Britta died a few months apart, fifteen years ago."

Irene couldn't help exclaiming. The pieces had fallen into place and she understood how it all fit together.

Tommy nodded to her and smiled. "You've figured it out. But Jenny and Katarina couldn't know about this, since they weren't born yet.

Sonya is my mother. Jacob and Britta, whom I always called Grandma and Grandpa, turned out to be my great-grandfather and his wife!"

Only Sammie's faint snoring under the coffee table disturbed the total silence that had descended over the room. Irene couldn't think of anything to say. Tommy had never told her about this. But really, why should he?

As if he had heard her thoughts he continued, "It was a shock for Mamma. She, who was confirmed and married in the Swedish Lutheran Church, suddenly found out that she was half Jewish and the product of a gang rape!"

Tommy fell silent and looked down at Sammie through the glass tabletop. When he spoke again, his voice was low and utterly serious. "Jenny, if you want you can borrow Jacob's diary. It's important that you understand why you and I can no longer be friends."

Jenny's eyes were wide with horror; her mouth stood half open, but she couldn't utter a sound. Irene's maternal heart writhed in sympathy, but she knew that this was between Jenny and Tommy.

He went on in a neutral tone, "You and Katarina attended the baptism of my children. We have spent vacations and weekends together. But because you have declared that you're a skinhead, play Nazi music, and advocate what they stand for, you are the enemy of me and my children. Our mortal enemy, literally! When the persecution begins, one drop of Jewish blood in our veins will be enough to have us killed. Even the suspicion that there may be one drop is enough to kill us! And I'm one-quarter Jewish, my children one-eighth. We don't have a chance. We will be killed."

Jenny tried to pluck up her courage and screamed, "That's the stupidest thing I've ever heard! We don't want to kill anybody!"

"Yes you do, Jenny. What is it they sing in the lyrics to the music you like so much? Since you say you love that music, you also have to stand for what the lyrics say. 'Death to niggers and Jews! Fight for a pure, Aryan Sweden!' Sound familiar? And to show even more clearly what you stand for, you've also shaved off your hair," he stated coldly.

"That was because of the band! Markus thought it would be cool if I dared to shave off my ha . . . hair!"

The last word came in a long sob. She sprang to her feet, rushed up the stairs, and slammed the door. They could hear her crying loudly. Sammie woke up when she rushed off and looked around bewildered. He sensed that the atmosphere was charged, not at all as cozy as it was when he went to sleep.

Krister leaned forward, put his head in his hands, and groaned, "Good Lord, this has been one of the worst experiences of my life! I almost stood up and yelled at you to stop. But now you've put the decision in Jenny's hands."

"It's not Jenny's fault; it's the fault of our forgetfulness. We forget what we want to forget, and the consequence is that we lose our history, and then we can't learn from it. It's an eternal cycle and everything is repeated," said Tommy in resignation.

Irene's mouth was dry when she asked, "Is this story really true?"

"Every single word. Do you want to borrow Jacob's diary?"

Hesitantly, she reached out and took the little book with the dry leather cover. But she didn't open it. Uncertainly she said, "My school German isn't that good anymore. I probably can't understand what he wrote."

Tommy gave her a big smile and a shrewd glance. "No, you probably can't. Because Jacob wrote his diary in his mother tongue. Polish."

JIMMY OLSSON had emergency neurosurgery at two o'clock in the morning. The examination earlier in the day had shown a small hemorrhage between the meninges that had not been visible on the emergency X ray taken the night he was admitted to the hospital. Jimmy's condition had deteriorated rapidly after he awoke at night with a splitting headache and began to show signs of failing consciousness. His speech had become slurred and his body was going numb.

SVEN ANDERSSON looked serious when he told Tommy, Irene, Birgitta, and Jonny about Jimmy. The superintendent said sympathetically, "The poor guy, it's evident a blood vessel was leaking blood."

Irene shuddered. Tommy looked angry when he said, "This is what really happens from hard blows to the head. In the movies the hero just shakes his head after a skyscraper falls on him, gets up, and quickly grabs his machine gun to mow down twenty gangsters!"

Jonny snorted, "Why don't you tell it like it is: This is what happens when you go out on a job with a chick. It's always the guy who has to take the worst lumps when things get rough!"

Irene was totally speechless, but she didn't need to get into an argument. Unexpectedly the superintendent came to her defense. "If Irene hadn't been there, Jimmy Olsson would be dead today."

"Thanks to her, in that case. She got them into the situation! Nobody asked them to drive out to Billdal. The dames lured poor Jimmy away."

The dames meant Birgitta and her. Irene knew that the accusation was groundless, but it still stung. She was the oldest, the one with the most experience and practice. All Jimmy had to do was follow orders and keep up with her. Was she to blame for what happened to Jimmy?

Andersson was bright red when he stood up, slammed his palm on the table, and yelled, "Shut up! Irene was doing her job, checking up on a possible lead to Bobo Torsson's hideout! Damn it, nobody in this department has to run in to see me every time something comes up that needs to be investigated more closely. That would be totally inappropriate! You're pros, after all!"

Wham! He slapped his palm on the table again, to emphasize what he was saying. Jonny was obviously unprepared for his boss's outburst, because he said nothing. Andersson took a few deep breaths to try to control his blood pressure. More calmly he said, "No one could have known that those punks would hide an alarm in a stack of lumber! And there was nothing to indicate that there would be Hell's Angels in Bobo's and Shorty's cottage. Jimmy and Irene ran into a damned unpleasant surprise at the site."

Andersson sat back down, but the grim expression did not leave his face. He scrutinized Jonny for a long time; Irene could see that Jonny was embarrassed. She felt that there was something else behind the superintendent's vehement reaction, but didn't have the slightest idea what it could be.

Andersson went on, "I don't want to hear this kind of shit again from you, Jonny. We can't attack each other. We have to concentrate on the job. Dump your anger on Shorty instead, and see if you can make him talk! Today is our last chance. Tomorrow we have to let him go. So far there isn't a single scrap of evidence that he did anything illegal. Even though that devil has never done anything else!"

"Now he's an honorable tobacco merchant." Irene gave Andersson a teasing look in an attempt to lighten the mood.

"Honorable tobacco! . . He sells drugs and nothing else!"

"But we don't have any proof," Irene countered.

"No. Everything points to Bobo Torsson alone. We don't have anything on Shorty."

"Tommy and I are thinking of paying an early-morning visit to young Fru von Knecht. Sylvia revealed yesterday that Bobo and Charlotte are old pals. We thought we'd check and see if she might be familiar with Shorty too."

A gleam came into the superintendent's eye. "That's interesting news. You wouldn't think she'd still keep up with Torsson. Funny girl, that Charlotte. Will it take two of you to interview her?"

"Two pairs of eyes see more than one. While one is talking, the other one looks around a little," said Irene.

"Are you suspicious of her?"

Irene hesitated a moment. Finally she said, "It's mostly a feeling I got when I talked to Sylvia yesterday. She has an idea who got the spare-key ring from Richard von Knecht. But she doesn't want to talk about it. And I'm convinced that it has to be someone in the family. Charlotte or Henrik. Sylvia also told me that Henrik had the mumps before meningitis. When I asked her whether he had become sterile as a result of the mumps, she broke down. So Henrik could be sterile. If so, who's the father of Charlotte's child? I want to feel out both of them on this."

IRENE AND Tommy drove slowly up Långåsliden. Big stucco functional-style houses predominated, but houses of both older and newer architecture were seen here too. Despite the fact that Örgryte and Skår were now considered the central and most exclusive sections of Göteborg, the large, showy gardens in which the houses stood were often marked by some neglect, probably because of the owners' lack of time for gardening. They probably had to work hard to be able to afford to live in these fashionable districts, Irene thought.

Henrik and Charlotte's house wasn't one of the larger ones in the area. But the garden was definitely one of the most overgrown. The house was a two-story yellow stucco with a vaulted oriel next to the balcony. It would have been beautiful if large chunks of plaster hadn't flaked off it. At ten o'clock in the morning, the venetian blinds facing the street on the upper floor were closed. The curtains on the ground floor were drawn in front of the big picture windows facing the porch. A new red Golf was parked in front of the garage.

Tommy slipped on the damp leaves that covered the slick slate flagstones. He had to watch where he set his feet, since many spring frosts had pushed the stones apart. The path up to the house reminded him of a miniature of the collapsed freeway in Oakland after the last earthquake.

Tommy nodded toward the house. "It looks totally dead. I don't think she's home."

Irene gave him a slightly mocking look. She pointed at the gleaming little red car. "And what makes you think the little lady is even awake at this ungodly hour of the day? She hasn't driven off in her new car, at any rate."

They slipped and slid their way to the once lovely teak front door. Many years without oil or maintenance had left the wood gray and cracked. They rang the bell repeatedly. After a good two minutes, they heard footsteps coming downstairs. A tired voice yelled from inside, "Yeah, yeah! What's this about? Who is it?"

Irene recognized Charlotte von Knecht's voice, but it wasn't as well modulated as it had been the last time they met. She waited to answer until she heard that Charlotte had made it to the door. Then she said in a loud voice, "It's Detective Inspector Huss."

For a moment there was utter silence before the lock began to rattle. The door was opened a crack and Charlotte whispered, "Do you have to stand there yelling like that? Think of the neighbors!"

Something had happened to her eyes. The radiant turquoise had become two ordinary bits of granite. She hastened to back up and let them into the surprisingly small entryway. She almost lurched when she turned quickly and swept the thick soft-pink dressing gown tighter around herself. Half choking, she said, "I didn't know it was you two. Wait here, I have to go upstairs!"

Before they managed to say a word, she slunk upstairs. But Irene recognized the smell of liquor. And sex. Charlotte smelled of sex. Pheromones are potent scent factors. Less than a fraction of a nanogram is enough to make the hormones run amok. Irene took a quick look at the clothes hanging in the entryway. She found what she was looking for. A light brown jacket of soft suede with fringes on the shoulders. A pair of boots with pointed toes, high cowboy heels, and shiny buckles at the ankles, size forty-two. Henrik von Knecht was thin, but he was also tall. In this jacket he would look like he was going to a costume party. His taste in clothes was more in the line of cashmere overcoats, not fringed jackets. Three pairs of men's shoes of excellent quality and design, size forty-four, stood in a neat row in the shoe area. Irene showed Tommy her find and he nodded in agreement. Naturally he had also registered the scent.

The sound of a shower was heard from upstairs. Irene quickly took a few steps into the hall. She chose the left-hand door. Out of the corner of her eye she saw Tommy sneaking through the one on the right. The left door led to a small kitchen. The kitchen implements were new and sparkling. The door of the dishwasher was down and revealed a full machine. On the drainboard there were plates and wineglasses.

Two salad plates. Two dinner plates. Two wineglasses. Two cut-glass tumblers. Two. The man was still in the house and it wasn't Henrik von Knecht.

She hurried back to the hallway. The door they had passed on the way in led to a small toilet. The shower on the top floor had stopped, and she could hear someone moving around up there.

Tommy returned and whispered, "Living room, dining room, and a den."

The Charlotte who came down the stairs was a completely different person from the one who had opened the door for them ten minutes earlier. This one had shiny brushed hair, smelled of Cartier, and gave them a radiant turquoise-shimmering look. Finally Irene understood. No one has eyes of that fairy-tale color. We live in the age of tinted contact lenses. Charlotte was dressed in black velvet pants and a short-sleeved, scoop-necked angora sweater the same color as her fantastic eyes.

With a courteous gesture that displayed a certain lack of enthusiasm, Charlotte invited them into the living room. It was clearly marked by Henrik's life and passions. Paintings and antiques were everywhere in the normal-sized room. They walked between urns and curved chairs over to a cream-colored silk sofa, which proved to be astonishingly comfortable. Charlotte draped herself gracefully in an overstuffed velvet easy chair with dark mahogany armrests. She crossed her legs demurely and gave the two detectives an unexpectedly calm look. Sparse daylight seeped in through the heavy drawn curtains and fell on her face. She had been in a hurry, because the foundation under her right eye had not been properly applied; there was a little brown smear on her cheek.

Irene decided on the tough approach and began, in a friendly tone of voice, "Charlotte, we've discovered a number of new details during the course of the investigation. We would be grateful if you could help us go over them."

Without the least quaver in her voice, Charlotte replied, "I'll try."

"First, a question that I'm asking now so I won't forget it at the end. When does your husband come home?"

"On Saturday night."

"Late?"

"Yes, around ten. Presumably, he's going straight to Marstrand. I'll be at a birthday party for a friend who's turning thirty."

"Henrik's not going?"

She hesitated before answering. "No, he's not so wild about big parties. Lots of people and all that," she said evasively.

"But you enjoy that sort of thing."

She looked surprised at Irene's statement. "Yes, of course I do."

"Do you often go out alone?"

Now her gaze wavered. "Usually. Henrik never wants to go. What does this have to do with the investigation of Richard's death?"

"Well, we know that you were often seen with Bobo Torsson. That you were good friends and that you worked together. We also know that you were the one who talked to your father-in-law and arranged for Bobo to rent the apartments on Berzeliigatan."

"That's correct. But Bobo has an aunt who owned the tobacco shop across the street. She gave Bobo a tip that Richard was renovating the apartments in his building. Then he asked me to ask Richard whether there was any chance he could rent one of them."

"Do you know that Bobo is dead?"

Now Charlotte's eyes glistened and she swallowed hard before replying. "I heard it on the news. How horrible!"

"Do you know if Bobo was involved in anything that might have made someone want to kill him?"

Something flared up behind the turquoise blue. Unease and wariness.

"No. Absolutely not!"

She crossed her legs harder and started to massage her bare forearms as if she were cold.

"Did Bobo sell drugs to you?"

Just like Lot's wife, Charlotte was turned into a pillar of salt. It took a long while before she replied apologetically, yet still aggressively, "Everybody uses a little smack nowadays. Everybody does it. There's nothing unusual about that. It's like using alcohol!"

"I see. But it falls under different legislation. Did he sell a lot?"

Now she was prepared and made a brave attempt to sound haughty. "Not at all! He was a prominent photographer. The little he sold was only to friends and at private parties."

She was almost successful, but not quite. Since Irene had a lot of other sensitive questions to ask, she changed the subject. "Do you know a man named Lasse 'Shorty' Johannesson?"

Charlotte was startled, but not scared. She pursed her lips and said, "That's Bobo's cousin. But I've never met him."

"So you don't know him at all?"

"No."

Clearly Irene wasn't going to get any farther with Shorty. Time to switch tacks. She continued calmly, "We also have information that you received a spare-key ring from Richard von Knecht this summer. Why did he give it to you?"

Her astonishment was not feigned. Or else she was a better actress than Irene thought.

"Spare keys? I never got any spare keys from Richard."

"Your father-in-law never gave you any keys?"

"No."

"Was it Henrik who got them?"

Now her gaze flickered before she answered, "I don't think so."

"You don't know if Henrik was given the spare keys by his father?"

"No."

"But you did know that there was a key ring with spare keys on it, didn't you?"

"No, I tell you! No!"

A new scent broke through the heavy Cartier perfume. Terror.

"Then we'll have to ask Henrik when he comes home," said Irene.

She pretended to look at something in her blank notebook. Out of the corner of her eye she saw Charlotte relax and sink a bit in her chair. She obviously thought the danger was past.

Thoughtfully Irene said, "Well, you know, Sylvia told me yesterday that Henrik contracted the mumps when he was in the service. Apparently he became sterile, since it also affected his testicles. I think that seems a bit strange, considering that you're pregnant, don't you?"

The question remained hanging in the air over their heads, like the blade of a guillotine. Charlotte turned pale as a corpse underneath her makeup. "What are you talking about? I feel sick!"

She got up and rushed toward the hall. On her way she knocked over a large Chinese vase. It shattered on the marble hearth in front of the open fireplace. They could hear her tear open the door to the toilet in the hall and slam it shut. Tommy pointed toward the upper floor. Irene nodded, because she had heard it too. A light thump, like a bouncing ball. Someone upstairs had dropped something on the floor.

After nearly five minutes Charlotte returned. She was composed, but they could see she had been crying. Her voice was ice cold when she said, "This is Henrik's child. I'm having a test, whatever it's called. The kind they do to determine paternity."

"DNA tests."

"That's it. But you'll have to wait until May! And I would like you to leave now. I'm not feeling well because of the pregnancy and your horrible questions. As if in some way I'm under suspicion!"

When they stood, Tommy smiled at her. Automatically she smiled back, but it was extinguished when he said in a friendly voice, "You are."

Rage glowed behind the contact lenses. Irene was almost afraid they were going to crack. She lied like a trouper, this young lady, but for the moment they would get no further with her.

Charlotte escorted them to the entryway. Demonstratively she opened the door wide to show them out. Tommy stopped and looked at the gaudy cowboy boots without saying a word. He caught her eye and smiled knowingly. It was more than she could handle. Her hands were shaking when she grabbed hold of Tommy's jacket and pushed him out.

Tauntingly he said, "Watch out, that could be assault on a police officer."

"Fuck that! I'm going to report you! The von Knecht family isn't just anybody! You're going to lose your job!"

With all her might she slammed the door shut.

They said nothing to each other until they were sitting in the car. Tommy looked at Irene. "We were tough on her. What if she has a miscarriage?"

"It would be more the fault of all the alcohol and God knows what else she's put in her body. And she won't be reporting it to any lawyer. By the way—the cowboy boots. And the jacket. We have to find out who's upstairs," said Irene.

She started the car, made a "Göteborg U-turn," and rolled down the street. When they were out of sight of the house, she stopped the car and asked, "Do you want the first shift, or shall I take it?"

"I'll take it. If anything happens I'll call you. Otherwise you can come back after you meet with the Narcs."

"Aren't you going to be there?"

"It's better if you go. You were the one out in Billdal."

"Yep, God knows I was . . . Okay, we'll do it like this. I'll be at headquarters in about half an hour. It depends a little on the streetcars and buses."

She climbed out of the car and headed off toward St. Sigfrid's Circle.

BIRGITTA WAS the first person she ran into at the division. She beamed and waved Irene into her office. There was restrained excitement in her voice.

"I've been looking for you. You said you were going to question Charlotte in more detail. That stirred up something in the back of my mind. I began rummaging through the little I have on Bobo Torsson. And I found this!"

Triumphantly she pointed at a list of names. Her index finger stopped on the name Charlotte Croona. Eagerly she went on, "I was startled when I saw this name the first time. But I had forgotten all your society gossip and never fixed the name in my mind. When you started saying that Bobo and Charlotte had some closer contact, it clicked. This is the list of the people busted in the raid in nineteen eighty-nine, when Shorty went to jail!"

"You've got to be kidding! Did Jonny ask Shorty if he knew Charlotte?"

"Yes. He says he doesn't have any idea who she is. But the interesting thing is that Charlotte was arrested for possession of half a gram of cocaine. She got off with a suspended sentence, since she didn't have a prior record. I searched, but couldn't find a thing on her after 'eighty-nine."

Irene sat and tried to think. She told Birgitta that Tommy was staking out the place, trying to find out who Charlotte's gentleman caller was.

Birgitta suggested, "Could it be the father of her child? If you're right about Henrik really becoming sterile after having the mumps. Can we check that out?"

"No. We have no chance of getting hold of those records. I'm basing my suspicions on Sylvia's reaction when I mentioned the possibility. And on 'Paul Fig-Ball.'"

"'Paul Fig-Ball'?"

Irene explained. Birgitta agreed that it was a long shot. But she had an idea. "What if Bobo Torsson is the father of Charlotte's child? Maybe they had a relationship the whole time."

"Possible. We'll have to check that out somehow. Do we have time to eat before the meeting?"

"Sure, if we wolf it down."

ASSISTANT SUPERINTENDENT Annika Nilsén and two inspectors from Narcotics were in place. Irene was taken aback when she saw them, and for a bewildering moment wondered if Nilsén had dragged along a couple of suspected dealers. But at the same time she knew that was how the undercover Narcs had to look in order to blend in. How great was the risk that they might actually blend in too well and start taking part in the activity they were assigned to monitor? To judge by the appearance of these two undercover agents, they were already a well-established part of Göteborg's narcotics scene. Which of course was the intention. From Violent Crimes, there were Superintendent Andersson, Irene Huss, Birgitta Moberg, and Hans Borg.

The latter looked as if he would rather lie down and sleep off his lunch. He had put his chair in the farthest corner and now sat with his head tipped back and his eyes closed.

Andersson briefly introduced everyone. The two Narcs were Stig Bertilsson and Daniel Svensson. Irene would have guessed Cheech and Chong.

Andersson began by reporting on what had led Violent Crimes to Billdal. He spoke for a long time about their suspicions and the evidence of Bobo Torsson's involvement in selling narcotics. Then he switched to talking about Bobo's death in the parking lot at the Delsjön golf course.

"The techs determined that the bomb on Berzeliigatan and the bomb that killed Bobo were constructed on the same principle. In each case the bomb was made from heavy iron pipe. The interesting thing is that it seems to be the same type of pipe, old-fashioned, heavy drainpipes, but of different dimensions. We had a good tip from a lady who lived in the building, but who wasn't home when it went off. She arrived right afterward, broke down, and had to be taken to the hospital. But she's okay now. Yesterday Fredrik met her by pure chance down on Berzeliigatan. They stood and watched as the men dug through the rubble. She started to ask how the bomb was constructed, Fredrik told me, and then she said something damned interesting. She had complained several times that there was a pile of old pipes left in the cellar from the renovation several years earlier. At that time all the drainpipes and water lines were replaced. But nothing happened. The pipes just stayed there. She had seen them as recently as two weeks ago."

Irene waved her hand and was recognized. "It must be possible to dig down into the cellar and find those pipes. And the lady who saw the pipes might know approximately where to dig."

Andersson nodded and rubbed his hands. "Precisely. That's already been decided. But first we have to pull out von Knecht's safe. How's that going, Borg?"

Hans Borg jumped. He was unlucky enough to have his chair slip out from under him as he sat leaning against the wall. With a crash it hit the floor, and he banged his head. Cheech and Chong exchanged glances.

Borg rubbed his sore head and tried to collect his tattered dignity. Apart from these two things, he didn't seem any the worse for wear. He picked up the chair and sat down again. Embarrassed, he said, "Excuse me. The boys are planning to pry the safe loose this afternoon, if all goes well. After that they'll start digging for the pipes in the cellar. It's going to take some time."

Andersson interjected, "How long? How soon can they start digging down there?"

"Tomorrow afternoon at the earliest. If they know exactly where to dig."

"Okay. See that the old lady is there to show them, so we don't waste a lot of time searching in the wrong spot. Have you got anything else?"

"Yes. This morning that teacher at Ascheberg High School called. The one who loaned me a felt pen and paper in the parking garage when I needed to put up a note that we wanted tips if anyone saw anything. He called and said that he had come upon something. He's a part-time teacher at the school and doesn't have a parking place right outside the building. That's why he's allowed to use a spot in the parking garage, which is about a hundred meters down the street. Last Tuesday night he worked late, until five-fifteen. When he set off for home, he rushed toward the parking garage. That's when he saw a light-colored car in the teachers' parking area that he had never seen before. Since it was after school hours he decided not to worry about it. But he remembered it now, because the newspapers said that no one had seen anything unusual around that time. And that was unusual! Only the teachers can use these parking places until six at night. And he says that none of the teachers who usually park there has a light-colored car. He's not sure of the exact color."

"What make?"

"He doesn't know. He was in a hurry in the pouring rain."

Irene could see that Andersson thought this was interesting. But the three from Narcotics looked so obviously bored that it was probably best to switch over to their domain. Andersson noticed this too and wrapped up.

"Keep checking, Hans. You're good at stuff with cars. Now we'll move on to Billdal."

Annika Nilsén nodded and immediately gave the floor to Stig Bertilsson. He started by telling them about the many years of work Narcotics had devoted to trying to chart the role of the motorcycle gangs in narcotics trafficking. It turned out that they had a surprisingly large share of the market. The small gangs didn't deal drugs. On the other hand, the gangs associated with the Bandidos or Hell's Angels did. And the membership of Hell's Angels Death Squadron No. 1 were being watched most closely at the moment. All kinds of narcotics poured in through them from Denmark and Holland.

Irene began to formulate a vague idea about a connection to Bobo Torsson and Shorty. She broke in with a question. "How do these gangs distribute dope to buyers?"

"Most often through dealers. It's not easy for a fat guy in leather on a big Harley to ride around selling dope to teenagers. He's too visible, and the risk of getting caught is too great. No, they take large quantities and sell to middlemen, who then distribute it to the market."

Irene nodded and said, "That sounds like Bobo Torsson. We know that he was dealing. And Shorty too, but we don't have anything on him since he got out of prison. Do you know if he's had any contact with this gang?"

Bertilsson shook his head. Andersson groaned out loud and everyone could hear him muttering, "We're going to have to release that scumbag!"

Birgitta patted him lightly on the arm and said consolingly, "I think I'll keep digging in the files. I'll work on it this afternoon. If there's any connection, that's where it'll be."

"All right. Keep digging," her boss sighed.

Irene leaned forward and patted Andersson on the other arm. She gave him an encouraging smile and said, "And you can ask Shorty if Bobo and Charlotte had a relationship. No doubt he won't answer, but maybe you can read something from his reaction."

"You mean a sexual relationship?"

"Yes."

Andersson raised his eyebrows and nodded. He turned to his colleagues from Narcotics and explained, "This is the only point of contact between Bobo and the von Knecht family we've found. Do you have the slightest indication that Richard von Knecht or anyone else in the von Knecht family might be mixed up with drugs?"

Annika Nilsén cleared her throat and said in her toneless voice, "No. That name has never come up in our department, as far as I know. Have you ever seen it?" She turned to the two agents, who both shook their heads.

Birgitta said eagerly, "But we've found Charlotte's name on a list from a raid in nineteen eighty-nine! She was single at the time and her last name was Croona."

Stig Bertilsson looked crestfallen. "But I was in on that bust! Charlotte Croona! She was doing a striptease on the table, so there wasn't much to search. For lack of anything better I had a good look at her necklace, a little carved cylinder. And when I unscrewed it there was snow inside. Freebase, not pure. That's why she got off with a suspended sentence. When we got to the station she was almost psychotic. Hallucinating."

He paused and grimaced at the memory. Then he went on, "I found out that she was a pretty well-known photo model, although there was never anything in the papers about her. But believe me, nobody who was there could forget Charlotte Croona!"

Andersson exclaimed, "And Bobo and Shorty were there too! It has to be Bobo and Charlotte who are the point of contact."

The others agreed.

Irene sighed dejectedly. "We have to find proof! We've got nothing but assumptions and guesses."

Andersson gave her an indulgent look and said, "That's fairly normal for an investigation. We just have to find some evidence that will hold up." He turned to Bertilsson. "What did you come up with in Billdal?"

Bertilsson shrugged. "Not much. Judging from the statements given by the neighbors along the road, the motorcycle guys were on the scene for three days. But no one ever saw more than two at a time. And no one suspected that they had broken into those two summer cabins. The gang had picked the locks. The only trace of drugs was a number of small plastic bags containing amphetamine. No hypodermics, but some paper towels with blood spots. Both places were a mess, and we found tons of fingerprints. Two pairs have been identified, belonging to Glenn 'Hoffa' Strömberg and Paul Svensson. Three pairs aren't in the records. One of them is so small that we assume it's from the girl. We haven't managed to identify her. We sent the other two sets to Interpol. We suspect the police in Holland may have those prints in their archives. Death Squadron had a visit from an Amsterdam club all last weekend and the beginning of this week. They came up via Malmö last Thursday. Twelve of them thundering up the coast of Halland. We followed them. Or at least we tried. They split up and stayed with various gang members. Yesterday they went back to Holland."

Andersson was frowning anxiously when he asked, "But how did Bobo, and possibly also Shorty, come in contact with the Hell's Angels? Shorty vehemently denies knowing Hoffa."

The investigators from Narcotics merely shrugged.

After a bit more discussion they decided to adjourn.

IRENE GOT a lift with one of the patrol officers and was dropped off at St. Sigfridsgatan. She brought along a sandwich and a light beer from the cafeteria for Tommy. He had moved the car, but she saw it, quickly walked over, opened the door, and climbed in.

"Hi. I brought you some chow. Anything happening?" she asked.

"Not a thing. I went off to take a leak an hour ago. I was gone ten minutes max. But nothing happened during that time. The Golf is still there, the blinds are closed. Man, stakeouts are sure boring!"

He unwrapped the sandwich from the plastic and opened the beer. It was already dark, and it was starting to get cold in the car.

Irene looked around. "Hey, maybe we should move. The old lady in the house across the street has peeked at us several times from behind her curtains. She probably thinks we're up to no good. Let's switch places, then you can keep eating."

She got out of the car and Tommy slid over to the passenger's side.

Suddenly a light showed behind the closed blinds on the top floor of Charlotte's house. After a few minutes a lamp was turned on downstairs. It was probably the hall lamp, because behind the curtains in the bay window of the living room it was still dark. They waited tensely, but nothing else happened. It was time to move the car; the neighbor lady was getting suspicious.

They drove off and parked on Förtroligheten. Irene stuck her arm under Tommy's and they slowly strolled back up Långåsliden. They talked softly as they walked.

Tommy asked, "Is Jenny going to the Karl the Twelfth demonstrations tonight? Or rather riots, in the worst case."

"No, she's never been that interested in going. That was a real eye-opener you gave her last night. She never really understood before that joining up with a group like that also meant that she might have to do things she didn't like or want to do."

"But what if her boyfriend demands that she come along?"

Irene hesitated. "I don't know. I honestly don't. But Krister says that we need to trust her judgment. She's a smart girl, but a little lost; she's had a hard time finding a real best friend. She has Katarina, of course, but they fight all the time, except when Krister or I say something to one of them. Then they gang up on us and stick together."

They were nearing the yellow villa, completely unprepared, when the front door suddenly opened and a figure rushed out, stumbling down the uneven garden path. The door closed quickly. Evidently Charlotte wasn't going out with him, which was lucky, considering she might have recognized them at once.

With great self-control Irene forced herself to continue walking at Tommy's side as if nothing had happened. They kept on talking as they discreetly observed the young man walk around the Golf. He was blond, of medium height, about twenty years old, and he was wearing the soft suede jacket and cowboy boots. The glow of the streetlight fell on him for a moment before he turned his back to them to unlock the car. He had a surprisingly young face with regular features, but he looked very grim. Was he angry? Had they had an argument? With an impatient gesture he pushed the hair out of his face. Irene caught herself thinking that he looked really sweet. Charlotte had gotten herself a boytoy. Although judging by his costume, he would probably prefer being called a cowboy. He got into the car and started fumbling in his jacket pockets. Apparently he was thinking of lighting a cigarette. Tommy and Irene passed the Golf and tried to increase their pace without being noticed. As fast as they dared, they hurried toward the Saab. When they opened the car doors, Irene looked back and saw the Golf swinging out onto the street. She let him drive by, hopped in the Saab, and then made one of her usual illegal U-turns.

He drove down toward Skårs Allé and then turned south on St. Sigfridsgatan. Before long he turned up Kungsbackaleden. Tommy groaned, half in jest, but said with a serious undertone, "Oh no! Don't tell me we're going out to Billdal again!"

But they weren't. At Mölndal the red Golf turned off and headed down Bifrostgatan. He drove a short distance and then parked outside a low apartment house. Irene quickly turned down a side street. They jumped out of the car and saw the young man calmly walk up to the street door and go inside. They jogged up to the door and opened it as cautiously as they could in time to hear a door closing on the floor above. The list of occupants was posted in the foyer.

She saw the name right away and started giggling. She said in a low voice, "R. Skytter. Robert Skytter. She's screwing her car dealer. And he's the one who gave her the alibi for the evening of the murder!"

THEY WAITED five minutes before they went upstairs. Tommy rang the doorbell with the nameplate "R. SKYTTER." They heard footsteps and the door opened. But it wasn't the cowboy. The man who opened the door had red hair and was taller, but about the same age.

"Hello, we're from the police. Inspector Irene Huss and Inspector Tommy Persson. We're looking for Robert Skytter."

The redhaired youth's eyes narrowed and he said with feigned non-chalance, "Do you have any ID?"

Both Irene and Tommy pulled out their laminated ID cards and held them up in front of him. He couldn't hide his disappointment when he said, "These can't be right. It's supposed to be a big gold badge."

Irene sighed loudly. "That's in the States. You've seen too many cop movies. Are you Robert, or is it the guy who came in five minutes ago?"

The redhaired guy looked like he was thinking about answering, but he never got a chance. Behind him the blond young man appeared. He smoothly greeted them, "Hello! What's this about?"

This was Robert. She recognized his trumpeting voice.

"Hi, Robert. Detective Inspector Irene Huss. We spoke on the telephone last week. May we come in?"

The redhaired guy moved aside reluctantly. Tommy turned to him and said, "And who are you?"

"Daniel Skytter," he replied sullenly.

Now Irene could see the likeness. They were brothers. In a friendly voice she asked, "Do you live here too?"

"Yes. Temporarily."

"Temporarily?"

Daniel Skytter showed signs of uneasiness, rocking back and forth on his feet. "I had to move here last week, when my girlfriend threw me out. It was her apartment," he said morosely.

"So now you live here. What kind of work do you do?"

"Collect unemployment. Out-of-work painter."

"Well, Daniel, we need to speak to Robert in private. Do you have any objection to taking a little walk?"

Daniel gave a start and then straightened up. His eyes narrowed as he snarled, "I sure do! No witnesses, huh? So you can work him over and make him confess to anything!"

Irene and Tommy sighed at the same time. In an exaggerated pedagogical tone Tommy said, "My dear Daniel, you really ought to stop watching those American movies. We just want to talk to your brother. He's an important witness in a very serious case that we're investigating."

A gleam of curiosity appeared in Daniel's suspicious gray eyes. Obviously he had no idea what it was all about.

Tommy continued, "Another option is that we take him downtown and question him there."

"You can't do that!"

"Yes, we can."

Uncertainly the brothers looked at each other. Robert nodded and motioned with his head toward the door. Daniel gave up. He took his jacket from the coat hook, put on a cap, stuffed his feet in a pair of heavy jogging shoes, and went out. The look he sent over his shoulders was brimming with distrust.

Irene turned to Robert Skytter.

"How old is your brother?"

"Eighteen."

"Eighteen years old, and already living with a girl?"

"It didn't even last two months."

"Why doesn't he move back home to Mamma, then?"

"He doesn't get along with Mamma's new man. So that's why he moved in with me last week. But I'm trying to find him a small apartment somewhere. Although he probably can't afford it."

"So it was because of him that you and Charlotte chose to meet at her house?"

Robert's gaze wandered, and then he turned abruptly to lead the way down the narrow corridor and into a small living room, furnished with "Balder" the sofa, "Runar" the coffee table, and "Diplomat" the bookshelf. Irene recognized them from her studies in home decorating: the '96 IKEA catalog.

Robert motioned them to the sofa. He chose "Tobbe," the armchair, for himself. But he got up just as quickly and asked nervously, "Would you like something to drink? Ramlösa? Light beer? Strong beer?"

"Ramlösa, thanks."

"A light beer, thanks."

He vanished down the hallway and into the kitchen. They could hear him clinking bottles and glasses. Through a half-open door Irene glimpsed an unmade bed. Two rooms and a kitchen. And his little brother. That was Robert Skytter's living situation for the present. Not great for inviting over his married lover from Örgryte. Again the familiar "why" popped up in her mind. Why did Charlotte need this sweet little boytoy? The object in question appeared with bottles and glasses in a precarious grip. Robert set his burden down on the table before he began to speak uncertainly and tentatively.

"So you were the ones at Charlotte's house this morning?"

Irene nodded. "It was after ten o'clock. Yes, it was us."

"It's like you said. There's not enough room here, and with Daniel . . . you know."

"Was it Charlotte who wanted you to come to her house?"

He looked down at the table and then nodded.

"How long have you and Charlotte been together?"

He looked up and seemed genuinely surprised. "We're not together! Well, okay. Last night."

"You've never slept with each other before?"

Now his hands were shaking and he picked sulkily at the label on his beer. Tommy repeated the question. Finally he said, extremely reluctantly, "I've already told you what happened last week when she picked up the car. What is she accused of, anyway?"

"She's not accused of anything. Possibly suspected of giving incorrect information regarding the murder of Richard von Knecht. We don't know for sure yet. That's what we're trying to find out," Tommy said in his best police tone of voice.

Irene decided to bring up what had been nagging at her subconscious. Jonny's flat tire had brought it to the surface. Sternly she said, "Robert, nobody ever cares about checking the spare tire. Nobody! Least of all Charlotte. What actually happened?"

Tommy looked very serious and stared right into Robert's eyes before he added, "Robert, if you lied about what happened that Tuesday afternoon, then you can be indicted for abetting a criminal. That can result in several years in prison. Is she worth it?"

Robert kept picking at the beer label and seemed completely absorbed by its artistic design. He swallowed several times before he replied. "She's so luscious. But she takes pills that she mixes with wine. She asked several times if I wanted some . . . but I don't use that shit. I've tried smoking grass a few times, of course. But this was big-time stuff. Finally, I didn't dare drink anything! In case she put some fucking shit in my wine."

"You didn't know that she uses narcotics?"

He shook his head vigorously. Suddenly he exclaimed, "I hardly know her! It was like a God damned sex fantasy! She was naked underneath! And I . . . it was impossible to resist her."

Heavily he rested his head in his hands. Since he didn't seem to want to go on, Irene decided to try to get him to relax and keep talking. In a mischievous tone of voice she said, "But Robbie, aren't you old enough to know that all women are naked under their clothes?"

He laughed and gave her a desperate look. "But not right under their coats!"

Irene motioned to Tommy. This looked like it was going to be man-to-man talk. He understood and turned with an expression of the greatest sympathy toward the young man. Tactfully he asked, "Robert, are you talking about the Tuesday evening last week, when Charlotte came to pick up her new car?"

"Yes."

"When did you and Charlotte first meet?"

"Three or four weeks before. There's a little waiting time for cars with special paint jobs."

"Does Charlotte's car have special paint?"

"Yes. Light yellow. A pale lemon yellow. A luscious color."

"What happened when you were supposed to deliver the car to her?"

"I called all day Friday and Saturday, because we got word that it wouldn't arrive until after the weekend, on Monday morning. She finally answered just before we closed. So then we agreed that she would come over on Monday afternoon. But she never showed up. On Tuesday I called her house in the morning, but she wasn't in. Then she called at three in the afternoon and said that she could come down in an hour to pick up the car. She said that she specifically wanted me to help her, nobody else. And I . . . was happy to oblige."

He stopped and looked down at his fingers picking at the label. He had scraped almost the whole thing off the bottle. Tommy leaned forward and said, "When did she arrive?"

"Right after four. She had one of those cloth raincoats on, with a belt drawn tight around her waist and high-heeled shoes. When we went over to her old car, which she was trading in, her coat slipped open and she was wearing some of those nylon stockings that stay up by themselves. And nothing else. When she leaned over the seat . . . then I saw . . . Naked. She was naked. Except for the stockings."

He stopped and his cheeks were red. He stole a glance at Irene. She responded with feigned indifference. But inside she was seething with emotion! This was a premeditated seduction.

Tommy ignored her presence and continued as though there were just two men in the room. "She made you hot?"

"What do you think? I'm a guy, after all!"

"So the two of you decided to screw?"

Robert was bright red in the face, but his expression became almost satyrlike when he replied. "You bet! We got into her new car and drove around to the back of the building where an old Ford Transit is parked; we have to fix it up a little before spring. They sell like hotcakes. People buy them as vacation cars. We hopped in the Transit. She brought a blanket and a bag from her old car. So we lay down on the blanket."

"You were hot, I know that. So it didn't take long before you were finished?"

To Irene's satisfaction, some of Robert's satyr smile was wiped away. "Well, yeah. But we couldn't take too long because they'd start to miss me in the showroom, you know. But then she said that we'd meet again soon. If I wanted to."

"And you did, I suppose."

"Did I ever! It's what every guy dreams about happening sometime in his life!"

"When did you hear from her again?"

"On Wednesday night. The next day. She said that we'd have to wait a while to meet. Her father-in-law had been murdered, you know. She also said that the police would probably want to get in touch with me. And that she had told them the truth. That she picked up the car. But not the rest. We agreed to say that we'd gone over the new car extra carefully. There are actually quite a few new details on this model. Take for example the new—"

"But that wasn't what you were doing. Going over new details. How does this fit in with the timetable you gave us? You said that you heard the news on the radio and that she said something like, 'Oh, it's the five o'clock news already! I have to hurry!' And she got her papers for the new car and drove off."

His whole young face radiated honesty.

"But the last part is true! When we were . . . finished . . . she put on the clothes she had in her bag. Then when she got into the car she turned on the radio. That's when we heard the news program. And then she said that part about the five o'clock news."

Both the detectives could hear that he was telling the truth. They got up, thanked him for the refreshments, and Tommy patted Robert lightly on the shoulder and said, "You probably know that she was using you. Tell me seriously—wasn't it really too good to be true?"

Robert hung his head, but nodded in agreement.

"If it hadn't been for the drugs . . . but she had to keep taking that shit all the time. Before I left this afternoon, I told her. That it's dangerous, I mean. I don't like stuff like that. She was mad and told me I could go to hell. I felt mostly relieved. Really!"

Thank God he was someone who hesitated about contact with narcotics. Charlotte had misjudged him, while Irene had been right. She had liked him after their first conversation on the phone. He had lifted her spirits on that rotten Friday. The Friday she had spent in Stockholm. Impulsively she decided to call Mona Söder as soon as possible.

THEY DROVE by Örgryte, but the house was empty. The garage door was unlocked and when they looked inside, the garage was empty. There was no yellow Golf. In a corner inside the door they found two empty plastic jugs marked "DISTILLED WATER."

At the department there was still feverish activity even though it was past six. Andersson wasn't in his office. Birgitta Moberg was deeply engrossed in her computer. On the desk lay stacks of papers and folders. They decided to go down to the pizzeria a few blocks away.

Before they left, Irene called home. Her mother answered. Yes, both the twins were home. They had rented a video, which they were watching. The girls had eaten dinner, and she was going to watch the rest of the movie with them. Before she hung up she said, "Be careful if you go out. It said on the TV news that there are young people rioting downtown. Good thing you're not involved with such dangerous things. When are you coming home?"

THE UPROAR in the center of town could be heard clearly. They went in the opposite direction and slipped into the pizzeria, whose owner was getting rich from the Göteborg police force. Besides pizza it served excellent dinners. They each ordered goulash and a large regular beer and had bread and salad while they waited for the main course.

As they sat stabbing at the salad with their forks, Birgitta said, "I found something really interesting this afternoon. Bobo Torsson and Hoffa Strömberg were in the same prison. At the same time, that is. There's the contact between Bobo and the Hell's Angels."

"What does Shorty say about that?"

"Naturally he doesn't know a thing about it, according to him. He did seven years inside, after all. But at a different prison."

"What was Hoffa in for?"

"Aggravated assault. The victim will never be a human being again. It was a fight between rival motorcycle gangs. We don't have any evidence against Shorty. He'll probably be released tomorrow. Andersson is frantic."

Irene and Tommy told her about their discoveries that afternoon. Birgitta didn't interrupt the story. She stared at them steadily, not wanting to miss a word. There was an intense gleam in her eyes when she leaned over her piping hot goulash and said in a low voice, "The beautiful people and their glamorous life. It's so enticing and enviable when you see it from a distance. But if you start to scratch the surface, the gold soon turns to dust."

AT NINE o'clock Irene called Mona Söder at home and left a message on her answering machine.

"Hi, Mona. This is Irene Huss in Göteborg. I want to thank you for telling me everything and letting me meet Jonas. It was a big help in the investigation that we didn't have to keep checking on you two. You've been completely eliminated from the suspect list. I've . . . been thinking about Jonas. Please give him my fondest regards. Tell him that the butterfly painting is the most wonderful I've ever seen. Talk to you later, Mona. I . . . we'll talk." Quickly she hung up. Then she drove home.

Chapter Sixteen

IT SMELLED LIKE COFFEE and gingersnaps at "morning prayers." Everyone had come, except for Hans Borg and Superintendent Andersson. The secretary had set up an Advent wreath, and the first candle was lit. In the windows stood the electric ones, spreading a soft, cozy glow. Irene was already into her fourth cup of coffee of the morning when the boss's steps were heard approaching down the corridor. They sounded determined. There was a sense of foreboding when the door was flung open and Andersson's bright red face appeared in the doorway.

Angrily he shouted, "Damn, it's dark in here. Turn on the lights!"

He stepped inside and poured himself some coffee, looked down into the steaming cup, and took a deep whiff.

"You'll have to excuse me. Happy Advent, or whatever it's called. But everything is going to hell! Shorty is going to be released this morning. And that God damned standalone has fallen into the cellar!"

Borg appeared in the doorway just in time to hear the boss's words. He nodded and said, "That's right. They called me when the standalone broke through. It's going to be salvaged later today. We decided to start digging for those pipes instead. Now there's a hole anyway. They have to redo the support work over the weekend. We won't have another chance to lift out the safe until Monday morning at the earliest."

Jonny Blom looked annoyed and urged, "Why don't we just knock down the walls with one of those big balls on the end of a crane? Quick and easy!"

Borg dismissed the idea with a wave of his hand. "Too rough. The whole building could come crashing down and then it would be hard to locate the safe."

"How are we going to open it?"

"We've checked it out with binoculars. It's a Swedish safe with a combination lock. A guy from Rosengren's is coming to help us. There's probably no bomb inside, but we're going to take safety precautions when we open it."

Andersson gave the group a grim look and said, "We're not getting anywhere. This is going too slow! Damn!"

The last had to be interpreted as a general comment on the state of things. No one ventured an opposing point of view.

Irene reported on her interview with Charlotte von Knecht and the conversation with her young lover. Tommy took over and told about Robert Skytter's revelations. By the time Irene presented Chong's story from the '89 raid, they had quite a different image of the charming Charlotte von Knecht, née Croona.

Andersson's face was beginning to return to normal, but his voice was strident. "That filly doesn't have clean oats in her feed bag. Or to put it more precisely, clean snow! Ha ha! *Ahem.* What did that guy from Narcotics call the stuff he found in her pendant?"

Birgitta hurried to his rescue and said pedantically, "Freebase. Cocaine mixed with bicarbonate of soda. That's what's sold on the street. Pure cocaine is too strong and too dangerous. And who can check how much baking soda they put in?"

Now that she had started, she told them about her visit to Väners-borg to see Bobo's mother. It had produced nothing of value. Mother and son seemed not to have had any contact in recent years. It had been almost two years since they last saw each other. But she had brought up the question again about the insurance payment in the event of death. Birgitta had referred her to the claims office of the current insurance company. The mother hadn't seen Bobo's father in more than twenty years, but she knew that he was a total outcast. She herself had remarried, lived in a house outside of Vänersborg, and worked in a candy store. Birgitta's final tidbit was the discovery that Bobo Torsson and Glenn "Hoffa" Strömberg had done time in the same prison, but she had been unable to find any connection between Shorty and the two Hell's Angels, except for Shorty and Paul Svensson's abortive participation in the bank robbery in Kungsbacka in the early eighties.

Andersson sighed heavily. "And today we have to release that son-of-a-bitch! Jonny and I have both grilled him, but it didn't produce a thing. Except that we suspect he knows who killed Bobo. That's why I want surveillance on him. Jonny? Hans? Fredrik? Birgitta?"

They all nodded. Only Fredrik looked enthusiastic. Andersson went on, "And how's it going with Bobo's drunken father? Did you get hold of him, Hannu?"

"Yes. At Lillhagen."

"He's been admitted to Lillhagen Hospital?"

"Right. He can't walk or talk. He's dying of liver cancer."

"But Lillhagen is a mental hospital. He shouldn't be there if he has liver cancer."

"Nobody would take him. He was admitted this summer. They found him passed out in a stairwell on the north side of town."

There was a brief pause as they poured more coffee and reached their hands into the plastic container to grab some gingersnaps. Andersson stacked up three cookies and bit into all of them at once. The result was a shower of crumbs. With his mouth full of gingersnaps he said, "Fredrik, did you find out anything new yesterday?"

Fredrik's face lit up, and he began energetically leafing through his notebook full of scribblings. "You bet! Two interesting new observations on Molinsgatan. I did another round with the tenants yesterday and asked if anyone had seen or heard anything at midnight on Friday, a week ago. Especially if anyone had seen or heard the Porsche. It's not a car you can sneak around in. A guy whose baby had a stomachache was up with the kid at that time. His living room window faces Molinsgatan, two floors above von Knecht's garage. He remembers that he heard a car braking hard outside the garage, then someone fussing with the garage doors. They're old and stiff and creak like crazy. Next he heard a car start up and drive out of the garage. After a while another car started and was driven into the garage. By then the guy was curious and went over to the window to take a look. There stood the Porsche parked on the street. He stood there almost fifteen minutes, rocking the kid by the window. The baby fell asleep and he put him to bed. Then he went to the john, and when he got back he heard the Porsche starting up. When he got to the window and looked out, it was gone."

"This is great! Did he see anybody?"

"No."

"Does he know exactly what time it was?"

"No. But he thinks the Porsche drove off sometime between twelve-thirty and a quarter to one."

Andersson rubbed his nose excitedly, so it shone Christmas-red. Irene spontaneously thought of a certain Rudolph with the red nose, but she kept her associations to herself. Pondering, the superintendent said, "Someone parks a car outside. Someone opens the garage door. Someone drives out the Porsche. Someone drives his car into the garage. Someone drives off in the Porsche."

Everyone nodded to show that they were following along.

"Someone also came back in the morning and drove out his own car and put back the Porsche. It wasn't on Berzeliigatan on Saturday morning, because then the man with the bedroom window facing the parking places would have seen it. It's those damned keys to the car and the garage that are haunting us again!"

Hannu nodded and said, "Which Pirjo had."

They all remembered the sooty key rings in plastic bags that the arson tech had shown them. Andersson began to rub his nose again.

"Why did Pirjo have these two key rings? She couldn't drive. She didn't have her own car. She had never been given her own key to von Knecht's apartment."

Fredrik interrupted him excitedly. "I think Birgitta was right the other day, when she said that somebody lured Pirjo to Berzeliigatan. The techs say that Pirjo never crossed the threshold to the apartment on Molins-gatan on Wednesday morning. First she had a hard time understanding when they tried to explain to her that Richard von Knecht was dead. She spoke very poor Swedish. When she finally grasped what they were telling her, she was utterly distraught. But she was never allowed in, because they had just started on the lower floor when she arrived. On the other hand, I got to hear something interesting from the guy who has that nice-looking clothing store on the corner. His name is . . . let me see . . ."

He feverishly leafed through his papers.

Jonny rolled his eyes and flapped his hands affectedly as he chirped in falsetto, "His name is Carl-Johan Quist. Q-u-i-s-t. I had the plea-sure of questioning him on Wednesday, after von Knecht's aerial escapade. He said he didn't know a thing. He just heard someone screaming outside his store and then '. . . ugh . . . oooh, so horrible . . . the poor wretch lay in a big nasty heap! I couldn't look, but I called the police at once!' I can see why he'd want to make himself interesting to you. But I guess you're probably his type."

Fredrik froze. A fiery blush instantly appeared on his cheeks, and the look he gave Jonny was annihilating. Then he slowly collected his wits and said with restrained rage, "Unlike you, I can talk to people with-out having to step on them. That's how I get results. You just strut off and think you've been damned witty when you've squashed someone! But all you've really done is boost your own rotten ego!"

That's when Birgitta did it. Right in front of her astonished colleagues she went over and planted a big kiss on Fredrik's mouth.

His blush deepened and his ears turned almost fluorescent. But his expression had brightened considerably. The same could not be said for Jonny.

Andersson felt he was about to lose all control of the situation. To take the initiative, he burst out, "What the hell are you doing? Stop taunting each other and . . . kissing! This isn't some playground, it's a homicide investigation! Colleagues and ladies . . . let's keep our work separate!"

After this, the group made a real effort to get serious. Fredrik smoothed out his paper again. He had wadded it up during the emotional confrontation. As if nothing had happened, he continued, "I have his name here. Carl-Johan Quist. He recognized Pirjo and knew that she cleaned for the von Knechts. She used to arrive at the same time he opened the store. That's why he reacted when he saw her on Wednesday morning. He thought no one would have missed the news that Richard von Knecht was dead! So he kept an eye out for Pirjo that morning. She came out about fifteen minutes later. Just then two reporters walked into the store. Not to buy clothes, but to interview one of the eyewitnesses to von Knecht's fall. Quist said that he hadn't seen much more than von Knecht hitting the ground almost on his doorstep. When he had to show the vultures exactly where von Knecht had landed, he happened to cast a glance toward the streetcar stop. He saw Pirjo leaning toward a rolled-down side window of a large light-colored car. She was talking to someone inside the car. He says that the image is etched on his retina, because in his wildest imagination he could never believe that someone would want to pick up that fat little woman! The memory reappeared as soon as Quist read in the paper that Pirjo had died in the fire on Berzeliigatan."

Excitedly Andersson leaned toward Fredrik and said, "What make of car was it?"

Fredrik shook his head regretfully. "Unfortunately Quist is useless when it comes to makes of cars. He doesn't know a thing. He has no driver's license and has never owned a car himself. But he thinks it was a BMW or Mercedes. I subscribe to Birgitta's theory from the other day: Somebody gave Pirjo the keys so she could go and trigger the bomb. And it was the person in the car."

The keys. The keys were flashing . . . what was it about those keys? Irene tried to capture the vague mental image, but it slipped away like soap between her fingers.

As if hearing her thoughts, Andersson echoed, "The keys. Always these keys! I understand that the killer gave her the keys so she could go and trip the bomb. But why the garage and car keys?"

Hannu squinted under his eyelids and said softly, "To get rid of them."

"The car keys? To get rid of them?"

Andersson paused and looked with increasing respect at his borrowed resource. "Of course! To get rid of the evidence he gives the keys to Pirjo! Maybe also to screw with our heads. And he certainly succeeded there. But not anymore! Now we know how it all happened! At least we have a good theory."

Birgitta looked angry and snapped, "What a horrifying person! Sending off a mother of three to a certain death! I can almost hear this monster saying, 'Dear Pirjo, will you be an angel and clean up Richard von Knecht's office apartment? He doesn't need it any longer, but it has to look nice when people come to look at it. And by the way, while you're there, could you please put back these keys? Thank you, I'll pay you double time if you do this for me.' And the murderer drives off with the secure knowledge that he will never have to pay that double time."

There was a silence as everyone played out the imagined scene in their minds. It was quite conceivable that it had happened exactly that way.

Irene spoke. "If this was what the murderer did, we know three things. First, the murderer had access to both key rings that were found with Pirjo after the fire. Second, Pirjo knew the murderer and trusted him. Or her. Third, the murderer had access to a light-colored car. Quite large, according to Quist. The teacher at Ascheberg High School also saw a light-colored car on the evening of the murder. Sylvia's BMW is red. As is the Porsche. The light-colored cars we know about in this case are Henrik von Knecht's Mercedes and Charlotte's light yellow Golf. Although a Golf isn't very big. And wouldn't a teacher have noticed that it was yellow?"

"Not necessarily. It's pale yellow. He was running toward the parking garage. Imagine that it was dark, pouring rain, and he saw it at a distance," said Birgitta.

Andersson gave Fredrik an urgent look. "You have to bring in Quist at once for an interview. He works with clothes and might be able to say something about the color, for God's sake! And try to get him to decide what make of car it was!"

"Will do. Although one thing occurs to me. Shorty has a white Ford Mondeo. Brand new, with dark tinted windows. Totally luscious," said Fredrik.

"All right, you might as well check out his car too. Although Quist probably can't tell the difference between a Golf and a Mondeo. Did he happen to see who was sitting in the car?"

"No. But he did say that the car windows were dark."

Irene remembered something. "The windows on Henrik's Benz are, too."

Andersson frowned and thought for a moment. "Okay. Fredrik, you work on that little ho . . . shopowner today. Jonny, Hans, and Birgitta will follow Shorty when he gets out after lunch. Like leeches! If we're lucky he might lead us to the killer. To Bobo's killer, in any case. You four will also take the weekend shift. The others who were on duty last weekend will have this one off. But today we'll keep checking and double-checking everything we've developed so far. Irene and Tommy, you can run up to Molinsgatan and find out if anyone else saw Pirjo talking to the driver of that light-colored Golf or Mercedes, or whatever kind of car it was. Speaking of cars: Ask if anybody saw the cars outside the garage on Molinsgatan on Friday night. It would be especially interesting to find out what kind of car was driven into the garage instead of the Porsche! Hannu, I want you to lean on Pirjo's daughter a little more. I have a feeling she might be hiding quite a bit. To protect her mamma's reputation or something. It sounds damned funny that she didn't say what place she was going off to clean."

Hannu nodded, but Irene saw him shrug at the same time. Apparently he didn't think he would get much farther with Marjatta.

The superintendent adjourned the meeting. "I'll be here all day and maybe part of the weekend. Otherwise you can reach me at home."

They all stood up. Birgitta and Fredrik slipped out to the corridor first, and the superintendent could hear their laughter sweep into the room like a warm and promising breeze. He felt a sudden pang. Was she going to start going out with Fredrik? How would that affect her trip to Australia? All her talk about independence and freedom from men's demands! Although they said the beer was good in Australia. But that's not somewhere he would ever go.

THE TEMPERATURE was just below freezing, and there was black ice on the roads. People were taking careful little baby steps on the sidewalks. The ambulances were making shuttle trips to the emergency rooms with broken arms and legs.

Fredrik rode with Irene and Tommy. In a bag on the floor he had an assortment of pictures of various car models. Carl-Johan Quist had categorically refused to come down to HQ to look at them. He was alone in the store and the Christmas shopping season was starting. He couldn't get away until Saturday afternoon after three at the earliest. Then he had unlimited time, if the inspector could make it then? So Fredrik decided that the mountain would have to come to Mohammed. He persuaded himself that the primary reason was the time factor. They had to clear up quickly what make of car they were looking for. Somewhere in the back of his mind Jonny's scornful comments during morning prayers were still reverberating. But then he remembered Birgitta's reaction to the verbal battle with Jonny and instantly felt quite satisfied with the way things had developed.

Irene managed to find a parking place on the other side of Aschebergsgatan. They agreed to meet back at the car at one o'clock on the dot. Anyone who didn't show up within fifteen minutes would have to take the streetcar back to HQ. Gingerly, Fredrik walked off toward the clothing store with his pictures in the dark blue bag. Irene and Tommy saw him slip and almost fall in the middle of the crosswalk.

Irene chuckled. "He doesn't really have his feet on the ground. He's still floating after Birgitta's kiss."

"No wonder! Who wouldn't be?"

"Would you?"

"Well . . . a little hop, maybe . . ."

They laughed, and it warmed them up. They decided to split up. Tommy would do a round and ask about the cars outside the garage on Friday night. Irene would take Pirjo and the light-colored car.

The streetcar stop where Pirjo had stood was about forty meters from Quist's store. There were always people waiting at the stop, since two streetcar lines and three bus lines passed by. It was probably no use to ask the people standing there now. Better to concentrate on the shops and businesses at street level.

Closest to her was a big art gallery. GALLERI UNO was written in curlicue letters on the show window and doors. When she tried to push open the door, it was locked. A note the size of a postage stamp was fastened with tape at eye level. "Monday–Tuesday closed. Wednesday–Saturday 12–17. Sunday 12–16." Okay, Uno would have to wait till last.

Uno's neighbor was a small foot-care shop. The woman behind the counter was wearing a nylon dress that had probably been white once upon a time. The only thing that gleamed white now was her hair. Irene was unsure. Was this a real business? In Sweden people usually retire at the age of sixty-five, but this lady had to be twenty years older. Yet her voice was strong and clear.

"Hello, how can I help you?"

"Hello. My name is Irene Huss, detective inspector. I'm investigating the murder of Richard von Knecht."

The old woman leaned over the counter and whispered so excitedly that her dental work clacked. "Imagine, how exciting, right at my doorstep! I've been following it on TV and in the papers."

"I suppose you've read in the papers that there is a possible link to the arson bombing on Berzeliigatan?"

"Well, it's obvious there's a connection! And that little cleaning woman who died in the fire! Since she cleaned here at the von Knechts' place, it's clear that she had something to do with the fire on Berzeliigatan!"

She crossed her arms and gave Irene a challenging look.

"That little cleaning woman is the key," said Irene. "We're trying to track whom she met on that last day of her life. Wednesday of last week. According to several witnesses, she was seen outside here at the streetcar stop at around ten—"

"That's right. I saw her. Three times a week for a couple of years I've seen her arrive on the streetcar. She usually rode home around three in the afternoon. But last Wednesday she went home at ten in the morning."

"Did you see whether she walked over to a car that had stopped?"

"Yes, she did. But they only talked for a minute. The car drove off almost at once."

"What kind of car was it?"

For the first time in their conversation the elderly saleswoman looked uncertain. "What kind?"

"Yes, what make of car."

"I'm not so good at makes of cars."

Irene sighed, but she tried to hide it. "Was it a large or small car?"

"I don't know. Pretty big, I think," she said and sucked pensively on her ill-fitting false teeth.

"Do you remember what color it was?"

"I don't remember. Maybe brown. Or lighter . . . But the little cleaning woman—actually she wasn't little—short, but not little. She was fat. She was wearing a white head scarf and a dark green jacket. And she had a big red shopping bag in her hand."

That jibed with Marjatta's description of what Pirjo was wearing. Irene decided to leave the car until later.

"Can you tell me what happened when Pirjo went over to the car?"

"She walked up to it. Bent down and began talking to someone inside the car."

"What side of the car was she standing on?"

"She was on the curb. The driver of the car rolled down the window on the passenger's side. But I didn't see much, since the car was hiding the cleaning woman from my view."

"So the driver had his back to you?"

"Yes. Although the windows of the car were so dark that I couldn't see very well. But I think the driver had on a light jacket or coat."

"Was it a man or a woman?"

"Couldn't tell. But I think it was a man."

"Why's that?"

"I thought the driver was fairly tall. And when the car drove off, the cleaning woman waved a little after it. Like this."

The old woman demonstrated a furtive wave. This reinforced Irene's feeling that Pirjo must have known the person who gave her the keys. Hopefully she said, "Anything else you can recall?"

The woman really tried, but drew a blank. Irene asked for her name, address, telephone number, and Social Security number. Her name was Ester Pettersson and she was eighty-two years old. Irene felt her curiosity reawakened.

"It's unusual for people to still be working at your age. Is it temporary?"

"Oh no, I've been in my shop for sixty-one years! My father used to own it, but he got T.B. and died. Mother was delicate. So I had to take care of the shop."

"Didn't you ever consider retiring?"

"Never! What in the world would I do?"

Irene declined her offer of coffee and promised to drop by again. A little bell tinkled when the door closed and shut off the olfactory symphony of foot powder, wart medicine, and liniment for tired feet.

BY ONE o'clock all three of them had returned to the car. Tommy had no new facts about the nighttime car exchange. Irene hadn't had any nibbles other than the old lady in the foot-care shop. Fredrik had made enough progress with Quist that he was convinced the car Pirjo had approached was a larger sedan. Light-colored paint. Probably white or beige. Dark tinted windows. And then Fredrik had been invited to lunch, but as politely and firmly as possible he declined. He gave the excuse that he was having lunch with his girlfriend. Not because he was going steady with any girl just now, but there might be a chance of changing that. He decided not to tell Irene and Tommy about the lunch invitation. They were decent colleagues, not at all like Jonny, but he'd still never hear the end of a juicy detail like that! All in good fun, of course.

Tommy was looking thoughtfully at the stately art nouveau facade on the other side of Aschebergsgatan. He glanced up at the marble balustrade of the top floor and the now famous little turreted balcony. He mused, "I wonder if Sylvia von Knecht is home? I'd like to look in the garage again."

Irene unlocked the car, took the card with Sylvia's phone number out of her jacket pocket, and punched the number on her cell phone.

"Sylvia von Knecht's residence," a female voice answered in a lilting Finnish accent.

"Hello, my name is Detective Inspector Irene Huss. I'm looking for Sylvia von Knecht."

"She's gone up to Marstrand. One of the horses is sick."

"When do you expect her back?"

"This evening."

"What time?"

"No idea." It was a cool but not at all unfriendly voice.

Irene decided to take a chance. "Are you Sylvia von Knecht's sister? Arja Montgomery?"

"Yes, I am."

"May we come up for a moment? We're right outside your building, on Aschebergsgatan."

After a brief pause she said hesitantly, "I don't know . . . Sylvia doesn't like having the police snooping around."

"No, I know that. She's a little fragile after all that's happened. But she has always helped us in our investigation. Our problem at the moment is something that can be easily solved with your help. We just need to get into the garage on Molinsgatan. The key is on Richard's car-key ring. It's on his nightstand, next to the case with the apartment keys."

Again a hesitant silence. Finally Arja said, resigned, "I'll go see if I can find them."

There was a clatter when she put down the receiver. After a couple of minutes she returned.

"I found them. But I'll have to bring the keys down to you. It's a little silly, but I don't know the code to the front door."

"That's okay. We'll be waiting outside."

ARJA WAS considerably younger than Sylvia. To Irene's surprise, she realized that she and Arja were about the same age. It was difficult to see the resemblance to her older sister. Almost ten centimeters taller, with a powerful and slightly stocky figure, Arja was good looking in a typical Finnish way. She had thick light blond shoulder-length hair, high cheekbones, big clear blue eyes, and a wide mouth with beautiful, even teeth, revealed in an apologetic smile. She motioned at the dirty men's shirt and worn jeans she was wearing and said, "Excuse me, but I'm helping Sylvia clean up. The funeral is on Thursday, so she wants the place to look nice."

What was it Sylvia had once said? "Only Finns know how to clean properly." It seemed as though she was sticking to that thesis. Arja pulled the keys out of her jeans pocket and asked, "Are these the right keys?"

"Yes, they are. And here are our IDs. It's important that you know who you gave the keys to."

Irene took out her police ID. Tommy and Fredrik followed her example, surprised. Arja glanced briefly at the card with the embossed metal seal and nodded.

Irene smiled and said, "After working on this investigation I know how Sylvia is. She'll scold you if you don't ask who you're lending the keys to. But now you've seen our IDs and know for sure that we're police officers."

At first Arja looked surprised, but then her sapphire-blue eyes began to glitter mischievously, and a warm smile spread across her face.

"I can see that you do know my dear sister. Or more correctly, my half sister," she said.

That explained the difference between them. Irene felt her curiosity urging her on. "Do you have the same father or the same mother?"

"The same mother. Sylvia's father was killed during the Finnish-German offensive against the Soviet Union in June of 'forty-one. Sylvia was born seven months later. Mother remarried a cousin of her late husband. My father, that is."

"Was it so that some ancestral estate would stay in the family?"

"No. The family's property was located in Viborg province, which was ceded to Russia. We were wiped out after the war."

"Is your father still alive?"

"No. He died of lung cancer ten years ago. Chain smoker."

"And how is your mother doing?" Irene nodded up at the apartment.

Arja laughed. "She's quite spry. Seventy-eight years old. She hears what she wants to, but otherwise there's nothing wrong with her. She's up there baking cookies for the funeral reception."

"Funeral reception? Isn't it going to be a large funeral, with pomp and splendor and a big dinner?"

It wasn't a cop's question, but a spontaneous expression of surprise straight from Irene's heart.

Arja pursed her lips significantly. "If you know my sister so well, you also know that she is very frugal. It's probably a remnant of our meager childhood. Keep up appearances, but it can't cost anything! Sylvia thinks that a funeral reception for the closest mourners is sufficient. Guess who has to fix the sandwiches!"

She gave another warm smile, said good-bye to the detectives, and closed the beautiful front door.

IT WAS a big two-car garage. The red BMW was gone, but the Porsche was in place.

They closed the garage door behind them and turned on the overhead light. The witness two floors up was right. The door creaked and screeched terribly when it was opened or closed. The garage was deep and wide. The cars had plenty of room in the forward part. The back was obviously used for storage. Shelves all along the back wall held cartons, ladders, snow tires, a hose, slalom skis, two racing bikes painted metallic green with curved handlebars, and a lot of rope, cans, and boxes.

Irene looked around thoughtfully and asked, "Have the techs examined the garage thoroughly?"

Tommy shook his head. "No, just the car. The only strange thing about it is that they found traces of dirt or sand and oil in the trunk and inside on the floor of the car. Both at the base of the backseat and on the floor in front of the passenger's seat."

They went over to the car and opened the small trunk. On the bottom they could clearly see some dark oil spots, as big as one-krona coins. A little gravel and sand had adhered to them. Inside the car there were similar spots on the floor mats. It was a very nice car to look into. And surely even nicer to drive. The black leather upholstery lent the car a masculine aura. The little leather-covered steering wheel and the high-tech instrument panel gave the sense of sitting in a cockpit, which was of course the intention. Irene felt a slight flutter in her diaphragm as she settled into the driver's seat.

"Excuse me, Irene, but have you entered nirvana or what?" It was Tommy's voice that abruptly brought her back to earth.

Dreamily she said, "You get a certain feeling sitting in a car like this."

"Go ahead and enjoy it. It's not often you wind up in a Porsche. But I found something over here. Come on."

With a sigh she hoisted herself out of the wonderful leather seat and followed him to the back of the garage. In one corner, wedged in between the end of the shelves and the wall, stood a large gasoline can of green metal. Tommy tried to wriggle it out, which he finally managed to do. He shook it and confirmed, "Empty. Only a little splash left."

"How much does a can like this hold?"

"Twenty-five or thirty liters. It's illegal to store gasoline in garages or similar spaces."

"But it's empty."

"Yep. But it used to have gasoline in it." Tommy unscrewed the lid and sniffed the opening.

"But maybe it was empty when it was put in here."

"Maybe."

He didn't sound convinced, and Irene agreed with him. She looked at the can and said, "Could it have been this gasoline that was used for the devil bomb on Berzeliigatan?"

"Exactly what I'm thinking. But there had to be more gasoline involved than this."

They went around looking at the junk on the shelves. All of a sudden Irene saw it. A yellow-and-black-edged snake that was trying to creep away under the bottom shelf plank. A cutoff piece of water hose. She pulled it out. It proved to be about a meter and a half long.

Triumphantly she said, "Check it out! A piece of the water hose, you say. Wrong, wrong! I say."

Both Fredrik and Tommy looked astonished. They stared dumbly at the hose and suddenly Tommy lit up.

"Yep! You're right. That's it."

Fredrik sighed, "I still think it's a piece of hose."

Both Irene and Tommy shook their heads and said at the same time, "It's a siphon!"

Irene stepped over to the coiled-up water hose. The piece had come from it. The fresh cuts fit perfectly when she put them together. Her heart was pounding with excitement, a familiar reaction to a riddle that was nearing its solution.

"That's it all right! This is what took time inside the garage. Our bomber cut off a piece of the hose and used it as a siphon, to transfer the gasoline from the metal can to the plastic can. Or the plastic cans, I mean," she added.

Tommy nodded his agreement and said, "Yep! But it would take more gasoline. Do you think he took it out of the car gas tanks?"

They looked at the Porsche. The BMW had also been in here. That was quite a lot of gasoline. Irene looked at the Porsche a long time. Finally she said, "I think I know why he took the Porsche and not his own car."

She took the car key, climbed into the soft driver's seat, and turned the ignition. The engine turned over. Her heart was pounding again as she pointed at the instrument panel.

"Look. The tank is almost empty."

"Shut it off so we don't die of carbon monoxide poisoning!"

Coughing, Tommy opened the garage door. It was doubtful whether the air outside was much better, but at least it wasn't as concentrated.

Feeling a pang of loss, Irene shut off the engine. It had purred as softly as a leopard. She sketched out her imagined scenario. "The bomb maker comes here after midnight. He knows that there's gasoline in the can and in the cars. He has just filled up his own tank. Once he's here, he discovers that the Porsche has almost no gas in the tank. It's only enough for less than fifty kilometers. He drives the Porsche out onto the street and puts his own car in the garage, so he can siphon the gas into the plastic containers undisturbed. But he leaves enough in his car that he won't risk running out on the way home. The oil spots in the Porsche probably come from the plastic containers he had set down on the floor in here. They got oily on bottom."

Fredrik interrupted her. "Why didn't he use his own car to drive down to Berzeliigatan?"

"Because he didn't want his own car to be seen in the neighborhood at the time. It would be hard to explain what he was doing there in the middle of the night. Von Knecht's own car would arouse some curiosity but not the same amount," Irene said.

That sounded reasonable. Tommy nodded and took the piece of hose. "Let's take this down to the lab, to confirm that gasoline actually ran through it. But take a whiff. It has definitely been used for gasoline. We'll have to ask the techs to come out here and take a few samples of the oil spots on the floor—if they haven't already—and compare them with the ones in the car," he said firmly.

They went out and closed the squeaky door behind them. Tommy looked thoughtfully at the solid, gray-painted door.

"Imagine if we could get hold of a witness who saw them loading the gasoline cans into the Porsche! But no one has come forward. It must have happened while the witness on the third floor was putting his baby to bed and going to the john," he sighed.

Irene patted him lightly on the arm. "Tommy, we've already seen plastic cans somewhere. Quite recently. In Henrik and Charlotte's garage. Let's swing by there and take a closer look. We'll keep these keys and give them to the techs. I think it's about time for another meeting with Sylvia von Knecht. Although I'm probably the last person on earth she wants to see. Things between us always seem to go a little off kilter somehow."

Tommy smiled. "Maybe it's time to call in some male expertise? Mine, that is."

"What a good idea."

THEY DROVE back out to Örgryte and went into Henrik von Knecht's still-unlocked garage. The two plastic cans, marked DISTILLED WATER, were still in the corner. Irene unscrewed the lid and sniffed, but smelled only stagnant water. Tommy looked at them and said, "Ten-liter cans. Perfect for the purpose. Easy to carry. Five or six of them would be enough for the devil bomb. We'll have to question young Herr von Knecht more closely about this. His wife is still away, isn't she?"

All signs seem to indicate that that was the case. No one answered when they rang the doorbell. They started to go around the house, looking in windows. When Irene stood at the edge of an overgrown flower bed in the backyard, she could look right into the kitchen. The dirty dishes were gone. Everything was clean and orderly. Henrik would never dream that his wife had had a visit from a cowboy. On the other hand, he was going straight up to Marstrand, according to Charlotte. While she herself was going to a party at a friend's house . . .

Irene's train of thought was interrupted by a gruff voice that shouted, "Don't move, or I'll shoot! The police have been called and will be here any minute!"

Startled, she turned toward the voice and stared straight into the barrel of a rifle. It trembled ominously in the hands of a fat, bald, elderly man.

THE THREE detective inspectors had almost managed to convince the armed man that they were actually police by the time the squad car arrived. The two officers came around the house with their weapons drawn. Fortunately one of them was Hans Stefansson. Or perhaps unfortunately, Irene wasn't sure. She *was* sure of one thing, though. The story of how a suspicious neighbor stood holding the three detectives in check with a moose gun while he waited for the patrol car would be all over PO1 before evening.

The poor elderly gentleman was terribly embarrassed when he realized his mistake. He defended himself in a shrill voice. "You can't be too careful these days. The wife saw some strange figures creeping around here and peeking into cars. A gang of burglars, that's what I thought!"

Irene suspected that "the wife" was the woman behind the curtain who had spied on her and Tommy the day before. *It's better to have them with us than against us*, she thought. *Some average citizen who thinks he has the confidence of the police might start telling us something that would prove useful.* As long as it was about someone else, that is. So in a confidential tone Irene said to the corpulent neighbor, "We've been trying to get hold of Henrik von Knecht, but with no luck. Do you happen to know where he is?"

There was no risk, since she knew he was in Stockholm. But the neighbor probably didn't know that. He shook his spherical head and said indifferently, "Henrik von Knecht? He's almost never home. For a while I thought he and his wife had gotten a divorce. But last week we saw him again."

"We met with Charlotte von Knecht yesterday, but would like to get hold of her again. You understand . . . everything has to be checked and double-checked in a homicide investigation."

The neighbor nodded eagerly in agreement. But when he thought about it, he turned grumpy. This was an excellent opportunity to complain. "We don't see much of the wife either. I mean . . . she's never out in the garden. Which really needs it! We always have to clean up the hedge between our properties. They never take care of their side. And I'm the one who has to clip it. Every year!"

"Don't they have a gardener to take care of their side?"

"No, and you'd think they could afford it! But they expect me to take care of their part too!"

Irene clucked her tongue sympathetically and decided to approach the actual target. Evasively she said, "If her husband is away so much, does she have a lot of friends and relatives visiting?"

The reply was curt and quick. "No."

There was something. Best to keep dangling the bait. She took a new tack. "But does she have parties occasionally? Otherwise she'd be pretty lonely in this big house, wouldn't she?"

The neighbor looked uncertain, and Irene thought she sensed some reserve when he replied. "No, there haven't been any parties all year. The house is empty most of the time. But sometimes she has had . . . visitors."

"Gentleman visitors?"

A light blush spread over the round cheeks and up toward his forehead. Probably about the person who had been standing behind the curtains and indignantly taking notice of these visits. Those lucky dogs who were allowed to visit the beautiful Fru von Knecht. For his own part it was out of the question, for several reasons. But he could always dream. And enviously keep an eye on those granted access to the beauty.

Irene clarified her question. "Have there been different gentlemen, or perhaps one special gentleman?"

The well-meaning neighbor began to have a vague sense that he was being subjected to a regular questioning, but it was too late to retreat. Once you've said A, you have to say B. Self-consciously he stood digging the toe of his worn-out loafer into the soft lawn and muttering indistinctly.

Quickly Irene said, "Excuse me, I didn't hear you."

He gave up and puffed, "There used to be various cars that picked her up. Sometimes they stayed overnight. But not very often."

"How often?"

"Well, maybe ten times."

If he said ten times, then it was ten. He probably kept track.

"There used to be, you said. Have things been different recently?"

Embarrassed, he twisted his voluminous body before he answered. "Well, yes. Early last fall a red Porsche would come to pick her up. The first few times we didn't think so much of it, because it was her father-in-law coming to pick her up. We recognized him from the newspapers. But one night he . . . spent the night."

"When was that?"

"At the end of August, maybe early September. It doesn't have to mean anything . . . inappropriate. We knew that it was him, Richard von Knecht, and he was her father-in-law, after all. But you start to wonder . . . He always came when his son, Henrik, wasn't home. And he's basically never home. But we've never seen the mother-in-law there."

Thunk! Thunk! Irene's heart was pounding wildly with excitement. She thought the others must be able to hear it. But the noise of their own hearts must have drowned out the sound, since all five officers were totally focused on the older man. Did he understand what he was saying? Probably. They could tell that he had been thinking about what this might mean and finally was forced to draw the only reasonable conclusion. It *was* something "inappropriate."

They thanked him for his valuable information and said that they would be in touch to go over things in more detail. As he was about to return to his own house, he suddenly put his chubby hand on Irene's arm. Embarrassed, he said, "Well . . . excuse me for pointing my rifle at you . . . but it's not loaded. I couldn't find the ammunition. But that wasn't . . . Do you have to tell Fru von Knecht that I was the one who told you this?"

Despite the freezing weather, his forehead was covered by a thin layer of sweat. Irene gave him a few calming pats on the hand, which she hoped would instill trust in him and said in her best official police voice, "Not unless it turns out to be of crucial importance for the investigation. At this point it's just one of many leads. If necessary, you may be called to testify in court. However, at present there is nothing to suggest it will be necessary. If it is, we'll let you know in plenty of time."

Statements that sound official always calm the public. They instill a feeling that the authorities have the situation under control. Which was hardly the case for the three inspectors at the moment. The whole investigation had been turned upside down!

After the neighbor had toddled back to his house, with the barrel of his rifle dragging through the wet lawn, Irene turned to the patrol officers and said, "Stefansson, you and I know each other well, don't we?"

Hans Stefansson nodded, at the same time giving her a puzzled look.

"Under no circumstances, and I repeat, under *no* circumstances will you and your colleague mention to anyone what this neighbor just told us! You will report precisely what happened out here, but not a word about the conversation. Word of honor!"

She held out her hand and they shook on it. Stefansson's colleague was a young assistant and he didn't seem to have understood a thing. But his expression was solemn and serious as he shook Irene's hand.

The two officers took off in their car, and the three inspectors were left standing in the overgrown yard. They looked at each other but were unable to make real eye contact in the gathering dusk.

It was Tommy who broke the silence. "We have to talk. And eat! It's almost three-thirty."

"China House on Södra Vägen?"

"Perfect."

As if by mutual agreement they didn't say a word during the ten-minute ride.

Chapter Seventeen

THEY WERE THE ONLY customers in the Chinese restaurant, but still picked a booth at the back. They selected "Four Small Dishes" and a large light beer each. Within a few minutes the food arrived. They didn't start talking until they could see the bottom of their bowls.

Irene began, "Henrik and Charlotte are probably the ones we need to talk to right away, not Sylvia. But it will be difficult, since we only have hearsay to go on."

Fredrik quickly broke in, "I think that guy Henrik is shady! I'd put money on it that he's the bomber! He could have easily arranged to get the keys to the garage and the Porsche, and he owns a big, light-colored car with dark windows. He also keeps plastic gas cans in his garage."

Tommy nodded and said, "I agree with you. There's a lot pointing to Henrik as the bomber. But why? Why try to blow up your own father? Why would he lure Pirjo over to trip the bomb? And why blow Bobo Torsson sky-high?"

Irene eagerly waved her hands to emphasize her theory. "I think the easiest question to answer is why he lured Pirjo to Berzeliigatan. Everything was turning to shit for him. If he's the bomber, that is."

"To shit?"

"Yes. Remember that the bomb was made almost four days before Richard was murdered. If he hadn't gotten a cold he would have gone down to his office on Monday. But he didn't. And not on Tuesday either. On Tuesday evening he was murdered. We know that Henrik couldn't have committed that murder, since he and Sylvia were down on the street when he fell. But Henrik knows that there's a devil bomb down on Berzeliigatan. It will kill whoever opens the door first. Who is most likely to be that first person?"

He looked at his two colleagues. They were both pictures of total concentration. Tommy answered after a moment, "Sylvia von

Knecht. It would obviously be Sylvia, who would go there to inspect her inheritance."

"Exactly! And Sylvia von Knecht is probably the last person in the world that Henrik would want to kill. As I said before, it was too bad that there wasn't a back entrance to the apartment. Then he could have gone in the back way and disarmed the bomb. Evidently he didn't dare even open the door a crack to unhook the wire to the detonator. So instead he chose to sacrifice an unimportant louse. Pirjo."

Fredrik got excited and leaned over the table, without noticing that he had put his elbow in a bowl with leftover sweet-and-sour sauce. Agitated, he said, "This fits with everything we found out today! Henrik von Knecht knows Pirjo's hours and knows that she won't be allowed in by the guys from the lab. So he shadows her and drives up when she's standing there waiting for the streetcar. Hold on a minute . . ."

He paused to wipe the sauce off his elbow. Absentmindedly he rubbed at the spot on his sweater. Irene was about to tell him to go out to the toilet and rinse out the spot properly. But she managed to stop herself. With his gaze fixed on a far corner of the room Fredrik continued, "How could Henrik von Knecht know that Pirjo was at Molinsgatan? The whole city, except Pirjo, knew that the guy was dead! Wouldn't it be more logical to assume that she knew he had fallen from the balcony? If so she would have stayed home."

Both Irene and Tommy nodded. Irene said firmly, "We have to go downtown and talk to the superintendent. It's probably Henrik we should be watching, not Shorty. Maybe we can get the Narcs to take over the stakeout."

She didn't pin great hope on her last remark, but it never hurt to ask. She continued, turning to Fredrik, "Have you guys made up a stake-out schedule for watching Shorty?"

"Yes. Birgitta is there now, until six. Hans Borg takes over and then I arrive at midnight. Jonny is taking Saturday morning. And so on."

"There wouldn't be anything wrong with us moving this stakeout to Marstrand, would there? According to Charlotte, Henrik isn't coming home until around ten o'clock—tomorrow night, that is."

Tommy sat sipping at his hot coffee. Pensively he said, "Do you think that staking out Henrik will produce anything? He comes home, tired and exhausted from his auction deals. He probably sits down and polishes some priceless trinket. And then he goes to bed. That's what I think."

Irene tried to persuade him. "But these are concrete leads in the investigation that we're following now! We aren't even sure that Shorty has a direct connection to the case. I propose that we take this up with the superintendent. What do you think about the neighbor's story? Did Charlotte and Richard have a sexual relationship?"

All three thought about it.

"It seems likely."

"There's a lot to indicate it. Especially the times he stayed overnight."

"At the start of this investigation I would have dismissed such testimony as utterly improbable. But considering what we've learned of Richard's and Charlotte's personalities over the course of the investigation, I would say that it's not at all inconceivable!" said Irene.

Fredrik again began showing signs of some excitement, so Irene leaned over and moved the bowl of sauce. Eagerness glinted in his eyes, and he leaned over the table to persuade them.

"That gives Henrik a motive. Jealousy! His own father is fucking his wife! That's a damned strong motive!"

Something started to stir in the back of Irene's mind and she managed to pry it loose. "I'm not sure that Henrik is capable of great jealousy. Or any emotions at all. He's hardly passionate about anything but his relationship to his antiques. But there's actually another very strong motive. The most ordinary of all—namely money."

Tommy looked surprised and asked, "But isn't it Sylvia who is her husband's heir?"

"Yes. Except for an insurance policy. Sylvia told me about it herself. She and Henrik get half a million each over a period of ten years, in the event of Richard's death."

Fredrik gave a low whistle. After thinking a while he said, "From what I understand from you, Henrik and Richard von Knecht didn't like each other much, right?"

"They weren't exactly enemies. But according to Sylvia, Richard could never accept that Henrik's personality changed after his meningitis."

Irene looked at the clock. It was past four-thirty. Resolutely she said, "We have to call and see if Andersson is still at HQ. We'll have to go there and present what we learned today. Then he has to decide the next plan of attack."

They paid and got up to leave.

//

IRENE DROVE, with Fredrik sitting next to her and Tommy in the backseat. After they managed to escape the rush-hour traffic on Södra Vägen, Fredrik leaned forward and turned on the radio. The Sven-Ingvar hit about "The Only Blonde in Town" filled the car. Loud and off-key, they all joined in on the chorus. They giggled when the music faded out. A pleasant male voice rapidly announced, "And that's all for *Melody Cavalcade* for today. This is Program Three. Time for *Today's Echo at a Quarter to Five*."

Out of sheer reflex Irene stomped on the brakes, and almost got a taxi in her rear bumper.

Her male colleagues yelled simultaneously, "What are you doing?" "Watch out for the cab!"

Demonstrating discipline, she put on the blinker and turned down Burgårdsgatan. The gods must have accepted some offering she had made, because she lucked out and found an empty parking space. She turned off the engine and turned up the volume of the radio, staring as if entranced by the tiny glowing red and green lights on the car radio that showed it was on. Fascinated she whispered, "Listen, you guys, listen!"

". . . no serious incidents in yesterday's demonstrations in conjunction with the anniversary of Karl the Twelfth's death. The police . . ."

Fredrik looked angry, mostly because of shock. "What was that all about? You could have caused an accident! Then they can say on the *Echo* tomorrow, 'Three cops in Göteborg were the cause of a serious accident in rush-hour traffic yesterday, due to an acute brain malfunction on the part of the driver!'"

Tommy started to laugh, but Irene just waved her hand and didn't take her eyes off the radio. Dramatically she said, "Didn't you hear the sound of something cracking?"

Fredrik and Tommy exchanged a glance, filled with male bonding. Fredrik's circling index finger next to his temple was enough. Irene saw it and started laughing too.

"What just cracked was Charlotte's alibi. There isn't any five o'clock news on the radio! It's called *Today's Echo at a Quarter to Five* because it's on at a quarter to five!"

The two colleagues realized what she was getting at. That would give Charlotte an extra fifteen minutes, which would be plenty of time to reach Molinsgatan from Mölndalsvägen.

Tommy was the one who recovered first. "Is there really no five o'clock news?"

"No, not on the big radio stations. And since Charlotte's Golf was brand new when she left the Volkswagen dealership on Tuesday afternoon, I doubt she had managed to set the button for any small local station that broadcast news."

Tommy leaned forward between the front seats and said, "I think you're right, Irene. We have to start keeping an eye on Henrik and Charlotte. But it's clear that they have already done what they intended. Now they just have to lie low. If only we could get hold of a single piece of evidence that would hold up! Somebody who saw Charlotte on Molinsgatan on the night of the murder. A witness who saw Henrik load his gasoline cans in and out of the Porsche. But no! They were God damned lucky! All we have are circumstantial evidence and guesses!"

Irene agreed and started the car again. She took great pains to be an exemplary driver. It wasn't good to subject her colleagues' nerves to any more stress than necessary.

SUPERINTENDENT SVEN Andersson blew his nose on a piece of toilet paper. He had a headache, and his eyes and nose were running. He was considering going straight home to make himself a hot cognac toddy and crawl into bed, when the three inspectors called and reported red-hot new information in the von Knecht case. Quietly snuffling, he listened to their accounts of the day's testimony and new leads.

He sat silent a long time and thought about what he had heard. Finally he said, "Well, I'll be damned. Charlotte and Richard von Knecht! That's a reasonable conclusion to draw after that neighbor's testimony. But we have to have proof! It's not such a good idea to watch Henrik or Charlotte. What they're doing now isn't as interesting as the deviltry they've already committed. We have to find more proof, and preferably the type that's binding. Could they have planned to murder Richard von Knecht together?"

Tommy shook his head and said, "We discussed that, but we don't think that's how it happened. There's plenty to indicate that the bombing was planned and carried out by one person and the actual murder by another. If Charlotte knew that Henrik had placed a bomb on Berzeliigatan, she wouldn't have had to take any risks by murdering her father-in-law herself! All she had to do was wait for Richard to walk through the door of his office one last time."

Andersson gave him a red-eyed look, wiped his copper-colored nose, and said thoughtfully, "You think that Charlotte is mixed up in the murder?"

Tommy nodded and motioned to Irene.

"We have no plausible motive for her, but Charlotte is the only one who doesn't have a really good alibi. Not anymore, since Irene figured out the part about *Today's Echo at a Quarter to Five*. So she left the Volkswagen dealership before five o'clock. It seems well planned, in view of the seduction of the little car salesman Skytter. She also had lots of opportunities to get hold of the keys," he maintained.

The keys. Again Irene's subconscious stirred. But nothing came to the surface. Annoyed, she had to try to concentrate on what the superintendent was telling them.

"Hannu talked to Pirjo's children again today. And one of the little boys suddenly remembered that a man had called and asked for Pirjo on Wednesday morning. But Pirjo had just left to go clean the von Knechts' apartment. The boy told this to the man on the phone. The daughter didn't know anything about this call, because she was at school. It was a stroke of luck that Hannu thought of questioning the boys one more time."

Fredrik did a double take on his chair and blurted out, "That's exactly what I said! How could he know that Pirjo didn't know the old man was dead, and that she would come to clean the place as usual that Wednesday morning? Now we know—he called to find out where she was!"

He paused, looked at his wristwatch, and continued quickly, "Excuse me, but I have to hurry to relieve Birgitta."

The other three grinned broadly without saying a word. Everyone in the room knew that Birgitta finished her shift at six o'clock, which was now, and that Fredrik's shift didn't start until midnight. The color of his face began to match the superintendent's nose as he nonchalantly said, "See you later. Have a great weekend, those of you who are off."

Tommy's response was swift, "Same to you, same to you. When you two are off."

Fredrik pretended not to hear but hurried out the door.

Tommy laughed and said, "That guy could play the role of Lucia this year. Someone could walk behind him whispering, 'Birgitta, Birgitta!' Then his ears would light up, so we could skip the crown of lights!"

Irene jokingly shook her fist at him. "We shouldn't tease them. I think they're cute," she admonished.

Andersson raised his eyebrows to his hairline. Not all the way, because then they would have wound up on the back of his neck. Vexed, he said, "Cute! We're talking about two cops here! They're not supposed to go around being cute on the job! That's not right. Trouble with . . . *aaah-choo!*"

Good thing he sneezed. Irene didn't have to listen to him say *broads*. But she could imagine it. In an unconsciously maternal tone of voice she said, "Now you should really go home and take care of that cold."

He glowered at her. He detested that kind of talk! "Yes, Mamma."

He meant it to sound sarcastic, but it fell a little flat. He was really tired. Maybe he had a fever. What else did he have to say? Suddenly he remembered.

"There was one more thing that Hannu found out today. After Richard von Knecht and Valle Reuter had lunch, Richard went to the bank and withdrew ten thousand kronor. It was around four o'clock."

The two inspectors looked surprised.

"Why didn't Valle say anything about this before?"

"Good question. Can you find out, Irene? He likes female cops. Hannu called in this information an hour ago. He was going to keep going around the square asking questions."

"What bank was it?"

"The SE-Bank on Kapellplatsen. The question is, what did von Knecht do with the money?"

He was interrupted by the phone ringing. He answered brusquely, "Andersson. Yes . . . I'll be damned! Meet Irene and Tommy outside the front door on Molinsgatan. They'll be there in fifteen minutes."

Energetically he hung up the receiver and clapped his hands together.

"That was Hannu. He was in the bakery by the square talking to them just before they closed. Richard von Knecht came in and bought two open-faced sandwiches on Tuesday afternoon. Around four o'clock. Barely an hour and a half before he was murdered!"

THEY WERE lucky. Valle Reuter was home. Irene was about to hang up when he answered after a great many rings. Over the phone she introduced herself as Detective Inspector Huss. Would it be all right to come over and check some new information that had just turned up in the investigation? Yes, of course, she was quite welcome to come by for a visit. Had she tried Neil Ellis yet? Irene was rather disconcerted, but muttered something that could be interpreted as both yes and no. Ho ho, how tactful she was! But he just happened to take out a few bottles. This could be quite a pleasant evening!

Somewhat baffled, Irene hung up. But she had an idea what was going on.

"He thinks I'm the charming Birgitta. I—or rather Birgitta—have been invited to a wine tasting this evening," she said chuckling.

Tommy gave a hearty laugh. "It would be a shame to disturb your little party. What do you say I go a round with Sylvia von Knecht? If I'm lucky she'll still be at Marstrand. And little Arja might be in need of some entertainment. She certainly wasn't hard to talk to."

"Not bad looking either."

"No. I prefer her mug to Valle's."

TOMMY CALLED Sylvia von Knecht from his cell phone. From his disappointed expression Irene understood that it was Sylvia herself who answered. She reluctantly agreed to a little "chat."

"But not too long! I have my elderly mother here!"

Irene could hear her hoarse voice, even though Tommy had the phone pressed to his ear. She snorted when he hung up. "The elderly mother who's well enough to bake cookies for the funeral! Even though there's an excellent bakery right in the neighborhood. I know. I've tried everything they make." With a shudder she remembered the coffee klatsch with the little dachshund owner.

Tommy asked, "Is that the same bakery where Richard von Knecht bought his sandwiches?"

"Yes, it is."

She slowed down and put on her blinker. A free spot just fifty meters from the building they were going to. No chance of hoping for anything closer. They parked and headed toward the beautiful front door. Irene had an idea.

"Don't forget to ask Sylvia about those sandwiches. According to her there weren't any sandwiches in the fridge when she came home on Wednesday. Richard promised in their last phone call that he would pick some up."

Tommy started to chuckle. "Imagine if the techs devoured them. So they wouldn't be wasted. Sylvia wasn't going to come home for a while, since she was in the psych ward," he said, giggling.

Irene stopped short. "Good Lord, it's not completely unlikely! We'll have to ask them. Remind me about it."

They had reached the front door. Hannu materialized silently at their side.

"Hi."

"Heavens, you scared me! Hi."

"Hello," said Tommy. "It might be best if you accompany me up to see the ladies. And you understand Finnish if it's needed."

Sylvia had exceedingly reluctantly given them the code to the front door, and now they punched it in. With a soft humming the door indicated it was unlocked. They pushed it open and turned on the stairwell light.

Even though Irene knew that the paintings would be there, she was still amazed by them. Springtime floated toward her in his flowered cart, and on the other wall the fiddler played so hard the sweat was flying. She hurried up the steps to spend a moment with the graceful black marble swan on the floor of the foyer. She glanced at Hannu but couldn't see the slightest glimmer of response. He stepped purposefully up to the elevator and opened the door. Irene thought it was silly to take the elevator up one floor, but she did anyway.

VALLE REUTER opened the door with a broad, welcoming smile on his face. It was extinguished at once when he caught sight of Irene. Disappointed, he said, "Who are you? And where is that sweet little police sister?"

"I'm Detective Inspector Irene Huss. Just as I told you on the phone. Apparently you're confusing me with Detective Inspector Birgitta Moberg. She was the one you talked to at headquarters last week. Right now she's busy with a major investigation concerning one of Sweden's worst narcotics criminals."

She couldn't help herself. It slipped out of her before she could think. It was in reaction to that "police sister" line.

Valle Reuter looked very impressed. He raised his eyebrows to his hairline and said, "Are you really going to send little Birgitta on such dangerous missions?"

He moved his shapeless body and made an inviting gesture toward the hall. It wasn't as big as von Knecht's. But the lovely carved closet doors were there, along with a magnificent mirror. Irene stepped in and hung her leather jacket on an ornate brass hat rack. At first she didn't notice it, but then she had an unpleasant déjà vu experience. A distinct smell of Ajax and cigars hung in the air. Involuntarily she shuddered. The last time she had been in this building surrounded by this mixture of smells it was due to an evil, sudden death.

Aloud she said, "There's a nice smell of Ajax. Have you already done the Christmas cleaning?"

He laughed and peered at her. "You could say that. As a matter of fact I've hired a cleaning firm. Three people were here all day yesterday.

Fantastically talented people. They cleaned the whole apartment and put up new curtains everywhere. I want the place to look good when my fiancée comes here for the first time," said Valle.

He smiled happily and glided before her into the large living room. It was somewhat smaller than the room upstairs at the von Knechts, but still about a hundred square meters. With a proud gesture he motioned for her to take a seat in a pompous-looking leather easy chair. The smell of new leather stung her nose. The leather furniture was heavy, shiny, and obviously brand new. Two sofas and four easy chairs. The glass table was the biggest one Irene had ever seen; it reminded her of an octagonal pool. In the large open fireplace of iridescent green marble and black slate a wood fire crackled. High cupboards with shiny glass doors towered on either side of the fireplace. Silver pieces glimmered behind the glass. Large paintings with heavy gold frames were reminiscent of the art in the von Knechts' apartment. Reuter also owned a paint-laden monster, like the one von Knecht had on the wall of his library—although von Knecht's was green and this one was blue.

At the other end of the room a large dining table with twelve chairs was enthroned. Above it hung a heavy crystal chandelier. Glittering light from thousands of prisms radiated over the room.

Valle Reuter stepped over to the wall and began twisting a small control dial. Softly the illumination was toned down; then with a quick twist in the other direction he bathed the room in light.

"They came to install this today. A dimmer, it's called."

With a thoroughly contented expression, he turned the light back down to a comfortable level.

"Your fiancée will like this apartment, I'm convinced of that." Irene said this with genuine honesty, because it was actually very pleasant.

"I think so too. Everything is new! It all came today."

"Everything?"

"Well, not the art and the carpets. Those are things that Henrik bought for me. Investments. The crystal chandelier is old too, very old, but superbly renovated. The furniture is new. You're the first one to sit in that chair."

"And all this you bought because your fiancée will be coming here for the first time?"

He gave her a long look and nodded solemnly a few times before he said, "She accepted my proposal last Tuesday. I was overjoyed! My life has been as black as night. Dreary years . . . alone . . . and then this thing with Richard. When Gunnel said yes, I thought a light was being lit for me too. I almost don't dare believe it! I decided to start a new life. Got rid of all the ugly old furniture that Leila picked out once upon a time! I'm not very good at cleaning . . . the place was a little dirty. But the cleaning company took care of that. Although I had to pay double because they had to come at such short notice. But it was worth it! The day before yesterday I went into that furniture gallery on Östra Hamngatan. I pointed out exactly what I wanted. Some of it wasn't in stock, so I took the display items. The dining room table and one of the sofas. 'I need it delivered Friday evening at the latest,' I said. It cost quite a bit, the whole thing. But it's worth every öre! I donated the old furniture to the City Mission. They came and got it yesterday. May I offer you a glass of something? No, I suppose not."

He looked disappointed, not unlike a pug dog that has his heart set on a treat but doesn't get it.

"We're not allowed to drink on duty," said Irene.

"But it's seven o'clock on a Friday night!"

"And I'm on duty."

"Oh."

"Naturally, that's why I'm here. But I would like to congratulate you on the new furniture. And wish you all the best in your new life together with Gunnel."

Valle lit up again. "A thousand thanks! You're the first to know. No one else knows yet. Sylvia was here and asked whether I was moving, but I evaded the question. She'll really love hearing my news! And my son doesn't care. Gunnel and I are getting engaged here secretly tomorrow night. It feels best that way, thinking of Richard. And we're getting married at Easter!"

Happiness shimmered from his round figure. Irene decided that it was time to get to the reason for her visit. She cleared her throat and said, "I would like to ask a few questions concerning last Tuesday. We received information that when the two of you took a taxi home from lunch at Johanneshus, you didn't take the direct route. Richard von Knecht stopped at the SE-Bank on Kapellplatsen around four o'clock and withdrew a large amount of cash."

Valle raised his eyebrows. "Indeed?" He gave her a friendly squint and seemed to be waiting for her to continue.

"Do you recall that he went into the bank?"

"Recall? I always sleep in the cab on the way home! Always! Richard wakes me when we stop here at the front door. Or used to wake me . . ."

His cheerful voice became subdued and sorrow was clearly evident in those last words.

To clarify, Irene went on, "So on the Tuesday afternoon in question you were asleep the whole time in the cab until it was time to get out?"

"Yes. I must have gone to sleep almost instantly. I was asleep until Richard woke me. As usual."

"Do you recall if he was carrying anything in his hand?"

Valle really made an effort. Irene was struck by his resemblance to a worried seal. He squinted his eyes and concentrated.

"I think he was . . . as a matter of fact. A small white object in one hand. A bag. Did he take out the money in a paper bag?"

"No. He went into the bakery next to the bank and bought two sandwiches."

"That could be right. He and Sylvia often did that on Tuesdays. Just had a sandwich for dinner. We always ate a substantial lunch, and then Richard had to deal with Sylvia's starvation diets again. She wanted to be as slim as a ballerina. Poor Richard almost starved to death!"

From what Irene could remember, there hadn't been anything in the autopsy report about severe undernourishment, but she decided to change the subject.

"Did he say anything to you about the money? It was quite a large sum, ten thousand kronor."

"He probably wanted to buy something. Clothing, perhaps."

Valle sounded uninterested. Evidently he didn't think it was a large sum. Irene suspected that the easy chair he was sitting in cost more than that.

"Did he usually take out cash when he was going to make a purchase?"

Valle thought about it with renewed interest.

"No, he always used a credit card. He didn't like carrying cash. He said you shouldn't have any, in case you're robbed. You never know these days, with all the skinheads and drug addicts."

For a second her daughter's bald pate swam before Irene's eyes, but she pushed away the image. She motioned toward the monster painting and asked, "Did Henrik help you acquire all these fine paintings?"

"Yes. A fine boy. Talented and competent. He also purchased the rugs. And the crystal chandelier."

He pointed at the painting with the blue-headed monster and went on, "He arranged the contact with Bengt Lindström, a noted Swedish painter in Paris. This is his portrait of me. I had him do Richard too—from a photograph—for his sixtieth birthday. Richard was overjoyed! Said it was the gift he valued most. But of course Sylvia didn't like it! She said that they had enough Bengt Lindström. She was mad because he liked the painting."

To her own astonishment Irene suddenly saw that it really was Valle Reuter in the painting. His expression of a jovial seal was right on the mark. The blue seal had a crimson-red glint in his left eye that clearly said, *Be careful you don't underestimate me!*

Since they so opportunely had begun to talk about Henrik, Irene decided to pursue the subject and pump Valle. In a tone of friendly interest she asked, "What did Richard think about his son's choice of profession?"

"Well, he was extremely disappointed after Henrik's illness. Probably thought he would continue in the financial world. Just as I thought about my son. Or more correctly, Leila's son."

His face clouded over and Irene sensed a trauma that she ought to avoid getting into. She swiftly said, "But Henrik went his own way, as we know. From what I understand, he stays up at his house in Marstrand most of the time, doesn't he?"

"Yes, that was the house that brought him back to life. He was apathetic and depressed after his illness. Had to fight to become reasonably healthy again. He was unhappy. But then Richard decided to build a guest cabin down by the water at their country place, and Henrik asked if he could have his own cabin. I assume he probably wanted to be left in peace. The two houses were built at the same time. Henrik was full of energy. He was with the workmen from the first dynamite blast to the last roofing tile! It did him good, both physically and mentally. Doing manual labor."

"Dynamite blast?"

"Yes, quite a bit had to be blasted out there on the rocks by the sea. For the building site. Henrik thought it was fun. He used to be a commando, you know. They learn a lot about explosives. Good grief, my throat is getting so dry with all this talk! Shall we have a little glass after all?"

She declined, friendly yet firm, as her brain worked in high gear. Henrik had both access to explosives and the knowledge to handle them. They had to go up to Marstrand and search for plastique explosive and detonators. And the det cord. Proof! That would be tangible evidence. Although there might not be any left. Maybe he used all of it for the devil bomb and Bobo's briefcase. She suddenly realized that Valle had started talking again.

". . . extremely lovely up there. But Charlotte doesn't like it. She thinks it's too isolated. At first she went up there often. But not so much lately."

"How was Richard's relationship with Charlotte?"

"Good. He didn't talk about her very often. Although he thought it was a shame that they couldn't have children."

Crash! The whole roof fell in on Irene's head. Mentally, at least. Without betraying her inner excitement she asked in a neutral voice, "Can't she have children?"

"It's Henrik who can't have children after his illness. He was tested several times, but he had no viable sperm. Richard told me the boy is totally sterile."

"Did Charlotte know about this when they got married?"

"Yes. But she didn't think it mattered. She didn't want to have children, probably didn't want to ruin her figure. If you're a photo model, you have to think about your appearance. Really a very beautiful girl."

"Did Richard also think she was beautiful? I mean, did he ever mention it?"

Valle gave her a surprised look. "Yes, I suppose any man can see that. Most normally constituted men probably consider Charlotte to be tremendously beautiful," he said with emphasis.

"He never talked to you about his relationship with his daughter-in-law?"

Now Valle looked annoyed. "Since he seldom talked about her, it must have been fine! What does Charlotte have to do with Richard's murder?"

Valle and Richard had been very close, had known each other for years. But clearly Richard had never mentioned to Valle any intimate relationship between him and Charlotte. Irene decided to drop the subject.

"You don't happen to know what taxi company you took home from Johanneshus, do you?"

"But of course! We always use the same company, Richard and I. The only company in the downtown area with nothing but Mercedes cabs. A small firm, but they operate twenty-four hours a day. Wait, I'll get you the number."

He toddled off toward a door that led into a den. A window lamp with a flower-shaped glass shade shone faintly over a large, bare desk of dark, polished wood. The light reflected in glass doors and shiny leather. The reading chairs resembled those in von Knecht's library. For a second Irene felt a longing to take a book from the shelves and sink down into one of the chairs. Just let herself be surrounded by its substantial leather embrace.

"Here it is!" Valle waved a slip of paper. He copied the number onto another piece of paper and came back into the living room.

"I always keep their card in my wallet too. It's good to have it along. This company has excellent drivers. Helpful and friendly."

Irene suspected that Valle was generous with his tips when he was in his cups, which would certainly be a contributing factor to the driver's helpfulness. But she kept this thought to herself. She stood up and thanked Valle for his kindness.

"Oh, think nothing of it! If I can assist in catching the person who murdered my friend, I am at your service," he said solemnly.

A little more of this attitude among those involved in this case and it would have been solved. Which made her wonder how the conversation at Sylvia's was going.

"SHE WENT nuts when I asked about the sandwiches. She screamed at us to stop badgering her. She certainly shut up when Hannu said something to her in Finnish just as we were leaving. What did you say?"

There was a little tug at one corner of Hannu's mouth as he hissed in a muffled voice, "This is about a murder investigation!"

Tommy laughed and turned to Irene, who was driving. "The conversation with Sylvia that preceded this didn't produce much. She wouldn't let us talk to her sister or mother. She told us that she had been up at Marstrand today. A horse had come down with bronchitis and a cough. But the vet had given it penicillin, so it would probably be fine. That was all the information we got. Otherwise she just grumbled. But she said something in Finnish to Arja just as we came in the door. Did you hear what she said, Hannu?"

"Yes. 'Not a word about the party.'"

"'Not a word about the party.' Are you sure about that?"

"Yes, I am."

"What party? She couldn't have meant the funeral, could she?"

Irene had an idea just as she turned into the parking lot at headquarters. She said, "Could it have been the celebration of their anniversary? Or the 'Thirty Years' War,' as someone referred to it during the course of the investigation."

Tommy pondered out loud as she was parking. "None of them who were there said that anything special happened. They agree that it was

an enjoyable party. Only Charlotte and Henrik seemed subdued, according to one account."

"No wonder! She's been knocked up by someone other than her husband. Maybe even by her father-in-law. And Henrik has just primed
a bomb to send his father to kingdom come! No wonder they were
subdued!"

Hannu put in, "Tense. Not subdued. Tense."

It took her a second to realize what he meant. The engine was turned
off, but they were still sitting in the car. She nodded. "Not subdued.
Tense. Precisely. Henrik was nervous that something would go wrong
with the bomb. And Charlotte had other things on her mind. Plans
to take the life of her father-in-law, her lover, her child's father? What
was his relationship to her?"

Tommy sighed and threw up his hands. "It's all circumstantial! We
need proof! Proof!"

THE SUPERINTENDENT had driven home, simmering with fever.
The three inspectors sat down and went over what the day had produced. On Andersson's desk was a fax from the lab. The techs reported
that the pipes in the cellar on Berzeliigatan had been located and "in
all probability match the pipes that were used in the fabrication of the
bombs in question. Additional tests for positive verification are ongoing."
They called the techs to ask about the sandwiches in von Knecht's refrigerator, but no one answered. So they sent a fax too: "Definite information
received that Richard von Knecht bought two ready-made sandwiches
an hour and a half before his death. Did you see these sandwiches in
the refrigerator? If so, were any of you hungry?"

Irene called the cab company. After lengthy explanations and fuss
it came out that the driver they were looking for was on vacation. He
was probably at his summer cabin in Bengtsfors. No, there was no telephone. But they could have the number of his apartment in town. Irene
thanked them and hung up. As she had expected, she got no answer
at the driver's home number. She turned to her two colleagues and said,
"Let's go home now. I'll take the number with me and try to get hold
of the taxi guy over the weekend. Although tomorrow morning I'll
be downtown with the twins. It's a tradition. We're going to look at
the Christmas decorations. I promised to go with them. I thought they
were too old to want to take their old mother along. But they actually
asked me to come with them."

Inside she felt both happy and flattered.

Chapter Eighteen

IRENE WOKE UP WITH a start. She thought she heard quiet sobbing. Was Jenny awake and crying again? Cautiously she sneaked up and listened at her daughter's door. All was quiet. When she cracked open the door, she could hear calm breathing and panting. The panting came from Sammie. He lay squirming on his back with his paws in the air. His "little mistress" lay dangerously close to the edge of the bed, but Irene felt no uneasiness, only tenderness. It was good for Jenny to have her dog close to her. It had been a difficult Friday for her.

IRENE HAD come home around ten. What she wanted most of all was to have a big cup of tea and a sandwich and then crawl into bed. But it wasn't to be. Not right away at least.

Sammie stormed toward her, but he wasn't himself. His tail hung anxiously straight down and he crouched down and whimpered instead of leaping and yelping. Was he sick or in pain? She bent down and started to babble to him as her hands slid over his body to see if he was sore anyplace. Then she heard sobs and Katarina's voice from the living room. "She looks like a God damned skag!"

"Skag"! What in God's name did that mean? And who looked like one? Irene got up, tossed her leather jacket on the hat rack as she passed by, and went to find her daughters in the living room. Katarina was hanging off the edge of the easy chair talking to Jenny, who lay prone on the sofa, shaking with sobs. She had hidden her bald head under a sofa pillow, which she was holding tight. Katarina hadn't heard her mother arrive and didn't notice when she came in the room. She was intensely involved in comforting her sister.

"There are thousands of other guys who are cooler and nicer! And thousands of other bands. With better music. And if you don't want to play skinhead music, you can let your hair grow out. In two months your hair will be as long as Marie Fredriksson's in Roxette! We can bleach it. Cool as shit! Pale stubble! Before it grows out we can say you had cancer. Your hair fell out because of all the chemo and all that radiation . . . Hey! Are you crazy?"

With a wail Jenny jumped up and threw the pillow straight at Katarina. She was furious. Tears sprayed from her wide eyes. Her stamina was running out, because she didn't pursue the attack. When she saw Irene she rushed over and flung herself with full force into her arms and sobbed. Sobbed inconsolably, wordlessly. Sobbed over her first betrayed love, her first betrayed hopes. Irene's crushed rib hurt when Jenny came flying into her arms, but she didn't show it; she started silently rocking her as she tenderly stroked her bald head.

A LITTLE later they were sitting around the kitchen table, drinking tea and eating open-faced egg sandwiches with Kalle's caviar. Bit by bit the story came out. Jenny had told Markus that she didn't want to go to the demonstrations on the anniversary of Karl XII's death. She didn't want to shout slogans that she didn't agree with. But she did want to stay in the band. Markus got furious and said, "If you don't believe in them, then you can't stay with the band. You've shown where you stand!"

Then he turned on his heel and left. Jenny was devastated, because she was in love with him, or so she thought anyway. He was the first boy who had kissed her so her knees got weak. When Katarina mentioned this, Jenny flared up again but soon calmed down. That was exactly how it had felt.

It had been Katarina's idea to rent *Schindler's List* that night. Grandma was coming over, and surely she would enjoy a movie that took place during her own youth. The movie was about a man who pretended to cooperate with the Nazis while he succeeded in saving hundreds of Jews from the extermination camps.

Katarina told her mother that after the movie Grandma had described in detail her own experiences as a seventeen-year-old at the end of the war. About the white Red Cross buses that emptied their cargoes of walking skeletons. At her school they had opened up the baths. Nurses had stripped the ragged clothes caked with filth off the human wrecks. They were treated with delousing powder and scrubbed with hot water and scrub brushes. A poor old Jewish man was so scared when they were about to delouse him that he had a heart attack and died! He thought it was poison. Like the poison the Nazis used when they wanted to kill lots of people at once. Although that was probably gas, Grandma said. Her job had been to hand out clean clothes and help those who couldn't even dress themselves. Strangely enough, Grandma didn't say a word about Jenny's clean-shaven head. It was as if she didn't even see it.

By then Jenny thought that her sister had been allowed to talk long enough. After all, this was mostly about her! Eagerly she broke into the conversation. "When Grandma finished telling her story, I asked her if she really had seen all those people who had been in concentration camps. She had. Then I asked if it was true that there were really extermination camps. And then she said 'Yes.' I asked why they let it happen! Why didn't the Swedes protest that millions of people were being killed in these camps? But she didn't know the answer. Then she said that in Sweden we didn't know about it during the war. It wasn't until the war was over and Hitler was dead that the camps were opened and people found out about it. I think that sounds incredible! I mean . . . it's not so strange that someone might not believe that the camps existed . . . since nobody reacted during the war. They just let it happen!"

She stopped and Irene sensed a slightly apologetic tone in those final remarks. Jenny sat running her fingernail along the edge of the table. That was a sign that she was holding back something that was difficult to say. Finally she took a deep breath and said, "Could you tell Tommy that I'm not a racist? We don't have to be enemies. I don't want that! Tell him. I'm not a racist, really. The lyrics are racist. I can hear that now. Totally. I gave my CDs back to Markus. He can give them to Marie!"

"Is she the one who's a 'God damned skag'?"

"Exactly! She *is* a God damned skag!"

It wasn't necessary to ask for an explanation of the word. Her tone of voice explained everything.

Cautiously Irene asked, "What happened to Markus?"

Jenny turned all crinkly around the eyes, but before Katarina could start to speak for her again, she said with a teary tremble in her voice, "Markus and Marie started going steady yesterday. She's in the eighth grade."

"Is she a skinhead too?"

"Naw, she has neon pink hair. Sometimes she makes lavender loops in it. And she got pierced too. She has a ring in her eyebrow, one in her upper lip, and one in her nose. Disgusting!"

Both daughters were agreed that it was "totally heinous," and Irene was grateful for that.

WHEN KRISTER came home at one A.M. the girls were asleep, but Irene was still up. After telling him about Jenny's troubles and about the impending end to her skinhead period, she tried to seduce her husband. But he was too tired and not at all in the mood. The Christmas rush at the city's restaurants had begun. She lay awake for a long time, her whirling thoughts of skinheads, millionaires, bombs, murderers, biker gangs, sexual relations between people who shouldn't be having any, and sexual relations between people who should.

From sheer exhaustion she fell asleep, until the sobbing woke her. But she must have been dreaming. Nobody in the house was crying.

THERE WASN'T a free parking place in the whole city. Finally Irene drove down to police headquarters and put her car in the lot. Both Jenny and Katarina were bursting with anticipation. They had a hard time maintaining their teenage dignity when the little kid inside them demanded to come out. Jenny had pulled a bright red chimney-sweep cap over her ears. Not just to hide her scalp, but also because it was very cold. Only a few degrees below freezing, but it was windy. That's when Göteborg feels like the Antarctic. Irene and the twins ran toward the downtown shopping district to keep their circulation going.

Garlands with lights and stars were stretched across the pedestrian-only streets. The tall trees in Brunnparken and along Östra Hamngatan glittered with hundreds of tiny lights woven into their leafless branches. But few people looked up at the crowns of the trees. Most of them burrowed their chins down into their collars and hunched their shoulders against the wind. They wanted to get into the lovely warmth, and the shopkeepers were rubbing their hands. That was exactly what they wanted too.

The girls popped in and out of clothing stores. Irene looked at a few jackets, but a glance at the price tags made her decide to wait until spring. She would only have to wear a winter jacket for a few more months. Spring and fall jackets could wait. But she missed her poplin one.

"Look, Mamma! Too cool, huh?"

Katarina's trumpeting woke Irene out of her reverie when she walked out of the dressing room like a runway model, dressed in a bright orange top that came down to her navel and a pair of moss-green bell-bottoms. First she just stared at her daughter. Finally she couldn't hold it back any longer and burst out laughing.

"What are you cackling at?" Katarina said. "This is totally modern! Try and keep up, okay?"

Jenny agreed and said patronizingly to her old fossil of a mother, "This is the latest thing, after all."

Irene tried hard to contain herself. "I'm sorry, but it's just that I recognized myself. I looked just like that when I was your age."

Both her daughters gave her a skeptical look and exchanged a glance heavenward. The hardest thing to believe was that Mamma was ever their age.

Just like all the other shoppers looking at the decorations and searching for gifts, they wound up in NK. Irene was tired and needed a cup of coffee, but the girls voted to go look around the department store first. With a sigh, after a mild protest, Irene had to give in. Whenever the girls joined forces, she was in the minority. All the lights and glitter began to drain the energy out of her. And the elves—! Wherever you looked you saw an elf. Tiny elves, giant elves, artificial elves, and live elves. One of them almost scared her to death when it bent forward and touched her arm and asked if she didn't want to buy a new shaver for the "little husband."

Worn out, Irene tried to catch her breath on the escalator up to the second floor. Above their heads hovered slowly rotating Christmas trees. Halogen lamps made them glitter and flash. One was done completely in silver rosettes, another in gold hearts, a third in silver icicles, a fourth in gold balls . . . all the gold and silver dazzled her and hurt her eyes. Gold and silver. Silver. Like shiny sardines in their can. Like shiny . . .

"Mamma! Lift your feet!"

Katarina was yelling at her. The girls were behind her and realized what was about to happen. But it was too late. She was on her face where the escalator ended. The bag of newly bought panties and stockings spilled out every which way, but Jenny quickly picked them up. Katarina was so embarrassed she was about to sink through the floor. How humiliating could a mother be, anyway?

All Irene's weariness had vanished. She swiftly gathered up her children, her packages, and her wounded dignity. Eagerly she said, "Let's go! I need a telephone!"

"Did you hurt yourself? Should I call an ambulance or anything?"

"No. But something did strike me, as a matter of fact. An idea!"

"Don't you have your cell phone?"

"No, I didn't bring it."

They made a U-turn and took the escalator back downstairs. On the ground floor Irene found a nice café and a pay phone. She parked the girls at a table furnished with hot chocolate with whipped cream and saffron Lucia buns.

Irene began searching her pockets for the piece of paper with the number on it; she found it and punched in the number.

"Sylvia von Knecht."

"Hello, excuse me for bothering you. This is Inspector Irene Huss."

"What do you want?"

It wouldn't be fair to claim that any great warmth flowed through the line. But it wasn't necessary either. What was important now was not to get Sylvia into a bad mood. Which Irene unfortunately seemed to have a real talent for. In as friendly a tone as she could muster, Irene said, "A piece of information has come up that I need to check. It will only take five minutes."

"Go ahead and check then!"

Irene was flustered until she realized what Sylvia meant. "No, I can't do it on the phone. I have to come up and talk to you at the apartment. It's very important if it turns out to be true," she said urgently.

There was a long silence.

"When would you be coming, in that case?"

"Would three o'clock be all right?"

"Fine."

Click. Hung up on her, as usual. If her revelation on the escalator proved to be wrong, imagine with what scornful laughter it would be scattered, like fog, into empty nothingness. In that case it would be a sweaty conversation with Sylvia.

JUST BEFORE three o'clock they went back to the car. All three had tired feet, but they were happily sated with purchases and impressions. There was no doubt about it: This year there would be a Christmas too. Irene started the car, and only then did she tell the girls that she had to run an errand at someone's apartment. But it was on the way home, not a detour. The girls griped but promised to wait in the car. Irene parked on Kapellplatsen so that they could stroll around and do some window-shopping. It wasn't that much fun, though, because all the stores were closed, except for the Konsum grocery store and the bakery. After NK all the other Christmas decorations were an anticlimax.

//

IT WAS Arja who opened the door. She smiled her pleasant smile but it faded rapidly when her sister's whiny voice was heard from inside the apartment.

"Is it that cop person?"

Before Arja could reply, Irene shouted back, "It's Detective Inspector Irene Huss from the Homicide Commission."

She'd be damned if she'd let herself be called a "cop person"! And there wasn't anything called the "Homicide Commission," but Sylvia wouldn't know that. It sounded good. Arja at least was impressed, when she stepped back to let Irene in, as evidenced by her wide eyes and slightly gaping mouth.

Sylvia came out of the kitchen with her lips pressed together in annoyance. Presumably she had gotten lost because the kitchen was not one of the places where she usually spent any time. Irene recalled the virginal kitchen implements over the stove. And the empty hook where a meat cleaver was missing. She tried to smile and look pleasant.

"Thanks for letting me come up and bother you for a moment. I just need to check on one thing. It's about the keys."

"Yes?"

"Can we go upstairs?"

Sylvia jerked her neck and began striding toward the stairs to the upper level. Irene assumed that it was all right to follow.

In the upstairs hall Sylvia stopped and turned. She coolly raised one eyebrow and said, "The keys?"

"Would you please get the spare-key ring? The one you said you keep in your desk drawer in your office. I'll go in and get your husband's key case. That is, if it's still on his nightstand?"

Sylvia snorted lightly before she replied, "In the drawer of the night-stand. The police just traipse around at will in my home! I don't suppose I can stop you. You've already taken his car keys, without returning them!"

She swiftly turned and glided away toward her office. Irene swallowed the words that were on the tip of her tongue. *Don't get mad, don't get mad . . .*

The room had changed. It took a fraction of a second before Irene noticed that the paintings were gone. There were a couple of paintings on the empty walls, but they weren't "sex pictures," as Irene in her ignorance had called them. A "collection of erotica," Henrik von Knecht had corrected her. Imagine how much useful information she had learned in the course of this investigation! The ones that were in the room now were completely normal paintings. Modern and eccentric, but not nudes. A sudden pang of sympathy for Sylvia went through her. She quickly went over to the enormous silk bed and opened the drawer of Richard's nightstand. It contained paper tissues, some ice-blue cough drops in transparent wrappers, and the shiny, black leather key case. Now she would see if she was right. She was surprised to see that her hands were shaking a little when she unsnapped the case. Out fell the six keys, hanging from their hooks. All were equally shiny. All were made of exactly the same type of metal. All had no numbers or markings. No wear whatsoever. This was the newly made set of keys, the one that Richard had had made at Mister Minit less than six months ago. A sigh of relief escaped her.

"Did you find anything of interest?"

Irene heard Sylvia's voice behind her back. You could have cut glass with it. Calmly Irene turned around, walked over to the rigid, thin little woman, and said, "Have you looked at Richard's set of keys since he died?"

Sylvia's eyes widened in astonishment but soon resumed their inimical attitude.

"Why would I do that? I have my own!"

"You haven't looked at his keys?"

"No, I told you! I just put them in the drawer."

"Look at this. Hold out your set of keys and compare them to the keys in Richard's case. That's it, hold them in your hand," Irene said in a friendly, persuasive voice.

Hesitantly Sylvia did as she was told. When the two sets of keys were held next to each other, she saw it too. Richard's new, shiny ones were as gaudy as Christmas tree decorations, while the keys in the spare set were different colors from age, wear, and oxidation. They also had various numbers and letters on them.

With tight lips Sylvia whispered, "Heavens!"

She was transfixed by the keys; she couldn't take her eyes off them.

Softly Irene said, "Somebody borrowed, or stole, Richard's keys last summer. He didn't get them back, but had another set made using the spare set as a pattern. Why did he do that? Why didn't he report the keys missing? Change all the locks? Why didn't he tell you?"

Sylvia just stared at the keys in Irene's hand. Her eyes looked unnaturally large in the narrow, transparent face. A wailing sound rose from her throat, and she started tossing her head from side to side. At first it was barely noticeable, then the motion grew more and more violent.

The wail rose to a shriek and Sylvia started shaking all over. Damn, she had done it again! Why, why couldn't she ever handle Sylvia?

Irene rushed over to the bedroom door and called for Arja. Then, with hard-won composure, she approached Sylvia and tried to calm her down. It was useless. Sylvia had worked herself up to a state of hysteria and was screeching like a siren. When Irene tried to put her hand on her arm, she screamed. Then she fainted. The woman could really collapse beautifully! Like falling swan's down she sank to the floor in a graceful rippling motion. One arm lay in an arc above her head and the other rested lightly across her stomach. This was the scene that greeted Arja when she came through the door.

"So, she's fainted again," she said calmly.

Without hurrying she crossed the floor to her sister. With a practiced motion she raised Sylvia's legs in the air and began to massage her calves. All the while she looked at Irene, who thought that her guilt feelings must be blatantly visible. Calmly Arja asked, "What made her so upset?"

"Upset? It was the keys," Irene said vaguely.

"Sylvia has always fainted when she gets upset. Her whole life! Sensitive artistic soul, you know."

Arja gave her a broad, pleasant smile of camaraderie, and Irene began to feel a little better. She decided to tell Arja exactly what was going on.

"It was when I showed her that Richard's set of keys was newly made. So the one we found in the door on Berzeliigatan was Richard's old key ring. He had lost it last summer and never said anything to Sylvia."

Arja gave her a long look. Emphatically she said, "There was a lot that Richard didn't tell Sylvia."

Now or never! Irene looked down at Sylvia, who was beginning to show signs of life. She said softly to Arja out of the corner of her mouth, "Tell me about the party!"

Arja started and cast a quick glance at Sylvia's pale face. She put one finger over her mouth and made a gesture toward her sister.

"Could we lift her up onto the bed?"

They helped each other lift the feather-light body. Sylvia began to mumble weakly and her eyelids fluttered.

"I'll call Mother," said Arja.

The words were barely out of her mouth before a thin little shadowy figure slipped in through the doorway. Irene was dumbstruck. That's exactly how Sylvia would look in twenty-five years. The little woman ignored the other two and tiptoed over to the bed. With her slender hands, in which the blue veins seemed to lie outside her white skin, she grasped her daughter's equally pale and bloodless ones. Gently caressing Sylvia, she murmured long strings of consoling words. To Irene's ears they sounded like magic incantations, but after a few moments she realized it was Finnish she was hearing.

Arja poked her furtively in the side and motioned with her head toward the door. Silently they slunk out and down the broad staircase. They continued into the entryway, and Arja took a key lying on the marble top of the ornate hall table. She opened the front door and gestured to Irene to follow. They hurried down the stairs to the floor below. With growing astonishment Irene realized they were on their way into the apartment below the von Knechts'. Arja unlocked the door. She motioned for Irene to enter and then silently closed the door and touched the switch on the wall. A naked lightbulb hung from the ceiling and cast a harsh light. The place smelled of paint and wallpaper glue.

Arja waved her hand and said, "Ivan Viktors is moving in tomorrow. The moving van is coming early."

"Do you know that Sylvia and Ivan Viktors have a relationship?"

Arja stiffened and gave her a sharp look. "So you know about it too? Yes, of course I know that. You certainly can't blame Sylvia. It wasn't always much fun being Richard's wife. He was a big shit!"

The way she said it with her Finnish accent made it sound quite pleasant. Irene decided to get right to the point to save time and skip the chitchat. With a hint of a smile in her voice, she asked, "Did he try to seduce you too?"

Arja pouted slightly and then gave Irene a big, soft smile. "Almost twenty years ago. But his charm didn't work on me. I told him like it is, that I'm a lesbian."

Irene gave a start. She hadn't expected this.

Arja said dryly, "I've been in a relationship for many years. But neither Mamma nor Sylvia will accept Siirka. She's not allowed to attend any of the family events, such as weddings and funerals. She couldn't anyway. She's a teacher, and it's hard to get time off."

Irene's thoughts flew to Mona and Jonas Söder in Stockholm. How was he doing?

Irene collected herself and tried to ask the right questions.

"And you're a journalist?"

"Yes. Freelance. I'm my own boss."

"Can you tell me about the party? The one Sylvia doesn't want you to talk about."

Arja took a deep breath and for a shaky moment Irene thought she had changed her mind. But she began to speak. "It was at Richard's sixtieth birthday party last summer. There were tons of people there. It was warm and lovely far into the night. But around two o'clock I was getting tired and thought I'd sneak off to bed. Mother and I each had a room in the guest cabin. Mother was feeling spry and still dancing. She had taken a nap in the afternoon. She loves parties! But I couldn't keep my eyes open. Too much wine and champagne. The guests had to be driven to various hotels in Göteborg. Limousines had been rented, but they weren't coming until three. No one would miss me if I slipped away. On the path down to the guest cabin I ran into Sylvia. She was tipsy like all the others, but she was also uneasy. People had been asking for Richard, but she couldn't find him. I suggested that she follow me to the cabin, then we could have a glass of the Arctic raspberry liqueur I had bought on the ferry. Sylvia loves it. And that's where we found Richard."

She fell silent and rubbed her eyes wearily, as if to erase an image from her memory. Or maybe to make it clearer. A bitter tone slipped into her voice as she continued, "We didn't just find Richard. Charlotte was there too. We saw them, but they didn't see us. On the floor of the great room they were engaged in filthy acts."

Irene was surprised at the choice of words. Did a lesbian consider heterosexual intercourse to be "filthy acts"?

Arja took her hands from her eyes and looked straight at Irene. Curtly she said, "They were sucking each other and . . . " She looked away and red flames shot down her neck.

"It was disgusting! We went back outside. They didn't notice we had been there. Sylvia fainted, of course, but recovered quite rapidly. She made me promise never to tell anyone what we had seen. Not anyone."

She paused and fingered the key to the apartment. In a low voice she said, "But I'm breaking that promise now. I think this has something to do with Richard's death."

"Why do you think that?"

"The keys. I know that Charlotte took them."

"Tell me."

"The next day the mood was naturally flat. Richard had fallen asleep on a sofa in the living room. He lay there snoring when I came into the big house. Mother had misplaced her little travel pillbox with her heart tablets. We found it later in the guest cabin, but not that morning. Mother swore that she had left it in Sylvia's bedroom when she went there for a little nap the day before. I tiptoed in as quietly as I could so I wouldn't wake anyone. Sylvia and Richard had separate bedrooms up at Marstrand. I sneaked into Sylvia's room and woke her, of course. She sleeps so lightly. She hadn't seen Mother's pillbox, and I couldn't find it either. When I left Sylvia's bedroom, I ran into Charlotte coming out of Richard's! We both stopped short and then she said, "Hi, I forgot my keys. But I found them." And then she stuffed the key case she was holding in her hand into the pocket of her dressing gown. I was tired and a little hung over, so I didn't give it much thought then. But I've thought about it many times since. Why would Charlotte leave her keys in Richard's bedroom?"

"Did you tell Sylvia about this encounter with Charlotte?"

"No. I didn't want to mention Charlotte too much in her presence."

"Do you think Henrik knew what was going on between Richard and Charlotte?"

Arja thought about it. She shook her head. "No, I don't think so. But Charlotte hasn't been up to Marstrand since the sixtieth birthday party, I know that."

"But Henrik goes there as often as he can?"

"Yes, he loves his cabin."

"Do you know that Henrik is sterile?"

"Yes. Sylvia told me."

"Do you know that Charlotte is pregnant and nearing her second trimester?"

Arja nodded and said, resigned, "Yes. Sylvia told me."

She took another deep breath and looked steadily at Irene. "I told you all this because I want the murder of my shithead brother-in-law to be cleared up. Sylvia needs rest. It has to be solved. But I will never testify in any trial. This is just between you and me," she said firmly.

"Not even the fact that you met Charlotte on the way out of Richard's room, with a key case in her hand?"

Arja thought for a moment. "All right, I could testify to that. But not the rest. Not a word about it! Sylvia would lose her trust in me. And rightly. I've already betrayed it. But I thought I had to. The murder must be solved, not swept under the rug."

WHEN IRENE came back to the car there were no twins, but a note on the front seat. "We went to Glady's. Hungry as hell! Hugs, K&J." She really couldn't blame them. She had been gone more than an hour and it was cold in the car. With a sigh she started the engine, rolled down Aschebergsgatan, and turned off toward Avenyn.

She parked in an employee parking space in the back lot of Glady's Corner and went in through the kitchen entrance. In the large restaurant kitchen there was feverish activity, and steam was pouring out of the huge saucepans. People were running around and shouting out orders. But everything was functioning smoothly; the big evening rush hadn't started yet. Not a sign of the girls that Irene could see. She managed to catch sight of Krister. He was lifting rolled-up fish fillets out of a wide sauté pan with a perforated ladle. His concentration was total, and he didn't notice her until she was right next to him.

She chirped in his ear, "Hiya, pal. Have you seen our kids?"

He jumped and the tender piece of fish plopped back into the pan.

"Damn, now it broke! Hi. I sent our kids off to McDonald's," he said, annoyed.

"To McDonald's?"

"Yes, the food here wasn't good enough for the ladies. And they kept buzzing around bothering people. So I sent them off across the street. A Big Mac is always a culinary hit according to our daughters. It must be your genes coming through."

He gave her a hasty kiss on the nose and dived for his fillet again, rescuing what he could.

IT HAPPENED unconsciously, but she did notice it. Her steps slowed when she saw the shiny motorcycles parked in a row outside the hamburger restaurant. A sense of uneasiness began churning in her stomach. Maybe she ought to talk to a shrink about her incipient—or manifest—phobia about motorcycles? Maybe it could be cured with a few doses of Porsche? This was something she'd have to figure out for herself. She gave herself a mental kick in the rear and began walking toward the entrance. The girls were sitting by the window and waved happily to her when they saw her. Just as she reached out her hand to push open the door, she saw him.

He was sitting with his back to the door but she could see his face at an angle from behind, since he was talking to a man on the seat facing him. The greasy hair curled thinly down his back and his shoulders jerked nervously under the padded leather jacket. It was the Thin Man, alias Paul John Svensson.

First she was mad as hell. He was pretty cocksure, all right! To sit in the open chowing down on hamburgers on Avenyn, when he had to know he was wanted by the police! A second later the fear came. She couldn't go in. He would recognize her. Her daughters were sitting inside, with a madman. Presumably he was fully tanked up on dope. And no doubt armed.

She spun around and tried to look like she had forgotten something. She hurried across the street and was almost run over by a streetcar in the process. *Calm down*, she had to try to stay calm! Safely on the other side she started jogging toward Glady's. She didn't have time to go around the back, but slunk in through the main entrance. The maître'd was new and didn't recognize her. She wasted a few precious seconds as she argued with him. Finally she had to wave her police ID at him, since the chef's wife apparently couldn't just walk in. She realized that it was her jeans and the worn leather jacket that had landed her in hot water. Authoritatively she shouted, "This is a police matter. I need to borrow a telephone immediately!"

With a disapproving expression he led her into the office. She and the owner were old acquaintances, but he also looked at her curiously as without explanation she grabbed the telephone on the desk. As she leafed through the Yellow Pages under RESTAURANTS, she snapped, "Police matter. I'll explain later. Here it is!"

She found the number for McDonald's on Avenyn. With shaking hands she first misdialed and then had to try again . . . ten, eleven, twelve. On the thirteenth ring a very young voice answered, "McDonald's, Tina."

"Hi, Tina. Would you please announce over the loudspeakers that Jenny and Katarina have a phone call? It's extremely important. There's been an accident, you see. I'm their mother. But don't say anything to the girls. Everything's under control."

"All right, yeah, I can do that."

There was a clatter when she put down the receiver and half an eternity passed before Katarina's querulous voice came on the line.

"Hello?"

"Hi, darling, it's Mamma. Don't say a word, but listen to me. I want you and Jenny to leave that place immediately."

"But we haven't finished our ice cream!"

"The hell with it! Do as I say! Dear Katarina, it's very very important!"

"Okay. But Jenny will be mad."

"Get her out of there. Come over to Glady's right now!"

Katarina must have sensed her panic. It was something she had never heard before in her mamma's voice.

"Okay. We'll be right there," she said quickly.

Irene's hands were shaking so much she could hardly hang up the phone. She ignored the owner's questioning glance. The direct number to the department was free, but no one answered. Five-thirty on a Saturday night, no wonder. Instead she called Dispatch. She got a connection fast. A confident voice answered, "Dispatch, Inspector Rolandsson."

"Hello, Irene Huss, inspector in Violent Crimes. I've spotted a wanted perp. He's sitting in McDonald's on Avenyn. Dangerous. Belongs to the Hell's Angels. Probably high, and armed. Name: Paul John Svensson."

Rolandsson was silent a moment before he said, "Roger. We'll send the team in the van and a patrol car. Armed, you said."

"Yes, that son-of-a-bitch probably has a SIG Sauer he took from me or Jimmy Olsson!"

"So it's one of those guys from the fray out in Billdal. We know what he looks like. The team has a photo. Can you stay there to facilitate the arrest?"

"Yes. I'll be across the street on the other corner, on Engelbrektsgatan. In front of the display window at KappAhl."

After she hung up she began shaking all over. Curiosity was written all over the restaurant owner's face, but she waved quickly at him and shouted that she'd explain later. Quickly, she went to the kitchen—and there stood her daughters. Krister looked annoyed and puzzled. Irene didn't have time to explain, but threw herself on the girls and said, relieved, "Oh, you girls are so good! Thank the good Lord! Just a little while more, and we'll go home to poor Sammie. Then the others will have to take over!"

Krister looked even more quizzical. "What are the others going to take over?"

"The bad guys and the bandits! God, I'm so tired of all this shit!"

He gave her an astonished look and said, "That's probably the first time I've ever heard you say anything like that."

She gave him a long look. To his consternation there were tears shining in her eyes when she finally replied. "This is the first time that my own family has been directly threatened because of my job!"

Like the wings of a brooding hen she spread her arms around the girls and admonished, "Stay here with Pappa. Don't go before I come back!"

She gave them each a hasty kiss on the forehead and crept out the back door. The owner came into the kitchen from the other direction.

He caught sight of Krister and gave him a questioning look. The head chef threw up his hands in a very French and telling gesture: *Women! What can you expect?*

THE PATROL car was about to park when Irene arrived at the rendezvous. After a few minutes the van arrived. To her relief Håkan Lund was in charge of the van squad. It didn't do him much good that the new uniform jackets had full-length, slimming white stripes. It's not easy to wish away a hundred kilos.

He greeted her cheerfully, "Hello! I heard you've got a bead on Paul Svensson! We're going to suck that scumbag right in. Here's the plan. Take this radio. Walk past McDonald's and locate Svensson. Make sure he doesn't see you. We'll move in as soon as you give us his position."

He pressed a little walkie-talkie into Irene's hand and waved her off. She walked along the outer edge of the sidewalk. Right outside the burger joint she stepped out into the street to gain some cover from the parked cars and motorcycles.

Irene saw him. He was still sitting, talking to his buddies. She raised the radio to her mouth and pressed the button. Exactly at that instant Paul Svensson got up. His lanky body began staggering around, until it suddenly seemed to remember its intention. He headed for the door marked with the international symbol for "Men."

She whispered in the radio, "Irene here. He went into the men's room."

"Excellent! We're going in."

Twenty seconds later the police went in the back way with their weapons drawn. They surrounded Paul Svensson's pals. Four officers went in the front and two of them took up positions on either side of the bathroom door. When the Thin Man came out he got two gun barrels stuck in his back. Even though he was as high as Kebnekaise Peak, he realized how lousy the odds were. Obediently he put his hands in the air. He was searched quickly and thoroughly. Irene saw Håkan Lund take a heavy pistol from a holster that Paul Svensson had under his jacket. A SIG Sauer. Hers or Jimmy's? She just didn't care. She wanted to go home.

SAMMIE WAS overjoyed when they arrived. He hadn't peed on the floor, even though he'd been alone for more than seven hours. Once outside the door he couldn't hold it any farther than to the rose bed under the kitchen window. He sighed with relief.

Irene tried to explain to her daughters what had actually happened inside McDonald's and why it was so important for them to get out of there. They were sitting around the kitchen table drinking a cup of hot O'Boy.

Katarina said excitedly, "Wicked exciting! Why couldn't we have stayed there and watched them nab him?"

"Because it's not TV or a movie! That guy is a murderer. He was armed with a pistol and maybe a number of other weapons. He wouldn't have hesitated to take the two of you hostage if he found that out you were a police officer's daughters. Mine."

Jenny was tracing her fingernail along the edge of the table again. "I thought they looked nice. The little I talked to them, I mean," she said sullenly.

"Nice! Sure, because he's tanked up on amphetamines and maybe some other shit!"

"You mean he could have killed us? I don't think so! They didn't seem dangerous at all, or like dope addicts," Jenny insisted.

Obstinately she tossed her head, where an extremely short stubble could be seen in the backlight from the kitchen lamp. Irene forced herself to speak calmly and tried to select her words with care.

"Jenny, do you remember when you and Katarina visited me at the hospital on Monday? Do you remember how I looked? Do you remember that a young colleague I had with me was beaten up so badly that he's still in the hospital?"

Jenny nodded glumly. Irene continued, imperturbable. "Do you remember that I told you about the grenade that was thrown into the house where my colleague and I were locked inside? Do you remember?"

"Yeah, yeah, you don't have to keep talking about it! Of course I remember!"

"If you remember that, what makes you think for an instant that this guy wouldn't kill you or Katarina? If the circumstances were right— or from your point of view, unlucky—nothing would stop him. He was there when they tried to murder me and Jimmy!"

Finally she couldn't stop herself. Her final words turned into a shriek. But she got them out. Jenny's eyes grew big and shiny. She got up and went over to her mamma and threw her arms around her. They didn't say a word, but they both felt that something was changing between them. It would take time, but it would heal.

They jumped when the telephone rang. Katarina got to it first and picked it up.

"Just a moment. Mamma, it's for you."

"Irene Huss."

"Hi, Irene. It's Mona Söder. Is this a bad time? No? I just wanted to tell you that Jonas . . . Jonas died early this morning . . . at two o'clock."

Her voice had been steady, but now it broke. Around two in the morning. That was when Irene thought she had heard somebody crying in the house.

Chapter Nineteen

SUNDAY MORNING WAS ROUGH. Irene woke up with an unpleasant feeling of being hung over. Unjustly, since she hadn't even had a light beer the night before. Krister was snoring loudly next to her in bed. He had come home around two in the morning. He had worked the extra shift he had traded with Sverker so he could take care of her after the beating out in Billdal. A wave of tenderness rose up inside her and she tiptoed out as quietly as she could so she wouldn't wake him. It was just after eight o'clock. The twins would sleep at least two more hours. And no doubt their father would too. The important thing was to make the best of these few hours to herself.

She put on her long underwear and jogging suit. Sammie lay playing possum. He was the biggest sleepyhead of the whole family in the morning. He didn't mind a brief walk to pee, but no running or jumping in the morning, please. She rattled his leash a little. Nature's call made itself felt, and he meandered out into the hallway. He gave a big yawn and stretched out his body, heavy with sleep.

It was a short walk. Sammie was eager to get home. He was thinking about an empty bed that was still warm.

It was dark and cold, but the air felt clear and crisp. She ran down toward Fiskebäck marina without meeting a soul. The salt-saturated wind blew the scent of seaweed into her wide-open nostrils and swept away the heavy feeling in her head. The flint-gray sea slammed its swells against jetties and wharves. The mooring ropes slapped and the shrouds fluttered on the big sailboats still in the water. The creak of some wooden fenders made her instinctively slow her pace. It was clear that they were protesting being squashed between a huge boat hull and the wharf. Although she had already run almost two kilometers she wasn't even short of breath. She turned around out by the rocks and ran back a bit, then turned off toward Flundregatorna and jogged the back streets up toward Skärvallsberget. She made it all the way out to the very edge of Hinsholmskilen before she turned back.

IRENE TOOK a long hot shower, followed by a short ice-cold one. A perfect conclusion to a jog of several kilometers. Gone was the earlier disgruntled feeling. She was bursting with energy. Breakfast for the family, including the dog, was fixed in a jiffy. It was harder trying to pry her weary family members out of their warm beds. Including the dog.

Irene had to explain one more time what had happened the day before. Krister apologized for not fully understanding the gravity of the situation. Irene shrugged it off and said that she was equally to blame. She had been too agitated to tell him what was actually going on. Her gracious spouse then tactfully told her what the restaurant owner had said. "Overstressed" and "perhaps a little too affected by her job" were hardly the comments his wife wanted to hear.

After breakfast her energy began to ebb. She began to notice her home. Piles of dirty laundry in the laundry room. Dust bunnies, dirt, and gravel that Sammie's long hair had dragged in. She had a vague feeling that she was seeing the whole house through a soft-focus lens. The dusty fluff was erasing all contours.

With a lot of sighing and protesting, the twins helped vacuum and dust. Krister had to take Sammie outside, because he was afraid of the vacuum cleaner. During the three years the dog had lived with them, he had tried to make his beloved family aware that there truly was a little dog locked inside the terrible vacuum cleaner. He could hear it whining! It had made things worse when Krister, in a fit of misdirected humor, sucked Sammie's whiskers into the nozzle. After that the dog was convinced. The vacuum cleaner was treacherous and lethal. It ate little dogs.

Irene set to work on the bathroom, the toilets, and the laundry room. All the beds had to be changed, all the towels replaced with fresh ones. This hadn't been done for two weeks. After Krister returned with Sammie, he left to do the grocery shopping. By then the vacuuming was done, but for safety's sake Sammie crept under Jenny's bed. He didn't quite trust things as long as there was activity in the house and the strong smell of household cleansers. All of a sudden somebody might decide to take out the vacuum again.

They went at it for almost two hours. Twice a month they went through the same process. All year round. There was never time for Christmas, fall, or spring cleaning. Irene's mother occasionally changed the curtains. She loved to change curtains. If she hadn't done it, the curtains would have never been changed. Well, maybe Krister would have taken care of it when he washed the windows twice a year. Irene herself wasn't much interested in curtains. She didn't know what the neighbor women thought about it, and it didn't bother her either. Some of them changed the curtains several times a year.

KRISTER FIXED a wonderful Advent dinner. The menu included an old-fashioned beef roast with steamed vegetables, black currant jelly, boiled potatoes, and a heavenly gravy. Irene's mamma was coming at four. Katarina had found the red ceramic Advent candelabra. Who had put it on top of the fuse box? Krister had remembered to buy four Advent candles of real paraffin. But they had to do without drip rings, because nobody could find them. Jenny set the table with the good porcelain and folded the napkins in intricate pleats and waves. It was the only napkin trick she knew, but it was amazingly sophisticated, excellent for impressing people. And Grandma was astonished at her talent, as always. She complimented Jenny without so much as a glance at her stubby scalp.

Katarina also seemed to have had a sudden change in attitude, because for dessert she had baked a magnificently gooey chocolate cake. Lightly whipped ice-cold cream was served with it, along with cups of freshly brewed coffee. They sat in the living room and ate the chocolate cake and drank coffee. The Advent candles glowed, everyone was full and content, and a warm holiday mood hovered over the room. The twins excitedly told Grandma about the thrilling events at McDonald's the day before.

Irene's mother gave her a sharp look. "I read about the arrest in the paper this morning. He's a thoroughly evil motorcycle gangster! Was it really necessary to take the girls along on this manhunt?"

Before Irene could open her mouth in defense, the telephone rang. Instinctively she looked at the clock. Almost five-thirty. She got up and went out to answer the hall telephone.

"Irene Huss."

"Hi, Irene. It's Birgitta. I'm calling from my cell phone. I'm following Shorty's car right now. The white Mondeo. We're on the way out E-Six to the north, and just passed Kärra. He stopped at Charlotte and Henrik's house in Örgryte and was inside almost fifteen minutes. Something tells me we're on our way up to Marstrand."

The connection crackled and crunched, but Irene could nevertheless hear Birgitta fine. She tried to get her food-sated brain to work and asked, "Did you get in touch with the others?"

"Yes and no. Just with Fredrik. He's swinging by his house to get his pistol. I've got mine on me. I haven't been able to reach the others."

Fredrik lived a few minutes from HQ. For him it was no big detour. But Irene decided not to waste any more time. The best thing for her would be to zip up the big freeways and not venture downtown. Two SIG Sauers should be enough.

She said curtly, "Okay, I'm on my way."

She hung up. An idea occurred to her. She took a few steps over to the hat rack and started rooting around in the pockets of her leather jacket. In the inside pocket she found her little notebook. She turned to the last pages with the heading "R. v. K." Richard von Knecht. The murder of that man had started this whole merry-go-round. Irene shook her head as she searched for the phone number of the caretaker, Lennart Svensson. She found it. The phone rang ten times with no answer.

She went back to her family in the living room. Doing her best to sound casual she said, "Sorry, but I have to run off. Things are happening in the von Knecht case."

Krister unconsciously pursed his lips and said, "And so you have to be there, of course? Even though it's your day off? Can't they get along without you?"

Her mother and the twins also looked disappointed. Irene felt a pang of guilty conscience, as usual, but steeled herself. Somewhat more authoritatively she said, "We're beginning to get close to solving the case. At least I think so. And Birgitta Moberg is in a bind. I have to help her out. She hasn't had any luck contacting anyone else. See you later, and thanks for a wonderful dinner."

She turned on her heel and made a flying start back out to the hall. Way too much time had already been lost. She grabbed her jacket and heavy jogging shoes on the way out to the garage.

THE SIGN HOLTA CHURCH flashed by and she slowed down. Now she had to make sure not to miss the exit. There it was! Tjuvkil. She turned onto the gravel road. There were no streetlights out here. The darkness was intense outside the field of her headlights. A little yellow arrow with black text said KÄRRINGNÄSET. She had to turn there. The road was narrow. The branches of the bushes and trees along the ditch scraped along the side of the car.

It was a good thing that Birgitta had the presence of mind to turn on her taillights, or Irene would have crashed into the rear of her car. True to form, she had been driving too fast. Birgitta had left the dark blue Volvo stakeout car in the middle of the road. There was no other place to park it. She turned off the taillights, hopped out of the car, and approached Irene.

"Good of you to come. And here comes Fredrik," she added.

Irene also put her blinkers on. The arriving car braked, and Fredrik jumped out even before the engine turned off. Eagerly he said, "It took a little extra time, but I slipped into Narcotics and borrowed a weapon. I was thinking of you and Jimmy. Too bad they couldn't spare another officer. So it's just the three of us. You didn't have any luck getting hold of Jonny or Hans?"

Birgitta shook her head and stretched out her hand so she could take a look at the famous night-vision telescope in the flashlight beam. Irene answered for her, "Borg is probably taking an after-dinner nap. And there's no hope of trying to get Tommy to come out here. He's in Borås at Agneta's parents' house."

They walked toward the two-meter-high gates of solid iron with inhospitable spikes on top. Fredrik shook the heavy iron bars to test them, but the gate was locked. The fence was just as high, and barbed wire ran along the top between tall iron posts.

After thinking for a moment, Birgitta said, "Irene, you've studied the map of this area better than we have. How far is it to the house from here?"

"Almost a kilometer. Close to the fence here are pastures for Sylvia's horses. A few hundred meters farther along the road—I'd say about five hundred—is the caretaker's house."

Birgitta looked around, pondering, and said, "Shorty's car isn't parked here, as far as I can see."

"Are you sure he was coming here?"

"Yes. I followed him up to Holta Church. He turned down toward Tjuvkil and then continued straight ahead. So I turned around and headed down the same road. I saw his lights in front of me. Then I switched mine off. He turned off here toward Kärringnäset. I didn't dare get too close. If he had stopped he might have heard my engine. So I parked for five minutes, right by the turnoff. When I got here there wasn't a trace of the Mondeo. He must have had a key to the gate."

"You said he made a detour over to Örgryte?"

"Yes. I was staked out at his place on Berzeliigatan. Right after five his car came zooming past. I got in my car, or rather the department's car. Mine is too clunky for tailing anyone. It couldn't keep up with a souped-up moped! He drove straight out to Långåsliden, jumped out of the car, and knocked on the door. Charlotte opened it. I saw her in the doorway. She let him in. He came out thirteen minutes later. I checked the time."

Irene said dryly, "Then they hardly had time for a quickie. That's where he must have gotten the key!"

Fredrik stood stamping impatiently and interrupted them, "We don't have time to talk right now. Let's get moving! How are we going to get over the fence?"

Irene thought of a possible solution. She went back to her Saab and opened the trunk. After some clanking and thumping amid all the junk, she found what she was looking for. Triumphantly she turned back to her colleagues.

"How about this—my towrope! Fredrik, you and I will give Birgitta a boost to the top of the fence. We'll toss up the rope so she can tie it to one of the iron bars, and we can hoist ourselves up. Then we just throw the rope over to the other side."

Fredrik and Irene placed themselves next to each other so Birgitta could climb up via their knees and shoulders. They tossed up the towline and Birgitta tied a good knot, as if she were making fast a sailboat worth millions. The other two rapidly clambered up, climbed carefully over the barbed wire, threw the line over to the other side of the fence, and slid down.

Birgitta asked, "Do we dare turn on our flashlights?"

"It's probably not dangerous out here. But point them at the ground. By the way, please hand me the telescope, Fredrik."

Irene strapped on the night-vision telescope. She could see the caretaker's house; a bit farther away a long, low stable was visible. She saw no activity in the house. There was a light in the stable windows.

"All quiet. We'll head up the road. It's easier to walk on," Irene decided.

They went as fast as they could. With some satisfaction Irene noticed that her two younger colleagues were panting a little when they passed the caretaker's house. For safety's sake they had turned off their flashlights. They didn't see a soul; only the outside light was on.

An icy cold north wind swept over the pastures, but their brisk pace kept them warm. The smell of salt and rotten seaweed was palpable, but there was also a distinct odor of horse manure. The distant roar of the sea and the whine of the wind were all they could hear. They stopped to catch their breath and plan a strategy. Before them loomed something that could have been a towering cliff. But Irene knew that it was the von Knechts' summer residence, designed by a famous Finnish architect. It was Jonny who had provided that information. He had also told her the architect's name, but she had forgotten it. Not important.

In a low voice she said, "About a hundred meters straight ahead is the von Knechts' little summer compound. To get to Henrik's cabin you have to follow the road to the left, around the big house. To the right the road ends at a small cliff. The sea goes into a little cove down below. So we'll go to the left. Use your flashlights, since it's pitch black here, but remember to point the beam down. Stay off the road; walk on the grass and use the bushes for cover. We don't know if Shorty has gone inside the big house or where he might be. By the way, was he alone in the car?"

Birgitta hesitated with her answer. "I honestly don't know. His car windows are completely dark. It's almost impossible to see in."

"Then we have to keep in mind that he may have had somebody with him in the car. It's about a hundred meters to Henrik's place. There are two identical houses right near each other, about thirty meters apart. I'm not sure which one is Henrik's, but I think Jonny pointed to the one on the right. The one closer to the boat docks. I suggest we spread out and approach the house from three directions. I'm unarmed. Someone with a weapon should take the windows and doors in front. It's important that we get inside fast."

As she had expected, Fredrik said briskly, "I'll take them."

"Good. Birgitta, you take the side of the house facing the big house and the back. I'll take the side toward the sea. But we'll start by checking out the lay of the land. We'll stop when we get past the big house. Then I'll look through the telescope and see if there's anything suspicious around Henrik's house. Starting now we have to talk as quietly as we can. When we get close to Henrik's house, we need absolute silence."

She sensed rather than saw that her two colleagues nodded in the dark. The light from their flashlights was pointed at the ground. They started walking toward the dark house; one by one they moved off the road. Irene felt her shoes sinking into the wet lawn; it was slippery and hard to walk. The splashing and sloshing of their hasty steps was drowned out by the angry slap of the sea against the rocks. The wind was a lot stronger out here on the spit and the roar was deafening. It bit fiercely at their earlobes and made their eyes water.

Irene turned the corner around the end of the big house at a good clip, but stopped short. Birgitta almost ran into her back. Taken by surprise, she snapped, "Yikes! What is it?"

Irene didn't answer but just pointed. A few meters in front of them a large white car was parked. There was no doubt that it was Shorty's Ford Mondeo. Irene darted behind the corner of the house and pulled Birgitta with her. She whispered in her ear, "There might be someone sitting in the car. Wait, I'll see if I can make out anything with the telescope."

But everything looked calm, with not a movement to be seen. Crouching down, they stole toward the rear of the car. Birgitta pulled open a back door and aimed her pistol inside the vehicle as Irene switched on her flashlight and shone it through the window on the opposite side. Empty. They each gave a sigh of relief.

Irene could just see Fredrik a short distance ahead. She put the telescope to her eye and saw him sneaking rapidly between the low bushes. He hadn't gone up toward the big house, but instead circled around to approach Henrik's cabin from the front. A good plan; this way he would have cover from trees and bushes all the way up to the house. It made it easier to use the flashlight. But he had missed the Mondeo. It wasn't possible for one person to see everything.

She directed her telescope at Henrik's cabin. There was a faint light in the windows. From that angle she could only see in through the window on the gable side. That was clearly the kitchen. No one was visible. She decided to try to reach her position by making a wider circle. It was extremely difficult to walk in the dark. There was a constant risk of tripping or falling. She swiftly followed in Fredrik's tracks. He gave her a hasty wave when she passed his position. It was strategically correct, behind a big boulder about ten meters from the illuminated window to the left of the front door. She stopped and cast an eye at the window. It was too high; she still couldn't see inside.

Her heart was pumping faster now. There was no sign of life inside the house, but she knew that Shorty was there. Her nostrils widened, and all her senses were on alert. She could smell the scent. A slight metallic taste in her mouth confirmed what she already knew. The hunt was on.

Cautiously she crept out on the slick rocks and looked up at the deck. The columns supporting the deck facing the sea were almost three meters tall. But that was the way she had to go. There was no stairway down to the rocks; you had to go through the house to get out onto the large deck. It certainly must give one "a genuine feeling of a ship's deck." Irene grimaced in the darkness.

The columns were made of granite blocks, cemented together. The mortar joints weren't wide enough to afford purchase for fingers or toes.

Under the deck lay a little upside-down dinghy. Even though it was small, it weighed a lot. Irene groaned as she slowly shoved and dragged it into position. She paused. Had anyone in the house heard her? But there was only the sea and the roar of the wind, and she was grateful for the cover it gave her. It was time to test whether her idea would work. The boat was now standing vertically, its bottom against the column. The bow pointed up, and the stern was securely propped against heavy stones. It probably wouldn't slip. She climbed up the stern and then farther up onto the little thwart. The last part was trickier. She put her right foot on the tip of the bow, grabbed hold of the bars of the deck railing, and was just about to kick off and lift herself up when a voice made her stop.

"Look up!"

She froze. Was it just the wind whining in her ears? As always she obeyed the voice. Balancing on one foot she peered through the bars toward the big glass doors leading to the house from the deck. The whole wall consisted of sliding glass doors. She could see a faint light farther inside the house, but the room adjacent to the deck was dark. A faint movement could be seen in one of the side curtains. Were her hyperalert senses playing a trick on her? The cold wind whipped around her jeans-clad legs, and the foot she was resting her weight on started to go to sleep. A cold sweat broke out all over her body. With infinite care she began to maneuver the telescope up to her eye.

Her breathing stopped and the roar of the sea and the wind disappeared. *He can't see you! He can't see you! You see him in the telescope, but he can't see you!* Good thing the telescope hung on its cord around her neck; otherwise she would have dropped it onto the rocks below. The curly hair over his shoulders. The shiny leather jacket with all the rivets; the enormous, compact body. And the satanic grin on his lips. Hoffa Strömberg stood gazing out into the darkness across the deck and the sea.

Only her face had been above the floor of the deck. She was peeking between the bars. He couldn't have seen her. Yet she felt residual fear from Billdal well up from the black hole inside her. The hole she thought she had sealed up forever.

Shaking, she climbed back down and collapsed on the frigid rock. She couldn't give in to the fear. She took a few deep breaths, closed her eyes, and tried to look inward and find the Point, when something began to claw urgently at her consciousness. At first she tried to shut it out, but suddenly she was totally present in the wintry wind. Her eyes opened and looked out into the darkness. The ice-cold wind whipped tears into her eyes. A desperate scream was faintly audible from inside the house.

It didn't take her long to climb up the dinghy this time. She positioned herself on the bow with one foot and looked between the bars through the telescope. Hoffa had turned his back to the deck. He, too, was listening, facing into the house. His next maneuver was very odd. To Irene's astonishment he slipped behind the curtain, still with his back to the deck. He stood quite motionless. Irene could see movement inside the house. Without thinking, she hoisted herself up and threw herself swiftly over the railing. She crouched, stock-still. After a few seconds she carefully pulled out the telescope and looked at the place where Hoffa had been standing. He hadn't moved. She cautiously stood and looked straight into the house. The illumination came from the ceiling light in the hall. She could see Fredrik in profile standing in the middle of the hall, with his pistol held in a two-handed grip and his arms out straight. He was aiming at someone who stood in front of him, out of her line of sight.

With infinite care she began to move toward Hoffa. Not because she knew what he was going to do, but driven by an instinct not to let him out of her sight. She was completely unprepared and almost screamed when she stubbed her toe on something hard. It hurt like hell. But it made only a low thud. She had kicked the heavy foundation of a patio umbrella. For several long seconds she stood motionless, on alert. Now she was so close that she could see him behind the curtain. No more than two meters separated them. But he was totally concentrating on what was happening inside the house. She was conscious of more movement in the hall. Birgitta came through the door, also with her weapon drawn. While Fredrik maintained his position, Birgitta headed for the room adjacent to the deck. She stopped in the doorway, felt along the doorjamb, and found the light switch. Light flooded the room from an elegant crystal chandelier over a dining room table.

Hoffa was suddenly visible in sharp relief against the white curtain. But the fabric of the curtain was heavy, so as to keep out the bright western sun in the summertime. Birgitta looked around without noticing the man behind the curtain. But Irene saw him. She watched him very slowly draw a knife from a sheath that was strapped to his thigh. A strip of light shone on the long, wide blade. A hunting knife for big game.

Afterward she didn't know where her strength had come from. Without wasting time to think, she bent down and took a firm grip on the base of the umbrella. She heaved it up to her chest, took a few steps forward, and threw it with all her might against the glass wall behind Hoffa. With an earsplitting crash the door exploded.

Birgitta screamed, but stopped as soon as Irene yelled, "Don't shoot! It's me!"

Birgitta hurried toward the door, found the key hanging on the inside, and unlocked it with shaky hands.

Hoffa lay in a big pool of blood. It was spreading with disquieting speed. A large piece of glass was sticking up from a gash in the side of his neck. Dark blood pumped out of the wound.

"Fredrik! Are you okay? Is everything under control?" Irene yelled toward the hall without taking her eyes off the man in the pool of blood. Her demon was about to die. Revenge was being exacted. Why did she feel no triumph?

"Everything's under control. I've got the drop on Shorty. But Henrik von Knecht needs an ambulance. Fast!"

Hoffa did too. Mechanically she yanked the curtain down from the other side of the glass door and went over to him. He yammered weakly when she carefully raised his head. She shoved the curtain under his neck and tied it. It was a clumsy and loose-fitting bandage, but it was all she could do for him at the moment. Fredrik was still positioned to shoot as she went to him. She stood next to him, turned her head, and saw the same scene he did.

In the middle of the room stood Shorty with his hands in the air and his palms turned toward the viewers. Blood was running down them. His face was expressionless, and the look he gave Irene was utterly uninterested. Only his lower jaw churned, as if he were chewing gum slowly. Across the double bed lay Henrik von Knecht. Or more precisely, she assumed it must be Henrik. The bedspread had once been white, but now it was so soaked in blood that it could have passed for a red batik. Henrik's face was swollen. With each breath he took, bright red bubbles came out of his mouth, and his naked body was covered with crimson swellings from blows and kicks.

Irene had seen plenty during her years of service, but this had to be the worst. A crazed beating, verging on slaughter. With a shudder she remembered how the murdered fourteen-year-old John had looked after the skinheads' senseless shower of kicks and blows. In the world of movies and videos, after murderous attacks, the heroes just shake it off, get up, and keep fighting. In reality the victims never get up again. They die. Anyone could see that Henrik von Knecht was dying.

Irene and Fredrik approached Shorty. Without revealing how she felt, Irene said, "Turn around! Head against the wall, spread your legs, and hands behind your back. If you don't obey, it'd be our pleasure to shoot your balls off!"

Still expressionless, he turned around and obeyed the command. This wasn't his first arrest; he knew when it was time to give up. These cops wouldn't hesitate, so it would be stupid to give them a reason. He preferred to keep his balls for a while longer.

Irene put the cuffs on him and ordered him to stay where he was. She barked out commands. "Birgitta. Call and get the chopper out here. Ambulances take too long. And we've blocked the road with our cars. It has to be a helicopter. They can land on the lawn in front of the big house."

Birgitta pulled the phone out of her pocket and did as she was told. There was a minor argument before Dispatch realized the extent of what had happened and who was involved. The constellation of Shorty Johannesson, Hoffa Strömberg, and Henrik von Knecht prompted some question about whether the whole thing was a joke. Not until Irene grabbed the phone and began bellowing and shouting just like the superintendent did the officer understand that it was urgent. It would take fifteen minutes at most before the helicopter arrived. With a glum expression Irene hung up. It was doubtful whether either of the two injured men would survive that long.

She looked around the room. There was blood everywhere. On the floor were smashed glass and ceramic shards that crunched underfoot when she walked over to the bed. Henrik von Knecht was almost unrecognizable. His face had been pounded to hamburger. His breathing was now shallow and fast. The blood bubbles came in gusts when he breathed. She leaned over toward him and said reassuringly, "Henrik. It's Inspector Huss. It's over now. He can't hurt you anymore. It's all over now."

His eyelids began to move faintly and he managed to open his eyes to small slits. In a whisper he gasped, "The h . . . ho . . . horse."

The horse? Irene vaguely recalled that Tommy had mentioned Sylvia's sick horse. Was Henrik worried about it? Apparently. With all the assurance she could muster, she said very softly and slowly, "Don't worry. The vet has been here and gave it a penicillin shot. It'll be well soon."

Again he began struggling to open his eyes, without success. A coughing fit threatened to choke him on his own blood. Fighting for breath, he gasped, "Idiot! The shattered . . . T . . . Tang horse!"

He lapsed back into unconsciousness. The shattered Tang horse? Suddenly she realized that she was standing in a pile of shards. She looked down at the floor and discovered a terra-cotta horse's head. Carefully she picked it up. One ear was broken off, but otherwise it had survived. It was a nobly formed horse's head that fit perfectly in her palm. Its nostrils were wide and its mouth open for a challenging whinny. The tensed muscles in its neck vibrated with vitality, power, and strength. But the body was gone. It was shattered and lay in bits on the floor.

Chapter Twenty

THE MOOD IN THE room was tense and feverish. Only Prosecutor Inez Collin looked cool and unharried in her dove-blue suit and white silk blouse. Superintendent Andersson was also excited, but not as ill as he had been recently. His fever had abated on Sunday evening, but his cold was hanging on in the form of loud sniffles and a whiskey-bass voice. He was glad not to have to talk. He could leave that to the three inspectors. Fredrik was the one who spoke the longest and gave the most details. His eyes flashed and his hair stood on end. He hadn't changed clothes in twenty-four hours, nor had Birgitta or Irene. They had each borrowed a dorm room at headquarters and slept a mere three hours. In Irene's case, less than that. The concern that Hoffa might die gnawed at her. In America, police who had injured Hell's Angels or been involved in firefights with them that led to fatal results had later been murdered for revenge. It would be stupid to broadcast her name too much and end up the first such victim in Scandinavia. So they had agreed on an edited version of events. Only the three of them knew what actually happened. No one else, at either high or low levels, would ever find out the exact truth. They didn't even exchange glances when Irene without a quaver in her voice related how Hoffa's accident had occurred.

"I was unarmed when I climbed up onto the deck. I had the night-vision telescope strapped on. Thanks to the scope I saw Hoffa, armed with a knife, sneaking up on Birgitta, who was standing with her back to the dark dining room and the deck. We thought Shorty would be alone! I had to act and just at that instant I stubbed my toe on the base of the umbrella. Somehow I managed to throw it through the glass doors. There was a regular explosion, and both Hoffa and Birgitta jumped sky-high. She spun around, caught sight of Hoffa, and aimed her pistol at him. He backed up with his knife drawn and suddenly slipped on the shards of glass. He pitched backward and . . . had bad luck. A large shard cut deep into the side of his neck."

She stopped and Tommy filled in, "From what I understood from the reports this morning, it cut a large vein. The blood loss was enormous. He's in a coma, and the doctors don't know his prognosis. On the other hand, it's quite clear that he will have lasting brain damage."

"Great! Then he can continue as vice president of the Hell's Angels!"

Of course Jonny had to draw attention to himself. Sulkily he had explained why no one could get hold of him on Sunday afternoon. He had taken his two youngest kids to see *Pocahontas*.

Hans Borg had wondered all Sunday evening where everybody had gone. Birgitta wasn't there when he came to relieve her outside Shorty's house at six o'clock. And no one was in the department when he called. He had also called both Birgitta and Fredrik at home. Where was he when Birgitta tried to get hold of him at five-fifteen? Well, yeah . . . there was a classic car exhibit at the Swedish Convention Hall and he stopped in for just a minute before he went on his stakeout shift . . .

Andersson sighed out loud. It's annoying to have people who mentally retire ten years too soon but still show up at work. To hide what he was thinking, he said in a scratchy voice, "All right. I myself was in bed with this cold. So now we know what everybody was doing yesterday. Hannu, we haven't heard about your day off. How was it?"

"Good."

What did he expect? A rapturous depiction of the fantastic tango evening at the Finnish Society's hall, or whatever it was that Hannu might find amusing?

Andersson cleared his throat again to conceal his embarrassment and began to sum up. "The situation looks like this: Henrik von Knecht died before the helicopter arrived. He had severe internal bleeding and both lungs were punctured from having his ribs kicked in. Shorty Johannesson was arrested for his murder. He's not saying anything, as usual, except 'That shit got what he deserved.' Hoffa is in a coma, prognosis uncertain. The other biker scumbag, Paul Svensson, we've charged with the attempted murder of Irene and Jimmy Olsson, in addition to narcotics offenses, since he had a lot of dope on him when he was apprehended. By the way, I'm pleased to announce that Jimmy is recovering well. I ran into the assistant superintendent of Narcotics, that Nilsson woman."

"Nilsén. Annika Nilsén," Irene corrected him. She was tired enough to burst and could feel that her tolerance level was low. It was a good thing she just had to sit and write reports today. She was going to try to leave early and go to bed.

Andersson pretended not to hear her and went on, "That Paul Svensson is starting to get a little disruptive. He's just about climbing the walls from withdrawal. That sh . . . creep hasn't had any drugs in two days and is beginning to fall apart. Maybe he'll start talking so we can use it against Shorty."

Irene raised her hand wearily. "I think that's the perfect strategy for solving this case. We have to play them off against each other. Make Paul Svensson think that Shorty has started talking and vice versa. The hardest thing will be to get Sylvia von Knecht to start talking and—"

Birgitta interrupted her discreetly, "Excuse me, but Sylvia von Knecht was taken to the psych ward last night. When her pastor told her what happened to Henrik, she had a total breakdown. This time it's serious. Her sister Arja called here a while ago."

An ice crystal glinted in Irene's eyes when she stated dryly, "Someone who won't break down so easily is Charlotte von Knecht. We'll have to convince her to speak."

Fredrik broke in excitedly, "But the key in the front door had a metal label with her name engraved on it! On the same key ring was a key to the gates and one to Henrik's cabin! Isn't that proof? I mean, her name was on the label!"

Irene shook her head and said wearily, "You can buy those engraved nameplates at almost any store or gas station. She could say that Shorty stole the keys without her knowledge. No, we need to nail this lady, and nail her good."

Andersson looked at her with his slightly bloodshot eyes and asked quietly, "You think she's the one?"

"I do. I think she's directly involved in the murder of Richard von Knecht. And was an accomplice in the murder of her husband."

Irene shut her eyes and pressed her fingertips lightly to her temples to try to stop her headache. Never in her life had she felt so tired.

"But you have no proof."

"No."

Inez Collin said thoughtfully, "Maybe we can make Charlotte believe that the other two we arrested snitched on her?"

Irene shrugged. "Maybe. But the question is, do they know that Charlotte was involved in the murder of Richard von Knecht? She may have even planned and carried it out herself. We have to find a motive and proof that ties her to the murder!"

Inez Collin thought for a moment before she said, "Couldn't we arrange a detention order for complicity in the murder of Bobo Torsson and the arson murder on Berzeliigatan?"

The others looked at her in surprise. She went on, "You did find some dynamite things . . . what are they called . . . Dynamex, thanks . . . and some detonators in a locked chest in Henrik and Charlotte's bedroom up there in Marstrand. The charge against her will be as follows: We don't believe that you, as the wife of the house, didn't know that your husband was storing considerable quantities of explosives in the bedroom you shared. Yet you didn't say anything when both the office apartment and Bobo Torsson were blown up. Why? You must have been part of it! Even covering up a crime is complicity."

"But she almost never went to that cabin," said Fredrik.

Inez Collin turned and smiled at him. "That's not something we know about. Officially. We have to go on the facts of the situation. The explosives were stored in their shared bedroom."

A trace of respect was visible in Andersson's eyes. Pensively he said, "That might not be such a dumb idea. Bring her in for something she had nothing to do with. Make her try to talk her way out of it. It's another person to play off against the others. Yes, by God, that might be the best way! Tommy, Jonny, and Hans will keep her under surveillance until it's time to reel the lady in. We really need to have our ducks in a row, because she's going to yell for her lawyer first thing!"

Hans Borg felt it was probably time to try participating in the investigation. He hummed and raised his hand. "I swung by Berzeliigatan on the way in this morning. The guys were already working. The stand-alone is making a new try at lifting out the safe this morning. If all goes well, I'll call Rosengren's and ask their guy to come over this afternoon."

"Okay. I hope the machine doesn't fall into the cellar again. We'll hold another meeting here after four. By the way, does anyone have any idea what the techs might mean by this fax that was lying on my desk when I came in? It says: 'No! We don't raid refrigerators!'"

OF ALL the long afternoons, this one took the cake. Irene tried to force her sponge of a brain to formulate a report, but progress was sluggish. At lunchtime she went out to eat with Birgitta. Afterward she couldn't remember what they ate. She should really have gone home. But at the same time she felt that they were moving toward a solution of the von Knecht case.

The standalone made child's play of pulling out the safe and loading it into a van. In triumph the safe was taken to the courtyard of police headquarters. There it was left in the back of the van to await the experts from the safe manufacturer.

After lunch the phone rang and Irene gladly interrupted writing her report. Someone hooted on the line. "Hello! It's Jimmy."

She was so happy at the sound of his voice that she couldn't think of anything witty to say, only a lame, "Hi! How's it going?"

"Much better. You nabbed both of them! I yelled out loud when I heard about it this morning!"

Confound it! She had that lump in her throat again. Jimmy knew and understood a great deal, but not even he would ever hear the whole truth. He obviously felt a strong sense of vengeful satisfaction. Why didn't she? Why did she only feel empty? Not happy, not sad, just tired and empty. She swallowed and managed to say, "Are you well enough to read the paper?"

He hesitated. "Well, not really. Remember the blond nurse with the braid who came in when you visited me last time? Her name is Annelise. She reads to me. There are newspapers on tape, but the news is several days old. I listen to the radio too."

"How's it going with the tail vertebrae?"

He sighed. "It's the next thing to deal with, I'm afraid. I'm having problems with the plumbing. I can't take a leak when I need to. And the pain in my legs is worse. There was a whole crowd of orthopedists here a while ago. They're moving me over there in a few days. They think I'll probably need an operation. But that'll go fine. I really do feel better now. Because you nabbed those shitheads!"

He seemed to know intuitively that she was the one who needed pepping up, not him. She managed to sound a little livelier as she said, "Take care of yourself. I'll come and see you tomorrow."

"Fantastic! No grapes, please. Twenty kronor worth of candy will do."

"It sounds like you're on the road to recovery."

THE NEXT interruption came when Birgitta stuck her head in and wondered if she wanted to see them open the safe. Irene gave her a wan smile.

"As long as it doesn't explode, sure. Hopefully, Henrik didn't manage to get into the safe."

It was almost two-thirty and already it was dark. There was a light sprinkle of small, hard snowflakes coming down. The back doors of the van were opened, and the man from Rosengren's stepped out. With a *click* he fastened a magnetic plate onto the safe. It was equipped with tiny lights and hooked up to a box that looked like a normal voltmeter. The expert turned some knobs, the lights blinked, and suddenly the safe door clicked. The icy vapor coming out of the mouths of all the onlookers stopped instantly. Cautiously the man opened the door. There was a collective sigh of relief.

The space inside the safe was small, about fifty by fifty centimeters. Birgitta had brought a carton, into which they packed folders, boxes, and envelopes.

They went straight to the conference room with the carton. The table there was the most suitable for spreading out and sorting the contents.

Andersson's face was reverential as he looked at the five inspectors present. Hannu Rauhala and Hans Borg were missing. With poorly concealed anticipation he rubbed his hands and said, "Finally! Now we'll see if there's anything useful here. We'll divide up the stuff and then go through it with the utmost care. We'll place everything that should be looked at more closely in the center of the table. If you're unsure of something, put it in the middle pile anyway!"

He swiftly divided everything into six stacks, which he passed out to those present. Irene got a hard leather case that turned out to contain a pistol. Impressed, she said, "Wow! Here's something. A Beretta Ninety-Two-S."

Andersson looked surprised. "Where the hell did he get that? Is it loaded? Check if he had a license," he said gruffly.

"Fifteen rounds in the clip. But there's no more ammunition that I can see."

They all looked through their stacks and boxes without finding any more ammunition. All they found were some medals from various sporting events. Plus an old gold pocket watch. It seemed to have belonged to Richard's father. On the lid of the old watch were the gracefully engraved initials "O. V. K." Otto von Knecht.

Irene was sitting and admiring the beautiful watch when she heard the superintendent gasp. The color began to rise in his face; his eyes were fixed on the pictures he had pulled out of a brown A4 envelope. Slowly he stood up and flung the photographs in the middle of the table.

There were ten color photos the same size as the envelope. All taken from the same angle. All with the same motif. An act of intercourse, with the man taking the woman from the rear. The woman stood leaning forward coquettishly, with her forearms supported on the back of a leather armchair. In the background there were large paintings on the walls and in one corner of the photos a crystal chandelier. The camera angle was from the side. He was dressed only in a leather helmet. It was pulled down over his face, with holes for his eyes. She wore thigh-high boots with stiletto heels and her legs were spread apart. Otherwise, naked. In some of the pictures she was staring straight at the camera, with a smile parting her moist lips. In one of them she pouted a little, as if she were sending the photographer a kiss. Her eyes were half closed with lust.

All the detectives in the room took a photo to study. Andersson's face was as red as a stoplight when he wheezed, "Well, my lovely chicken! We've got you now!"

Irene almost didn't believe it was true. Finally something concrete to present! Proof against Charlotte von Knecht.

Jonny gave a stifled moan. "What a delicious body she has! My God, I can see why little father-in-law couldn't keep his fingers off her. All eleven of them!"

Nobody giggled, but nobody protested either. Fredrik looked closely at his picture and said after a while, "Is it really certain that it's Richard von Knecht in the picture with her? I mean, couldn't it be Henrik? Or somebody else?"

Irene looked carefully at her photo. All her weariness seemed to have evaporated; she felt the thrill of the hunt pulsing inside her. The trail was hot again and smelled strongly of pheromones.

Meditatively Birgitta asked, "Where were the pictures taken? Does anybody recognize the room?"

They all took another look at the photos, then shook their heads. No one recognized the interior. Irene's attention was captured by the background. The paintings. One of the paintings.

Irritated, the superintendent slammed his palm down on the picture on the table and exclaimed, "It's damned weird behavior, putting a leather hood over his head! It'll be hard to prove that it's Richard von Knecht in the pictures. Not to mention proving where they were taken."

Irene's brain suddenly felt amazingly crystal clear, and abruptly she knew. She started laughing out loud.

Jonny said to Andersson in a stage whisper, "Now that one's having a breakdown too!"

Ignoring him, she said triumphantly, "I know where, by whom, and how the photos were taken. And I know that this is definitely Richard von Knecht in the pictures. His whole face is there!"

Jonny tapped his index finger on his temple and shook his head. Irene ignored Jonny's gesture and turned to Andersson.

"Keep Charlotte under surveillance today, just as we planned. At seven in the morning we'll bring her in and accuse her of knowing about and participating in Henrik's bombing of his father's office. Hammer away at her and let her try to explain herself, precisely as Inez Collin suggested. After an hour or two I'll come in. And then I'll nail her for the murder of Richard von Knecht!"

Andersson groaned out loud, "Would you please explain to us, your somewhat less gifted colleagues, how the hell you plan to airbrush out the leather hood on the guy and show his face?"

She did. Her colleagues gave her looks filled with respect. Even Jonny's eyes reflected grudging admiration.

THE REST of the afternoon was hectic, but when she drove home at around six everything was ready. It had gone well. The people she wanted to get hold of had been available and those she needed assistance from were helpful. She was pleased. And exhausted.

She had to recount the events out at Marstrand one more time for her family. The edited version. In the middle of the evening news she felt her eyes close. She took a long hot shower and crawled right into bed. Her sleep was deep and dreamless, undisturbed until the alarm clock rang.

Chapter Twenty-One

PAUL SVENSSON LAY CURLED up in a fetal position on the bed, with his face to the wall. Through the hole in the locked cell door Superintendent Andersson could see powerful tremors rippling through his skinny body. Low whimpering and sobs were heard even out in the corridor. There was nothing left of the tough Hell's Angel. What remained was merely the remnants of a dope addict with severe withdrawal symptoms.

The guard opened the door and Andersson stepped inside. There was a rank, sweaty smell of fear coming from the man in the detention cell, who could actually use a shower. Paul Svensson didn't seem to notice that he had a visitor. Or maybe he did, because his whines of complaint increased in volume.

Andersson assumed a brisk tone. "Hello, Paul. Time for another chat."

Svensson turned his face dripping with sweat toward the superintendent. He had a hard time focusing. His eyeballs were rolling around in their sockets like panicked eels. His tongue kept licking his dry, shredded lips. Weakly he managed to croak, "A doctor! Get me a doctor. I'm dying! I'm dying! Don't you get it?"

Over the years Andersson had interrogated far too many dope addicts to let it affect him. On the contrary, he viewed the situation as very favorable. Now the thin man should be ripe and ready to pluck.

"If you help me with a few new things that have come up over the past few days, maybe out of the goodness of my heart I'll see that we get you a doctor. But I want some real help in return!" said the superintendent in his friendliest tone.

"Go to hell!"

"If that's the way you want it. But then it's going to be a long wait before we call the doctor. An unnnn-believably long wait . . . for you."

Paul John Svensson's lanky body convulsed in a fit of cramping. All he could do was moan. Fear and pain were pulsating in the cell. When the spasms passed, he whispered, "What . . . what's it about?"

Keeping in mind that Svensson could only reveal those things he actually had knowledge of, the superintendent speculated about confusing the issue and letting Svensson try to talk his way out of the erroneous suspicions the police might have. Nothing in Andersson's voice revealed how precisely planned his first sentence was. Nonchalantly he said, "New information indicates that you and Hoffa were mixed up in the explosive fire on Berzeliigatan and naturally also in the bomb that killed Bobo Torsson. So the grenade and the attempted murder of those two inspectors out at Billdal isn't the only thing we can send you up for. Damn it, Svensson, you're looking at the bunker in Kumla prison!"

Dread spilled out of Svensson's wide eyes as he cried, "It was that upper-class shit Henrik von Knecht! He's the one who blew that Bobo Torsson to hell!"

"Why?"

Svensson jumped at that single word, tried to stop himself from snitching, but his fear of the rock-hard narcotics-free Kumla bunker— Hell on earth for a drug addict—won out. He replied curtly and nervously, "Torsson was supposed to get some dough from von Knecht. But there was a bomb in the briefcase instead!"

"Why was Torsson supposed to get dough from Henrik von Knecht?"

"Hoffa . . . I don't know."

His fear of the vice president of the Hell's Angels was clearly stronger than his terror of the Kumla bunker. But Andersson had no intention of loosening his grip yet. So he snapped harshly, "You're not going to see any doctor until tomorrow morning at the earliest."

"Noooo, wait! I know that Torsson was supposed to extort money from old man von Knecht. But it turned to shit. Hoffa was mad as hell, but the guys from Amsterdam were still coming up here with the stuff. There were other people interested."

"'Old man von Knecht'? You mean Henrik's father, Richard von Knecht?"

"Yeah, that's what I said, for fuck's sake! But that asshole didn't pay. After a few days Bobo called us back and said it would be okay with the bread. Henrik von Knecht would cough it up instead. Sounded screwy as hell, but Hoffa said we didn't give a shit who paid. As long as we got the bread."

"How much money were they talking about?"

"Half a mil."

"*Five hundred thousand?*"

"Are you dense or what? That's what I said!"

"What was Bobo Torsson going to do with another half a million? And why would he give it to Hoffa?"

Now Svensson's gaze began wandering again, but he knew that he had already spilled too much. He might as well go whole hog and get a doctor. Right now he didn't give a shit about anything to do with the Hell's Angels. He was dying and he needed a fix . . . of anything at all. Right now.

Resigned, he said, "Junk. Half a mil worth. Torsson wanted to be a big-time operator."

"Together with Shorty?"

Svensson shrugged his shoulders and muttered, "Dunno."

Annoying, but what he *had* said was interesting enough.

AT SEVEN-THIRTY Irene walked into Andersson's office. Hoarsely, he was yelling into the intercom, "Tell them that the press conference will be at one! Not a word before that!"

He was pale and tired, and for the first time Irene thought he looked ancient. A few days in bed wouldn't be a bad idea. But the von Knecht case was nearing a resolution and he had no intention of missing it.

He looked at her with bloodshot eyes before he wheezed, "'Morning. Charlotte von Knecht is expected anytime now. Hope the plan holds. I put Jonny and Tommy on her. They're picking her up."

"Then I'll stay out of sight. Any news from the interrogations of Shorty and Paul Svensson?"

He coughed and stuck a cough drop in his mouth. "Good news, actually! Svensson started to talk."

Irene laughed and said, "You got him to talk. Threatened him with the Kumla bunker."

"Cruel, but effective."

"How much money are we talking about?"

"According to Svensson, five hundred thousand kronor."

"Five hundred thousand! Henrik's fortune wasn't that big."

"Precisely. We know that because we've already checked it out. But Bobo didn't know that. And we know how Henrik pulled it off. Paul didn't have much more to offer. He got sick last night, and the doctor's been looking in on him regularly. He got an injection and went to sleep. He hadn't slept since we nabbed him on Saturday. Why don't we get a cup of coffee before we continue?"

"Continue? Is there more?"

"You bet! There's plenty more."

They had to settle for coffee from the vending machine. Since both of them were caffeine addicts, taste played a minor role. It was possible to get used to almost anything. Andersson stopped by the toilet. From out in the corridor she could hear him blowing his nose.

Back in the office he pulled out the top desk drawer and took out a little tape recorder. With a satisfied smile he said, "Yesterday's interrogation of Shorty. I went to see him right after my talk with Paul Svensson. The strategy was the same. Play them off against each other and get them confused. And I took along an envelope with one of the photographs from the safe."

He began fiddling with the buttons on the tape recorder. His contented smile turned into an angry grimace. Half-stifled oaths and groans filled the air before he finally succeeded in pushing the right button. The superintendent's voice was heard saying, ". . . a good deal now. Paul Svensson has talked. We know that you and Bobo were planning to extort five hundred thousand from Henrik von Knecht so you could buy smack from the Hell's Angels. We know that there was a bomb in the briefcase instead of money. We know that's why you pounded the life out of Henrik on Sunday, as revenge for killing Bobo."

Silence. After a while there was a dull muttering, "Fucking idiot."

"Svensson denies that he or anyone in the Hell's Angels would have had anything to do with a contract on Henrik von Knecht. Or the bomb on Berzeliigatan. He thinks it's you and Bobo who did the job for them."

Silence again. Then a stream of invective poured out of the minuscule machine. If even half of the abusive words were correct, Paul Svensson ought to be picking out a nice, pleasant grave site.

Shorty's outpouring was interrupted by Andersson's voice. "Why isn't what Paul Svensson told us right?"

"We didn't have shit to do with any bombs or the murder of Pappa von Knecht! We needed the bread to do business. That's all."

"It was these pictures that were going to get you the five hundred thousand, right?"

Light rustling was heard from the tape recorder. Shorty took a very deep breath before he wheezed, "Where the fuck did you get hold of those? That shithead said he burned them!"

"As you see, he didn't. Why didn't Richard von Knecht pay?"

Sullen silence. Then came a petulant, "Because his God damned pig-face didn't show. We couldn't prove it was him."

"So that's why you tried to extort the money from Henrik von Knecht instead?"

"Fucking dumb idea. We didn't have much time. We should have knocked over a bank instead!"

Then Andersson pushed the off button. Chuckling, Irene said, "I can imagine that discussion, between the two cousins."

"Me too. I asked when they had contacted Henrik von Knecht. Shorty wasn't sure, because it was Bobo who was taking care of that part. It was probably on Thursday. It must have been two days before the party that Sylvia and Richard had, celebrating the Thirty Years' War. And on Friday Henrik primed the bomb, if it all went the way we think."

"Actually a brilliant plan. If he'd been lucky, both his father and Bobo Torsson would have been blown up in the same explosion! It didn't happen, but you can understand what Henrik was thinking. He knew that he couldn't pay the amount the extortionists were demanding. When he saw the pictures he also knew about the relationship between Richard and Charlotte. If the bomb had been triggered by Richard, Henrik would have solved at least one of his problems. In the best-case scenario, both of them."

"Why did Henrik bother to pretend to pay? His revenge could have been to let the world see the pictures of his unfaithful wife and his lecherous father."

"He was probably concerned about the family's reputation. And Sylvia would have had a breakdown!"

"There's still the murder of Richard von Knecht."

"That's where everything started and that's where everything will end. And we're going to crack the last part too."

"One more thing. Jonny traced Charlotte's phone calls on Sunday. After Shorty came by she made a call. To reserve a table at Brasserie Lipp."

Andersson leaned over and pulled out the bottom desk drawer. In a subdued voice he said, "Here are the pictures you asked for from Pathology. Disgusting. He's a murderer and deadly arsonist, but the question is whether anyone deserves this. The poor devil is completely mashed. He could pass for the chop suey special at a Chinese restaurant. God damn!"

She took them and stuffed them into the interdepartmental envelope along with the other pictures she had gotten from the lab earlier that morning.

AT EIGHT-THIRTY Irene went into the interview room where Jonny sat with Charlotte. Jonny loved the whole setup. He would get to play his favorite role, the bad cop. It would be a shame to bother a great actor during his big scene, so Irene sat passively in a corner and made herself invisible. The time for her entrance would come soon enough. Her role would be determined by the progress of the interview. Nothing must be allowed to go wrong. Charlotte wasn't exceedingly intelligent, but she was cunning and totally self-centered. Those were dangerous characteristics combined with a beautiful body.

Charlotte ignored Irene's entrance and concentrated completely on Jonny. The moist film over her turquoise eyes shimmered, and she ran her tongue over her lips, carefully, so as not to disturb her lipstick. Irritated, Irene noticed that she had taken time to put on her contacts and some makeup. There was a strong scent of Cartier in the room. Charlotte tilted her head and glittered turquoisely at Jonny.

"My dear man, I want an attorney and I don't have to answer these horrid questions. I don't know anything. And I need some breakfast. I'm pregnant," she said in explanation.

Jonny showed his teeth in a reptilian smile. "Calm down, little lady, we'll get to that too, eventually. Of course you'll have an attorney. Do you have one of your own?"

"Well . . . no . . . Father-in-law did . . ."

"But you and Henrik don't have a family lawyer?"

"No."

"Why do you think that the attorneys at the firm Eiderstam and Sons would have any great desire to take on your defense? There's reason to suspect you were an accessory in the arson murder on Berzeliigatan and the bombing murder of Bobo Torsson. As well as conspiracy to murder your own husband, Henrik von Knecht. Deeds that were indirectly aimed at one of their biggest clients, Richard von Knecht, who has also been murdered. We'll come back to that later. If I may give you some advice, ask for a public defender."

Charlotte's lips began to tremble, and for a moment Irene thought she was about to cry. But she crossed her arms firmly under her breasts, making sure to push them up a little at the same time as she paused to think. After about a minute her strategy was decided. With her eyelids lowered and in a soft voice, she cooed, "I'll follow your advice. I'm sure you know best. I would like to have a public defender."

"We'll arrange that. But until then you have to answer my questions. If you don't I'll take it as an indication that you have something to hide. And then there will be a very tough interrogation!"

Her eyes widened slightly and the hint of a satisfied smile tugged at the corners of her mouth.

"So . . . this isn't an interrogation?"

"No. You just have to answer my questions."

Would she bite? Did she really believe that it wasn't an official interrogation? She might be lulled into feeling safe for the time being, but she would find out otherwise.

"Let's begin with the bomb on Berzeliigatan. Why did you never mention to us that Henrik stored a large quantity of explosives in a box in your bedroom at Marstrand?"

She rolled her eyes so they flashed turquoise lights, and made sure to expand her bust by sighing deeply. "I didn't know that Henrik had explosives in the box. He always kept it locked."

"Didn't you ever ask him what was in the box?"

"No."

"Why not?"

"Why should I?"

"I'm the one asking the questions. Why didn't you ever ask him what was in the box?"

For the first time she looked uncertain before she replied. "I wasn't interested. He had so many gadgets and so much junk all over the place."

"So you never cared about finding out what was in the box?"

"No."

"Then you must understand that the prosecutor has good reason to suspect you of complicity in the bombings. A married couple can't live together for years without the wife knowing that there are explosives in the bedroom."

"But God da . . . I'm almost never there!"

"Almost never there? At the cabin at Marstrand?"

"Yes."

"But you have keys to it? To the gate and the cabin?"

A clear glint of fear behind the turquoise film. "Yes . . ."

"Where are they?"

She knew it was serious now. The smell of fear broke through the perfume.

"I don't know. I haven't looked."

"No, of course not. Shorty had the keys yesterday. He says you gave them to him."

"He's lying! He must have stolen them!"

"When?"

"I don't know."

"But we do know a few things. We know that Shorty drove by Långåsliden on Sunday evening, stayed barely fifteen minutes, and then drove straight up to Marstrand and killed your husband."

"How do you know . . .?" She cut herself off and quickly bent her head. Her hair slid forward like a curtain in front of her face, a move she had learned from her mother-in-law. Irene recognized it at once. After a while she looked up and said in a low voice, "He came by to ask if I was planning to come to Bobo's funeral next week."

"Funny. He didn't tell us that."

Basically, Shorty had refused to say anything as soon as they started asking about Henrik's murder, but Charlotte couldn't know that. With an audible quaver in her voice she asked, "What did he tell you?"

"That you gave him the keys and directions to Marstrand."

It was a long shot, but Irene could see that it struck home.

"He said that? He's lying!"

"Why would he lie? He'll be doing hard time for your husband's murder and has everything to gain from putting you away too. You'll be sent up for instigation of homicide, and he'll be sentenced for doing the job at your request. It'll be a lighter sentence. For him."

A person familiar with the law wouldn't have fallen for it. But Charlotte was both ignorant and scared.

"That asshole! He threatened me! He wanted to get hold of Henrik, and he forced me to tell him where Henrik was. If I didn't give him the keys he was going to kill me."

"Why didn't you call Henrik on his cell phone?"

"I couldn't remember the number. It's a new phone."

"So why didn't you call the caretaker and ask him to warn Henrik? Or the police?"

Now the scent of fear pervaded the room.

"I did! But the caretaker wasn't in."

"We checked your phone calls from Sunday evening. None were made to Marstrand or the police. On the other hand, one was made to the Brasserie Lipp, to reserve a table. And that's where you went later that evening. We checked it out. You were a lively bunch, from what I understood from the owner. He wanted to get hold of the guy who pulled down the lamp; it's going to cost five thousand to replace. All right, one more time. Why didn't you call Henrik and warn him? Or the police?"

"I didn't dare. Shorty said he'd cut the baby out of my belly if I contacted anyone."

"But you weren't so upset that you couldn't go out and party with your friends later that evening."

She had no reply to that. She looked down at the table, under which she was hiding her shaking hands. Neither she nor Shorty had suspected that they were under surveillance. The police wouldn't have known about his quick visit to Örgryte if they hadn't been tailing him. She would have had a neat alibi at the restaurant with her pals and plenty of other people all around. Cunning, but not intelligent. Cunning approaching boldness, bordering on recklessness. All the ingredients necessary for successfully murdering Richard von Knecht. Add a little intelligence to the mix and the murder would have been much harder to solve. Maybe impossible.

Jonny continued pressing her for almost half an hour about the bomb on Berzeliigatan. When she protested that she didn't know a thing about it, Jonny pressed even harder. After a while she turned chalk white, and Irene decided the time was ripe for the entrance of the good cop.

In a softly admonishing tone she interrupted the interview. "Okay, Jonny, time for you to take a break. Can't you see that she's completely worn out? Would you like some breakfast, Charlotte?"

"Yes, please. Tea and a sandwich. And I have to go to the bathroom."

"Okay. But no more than ten minutes."

Jonny was in his element as the bad cop. A certain natural talent for the role, Birgitta would probably say, but Irene thought he had conducted himself brilliantly. If he had gone on to study law, he would certainly have been a feared prosecutor.

After a visit to the toilet and a cup of coffee, Charlotte had plucked up her courage again. But Jonny and Irene had made good use of the break. Tactics had been planned, and she had given Jonny the pictures showing Henrik beaten to a pulp.

Charlotte said curtly, "Now I'd like to have an attorney. I won't say any more."

"Good idea. But you'll have to wait in this room. Meanwhile I think you should take a look at these pictures."

Jonny shoved the photos across the tabletop with a flick of his wrist. Purely out of reflex, Charlotte caught the pictures and then glanced at them. Her eyes widened and her breathing grew heavier. She seemed unable to tear her gaze away.

Jonny said in a low voice, "Was he really such a pig that he deserved this?"

She didn't seem to have heard the question. He slammed his fist hard on the table and screamed, "Answer me! Did he deserve this? Was he a pig?"

She seemed to wake up and looked at him in bewilderment. Her eyes narrowed and she had to clear her throat before she replied. "Not a pig. A . . . sawhorse. A wooden sawhorse is what he was!"

"And now you're free of him. Does it feel good? Look at the pictures! Does it feel good?"

No reply. She stared straight ahead, into the wall. But Irene could see her hands twisting under the table. Soon, soon . . .

Jonny was merciless. For the next half hour he went over all the events of Sunday night and the early hours of Monday morning once more. She had no explanation for Shorty's visit to her before the murder, no explanation for how he got hold of her keys, no explanation for why she went out to eat with her friends instead of warning Henrik. Charlotte was in the frying pan, and she knew it. She lamely tried to prevaricate, but there were no more lies for her to tell.

The time was ripe. Irene got up and walked across the room. In wordless agreement Jonny stepped aside and left the room. Birgitta slipped in and took over the listener role.

Irene began. "Charlotte. I've been working on the investigation of the murders of Richard von Knecht and Bobo Torsson, the two arson fire victims on Berzeliigatan, and now Henrik's death. A lot has come out in the course of the investigation, strange connections and relationships. As you no doubt know, we have arrested both Shorty and one of the Hell's Angels gang. And they're telling us everything now. Both of them!"

Charlotte started and terror danced in her eyes. Irene calculated coldly that she didn't know Shorty very well and consequently didn't realize he had a reputation for always keeping his mouth shut. She had apparently never met Paul Svensson. The Hell's Angels were Bobo's contact. She also didn't know about Hoffa's fate, since she couldn't have had time to read the morning paper or listen to a news program. If she ever did. Still in a friendly tone, Irene began to run down the facts for the terrified Charlotte.

"We know that Bobo and Shorty planned a major narcotics purchase, via Bobo's old friend Glenn 'Hoffa' Strömberg, vice president of the Hell's Angels Göteborg chapter. The guys from Holland were supposed to deliver it. Everything was arranged and ready, when suddenly Bobo had trouble raising the cash. We now know why. Richard refused to pay."

Charlotte was pale gray beneath her makeup, but her eyes were fixed on Irene. Slowly Irene continued. "Five hundred thousand. Half a million. For pictures in which Richard's face can't be seen. No wonder he refused to pay!"

With these words Irene whipped out the sex pictures, in which there was no doubt who the female participant was. For a moment it looked as though Charlotte was going to faint. Irene declared, "We know that it's Richard you're having sex with in these pictures."

"No! It's . . . someone else!"

"Who?"

"I don't remember."

"So . . . you don't remember. Are you accustomed to having sex with men whose names you can't remember afterward?"

Charlotte raised her head defiantly. "It happens!"

"And this man isn't Richard?"

"No."

"Then I can tell you that his face is actually in the picture. And it *is* Richard."

"No. His face can't be seen."

"Yes, it can. Do you see the big painting in the background of the picture? Yes, that one. One of Bengt Lindström's famous 'monster heads.' I had our technician blow it up and make a copy. Then I took it to Valle Reuter last night. He identified the painting as the portrait of Richard von Knecht that he gave to Richard for his sixtieth birthday! Since Sylvia thought they already had plenty of Bengt Lindström's paintings on the walls, Richard hung the painting in his office apartment. How do we know that? Because the pictures are of Richard von Knecht's office apartment, taken with a telephoto lens. Where from? From across the street. Who lives there? Why, Shorty Johannesson, cousin of your pal Bobo Torsson! Who took the pictures? Bobo, obviously! Don't try to tell us that the man you're fucking is anyone other than Richard von Knecht!"

One look at Charlotte was enough. Her face was a clay mask. It was inconceivable that it could ever have been considered beautiful. Her features were distorted with loathing. Half choking she said, "I was forced to do it. I didn't have any choice. I owed Bobo money. A lot of money."

"Drug debts?"

"Yes. I thought I could get a little money over at the car dealership, but Henrik managed it all through his account. I was desperate. I didn't have a cent."

"Didn't you get money from Henrik? For the household, I mean."

"Sure. Ten thousand kronor a month. But it wasn't enough. At first I had my own money, from my modeling days. But that ran out. Henrik took care of all the payments for the house and the cars and that was all."

"How much did you owe Bobo?"

"Eighty-five thousand."

"Cocaine and amphetamines, I suppose."

Charlotte nodded.

"How did Bobo find out about your relationship with Richard?"

"He met me a few times on the stairs, on the way to or from Richard's apartment. And at a models' party in September he asked me straight out. And I was dumb enough to tell him. I'd snorted a lot and was babbling."

"And so he got the bright idea to blackmail Richard by taking pictures of the two of you."

"I didn't want to. He forced me. And I owed him money."

"But you did it. Tell us."

"I actually liked Richard. At first. He was cool and loved sex. Henrik didn't at all. The past year we've hardly touched each other. He's . . . was abnormal, I think. And boring. Boring in bed."

"But Richard wasn't?"

"No."

"How and when did your relationship with Richard start?"

"Last summer. At the end of July. Sylvia had gone to Finland to visit her mother and sister. Henrik was at Marstrand, of course. Richard called and asked me out to dinner. There was nothing strange about it. But it turned into something more. We suited each other, in some way."

"How did you manage to get the pictures taken?"

"We used to meet in Richard's office apartment. But we usually did it in the bedroom. It was a great room for . . . that. The only time I managed to lure him into the living room, he had to put on that damned hood! Or 'Roman helmet' as he called it. He called himself 'the Roman commander' when he had it on. Ha!"

"And that's why he refused to pay when he saw the photos?"

"Yes. He said that Bobo could never prove who the man in the pictures was. Laughed right in his face. Although it was over the phone, of course."

"And then you two got the brilliant idea of blackmailing your husband for the money instead?"

"I didn't know anything about it. It was all Bobo's idea. He didn't mention anything to me."

"When did you find out that Henrik had seen the pictures?"

She put her hands to her face and whimpered. When she took them away there were no tears. Tonelessly she said, "The Thursday before Richard and Sylvia's anniversary party. The Thirty Years' War, you know. All the men said that in their dinner speeches. It was the worst thing I've ever been to. Henrik knew that Richard and I . . . and then to sit there and pretend that nothing was going on."

"What happened on Friday?"

"Henrik drove up to Marstrand. In the morning."

"And you went to the gynecologist, to get confirmation of your pregnancy?"

"No. I knew that I was pregnant two weeks earlier. But I didn't know what to do about it."

"Whether you should keep the child?"

"Exactly."

"Let's return to Henrik and Friday. When did you see him again?"

"On Saturday afternoon. We were supposed to go to the party that evening."

"Had he taken the keys from you on Friday?"

"The keys?"

"The keys you took from Richard, after his sixtieth birthday party at Marstrand. Arja stated that she saw you coming out of his bedroom, with his key case in your hand."

"That fucking dyke!"

She slumped down in her chair and said, resigned, "Richard didn't want to give me any keys of my own, but I saw them lying on the nightstand that morning. I figured it might be good to have them."

"Did Henrik take the keys from you on Friday?"

"Yes, I discovered that the keys were missing on Friday. I usually kept them in my handbag, but they were gone on Friday evening. I immediately suspected it was Henrik who took them. On Sunday I found them again."

"In your handbag?"

"Yes, he had put them back."

"When did you find out he really had taken them? Or did you just have a hunch?"

"No, I knew. He wanted to have them back on Wednesday morning, the day after Richard died. He just took them out of my handbag, dangled them in the air, and said something like, 'You've never seen these keys! Get it?' And then he left."

"Do you know what he did with them then?"

She nodded. "Yes. He gave them to that cleaning woman. The Finn. I didn't figure it out until Bobo was blown up too. But I had nothing to do with those bombs. It was Henrik. He was jealous of Richard. He wanted revenge. And he refused to pay for the pictures."

"What about your baby, Charlotte? Who's the father?"

"Henrik."

"No. We've learned that he became sterile after having the mumps. And don't forget that we have him up in Pathology. We've already asked the postmortem examiner to check to make sure."

She had fought as hard as she could but finally collapsed over the table and buried her head in her arms. For a long time she stayed like that, without moving. Once again Irene noticed that there was no trace of tears when she showed her face again.

Charlotte said harshly, "It was Richard's. The child is a genuine von Knecht."

"So that's why Henrik chose to kill his father and not you. Isn't that right? This was his chance to become a father, as biologically close to the real thing as he could get. Father to his own half sibling. The continuation of the line would be secured. But he wanted revenge."

"Yes." She answered in a whisper.

In a low, neutral voice Irene asked, "You knew nothing about the bomb on Berzeliigatan?"

"No."

"That's why you decided to murder Richard yourself. Isn't that true?"

"No! That's not true! I have an alibi! I was out picking up my car from the dealer."

"That alibi has been cracked wide open. Your little cowboy from Mölndal, Robert Skytter, told us exactly what happened. How you missed the appointment on Monday. Suddenly you called on Tuesday and demanded that he had to be the one to handle the delivery of your new car. Then the cunning seduction; naked under your coat, wearing only stockings and high-heeled shoes. Not a very original move, but it worked on a young man like Robert."

"But the time. I could never have made it back in twenty or twenty-five minutes max."

"No. But in forty or forty-five, yes. You gained fifteen minutes with that remark, 'Oh, it's the five o'clock news already! I have to run!' And little Robbie was probably still giddy from fucking in the Ford, so he didn't react. Clever. But you made a mistake." Irene paused.

Again Charlotte's eyes were fixed on her lips; she was incapable of tearing her gaze away. A barely audible whisper, "What kind of mistake?"

"There isn't any five o'clock news on the radio. *Today's Echo at a Quarter to Five* is what it's called. Why do you think that is?"

Charlotte's voice failed her when she replied, "It's on at quarter to five?"

She was sitting erect, with her arms hanging down at her sides and her eyes fixed on Irene's face. She knew it was over.

Irene tried to appear unmoved, even though inside she felt as if a volcano was about to erupt.

"Why, Charlotte? Why? Tell me."

"Richard . . . two weeks before he . . . died . . . I told him I was pregnant and that he was the father. At first he tried to wriggle out of it. He didn't know who I'd been sleeping with, and stuff like that. But I actually hadn't been with anyone else since July. So I insisted, and I read about this technique of determining paternity with . . . DNA. When I told him I wanted one of those tests, he backed down. He promised to give me money every month. I thought that sounded fair. But then this thing with the photos came up . . . those lying on the table. He asked if I knew anything about them, but I denied it. You see, he didn't know that Bobo was the one who took them. Bobo contacted him anonymously, by telephone. But I think Richard suspected something. He didn't want to see me."

Charlotte's hands were twisting and turning now, though she was unaware of it. Irene sat in silence, waiting for what she knew was coming.

"But then Henrik ended up getting the pictures instead. He showed them to me and . . . he was out of his mind! He recognized Richard and me. I told him everything. He didn't say a word. Wouldn't speak to me, and then he left for Marstrand on Friday afternoon. I thought it was great that he left. Right after that I noticed that Richard's keys were gone from my handbag. On Saturday around three he came home. He didn't say a word, just got ready for the party. We went to it. It was abominable. But Henrik put on a good act. All those old fossils."

She stopped talking, looking angry. A thin film of sweat appeared on her skin. Her gaze was still fixed on Irene, but it was doubtful whether Charlotte saw her. Her voice was strained when she went on. "On

Sunday Henrik was supposed to fly to London. Right before he left, Richard called about some auction catalog that Henrik had forgotten to give him. Then Henrik said to me, 'You can take it over to him tomorrow, since you have a key!' And then he left. So I did. I had to talk to Richard. But when I arrived on Monday, the cleaning woman and her daughter were there working. Richard had a slight cold and was home, taking it easy. But when I handed him the catalog he whispered to me to come back later, around seven. And I did. And stayed overnight."

"Had you ever been together in the apartment on Molinsgatan on previous occasions?"

"No, never. And on Tuesday morning, as we were sitting, eating breakfast, that shithead says, 'I think we've had enough fun with each other so it's time we call it quits. We won't meet anymore, but will go back to being daughter-in-law and father-in-law. And you can raise the child as my grandchild. Ha ha!' He laughed at me! That fuck laughed at me! Right in my face! He was dumping me like an old slut! But I didn't let on, just asked him what financial arrangements he contemplated. He said I'd get five thousand a month. Five thousand! That's not enough for anything. I gave him a piece of my mind. He kept on laughing at me, but finally he said . . ."

She paused, stretched, and assumed an arrogant tone of voice to imitate Richard von Knecht. "I understand that you're a little oversensitive right now. Let's do it this way. Valle and I are going out for our Tuesday lunch today. If you clean the whole apartment so that Sylvia can't see the slightest sign that you've been here, I'll give you ten thousand kronor this afternoon. But that's all you'll get during the pregnancy. You won't get the five thousand a month until after the delivery. We're coming home around four o'clock. See that the apartment is ready in time, because Sylvia will be here between five-thirty and six."

She slumped down again and spat out, "'The delivery.' As if I was some breeding sow. And I knew that he wouldn't give me any more money. He was kicking me out like a piece of worthless shit. That's when I decided that he had to die! It would be much easier to get money out of Henrik. Now that the child is on the way . . . You wouldn't believe how thoroughly I cleaned the rooms we'd been in. For safety's sake I even wiped off the light switches and changed the sheets and towels. Gave the place a real once-over. Then I did exactly as you said. Called Robbie and . . . picked up the car."

She fell silent and started breathing harder. Unseeing, her eyes gazed straight ahead; her voice seemed to come from a long way off when she continued, "I deliberately went to see Richard very late. He would be more rushed then, I thought. Clever. I was very clever. I parked by Ascheberg High School. Since all the front door keys fit all four doors in the building, I went in on the Kapellgatan side, walked across the courtyard, and went in through the courtyard door. Then I took the elevator up and opened the door to the apartment. I didn't have gloves on. That's why I wiped off everything with a rag when I left . . . later . . . after . . . Then I threw the rag and the vacuum cleaner bag in a trash can in the garbage room. I watch TV, after all. It's important not to leave any traces. I went back the same way across the courtyard. You didn't find a thing!"

Triumph shone in her turquoise eyes. Eagerly, as if to reveal how clever she had been, with her words practically falling over each other, she turned to Irene and continued her story. "He didn't hear a sound when I opened the front door. I went through the kitchen and took a little meat cleaver that was hanging over the stove. I stuffed it under my trench coat. I went upstairs and there lay Richard on the sofa, resting after a sauna. He was pretty drunk. He jumped up, nervous as hell because of the time. Sylvia would arrive any minute. He ran off to get the envelope with the money. When he came back and gave it to me, I said, 'Come on, you have to see my new car! It's parked right under the balcony. It looks really great in the light from the display window.' At first he didn't want to. But at the same time he wanted to get rid of me before Sylvia came home. So he went out onto the balcony with me. He leaned over the railing so he could see the car. I whacked him on the back of the neck as hard as I could and shoved him over!"

She showed not a trace of regret or remorse. Nothing but pure triumph.

Cautiously, Irene asked, "He had a cut on the back of his hand. How did he get that?"

"That wimp was afraid of heights. He was holding on with one hand. I had to give it a whack so he'd let go."

She began to laugh. A hysterical giggle that grew into a howl.

"Charlotte, one more thing. The sandwiches in the refrigerator. Were you the one who took them?"

"Yes. I was hungry afterward. So I took them with me and ate them at home. You get hungry all the time when you're pregnant."

"MAMMA! WHERE'S THE LUCIA crown? Guess who was chosen Lucia by our class? They picked me. Super to have a bald Lucia, they thought. Do you know where we put the crown last year?"

"Wasn't that the one that short-circuited?"

"No, that was Katarina's electric light candleholder. Do you think I need to shave my head again? I mean, the point is that I'm bald, after all."

"No. Dear Jenny. No!"

"Damn, you're grumpy when you get home from work. You're always so tired and useless."

Annoyed, Jenny slammed the door to her room. Irene sighed and looked up at the closed door on the second floor. Jenny was right. She was always tired and useless when she came home. She had to be sharp and energetic when she was at work. There were no reserves to call on when she was home with her family.

Jenny opened her door a crack. "Maybe you'll be in a better mood after you open the package in the living room. It came by delivery van a while ago. And you could say congratulations to me. Not even Katarina has ever been Lucia for the whole class!"

"Congratulations, sweetie."

She spoke to a door that was already closed. With a sigh she went into the living room. The thought occurred to her: *Could be a bomb.* After all, she had screwed things up for the Hell's Angels, and she knew what they were capable of. The package was big and flat. Sent by Mona Söder, Stockholm. She took down the framed Miró print from the wall.

TWO BIG yellow butterflies with black markings on their wings hovered over a vast landscape, a shimmering stream in the valley and blue-tinged mountains in the distance. In the foreground there were beautiful meadow blossoms. The blue of the forget-me-nots was dominant, but there were also splashes of white and pink flowers that she recognized but couldn't name. They came so close to the observer that it felt as if she were lying on her stomach among the meadow flowers and peeking over the edge down into the long valley, up toward the two gaudy butterflies. The sky was not blue, but a silvery white circle above the mountains dispersed a strong light that became a warm pink at the outer edges. It was not the sun and not the moon. It was the Light.